THE PATH *of* THE STORM

The Evermen Saga, Book 3

OTHER TITLES IN THE EVERMEN SAGA:

Enchantress

The Hidden Relic

The Lore of the Evermen

THE PATH *of* THE STORM

The Evermen Saga, Book 3

JAMES MAXWELL

47N⭘RTH

Text copyright © 2014 James Maxwell
All rights reserved.

Published by 47North, Seattle

www.apub.com

Amazon, the Amazon logo, and 47North are trademarks of Amazon.com, Inc., or its affiliates.

ISBN-13: 9781477824221
ISBN-10: 1477824227

Cover design by Mecob

Library of Congress Control Number: 2014932660

Printed in the United States of America

This book is for my wife
Alicia
with all my love and gratitude
for the dreams we share together

THE TINGARAN EMPIRE

IN THE YEAR OF THE EVERMEN 545

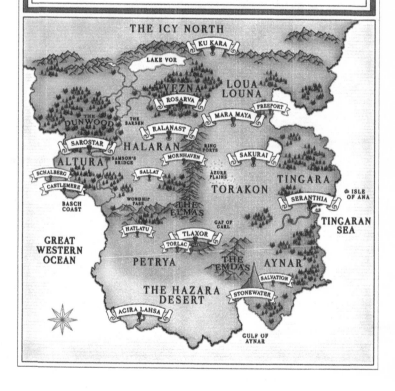

THE ICY NORTH

KU KARA

LAKE VOR

VEZNA · LOUA LOUNA

ROSARVA

THE DUNWOOD · THE SARSEN · RALANAST · MARA MAYA · FREEPORT

SAROSTAR · HALARAN · RING FORTS

ALTURA · SAMSON'S BRIDGE · MORNHAVEN · SAKURAI

SCHALBERG · SALLAT · AZURE PLAINS · TINGARA

CASTLEMERE · TORAKON · SERANTHIA · ISLE OF ANA

BASCH COAST · WONDHIP PASS · THE ELMAS · TINGARAN SEA

HATLATU · GAP OF GARL

GREAT WESTERN OCEAN · TLAXOR · TORLAC

PETRYA · THE EMDAS · AYNAR

SALVATION

THE HAZARA DESERT · STONEWATER

ACIRA LAHSA

GULF OF AYNAR

PROLOGUE

It was the first time in Sentar Scythran's memory that he needed to survive on his wits alone. Essence had always filled his body with vigor, given him powers the pitiful humans could only dream of, and now he had none of the black liquid. Yet his brother Evermen had chosen him for a reason. They knew Sentar was single-minded, ruthless, and intelligent. The Evermen knew that, of all of them, he had cunning.

He'd come far since his return, traveling through lands, now foreign to him, where once he'd ruled as a god. Without allies and with no gilden, he'd managed to feed and clothe himself, no mean feat, finding his way alone through forests and over hills, surviving heartless cities and wary villages, heading ever north.

Now Sentar stood in front of a hunter's log cabin, the first sign of habitation he'd seen in days. Two hunters stood in front of him, crude men in crude clothing. Sentar himself wore a fur-lined gray cloak over his black velvet shirt and trousers, the hood pulled forward over his head to cover his bloodred hair. Snow covered the earth and blanketed the trees white while mist swirled and eddied through the frosted evergreens. It was unbearably cold.

Sentar had come far, but cunning couldn't combat the weather.

"Snow's closin' in," the old hunter said, leaning on his tall bow. "You can't go north in this weather. You'll have to wait."

"How long?" Sentar said, his words spoken through crusted lips, mouth turned down in displeasure.

"A month. Might be longer," said the hunter's broad-shouldered son.

Sentar cursed.

He had to go north. His quest consumed him. His brothers were still in that world of horror, and it was his duty to bring them home. He alone had been entrusted to watch over the portal in case the way to Merralya opened. When the beacon had awoken him from his slumber, there had been no time to wake his brothers; he had traveled to the portal only to see it would be open for the briefest moment. He would bring them home. He must not fail in his duty.

"No," Sentar said. "I must go north, to the ice city, now."

"You're welcome to try," the old hunter said. "You won't make it, though."

Sentar's mind turned to essence. With essence the cold could never touch him. Yet it wasn't just he who had been forced to survive without essence; it seemed no one had any. Not those people who called themselves Tingarans, or the Louans, or those in white from the land of Aynar. Sentar had seen it for himself; it was the first place he'd gone to—the great machines at Stonewater had been destroyed.

It was grim news, but Sentar always found a way where others failed, and hope was not lost. Some inquiries led him to those who once held the Lord of the Night close to their hearts and who were likely the only people to have their own supply of essence: the Akari.

To fulfill his quest and bring his brothers home, Sentar would need essence—essence to open the portal and essence to crush the humans. He had no wish for his brothers to return to a land filled with human soldiers, innumerable as insects. He would need to conquer the people of this Tingaran Empire and to harvest their life energy. Only then would he have the essence he required. Only then would this land be ready for his brothers' return.

Looking at the hunter and his son, Sentar set his mouth with determination, ignoring the bite of the cold.

"How do you and your family survive in this weather?" Sentar asked.

The old hunter shrugged. "Cunning," he said.

The son smiled. "We trade furs with the Akari, and in return they give us bows. We use the bows to hunt."

"I must go to the Akari." Sentar stepped forward, his ice-blue eyes intent.

"Who says they'll have you?" the old hunter asked, his wrinkled face curling into a scowl. "They don't take kindly to strangers."

"They'll receive me," Sentar said. "I'm important to the Akari, and they're expecting me."

Sentar held the cudgel buried inside his cloak. As close as he was now, the old hunter wouldn't be able to react.

As father and son exchanged glances, Sentar took his hand out and swung.

He didn't want them dead; he needed their help too badly for that. He went for the father first—the old man was wary. The cudgel hit the old man's temple with a crack like an axe on a tree. Sentar then turned to the son and punched the tip of his club into the younger man's throat.

Both hunters crumpled to the ground, the old man bleeding from the head, instantly unconscious, while his son gasped and choked, holding his hands to his throat, the youth's face turning red.

Sentar immediately turned to their tall bows, now fallen from the two hunters' hands. Picking them up, he broke first one and then the other, over his knee.

"Come with me," Sentar said to the young hunter, grunting as he crouched and hooked an arm around the youth's neck. Sentar rose to his feet, pulling the youth along behind him, dragging the young hunter over to the entrance of the log hut.

Sentar still clutched the broken bows in his other hand. Lifting up a leg, he sent his black boot into the door, kicking it open with a crash.

Without waiting for his eyes to adjust to the darkness within, Sentar tossed in the young hunter. The man wheezed on the floor, coughing; Sentar would find no trouble from that quarter.

Sentar looked around, seeing the red embers of a fire and a grubby house. He wrinkled his nose; the hut reeked of smoke and animal sweat. An old woman sat on a chair, a threaded needle in her hand and a furred skin across her lap. Her face registered shock.

Sentar walked over to the fire and threw the broken bows into the hearth.

"Where are your other bows?" Sentar asked.

The old woman didn't open her mouth, but her eyes moved, and Sentar saw a place on the wall where two more bows hung fixed to the wood.

Sentar took the first down and held it poised over his knee.

"Please," she begged, "we'll starve."

Sentar broke the bow, quickly following it with the second; both bows, now in splinters, were thrown into the growing fire.

He went back outside and took the old hunter under his arms. The old man was heavy, and Sentar grunted as he pulled his unconscious body into the hut and threw him beside his son, now nearly recovered.

"Tend to your husband," Sentar said to the woman.

She ran over to the old man and brushed the hair away from the wound on his temple. Blood welled on her hands, and tears ran down her face as she pulled his head into her lap.

The hunter's son sat up and glared at Sentar. "We'll die without our bows."

Sentar crouched close to the youth and tapped his cudgel into the palm of his hand. The young hunter looked on, fear in his eyes.

"So you need new bows, I should think," Sentar said, "from the Akari."

"We don't have furs to trade for them. The weather's closing in. You've killed us."

"No, that's not correct. You have a problem: You don't have any bows, nor will you have furs to trade for them, not for many months. I also have a problem: I must travel to the ice city, but I will need help finding it and help to survive in this cold. I think we should make a bargain."

"He is an evil man," the old woman said from where she tended her husband, directing the words at her son.

"I make opportunities—that's all," said Sentar.

"Druin, please, do not help this man," the woman said to her son.

"Mother, without bows we'll all die. We've only food for another week. I think I can make it back in two."

"A bargain means nothing to one such as him. He'll kill you without a thought."

"If I don't go, we're doomed anyway."

"All I need is for you to guide me to the ice city," Sentar said. "It's in your interests that I arrive there safely. I'll instruct the Akari to give you new bows, and soon you will be back in your hovel."

The light in the room grew as the broken bows blazed.

Sentar smiled as the young hunter slowly nodded. Cunning had won again.

As he traveled ever onward into the cold, Sentar realized that, for all his abilities, he was dying. In the twilight world of Shar, he had fought nightmarish creatures, endured horrors beyond imagining, and seen the shadows in his brothers' eyes when all hope was lost. Yet now he was here, returned to Merralya, a world warm and golden in comparison, and he was going to die.

The snow now came up to the top of Sentar's high boots, making each step an agony of effort, dragging at his legs. The wind grew in strength, driving the crystalline snowflakes hard against his face, stinging his cheeks and gathering around his nose and mouth. The dim light reminded Sentar unpleasantly of Shar, and shielding his eyes against the wind, he could see even the hardy pines growing scarce.

The days had become grueling marches, consuming Sentar's thoughts with the simple task of putting one foot in front of the other. The nights were the worst, spent huddled under pine trees if he could find them, where the branches at least blocked the snow from overhead. If there were no trees, he found icy overhangs and stuffed his hands under his armpits, shivering his way to a twitching sleep.

He had long ago killed Druin, the young hunter who was supposed to ensure his survival. The youth had insisted on turning back, and Sentar knew he needed extra sustenance as well as the young hunter's blankets. Sentar had forced Druin to give him directions before he'd ended the young man's life and taken his provisions.

Sentar had now covered such distance that if he tried to return south to warmer lands, he knew he wouldn't make it. So he continued onward, and finally he realized he was going to die.

The blizzard came down from overhead, plunging from the perfectly white sky with the force of an ocean wave. It knocked Sentar to his knees, and he felt a sudden calm descend on him. It would end here, he knew.

Even so, the thought of the weight on his shoulders spurred him on.

"My brothers!" Sentar screamed.

Sentar tried to rise, but the wind pushed him down. He knew from bitter experience that the blizzards could last for days. The shortest would persist for hours.

Sentar lifted his chin and looked into the white, determined to face his death with eyes open.

And then, moments after it arrived, the blizzard was gone.

The sky was still white, but a small patch of blue appeared. The patch grew, and with it Sentar's vision cleared. It was late in the day, he now realized, rapidly descending to night. He could see his hands and then the clumps of snow in front of him, and then could see farther, to a pathway—no, a road—lined with markers of gray stone. As more of the landscape revealed itself, Sentar looked farther still.

He suddenly knew he'd made it.

Two tall towers thrust out of the ground ahead, so pure of color they were almost blue. A ring of spikes topped each tower, wider than the tower's base, like the crown of a monarch. The towers were made of ice, and the road passed between them.

Sentar took a deep breath and with an effort of will brought himself back to his feet. The first step he took was more of a stagger, and the second little better. Walking was agony until he reached the marked road, and then the packed snow under his feet offered blessed relief. As he finally passed through the towers, Sentar saw the name of the city announced, with one word on each tower: "Ku Kara."

It wasn't a walled city; the cold was protection enough for the Akari. Nor were the streets narrow and winding; there was space enough to build big. As Sentar walked, he saw broad avenues uniformly marked by short pillars of gray stone. The single-storied buildings were all made of ice, with heavy doors of dark wood and inset windows the size of a man's hand.

Sentar staggered through Ku Kara in a daze. This city hadn't existed when he and his brothers ruled Merralya. The Akari had been his people, and now they had built a home of their own. He'd thought Seranthia to be an aberration. How could mere humans build such a city? But with all he'd seen, Sentar now knew: The humans had grown from childhood to adolescence.

With a shake of his head, he stopped. He was Sentar Scythran, the Lord of the Night. He had ruled this world, and he had survived Shar. The lines of resolve in his mouth and forehead returned. He would rule again.

Sentar scanned the street and scratched his chin in thought. A few houses along, at a dwelling larger than the others, a withered tree made of silver wire decorated a front door. Some things may have changed, but Sentar knew that symbol.

Reaching the house, Sentar stood in front of the door and instantly began to pound at the wood. Moments later he nodded with satisfaction when a man in a gray robe opened the door.

"Who are you?" the robed man asked, his brow furrowed with suspicion. "You are not one of us. What are you doing here?"

The robed man wore his black hair close cropped . His face and hands were fine boned and delicate, and his high forehead suggested intelligence. He wore a necklace of bones around his neck, and his robe bore a matching symbol to that on the door.

"Surely you know me," Sentar said. He raised a wrist and brushed the snow off a device of worked silver he wore on his collar. The withered tree was a match to the symbol on the door. "You wear my symbol on your robe. You bear my mark on your dwelling. Let me in from this cold, and I will show you who I am."

8

Sentar pushed past the man in gray robes, who was too stunned to react. The warmth from the interior hit him with such force that he could have wept, and the contents of the man's house were suddenly irrelevant as Sentar strode to the red embers of the hearth. It wasn't until he'd removed his gloves and felt the blood return tingling to his limbs that Sentar turned back to the robed man and took note of his surroundings.

The house was larger than it appeared from the outside. The floor consisted of wide planks of the same dark wood as the door with soft animal furs covering its surface. A human skeleton stood in the corner, teeth bared in a permanent smile, and from the workbench and bookshelves Sentar could see this place was dedicated to work rather than leisure. The robed man had closed the door and now frowned at his unwelcome guest.

Walking around slowly, Sentar passed a bronze mirror, and seeing himself, he grimaced. "I will admit I have recently been a victim of circumstances and do not look my best. You can be forgiven for not knowing me"—Sentar paused—"this time."

Sentar pulled his hood back and unclasped the cloak, letting it fall to the floor. He brushed his elegant clothing of black velvet, ignoring the scattering of snow and ice that fell to the ground. He straightened his shirt and ran his fingers through his hair.

Finally, Sentar rested his eyes on the other man. "What is your name?"

"I am Renrik. And you are?"

"From your garb you are one of the chosen, are you not?"

"Chosen?"

"One of those chosen to receive the knowledge . . . I taught your kind to give life to the dead. You are a necromancer."

"I . . . I am," Renrik said.

"Do you possess essence, Necromancer Renrik?"

Renrik's eyes narrowed. "I do . . . a small amount."

Still wandering around the room, Sentar found a basin and ewer. He washed his face and slicked back his hair. "Bring it to me," he said.

"Stranger, I do not know who you are, but . . ."

"Has it been so long? Are your memories so quick to fade?"

Sentar turned and leveled the full force of his gaze on the necromancer. He could see Renrik noticing the bloodred hair with black streaks at the temples, the blue eyes, like ice. "The essence," Sentar said, "give it to me."

Renrik disappeared into a second room. Sentar heard the necromancer mutter, and then a click as a locked cupboard opened. Something clinked, and Renrik came back into the room, holding a tiny vial. Sentar opened his hand, and in that moment Renrik stumbled. Sentar knew it was pretense when he felt a prick on the skin of his right hand.

Sentar smiled without humor. Along with the vial, Renrik held a scrill. A blue mark appeared on the back of Sentar's hand where the scrill had touched essence to his skin.

Such a touch would kill any man. He would fall to the floor and scream as he died the most agonizing death imaginable.

Sentar merely felt a tingling sensation in the region of the blue mark.

Renrik stared at the mark, his eyes wide with shock. He slowly looked up to meet Sentar's cold eyes.

Sentar watched and waited, as the thoughts crossed Renrik's face. Sentar's own eyes flickered to a stylized portrait on the wall. The man in the portrait had hair the color of blood, with streaks of black at the temples.

The necromancer fell to his knees.

"Master!" Renrik cried.

Sentar crouched and put his fingers under the necromancer's chin, tilting Renrik's head and looking into his eyes. The devotion was genuine.

"Let that be the last time you distrust me, Necromancer Renrik," Sentar said. "I am Sentar Scythran, the Lord of the Night, and I have returned."

"Forgive me, Master."

"As one of the chosen, you may serve me, and you may live," said Sentar. "Those of your order will be the only kind to survive when my brothers return. Serve me well, and you may have a special place in the new Merralya and be raised up to rule the others of your kind."

Renrik kept his head down, but Sentar saw him take a tremulous breath. "Master, I will serve," the necromancer finally said.

"Stand," Sentar said. "I need to ask you some questions."

Renrik stood but kept his eyes lowered. "Ask," he said.

"Your people, the Akari, will they serve me?"

Renrik was silent for a while before speaking. "I . . . I am afraid there are many who will not. The Dain, Barden Mensk, has poisoned our people against you, saying you ruled as a wolf rules the sheep. There are some, in my order, who still believe, but they don't dare speak out against the Dain."

Sentar was pensive for a moment. "Even my own people," he muttered. "Perhaps a new people . . ."

Renrik kept his head bowed while the Lord of the Night made his plans.

"How much essence can you gather?" Sentar asked.

"I cannot get to the stockpiles without the Dain's permission."

Sentar's mind worked. With essence he could destroy the Dain and many of the Dain's followers. But how many would he face? And what purpose would it serve? The amount of essence he needed . . .

Sentar spoke. "I need to build an army to conquer this Tingaran Empire so that the blood of the dead will enable my brothers to return to a defeated world. I thought your people might be the followers I need, but it seems I was wrong."

Sentar made a decision.

"I know where there are those who will be easy to dominate. We need weak humans, multitudes of them, ready to subdue. Necromancer Renrik, can you take me to a ship, an ocean-going vessel?"

"We have only a few, but yes. The *Icebreaker* is big enough . . ."

"I need you to gather those of your order who will follow," Sentar interrupted, "and get together as much essence as you can, enough to build the vats anew."

Sentar took the vial of essence and scrill from Renrik's hands. He began to draw on his skin, the movements deft and precise. As the Akari necromancer looked on in wonder, Sentar spoke an activation sequence, and moments later the symbols lit up. Sentar felt his skin tingle with suppressed power.

"We will leave some followers here to work on our behalf and stay abreast of what transpires in this supposed empire. The rest will come with me."

Renrik bowed and nodded.

"Show me to this ship," the Lord of the Night said. "Time is our enemy."

Sentar may not have found the beginnings of an army, but he now had allies, and he had essence.

The rest would be easy.

1

Miro was terrified. His hands shook and his heart beat so loudly in his ears that he wondered that Amber couldn't hear it. His palms sweated even though the air was cool, and his lips seemed to dry, no matter how many times he moistened them.

"You're not afraid of heights, are you?" Amber asked with a grin. "You look anxious." She gazed out over the expanse below. "Lord of the Sky, I can see why you brought me here. It's beautiful."

Miro had never been to this place, but Ella had given him directions. She'd told him words couldn't describe the valley's beauty, and as soon as Miro saw it, he knew she was right.

The view was incredible. Below them a turbulent river twisted and turned its way through rocky chasms and glades of emerald trees. Its source was a majestic waterfall, sprouting from the cliff face and pouring out into the open air before disappearing in a cloud of spray. In the distance, three other waterfalls cascaded down the smooth shining rock, and the roar of the water combined with the sound of insects to form a soothing hum. Miro could see butterflies the size of a man's hand, fluttering around the lush trees like brilliant jewels.

As preoccupied as he was, Miro's thoughts were on anything but the rainbows dancing on the spray. He focused on the carefully rehearsed words, and the great flurry of activity his actions would precipitate. Most of all, his thoughts were on the woman by his side.

"I can't believe how warm it is here," Amber said. "Back in Sarostar there's still ice on the Sarsen."

Miro silently thanked Ella again. He'd feared rain and icy cold, yet here in this valley they could feel the sun warm their skin.

It had taken Miro and Amber most of the day to find a path down from the heights, and they were now on their descent into the valley. "Look," Amber said. "There—can you see it? There's a thin line hanging down from the top of the cliff."

Miro searched for a moment. "A rope?"

"That's how Ella said she climbed down the cliff. I can't believe she did it. She must have nerves of steel."

Miro smiled. "Sounds like Ella."

"And to think, she never would have found this place if the Lexicon hadn't been stolen."

"Good things can always come out of the bad," Miro said. "Should we keep going?"

"Lead the way."

The path they'd found was meandering, but not treacherous—still Miro was nearly bowled over when a small form swept past him, squealing with delight.

"Tomas," Amber called, "slow down."

The child grinned back at them, his eyes twinkling with mischief. "Papa!" he cried. "Race me!"

Running in chase, Miro felt a root grab hold of his foot, and before he knew it, he'd landed face first in the dirt. Tomas paused in his game, the toddler stopping in astonishment.

"Are you all right?" Amber asked, and then laughed when she saw Miro's expression. "You're never normally this clumsy." She started to help him up.

Crestfallen and evidently believing he was the cause of Miro's fall, Tomas came over and tugged on Miro's clothing. "Up!" he said.

"How can a two-year-old be so quick?" Miro muttered, dusting himself off.

"Two-and-a-half," Amber said. "You don't have to tell me, though. I can hardly keep up with him anymore."

"Two and a half years. I can't believe it's been so long," Miro said. He looked down at the boy who was now his son and was currently absorbed with pulling lichen from a tree.

"We've been busy."

"I know, but it doesn't mean we shouldn't find time for each other. I . . . I'm sorry Amber, if I haven't always been there for you."

"Miro," Amber sighed, "what are you talking about?"

"Every time I go to Halaran or Tingara, when I return, I feel like Tomas has grown so much, and I know I've missed it. Every time I sleep in a strange bed, I wonder why you're not there beside me."

Amber smiled and squeezed his arm. "We've got today. Come on."

Amber led the way along the narrow path down to the valley floor, and following her, Miro cursed his tongue. Why could he never find the right words? Amber and Tomas had made him happy—happier than he had ever thought he could be. Yet there were always more demands on his time.

In the years since the primate's death, the Empire had settled, but it was an uneasy peace. The world economy was in ruins, with the price of essence so high that trade between the houses had completely dried up. Reconstruction from the war employed some, but with no drudges to haul goods in quantity, countless people were underfed, from Altura to Aynar, and Miro was constantly firefighting, dashing from one explosive situation to the next. Tingaran soldiers now worked alongside Alturans, but there were many who

15

spoke of the despotic rule of the emperor with nostalgia. At least then there was food on the table, they said.

Miro's message was simple. He felt that he was repeating himself again and again, yet if he kept trying, the words would get through. The situation they were all in was the inevitable result of the war. What had been done was in the past. The oppressed people of Aynar and Tingara deserved as much of a chance as the war-torn multitudes of Halaran and Petrya. The machines would be rebuilt, and when essence again flowed through the Empire, prosperity would return.

Amber said she understood Miro's pressures; still, Miro wanted to give her more. As he watched her, she laughed at something Tomas said, the sound girlish and free. But she was no longer a girl; Amber was a woman, and she'd been through more than any person should have to go through. Miro was constantly amazed at her resilience. Even now, when people met her, they saw her beauty and warmth without realizing the trials she'd been through, the strength she carried within.

"You really are somewhere else today, aren't you?" Amber said. She took his hand. "Are you coming?"

Miro realized they had made it down to the river. Tomas chased butterflies, his fluffy brown hair only a little darker than Amber's auburn, catching leaves and twigs. "Sorry." Miro grinned shakily. "Let's head down to the water, shall we?"

"Sounds good to me," Amber said.

Amber kept hold of Miro's hand while they walked, but he could see her expression was a little puzzled. Miro's other hand felt down to the back pocket of his trousers, patting the little bulge there comfortingly.

The pair reached the water, where grassy banks led down to the plunging peaks and troughs of a turbulent river.

"Ella said she tried to swim across," Amber said. She shuddered. "She could have been killed."

Miro took a deep breath. There was a sudden roaring in his ears, his heart beating so hard he thought it would burst out of his chest. The feeling was completely foreign to him. This wasn't the fear of the battlefield, with instant decisions leading to life or death. This was something altogether different. He clutched at the ring in his pocket.

Miro made sure he had Amber's attention before speaking. "Amber . . . I . . ."

"Tomas!" Amber screamed. She put her hands to her face in horror. "Get down from there!"

Miro turned, seeing a tall rock poking its head from a grove of trees. The rock leaned out over the water.

Tomas stood on the summit of the rock, waving a hand at them, completely unaware of the danger. If he took another step, and fell into the river, he would drown.

Even as he was moving, Miro cursed himself for becoming so distracted he'd jeopardized his son's safety. His muscles freed by action, he ran at the grove, ignoring the cuts to his arms as he pushed through the trees. He lost sight of Tomas as he thrust his way through the grove, desperately looking for the rock, but finally saw the gray of stone through the branches and leapt forward. Miro stopped in his tracks.

A small woman with ruddy features sat just below the summit of the rock, the child in her arms. She wore the garb of a Dunfolk healer, with a soft mantle of precious fur on her shoulders. Tomas was giggling as she tickled him. Neither of them seemed troubled in the slightest by their precarious position.

"What are you doing here?" Miro demanded. "Did you follow us?"

"I came to watch," Layla said. "Have you asked her yet?"

"Layla," Miro said, clambering up the rock to sit beside the Dunfolk healer as the water roared below. "This is a private moment between Amber and me . . ."

"Oh, I see." Layla pretended to ponder. "Should I have let him fall, then?"

"No, no, I'm sorry. Thank you. I'm just nervous."

"You have fallen over twice. I've been watching. You're clumsy today," Layla said.

"Thanks," Miro said wryly. "Can you at least stay out of sight?"

Layla snorted. "You couldn't find me if I was right in front of you. I will stay out of sight, but I am going to keep an eye on your son. You are fortunate the Eternal brought me here."

Calmly and confidently, Layla took Tomas from the peak down to the base of the rock. As Layla looked up expectantly, Miro stood, wobbling as his feet sought purchase on the jagged surface, suddenly terribly aware of the drop.

As the reflexes that had seen Miro survive desperate battles deserted him, he slipped, tripping backward.

Miro's last sight as he fell was Layla regarding him with an expression of astonishment. He tumbled through the air, hitting the water on his back with a mighty splash.

The fall took the breath out of his lungs, and he coughed and gulped at the water as he went under. Miro's head popped above the surface, and he grabbed a hasty breath before the plunging waves pulled him back down. He felt water fill his boots and soak his clothes, adding to the weight threatening to drag him to the bottom.

The next time his head came up, Miro pulled at the water with his arms. He kicked out with his legs; fortunately, he was close to shore, and his foot found purchase on a rock below the surface. He thrust with his foot while simultaneously paddling. The current almost took him, but he got a foothold, and then he felt a hand take his wrist to pull him out of the water.

Finally, Miro flopped onto the bank, thanking Amber with his eyes as she let go of him. Rolling and coughing, he finally spluttered river water onto the ground. He pulled himself up farther onto the bank, heedless of the mud, and lay dazed.

"Miro! What happened? Are you all right?"

Amber held Tomas by the hand, Miro was pleased to see. Miro raised his head and shook it from side to side to clear it.

"I'm fine," he panted.

A sudden stab of fear hit him, and his eyes went wide. Miro clutched at his trouser pocket, his hand grasping empty cloth. He began to search the muddy bank, his hands grasping at one handful of silt after another.

"Miro, what are you doing?"

When his hand clutched onto a smooth circle of metal, Miro thanked whatever deity was looking out for him that the ring had fallen out only at the end. He washed it off in the water. He might be covered in mud, but at least the ring would be clean.

"Lord of the Sky," Miro muttered, "nothing ever goes according to plan."

As both Amber and Tomas looked on in astonishment, Miro stood shakily and faced them both. Covered in mud and with chest heaving, he turned to Amber, sinking to one knee.

Miro held out his hand. The ring was of bright yellow gold, with a central emerald stone in the shape of a droplet bound by tiny diamonds.

Amber's mouth dropped open. Miro's hand shook.

"Amber, I tried to make this day perfect, but I know I'm covered in mud, and I know Tomas almost fell into the river. I know I'm not perfect, but you've made me incredibly happy, and I want to give you more." Miro took a deep breath. "This ring was Lady Katherine's . . . I didn't know her, but she was my mother. It's not the ring she married Tessolar with—it's the ring she wore when she married my father, High Lord Serosa. I'm sorry. I know it's not about the ring. What I'm trying to say is . . . you and Tomas . . ."

Amber put her fingers to Miro's lips. "Shh," she said, her lips curved in a smile. "Yes."

Miro looked up. "Yes?" He grinned.

Amber laughed. "Of course yes, you crazy man. I'll marry you. Mud and all."

Miro slid the ring onto Amber's finger and then stood. Still grinning like a fool, he kissed her, long and slowly, before breaking away when he felt moisture on her cheeks. Drawing back he saw tears in Amber's eyes, but she was laughing and crying, all at the same time.

Miro squatted down and hugged Tomas while the boy squirmed. He stood again and held them both for a long moment, realizing the day was perfect after all.

Miro looked past Amber's shoulder, and between some branches he saw white teeth and sparkling eyes, and there was Layla, for once smiling broadly.

Thinking about the mud on his clothes, Miro thought about Tomas on the edge of the rock, and realized how little the mud mattered.

Miro reminded himself to thank Layla.

He was glad she had come.

2

It was situated high in the mountains, in the very center of the Empire. It was encircled by the Ring Forts, the five fortresses that had never been taken by force while in Halrana hands, only by treachery. Grand, yet small, the town of Mornhaven's unique geography was only exceeded by its place in history.

Long ago, the Western Rebellion had ended here, when Tessolar's betrayal of Serosa, the Alturan high lord, ensured the surrender of Altura and Halaran to the emperor. The crushing Treaty of Mornhaven that the emperor enforced on the two rebel houses resulted in peace—but only for a time.

Twenty years later, it was at Mornhaven that Miro, Serosa's son, confronted Tessolar, revealing Tessolar's treachery to the world. At Mornhaven Miro was made lord marshal, rallying the last free men to his cause.

Now, over two years after the death of Primate Melovar Aspen, Mornhaven had a new place in history. The town no longer flew the flag of Halaran, nor did the five Ring Forts—Manrith, Penton, Ramrar, Charing, and Sark. High Lord Tiesto of Halaran had gifted this part of his domain not to one nation, but to the Empire as a whole. Soldiers of all nations traveled daily on the winding mountain roads, and a strict rotation system ensured the different houses occupied the Ring Forts evenly.

It was here, at Mornhaven, that the strange man known as Evrin Evenstar was building the new machines.

The common soldiers didn't actually know where the work was being done, but those who'd been at Mornhaven and the Ring Forts the longest tended to look nervously down at the ground. There were catacombs deep beneath the mountains, connecting the town with its protective circle of fortresses, and the locals said the tunnels stretched for miles, with some caverns so huge, they contained actual lakes.

Only a few knew if the rumors were true: that a new harvesting plant, extraction system, and refinery were being built down there. But occasionally a rumble could be felt, and there wasn't a man who didn't believe lore was the cause. Many a brave soldier walked gingerly, half-expecting the earth to erupt beneath his feet.

Ella herself was uncomfortable, but in her case it was with the sensation of weighty rock resting above her head. She walked through a glowing archway, reading the runes she'd inscribed herself, lore that would provide light and help to regulate the environment of the chamber beyond.

Ahead, Ella was confronted by a bright device that sparked and blinked on and off intermittently. Ella put her satchel down at the foot of the archway and watched Evrin work.

Evrin was manipulating a pointed cylinder, but rather than touching it, he sang to it softly, his eyes watching intently. The cylinder stood on an arm of blue metal, and a thin beam of light shone from the cylinder onto a great crystal that buzzed and hummed, seemingly suspended in the air. Light also shone from the jewel's glittering facets, and Ella knew the light should focus onto a point underneath. Instead, the light was a wan shade of pink, diffuse and lacking power.

"Need the scratched energy tables," Evrin muttered.

Ella walked over to a workbench at the side of the chamber and searched through the books stacked haphazardly until she found what she was looking for. She walked over to where Evrin glared at the cylinder.

"Here," she said, opening the book at the right page.

"Ah." Evrin's eyes lit up. "You're back, my dear. I could use your help with this. Two years, and we're almost there, but I always knew the problem would be with the scratched refinery, and here we are."

Ella looked once more at the wondrous floating crystal. "It seems unfair that it takes all this work to extract essence from lignite, while the vats that extract it from the dead are simple in comparison."

"What can I say?" Evrin responded, peering at Ella from under gray eyebrows. "There's more life energy in people than in plants. It's easier. But this way is better for us."

"It is." Ella grinned. "And we're nearly there. What can I do to help?" she said.

She worked with Evrin for over two hours, rarely understanding the things he directed her to do, yet, as always, learning all the time. She felt herself losing track of time, a frequent occurrence when working down in the catacombs, and it was Evrin who finally noticed the satchel resting on the ground at the foot of the archway.

"Oh." He looked abashed. "Is it Lordsday already? Why didn't you say something?"

"I wanted to help," Ella said. She smiled. "It's fine. I'll still make it in time."

"Well," Evrin harrumphed. "So you're off then."

"Are you sure you won't come to the wedding?"

"Too much to do here," Evrin said. "Tell me what the food is like, though, won't you? Do you think they'll match wines? There are some lovely wines in Altura's south . . ."

Ella laughed. "Just come. We'd all be happy to have you. You can't work all the time."

"No," Evrin said, uncharacteristically abrupt, and as he turned away, Ella saw through his façade as she only had a few times before. "Weddings aren't my thing."

Ella's face fell as she remembered Evrin's story. To her it was centuries ago, but to him the loss of the woman he loved was still raw.

"I'm sorry," she said. "At least you had someone special. Not many people can say that. Perhaps one day you'll find another." She hoped it was the right thing to say. Ella wished she had Miro's way with words. Her brother never appeared flustered or uncertain.

"For me there isn't anyone else, Ella. I betrayed my brothers for her. Yet it was she who showed me it was right." Evrin brightened, though Ella knew it was only a front. "Have a wonderful time, my dear, and don't mind me. Please give your brother and his new wife my best." He reached over to touch Ella's shoulder, a rare gesture of affection. "You've been a great help. I wish I had time to teach you more, but this must take priority. The world needs essence." He turned back to the apparatus in front of him. "You'd best be going now."

Ella took one last look at the distant peaks of the Ring Forts before turning her back away from Mornhaven, and away from her work for the first time in what seemed like an eternity.

It was strange: Here she was, working with someone whose knowledge was so far beyond her own it scared her, yet she still wasn't learning what she wanted to learn. She knew the most important task at hand was to build the machines, and she would give everything she could to that goal, but the desire had never left her to bridge the different schools of lore. Ella had started down the path: She had made Miro armorsilk that could project an illusion and devised an enchantment that used Petrya's lore to turn the boiling water of Lake Halapusa to ice. What else could be done? Would she ever have the opportunity to find out?

"Stop working," Ella said to herself, smiling.

She deliberately turned her thoughts to the journey she had ahead of her. Ella hadn't told Evrin she was making the journey from Mornhaven to Sarostar alone, and the preoccupied old man hadn't thought to ask, but she was pleased she'd made the decision. She felt excited and free to be traveling, and she knew that her solitude would soon come to an end when she saw all of her friends at the wedding.

Spring was in full force, with summer just around the corner. The sun was warm on Ella's back, and the smell of new growth filled the air. As she descended down the winding road, leaving the mountains for Halaran's fertile lowlands, Ella passed through small farming villages, feeling comforted by the signs of normal life. On a field to her right, a group of men were walking down a row of vines, trimming the loose leaves and calling out to one another. She followed an arched stone bridge over a bubbling river and stopped for a moment to watch a water-powered mill grinding grain into flour. The water sluiced through the great paddles, splashing and sloshing ceaselessly.

Ella spent her first two nights at village inns, surprised at the way the proprietors fawned over her and gratefully took her gilden. She wore traveling clothes rather than her enchantress's dress, but she realized that to these people she was a wealthy guest, with clean skin, delicate hands, and a well-cut brown dress of thick wool. The food was good: hearty country stews seasoned to a dark red color and served with plump dumplings. Each time Ella made sure to stay in the most expensive room, and earnestly thanked each innkeeper as she left.

As Ella's journey took her closer to Altura and deeper into Halaran's heartland, traffic on the road increased and she kept a wary eye out for brigands. With more people around, she saw more visible signs of poverty. Stomachs were shrunken and fields were left fallow, the workingmen listless. Gone were the ubiquitous drudges of Halaran's merchants, bringing goods from one end of the Empire to the other. It was sad to see the inns using candles rather than nightlamps, and the Halrana struggling with goods on their backs where once they would have sat proudly atop a drudge-pulled cart.

After the large Halrana town of Carnathion, Ella's path took her onto the New Road, still under construction, some of it paved, some of it dirt. The New Road led to the recently completed bridge, built to connect Altura and Halaran after the Bridge of Sutanesta had been destroyed in the war. It had been named Samson's Bridge, in honor of the man who gave his life to destroy the emperor.

Just outside Carnathion's walls, Ella idly looked at a marble column at the side of the road, waist high and as thick as a tree stump. She suddenly stopped and stared.

This town was liberated by the allied forces of Altura and Halaran under the leadership of Lord Marshal Miro Torresante. May we never forget those who died so that we may be free. In the Year of the Evermen 544.

Ella touched her fingers to her brother's name and smiled, wondering on how many of these plaques Miro's name was forever immortalized. She was eager to see him; it had been too long.

She wondered who would be at the wedding of the commander whose name was synonymous with the fight for freedom. Who wouldn't be there? Most, if not all, of the high lords would be there, as would Rogan Jarvish, lord regent of the Empire.

Rogan shared the temporary leadership of what had been known as the Tingaran Empire with one other, in a power-sharing arrangement that must be difficult indeed.

Particularly when the other man was Ilathor Shanti of House Hazara.

Would he be there?

Ella had only seen the desert prince once since the events at the Sentinel in Seranthia. Rogan had asked for Ella's help in dealing with the Tingaran loremasters, and Rogan was someone Ella could never say no to. She'd known Ilathor was in the Imperial Palace, and she'd kept clear of him, but then she saw the tall prince in his elegant desert garb, striding down a corridor toward her, an aide at his side. Ella knew he'd seen her, but she'd turned, walking the other way. He hadn't followed.

Ella would be attending Miro and Amber's wedding unaccompanied, and that was the way she wanted it. Killian had made a journey he could never come back from; the orphan who had only wanted to discover his heritage had sacrificed himself so the world could be safe from the Evermen, those who had once enslaved humanity. With Killian gone forever, Ella just wanted to be alone. For her that meant work, and the construction of the new machines at Mornhaven provided the perfect opportunity.

Ella sighed and her thoughts returned to the present. Her back was growing sore, and she hoisted her satchel higher on her shoulder.

Soon she would be at Samson's Bridge, with Altura just beyond, but it would be dark soon, and she would need to find a place to stay.

Ella noticed a dust cloud ahead, big enough that it must be raised by a large contingent. She was making ground on it and wondered if she should be worried, but this was the new Empire, and these lands were finally at peace. As she grew closer, Ella saw soldiers in Tingaran purple and Halrana brown, marching side by side.

A standard bearer carried a tall pole with a black flag borne high above the dust. The image on the flag was a nine-pointed star, each point of the star rendered in a different color to represent the nine houses: green for Altura, red for Petrya, blue for Loua Louna, brown for Halaran, purple for Tingara, tan for Torakon, yellow for Hazara, orange for Vezna, and even the coral pink of the Buchalanti. The center of the star was white, bordered with gray: white for the templars, and gray for the Akari.

Ella knew this standard; she had last seen it in Seranthia. She knew the arguments had been bitter, but Rogan insisted that none be unrepresented. It was the symbol of the new Empire.

Ella smiled and quickened her step. As slow as the contingent was, she would catch up with it soon, and there was only one person who could be on his way to Altura carrying that banner. She ignored the curious glances of the soldiers as she made her way through the column. A tall man, his hair nearly entirely gray, led the group, his back straight and bearing proud.

"Rogan!" Ella called.

He turned at her call, and in the afternoon light Ella could see his smile.

"Enchantress Ella," Rogan said. He held up his arm. "Men, halt!" Soldiers from across the Empire came to a standstill at Rogan's command.

"Just Ella," Ella corrected, laughing when she came close. "It's good to see you."

"'Just Ella' is good for me," he said. "I've never been one to stand on ceremony."

"Where's your family?" Ella said.

"Right here," Ella heard a matronly voice say.

Ella hadn't noticed Amelia and Tapel beside the tall soldiers. Amelia placed her hand over her heart in the Halrana manner, and Tapel gave a mock bow.

"I can't get away from them," Rogan muttered.

Rogan had aged, Ella could see. There were more lines and creases on his face than ever. By contrast, Amelia's golden hair was still the color of wheat in the sun. Tapel, Rogan's adopted son, looked dirty even in his fine clothes, and Ella guessed it likely that he'd intentionally mussed up his mousy brown hair.

"You're looking well," Amelia said. "Not a young girl anymore, are you?"

Ella blushed. The few times she'd met Amelia, the woman had exhibited a habit of quizzing her about her love life.

"We might as well make camp here," Rogan said. "It's as good a place as any."

As the dust settled, Ella turned to try to catch a glimpse of Samson's Bridge ahead. Suddenly, she felt herself lifted as Rogan picked her up in a bear hug. It was so uncharacteristic that she almost shrieked.

Married life must agree with him.

———◆———

Ella felt nervous. She stood outside Rogan's command tent, where she knew he would be conferring with his aides and marshals. She had announced herself to the guard, who finally exited and nodded to her, holding the flap of the tent open wide for her to enter.

Rogan sat at a table with four men Ella didn't know. One was in Louan blue, another in Tingaran purple. The third was in the brown of Halaran, and there was even an officer in the red of Petrya.

"I don't mean to take much of your time," Ella said. "Rogan, may I speak with you for a moment?"

"Of course, Ella," Rogan said. He nodded at the men, and they each bowed in their own way, first at Rogan, then at Ella, before filing out of the tent.

As soon as they were gone, Rogan sighed, and Ella saw him slump. "I wish I'd never let your brother talk me into being regent, Ella. I knew it would be hard, but . . . Lord of the Sky. Here, take a seat."

There was a bottle of Louan red wine on the table, and Rogan poured himself a liberal glass. He raised an eyebrow to Ella but she smiled and shook her head.

"I try to keep the worst of it from Amelia, but it's dangerous there. The east is different. The people there need a stronger hand, a firmer touch. They're used to leaders like Xenovere and Moragon. Even the primate. Men who rule by fear and faith. I'm just an Alturan soldier."

Ella felt honored that a man like Rogan Jarvish would confide in her, but at the same time she felt worried for him. He was the strongest man she knew.

"There's a man—Bastian, his name is. He's rousing the common people and making my job harder. Bastian's just a tradesman—not a templar; I don't think anyone will be following one of them any-time soon—but he's a man of faith. And common people of faith will listen to him where they might ignore an old Alturan soldier like me."

Rogan took a long draught of the wine and then topped up his glass again.

"Ella, your brother thought it would be best to tell the world what Evrin told us at the Sentinel. That the Evermen were never gods and that instead, long ago, it was we who were their slaves. I'm not sure if he was right. I'm sure Miro thought it was for the best, but the people of Tingara and Aynar are devout, and without the Evermen to follow, they feel lost. Even we still call out to the Lord of the Sky. We're lucky he was"—he smiled—"*is* one of the good ones."

Rogan wiped his hand over his face. He looked exhausted.

"You can't simply change centuries of tradition and belief in an instant. Bastian says there's a conspiracy, and even if he's not a templar, I'm guessing some of them are supporting him. He says the war was Emperor Xenovere's fault and we've simply blamed it on the primate to discredit the priesthood. This 'revelation' about the Evermen is yet another attempt to take power away from the Assembly of Templars."

"People are stupid," Ella said.

"Yes, but people have power. And they're listening to Bastian. There have been riots. Nothing we can't deal with, but I worry about what comes next. The army is holding together, but even some of my men aren't sure what to believe."

Ella reached out and squeezed Rogan's hand. "Don't worry," she said. "You'll think of something. You always do."

"I hope your faith is justified," he said, smiling thinly.

Ella took a deep breath. "What about the Hazarans? Are they helping?" It was dangerously close to what she'd come here to ask.

"They're surprisingly good at dealing with the Tingarans," Rogan said, "perhaps because the Tingaran officers prefer not to work with us Alturans. I suppose that's not surprising, given our past. But since Prince Ilathor left, the Hazarans themselves have been more difficult to lead. They're not interested in following a foreigner, no matter what their prince says."

"Prince Ilathor left?" Ella said. "I thought you were both joint regent?"

"He did." Rogan turned his piercing gaze on her, and Ella remembered he wasn't an easy man to fool. He could probably see right through her. "His father, the kalif, is ill, and he was called back to the Hazarans' new capital, Agira Lahsa."

"So he won't be at the wedding, then?"

"No, Ella. He would have been on his way home when we received the news, and I'm sure he has bigger things to worry about.

Not only are we trying to find a new Tingaran high lord, but if Ilathor's father dies, he'll be the new kalif. Marshal Beorn is back in Seranthia trying to hold things together, as much as he'd like to be at your brother's wedding. I don't envy him."

"I see," Ella said.

"I'm sorry if you're disappointed, Ella."

"I'm not disappointed. I'm excited. We're going to the wedding of the two people I love most in the world."

"Ella?"

"What?"

"Prince Ilathor. He's a hard man . . . He would be a difficult man to love."

"Thanks, Rogan," said Ella. "I know."

3

Guests and well-wishers came to Sarostar from far and wide for the wedding of the now famous Alturan lord marshal, Miro Torresante, the man who had kept hope alive through the darkest days of the war, and his childhood love, Amber, an enchantress of the Academy.

The wedding would take place on the banks of the Sarsen, below the Crystal Palace, where people who had journeyed from all over the Empire could watch from one of Sarostar's tall bridges. There would be music at the palace fountains to start the day, followed by a river parade of flower boats. Four Alturan bladesingers would lead a procession of the elite palace guard through the garlanded streets, and finally the ceremony would take place exactly an hour before sunset, when the Crystal Palace began its evening display of colors. The ceremony would be followed by the performances of acrobats and musicians scattered throughout the cobbled streets of the Poloplats and Woltenplats. With feasting and ale, the revelry would continue into the early hours of the morning.

The guests were a roll call of the most powerful people in the Empire. They arrived in the city with their retinues until every inn and guesthouse in Sarostar was filled to bursting.

High Lord Tiesto Telmarran came with the Halrana high animator, Salvatore Domingo, along with a squad of handsome dark-haired soldiers in brown.

Jehral, Prince Ilathor's right-hand man, arrived with a score of dark-skinned Hazaran horsemen in black and yellow.

High Lord Rorelan and High Enchanter Merlon would, of course, be attending, as would the Tartana of the Dunfolk, whose arrival was perhaps the most exciting of all, with children skipping along behind and hiding from the mischievous glares the wizened old leader of the small forest denizens gave them.

Sailmaster Scherlic came via Castlemere, regretfully docking his Buchalanti storm rider, the *Infinity*, and setting foot on land with a shudder.

Ameet Ptolmec, the new high lord of Petrya, arrived with a dozen elementalists in bloodred robes, and the high lords of Torakon and Loua Louna came together in a display of unity. The isolationist Veznans, as was typical, declined the invitation, sending their regrets.

Then one came who surprised everyone.

Dain Barden Mensk of the Akari arrived with a small personal guard of tall, blonde-haired, pale-skinned warriors. The ice-dwelling men and women strode through the streets of Sarostar, proud and tall, with weapons of all description at their sides, from war hammers to broadswords. People drew back into doorways, whispering as the Akari passed, looking fearfully for decaying revenants, scanning for dead soldiers brought back to a semblance of life. Fortunately, the Dain had the presence of mind to bring none with him. The Dain looked uncomfortable in thick gray clothing and silver furs—much too hot for spring in Altura. Ill at ease in the city, he was quick to retreat to his lodgings.

On the day of the wedding, chiming music filled the air, and the scent of flowers wafted on the warm breeze. Inhaling the fragrance, Ella looked out from the fountains and up at the multitude of people who lined every bridge, watching the happenings below. The fountain display had been mesmerizing, timed to an orchestra of fifty musicians, and food had been served. Guests now mingled; the ceremony would soon take place, and a sense of anticipation hung in the air.

Ella knew she was nervous for Amber and her brother, but another feeling steadily crept up on her, a strange sense of dread she couldn't place. Perhaps it was seeing all these powerful people gathered in the one place. What an easy target they would be!

She tried to shake the sensation.

Hearing her name, Ella turned and saw Shani, the Petryan looking scandalously snug in a burgundy dress. Ella always felt drab beside her voluptuous friend, but Shani hugged her and then stopped, pushing Ella back and looking her up and down.

"Look at you," Shani said, shaking her head and grinning. "Lord of Fire, if there's a noble or soldier whose eyes aren't on you today, he's not a healthy man."

Ella blushed. She'd forgone Alturan green for a sleeveless dress of sky blue. It had been a long time since she'd cut her pale blonde hair, and it now spilled down nearly to her waist, straight and shining. She'd drawn around the edges of her eyes with a thin black pencil, something she'd never done before, and on her feet she wore silver slippers, matching the silver chain she wore around her neck.

Shani noticed the necklace. "You're still wearing Killian's pendant. Ella, it's been over two years. What about your desert prince? You two seemed to have something going there, although I'm not sure what it was."

Ella defensively took hold of the chain and opened her mouth, although she wasn't sure what she was going to say, when Bartolo walked up and slipped his arm around Shani's waist. "And what are you two lovely ladies talking about? Ella, your brother and soon-to-be sister-in-law are quite the organizers. I'm already flabbergasted and the day is young."

"Miro likes things to be perfect," Ella said, "and Amber's always thinking about other people when she should be thinking about herself. They make a good couple." She grinned. "And how are the two of you finding married life in Petrya?" It was her turn to make Shani uncomfortable. "Any little surprises coming your way?"

"We keep trying," Shani said, poking the bladesinger in the ribs, "but Bartolo here still hasn't put a child in my belly. The trying is fun though—a lot of fun. And there's still so much territory to explore."

Ella and Bartolo both looked at each other and then down at the ground while Shani laughed. "You Alturans are so prudish. Get a man, Ella. You deserve one."

"I'll leave you both to catch up," Bartolo said, touching his fingers to his heart and retreating somewhat clumsily.

"Where's Amber?" Shani asked, for once turning the topic to something Ella was comfortable with. "I'd imagine she's nervous."

"She sent me away," Ella said. "We spent the morning together, and now she's said she wants some time alone to think about things. Seeing her so happy . . . I can't tell you how it makes me feel. I'm going to go and check on her in a minute."

"And Tomas?"

"They're putting him into his costume, as much as he squirms." Ella grinned.

Shani looked wistful. "He's adorable." She gazed around. "I can't believe all the people who've come. You and your brother . . . You're famous, Ella."

"Well, my brother certainly is. I'm not sure if fame is what I'm really after. Shani, may I ask you something?"

"What?"

"Does it trouble you at all?"

"Does what trouble me? Speak plainly."

"All of these powerful people. All in one place."

"Ella, the war's over."

"I'm worried, though. Maybe I should say something . . ."

"Don't. It's a happy day, and people don't want to think about those times anymore."

"You're right." Ella nodded. "I think I'm just nervous. I need to go and check on Amber." She smiled and touched Shani on the arm. "I'll speak with you later."

On her way to the Crystal Palace Ella felt a hand clutch her arm and saw Amber's mother. They had never been friends; Ella had lived without strong parental guidance her entire life, something the stern woman disapproved of, whereas for Ella it was Amber's mother who years ago had pushed her daughter into a marriage Amber wasn't ready for.

"Ella, there you are. I was just looking for you. The men are ready. You should fetch my daughter."

Ella wondered whether Amber's mother realized Ella was walking in a direct line for the chambers where she'd left Amber preparing herself. "I'm on my way now," she said. Forgetting her talk with Shani, she blurted out without thinking, "I'm worried something's going to go wrong."

"Nothing's going to go wrong, Ella, and don't voice any of that talk where Amber or your brother can hear it. This is a big day for them."

I know that! Ella wanted to scream, but bit her tongue.

This was the day Amber had dreamt about since she was a young girl watching Miro in sword practice at the Pens. Ella didn't want to spoil it on a hunch. She was practical, valuing knowledge over all else. Yet, when she'd stood looking at all of the powerful guests gathered, she'd suddenly had a premonition, a flash of intuition she couldn't ignore.

"Ella, I know you haven't been lucky in love. But one day your time will come."

Ella stared at Amber's mother, dumbfounded. "This isn't about me."

"That's right. This is about my daughter."

"I need to get going," Ella said.

She moved past and began to ascend the broad stone steps leading up to the Crystal Palace.

"Ella!" she heard her name called behind her.

Ella turned and spotted Miro. Seeing her brother dressed in his finery, anxious and happy all at the same time, she momentarily forgot her concerns. "Miro,"—she took his arm, but he swept her up in an embrace—"I'm so happy for you. What are you doing up here? You should be down on the riverbank with the guests."

He wore a short white cloak over his green armorsilk, the *raj hada* of a lord marshal displayed on the breast. Miro wore it well, and suddenly Ella saw he was tall and regal, rather than lanky the way he was in his youth. The thin scar down to his jawline made him look dashing rather than sinister—like a war hero rather than a fighter. His long black hair was, for once, held back by a circlet of silver.

Miro seemed nervous, and Ella guessed mingling with the guests was probably the last thing on his mind. "I saw you walking up here, and I just wanted to see you before the ceremony. Do you remember the day the three of us—you, Amber, and I—sat on the lawns of the Academy? It was the last time we were together before the war, the day of your graduation."

"I'm not going to forget my own graduation," Ella said, smiling. "But I know what you're talking about. I think that was the day you realized what a fool you'd been to lose her."

"But not lost forever," Miro said.

Ella gave him the best hug she could, feeling a catch in her throat. "I always knew the two of you would be together. Now, you'd better take your place. I'll be bringing her soon."

As Miro turned, Ella suddenly stopped him with a word. "Miro, what's that?"

Guests were busy finding their places, yet the cleared space where the ceremony would be held was kept carefully empty, as if to walk through it would be somehow sacrilegious.

The large, pointed shrine couldn't be missed. It was as tall as a man, and although its gold trim and the intricate detail of the woodwork was impressive, to Ella's taste it was somewhat garish. Something in the design reminded Ella of the architecture within the Sentinel. More than anything it looked like a miniature version of one of the great temples she'd seen in Seranthia, dedicated to the Evermen.

"It's a gift from Evrin Evenstar," Miro said. "The Lord of the Sky has always been our deity, and we thought it fitting that even if he couldn't be here, we'll be married with his blessing."

"Evrin sent that? Are you sure?" Ella thought again about all the powerful people present. "Has it been examined?"

"High Enchanter Merlon checked it himself. He used something called a . . . divinity wand?"

"Divination wand," Ella said. "It alerts when near the presence of anything made with the slightest amount of essence."

"Yes, divination wand, that's it," Miro said. "Master Goss was there also, and they both announced there was no lore in the object at all."

"I'm glad to see they're not taking any chances with security," Ella said.

"We have bladesingers, the palace guard, and half the army scattered through Sarostar, not to mention the additional numbers of our guests' personal retinues. We have checkpoints on all the major roads and even the river. It would take an army to disrupt this wedding."

"It's already a wonderful wedding, and it's only going to get better," Ella said. "Good luck."

———— ◆ ————

"Amber?" Ella called out as she stepped into the dressing chamber.

Afternoon light shone through the walls of the Crystal Palace, and Ella smelled the sweet scent of roses. She turned a corner to find her friend sitting, composed, on an ornate chair, regarding herself seriously in the wide mirror.

Ella had spent all morning with Amber and only left her for a few moments, yet once again she was nearly breathless. Amber looked beautiful.

"I can't tell you how incredible you look," Ella said.

Amber turned to Ella, and there were tears in her eyes. "Thank you for leaving me. I just needed some time to think. People were probably asking you why you weren't with me."

"Well, your mother accosted me. Miro's more nervous than I've ever seen him. Bartolo and Shani are enjoying their efforts to make babies, and apparently I need to find a man. It was an eventful few minutes."

Amber laughed. "Thanks for making me laugh. You know, during the planning and the organization I've felt fine the whole time, and then suddenly it hit me now, and I'm terrified." Her smile was shaky. "What if something goes wrong?"

"Amber, you're the strongest woman I know, and you can do anything. You don't have to face any enemies, only your friends and family, and the man you love, waiting on the bank of the Sarsen, desperate to make you his wife. You can do anything you set your mind to, and together you'll make an unstoppable couple."

Ella took her friend's hand and helped her to her feet. "Thank you," Amber whispered, squeezing Ella's hand.

"Let's go show the world," Ella said.

───◆───

Ella couldn't believe she was finally watching her brother and her oldest friend become one. Not only watching but participating. Her own heart raced, so she could only imagine how they must feel.

Miro took a step forward, with Bartolo behind him. Bartolo's sword was bared and held upright to demonstrate that he would fight anyone who tried to disrupt the wedding. Few would take that chance with the battle-hardened bladesinger.

In contrast to Bartolo's naked threat, Miro held a summerglen in his hand. The petals shifted hue between blue and green as the flower caught different aspects of the slanted afternoon light.

As Miro stepped forward, Amber took a step toward him. Her dress was brilliant white, the color of crystal, and off her shoulders, leaving the milk-white skin of her throat and neckline bare. Her auburn hair was piled on top of her head in intricate ringlets that complemented her warm brown eyes. Dainty white slippers covered her feet, and as she walked, she looked at Miro and then down at the ground, the tip of her tongue moistening her lips nervously.

First one, then another guest made a sighing sound, an expression of appreciation, like the wind in the trees. A blush came to Amber's face, and then she began to smile. Once she started, it was clear she couldn't stop, for the smile broadened, and she looked around her, meeting the eyes of the guests, who all started to smile along, until all present, Ella included, smiled together.

Amber carried Miro's scabbarded sword in two hands, and behind Amber walked Ella, carrying a scroll. On it were the words she'd written, words about Miro and Amber she would speak at the end. She'd been writing for weeks and only hoped that when the time came she wouldn't falter.

Miro and Amber took another step toward each other, drawing ever closer, and between them Tomas tottered about, scattering flower petals and then falling down as he tripped over his shiny black boots. Ella looked out and saw the friends and dignitaries smiling. Out farther still, the opposite riverbank was packed with onlookers, as were the bridges and even many of the roofs of the buildings. The Crystal Palace began its evening display of colors, and a rising cheer came from the crowd.

At exactly one hour before sunset, by precise Louan timepiece, the two lovers would exchange the sword and flower.

Two more steps forward, and Miro and Amber now faced each other. Father Morten, the priest who had helped Amber bring peace between Altura and the Dunfolk, stood smiling beside the gaudy golden shrine. Bartolo looked stern and noble. Ella wished she could see Amber's face, but she was pleased she could see how happy Miro looked.

Father Morten began to speak, but Ella didn't really hear the words. She was drinking in the details around her and thinking about the words of her speech, rehearsing them in her mind. Ella glanced at the most important of the guests, seated in tiered semicircles around the happy couple. She saw High Lord Rorelan, wearing formal dress and for once smiling as he met her eyes and nodded.

Turning back to the ceremony, she saw Tomas actually behaving himself as he stood beside Father Morten.

Ella realized the words had stopped, and Miro held out the summerglen. He took the scabbarded sword from Amber as she took the flower.

They kissed, and Ella heard the great timepiece on the Green Tower at the Academy of Enchanters start to ring in the distance. The nearby fountains shot up ever higher, and the Crystal Palace brightened to an intensity Ella had never seen before.

The crowd cheered wildly, a mighty roar that drowned all else, so that Ella thought the whole city must have mouths opened wide.

Miro and Amber broke their kiss and both turned to wave at the crowd.

Ella smelled burning.

She looked at the shrine and suddenly thought of Evrin.

"We weren't gods," he once said, "but we thought we were."

The Empire's most powerful people were all here.

Why would Evrin give Miro and Amber a shrine devoted to himself? Ella knew Evrin; it wasn't like him.

"Weddings aren't my thing," he had said.

Ella thought about working with Evrin, and his sense of majesty and splendor in everything he did. He loved everything beautiful, from food and wine to art and the face of a child.

Evrin did not give this gift.

Ella looked at the shrine, so close to everyone she held dear, so close to the Empire's leaders.

"Everyone get back!" Ella screamed. The smell of fire was unmistakable. She could hardly be heard above the din.

All eyes were on the couple, but Ella saw High Lord Rorelan stand up from his chair, an expression of alarm on his face.

The smell of burning grew stronger.

Ella thought furiously, wondering how she could force everyone away from the shrine. Her eyes rested on Miro's zenblade. She knew the activation sequences for Miro's sword. She'd made it herself.

Something terrible was going to happen.

Ella called the words that would call the zenblade to life, chanting, her voice rising in strength. Under the scabbard the activation rune lit up, red lines traveling from one symbol to the next, colors changing, moving through the spectrum.

Amber had only moments ago exchanged Miro's flower with the sword. Ella stood directly behind Amber, and the zenblade heard Ella's call. She didn't want to burn Miro's hands off, but she wanted to clear the area. Fast.

Miro cried out and dropped the zenblade as the scabbard melted away. An impossibly bright searing light shone from the sword. Then came the sound: Ella had chosen it to be the most disruptive sound the sword could produce. The deafening shriek pierced Ella's eardrums.

Those in the distant crowd who thought it part of the show clasped their hands with delight, but many shook their heads and clapped their hands to their ears.

On the riverbank at the site of the wedding, it was pandemonium.

The guests fled the area, chairs knocked aside and hands held to heads as they ran. Looking at the shrine, Ella saw smoke pouring out in a widening plume. Igniting flames made the danger unmistakable.

Time slowed.

Bartolo grabbed Miro and pulled him away, activating his armorsilk and enfolding his friend in his arms as he did.

Rorelan lunged for Tomas and lifted the child in his arms.

Ella took Amber's arm and ran, tumbling them both into the walled pool of a fountain.

Behind them, the shrine exploded.

It was unlike anything Ella had ever experienced; the explosion was concussive and forceful, almost primal, like a volcano erupting. Above it all, Amber's scream stayed with her.

"Tomas!"

4

Father Morten died instantly in the strange blast. His body lay burned beyond recognition, flesh charred and eyes ruined. The fleeing guests were saved, with a wide black circle scorched into the earth where the closest had once been seated.

Bartolo and Ella's swift actions led to both Miro and Amber escaping unharmed.

High Lord Rorelan, after taking Tomas in his arms, caught only the edge of the blast as he fled, yet even so Rorelan's back was red and raw, with layers of skin melted to reveal pink flesh underneath. Nestled as he was in Rorelan's embrace, Tomas blessedly escaped the explosion, and only the backs of the child's little legs displayed mottled crimson and purple.

But the situation had worsened. Now both Rorelan and Tomas were vomiting blood, and white spots appeared on their fingernails. Investigators discovered a yellow residue on the scorched earth, and the same sickly color surfaced on the wounds of both man and child.

Miro ordered the city of Sarostar locked down, with soldiers blocking the exits and patrolling the streets. But the messenger who had claimed to be from Evrin Evenstar was long gone, and with no rationale behind who stood to gain from such a deadly attack against the Empire, a plan of inquiry had yet to be formulated.

As the days passed, Miro considered refusing the guests permission to leave, but Rogan talked him out of it. The guests were targets as much as anyone else, and suspicions were already growing between them. Some of the dignitaries pointed to the fact that the Veznans hadn't come to the wedding, and others whispered about the seating plan, marking out those who were conveniently placed far from the blast. Better that they go. Rogan's difficult task of keeping the Empire together was now made even more so.

After offering Miro and Amber their sympathies, the dignitaries left Sarostar in small groups and large contingents. Miro was forced to be polite and respectful, thanking them for their support and for traveling what for some had been a very long distance. Miro was surprised by the sincerity of Dain Barden Mensk of the Akari, whose deep-set eyes showed hidden compassion. High Lord Tiesto of Halaran was one of the last to leave, but eventually even he was called back to his homeland by his responsibilities. Rogan Jarvish had so far stayed and was a rock Miro could lean on, and Amelia's support of Amber was invaluable.

Initially relieved beyond imagining when Tomas escaped relatively unharmed, Amber was now distraught as her son's condition worsened. Her new husband consoled her, and neither cared that they were now officially married.

As she treated both Rorelan and Tomas in the Crystal Palace, Layla, a skilled healer, said their sickness wasn't natural. When Layla spoke of poison, Ella looked down at the ground, unable to meet Amber's eyes as the healer said there was little she could do to help.

Miro dispatched a messenger to Evrin Evenstar, but it would be weeks before the fastest courier could return. No one seriously suspected Evrin, but perhaps he could shed light on the strange blast and even deadlier poison.

With so many mysterious phenomena at hand, and no answers to be found, Ella buried herself in the libraries of the Academy of Enchanters.

Four days passed and Ella had found little to go on. She strode through the Great Court, heading from the Melton Library to the Wrenright Library, her footsteps quick and the sandstone buildings on either side passing her in a blur. She thought about what she knew, so preoccupied she almost ran into a centurion tree, stumbling around it at the last instant.

Ella was quite sure the device had utilized some kind of chemical explosive, which explained why the divination wand hadn't found anything, yet she'd never heard of a people with such knowledge of the physical world easily surpassing the masters at the Academy of Enchanters.

Even so, the makers of the device could harness strange forces, combining their explosive with a precision timer and a powerful poison. If someone, anyone, had encountered such mastery of the elements, there was no better place to look than the Academy.

Ella kept running the events of the wedding day through her mind. She didn't know how she'd felt something was wrong, but she'd learned to trust her intuition; only this time she hadn't listened.

She was now terrified of facing Miro and Amber and telling them she'd had a premonition but hadn't said anything.

Looming over the expansive court, the Green Tower was a dark square against the night sky, blotting out the stars. Ella didn't bother reading the glowing hands on the great timepiece. She knew it was late.

In the very center of the Great Court stood a tall marble statue, newly erected after the war. Given prominence over all the other statues spotting the Academy, this woman had been someone important indeed.

The carved woman wore a hooded dress decorated with a myriad of tiny symbols, although the runes were an artist's interpretation and not the real thing. Her hair was long and straight, flowing to her waist, and in the starlight it didn't take Ella much effort to picture the way it had been, shining silver.

Ella found herself in front of the statue. She looked down and took a deep breath, before gazing up at the face of Evora Guinestor, the late high enchantress.

"Evora, you always knew what to do. There's something buried in these books that tells me what I need to know. Please show me the way. You always said we focus too much on lore and too little on the physical world. Where should I look?"

"I hope she answers you," a voice came from behind Ella.

Layla looked haggard.

"There's nothing I can do," the Dunfolk healer said. Ever serious, Layla's ruddy face showed an expression more grave than Ella had ever seen her wear.

"How . . . How are they?"

"The wounds of the big one, the high lord, are grave, and he will not wake—the poison seems designed to induce a comatose state. Ella, I know the properties of many plants and mosses, but I have never seen anything like this poison. For now, though, it is the burns of the high lord that concern me most. His wounds are crippling, and internally his body slowly fails him. The fluids he expels are tinged with red. I hold little hope."

Ella put her hand to her mouth. "How . . . How long?"

"I cannot say. The high lord can hold on for a few weeks. Not long."

Ella's heart lurched, beating out of time. She couldn't imagine how Amber and Miro must feel. She dreaded asking, but she had to know. "And Tomas?"

"The child is stable, but the poison has him firmly in its grip. He will stay like this for a long time," Layla looked up at Ella, "however I do not expect him to wake without an effective antidote. All I can do is make sure the child continues to receive sustenance."

"Lord of the Sky," Ella whispered. If Layla didn't know what to do, Rorelan and Tomas's chances of recovery were slim. "Thank you . . . Thank you, Layla. For trying."

Ella forced down her emotions. There must be something she could do. She took a slow breath before speaking again. "Has anyone learned anything new about the attack?"

"They say there was no lore involved, but none know of anything that can create such destruction. The device also projected this poison." Layla shrugged.

"There must be something here to explain it," Ella said, looking out over the buildings of the Academy.

"Yet the wisest of your people do not know the answer. Perhaps you are searching too close to things you already know. Perhaps you need to look further, to where mysteries still remain."

"What are you saying?" Ella thought about the libraries she'd been searching. She'd been lost in all the treatises on lore, daunted by the volume of information on the peoples of the Tingaran Empire. Should she shift her focus?

"Also, there are those who say you should be with your brother and your friend right now."

Ella sighed. "I have to try. Something here could help them . . . Tell me, Layla, what do you believe?"

Layla met Ella's gaze. "I trust you, Ella. You are my friend. And I think you might be the only hope that remains."

It was some hours before dawn as Miro walked the corridors of the Academy, looking for his sister.

It was now the fifth night since the wedding, and he'd hardly slept. Rorelan's state had steadily worsened, and Tomas was still and unresponsive. Amber hadn't left her child's side, and Miro needed to see someone—anyone—in whose presence he could let himself be a powerless wreck, rather than strong for his wife's sake.

At this late hour guards patrolled the grounds and halls, and a uniformed soldier started to question Miro, but seeing who he was, let him past with a sympathetic nod of his head. Miro wandered the libraries for hours as he searched for her.

Finally, after pacing endless rows of shelves and waking up half the Academy's resident staff, Miro had searched all the libraries except one. A librarian pointed him in the direction of the Trenton Exploration Library, which apparently dealt with, of all things, discovery and travel.

Miro saw the glow of a nightlamp before he rounded a corner and spied his sister, hunched over a desk. Ella pored over a book, muttering under her breath and turning the pages so rapidly, Miro wondered she had time to scan them.

She obviously hadn't eaten in days. Her face was gray and pale, yet there was an animation in her expression Miro recognized immediately. This was the Ella who'd left the temple school at fourteen, yet had been admitted to the Academy four years later after a short verbal examination, dazzling the masters in the process.

"Ho, Ella," Miro said wearily.

"Just a moment." Ella looked at Miro and frowned before turning back to the book.

Taken aback, Miro looked down at the book she was reading and snorted humorlessly. He could read the title from the top of the page: Toro Marossa's *Explorations*. Toro Marossa's adventures were famous throughout Merralya, yet he'd lived long ago, and Miro could see nothing linking the explorer's well-known journal and their plight.

Miro moved to stand close beside his sister and tried to read the page she had open. Ella brought her face close to the page, reading every word as if committing it to memory. She then stopped, sighing and closing her eyes momentarily before smiling and leaning back in her chair. She made way for Miro to see what she'd been reading.

The islands I have come to call the Ochre Isles were once occupied. I have no doubt whatsoever. Abandoned buildings stood scattered throughout all three islands, in particular the largest, the one I named Sofia in honor of one who was once dear to me.

We spent most of our time on Sofia. The men thought we were searching for treasure, but it was signs of those who were here before that I was most interested in.

The native people had abandoned the isles many years ago, yet I knew I had found the remnants of a hitherto unknown civilization, for the buildings were all of an exotic design. We found several items of interest, including a large ocean-going vessel, much larger than our caravels, larger even than a Buchalanti dreadnought. This foreign ship was in a terrible state of repair, but fascinating nonetheless. Bronze tubes lined the sides, their purpose unknown, and the ingenuity of its construction was far beyond anything I'd seen.

We abandoned our exploration of the vessel when one of my men discovered some barrels marked with the symbol of a flame. He poured out a strange black powder, ran it between his fingers, and then took quite ill. After vomiting for some time, white spots appeared on his fingernails.

We took him off the ship, but before we left I noticed some of the barrels bore a second symbol beside the flame. The universal language of symbols told me we were being warned the contents of the barrel were poisonous. I instructed my men to stay away from the barrels.

We resumed our explorations elsewhere, first, of course, taking the sailor to the ship's surgeon. The man entered a deep sleep from which we could not wake him. I instructed the surgeon to give him the best possible care.

My first voyage to find what lies across the Great Western Ocean has been a success, yet has opened up more questions than answers. Who were those who built these structures? Why did they abandon these islands? Where did they go? What is this black powder? I'm resolved to return to these islands and to explore further still . . .

"There's more," Ella said. "Later in his journal, Toro Marossa mentions visiting the sailor's family back home. He was surprised to find him still alive but still in the same deep sleep. Miro, this was months later."

"Did he ever recover?"

"I'm sorry," she said, her voice softening. "It doesn't say."

"How . . . how did you find this?"

Ella flicked through the pages again. "I wish I'd found it sooner. I read this book when I was younger, but still, if it weren't for Layla . . ."

Miro shook his head. How long had Ella searched to find this one account? "Don't be sorry. Lord of the Sky, I can't believe . . ."

Ella rubbed her eyes. "I can promise you this chemical explosive isn't mentioned anywhere else in the Academy, and this explains why. We know something now about what the poison does, and we also know something about where it's from. The islands were abandoned when Toro Marossa found them, but that doesn't mean they still are. The creators are out there somewhere—the poison proves it—and they're not in the lands of the Empire."

"And the closest land to these Ochre Isles . . ."

". . . is Altura," Ella finished.

"Why would these people show themselves after being silent for so long?" Miro asked. "And why would it be with an attack against the Empire?"

"I don't know," Ella said.

Miro rubbed his temples. He needed to think. Why would these people from across the sea attack his wedding? How could he find the cure that Tomas needed? How much of a threat did people with such skills pose to his homeland?

"Please—come, Ella. You need some proper sleep."

"Don't worry about me," Ella said. "How are you holding up? I can't imagine how hard it must be."

"Amber's strong," Miro said. "You know that. She's sleeping right now. Layla gave her something."

"You need to sleep too," Ella said.

"I know."

Even as Miro picked up the heavy book and helped his sister out of her seat, his mind worked. Always a man of action, feeling impotent from his inability to do something—anything—he now had somewhere to focus.

He needed to find the people who'd built the device, and he needed to find a cure for this poison. Any people with the knowledge to make this powder might also have a cure. He had to find those who had tried to murder him and those he loved most.

Miro's eyes caught a huge map of Merralya as he exited the Trenton Exploration Library. To the west of Altura, the symbols of waves stretched endlessly.

"What are you planning?" Ella asked, seeing the direction of his gaze.

Even as Ella spoke, Miro made his decision. "It's a short distance from Sarostar to the free cities, and then you're at the ocean. Someone from the west crossed the Great Western Ocean to make this attack. It stands to reason a voyager can cross back the other way. You don't win battles by staying on home territory."

"You don't even know where to go."

"Does Toro Marossa give directions?"

Ella nodded reluctantly. "Yes . . . but he never returned from his second expedition and no one since has ever tried . . ."

"Then I'll find these islands, and if need be, I'll voyage beyond. It's time someone found out what's there."

"With Rorelan ailing, Altura's without a leader."

Miro felt the strength go out of him. "You're right. I shouldn't go myself. I'll send . . ."

"Miro, I'm your sister. I know you. You'll never forgive yourself if you don't go. The Council of Lords can administer Altura, and with the borders quiet, Marshal Scola can take over in your stead. It's terribly dangerous, and I don't like the thought of you going, but I can't imagine what you must be feeling right now. You need to find a way to help your son."

With the prospect of action, Miro felt a surge of adrenaline course through his veins.

Someone had attacked his wedding, an attack not only directed at him but at the Empire as a whole. With Altura's eastern borders safe, the danger in the west heralded a great potential threat to Miro's homeland.

The attack utilized a powerful chemical explosive, nothing ever seen before and no product of lore or essence.

To make the attack as deadly as possible, the explosive was laced with a poison.

Tomas needed a cure.

Miro's jaw set with determination as he made up his mind. He was going to find the Ochre Isles and follow in the footsteps of Toro Marossa. He would find these people and get the answers he needed. The thought filled him with apprehension, but nothing would stop him in his quest.

Miro was going to cross the Great Western Ocean.

5

Perched on the coast to the south and west of Altura, the free cities of Castlemere and Schalberg jealously guarded their status as the chosen home for hundreds of independent merchants and traders.

Relations between Altura and the free cities were amicable—Alturans were forest and plains dwellers, and when they traveled on water, it was in flat-bottomed riverboats. Altura was the land of enchanters, whereas the people of the free cities used no lore and were part of no house. There were no Alturan towns or cities on the coast, and the Alturan high lord commanded no navy. It was a void the free cities filled perfectly.

History said the founders of the free cities were of Buchalanti stock, and the denizens certainly had the round features, strange names, and guttural way of speaking. Yet there were fundamental differences. The sailors and sailmasters of House Buchalantas gave birth, lived, and died on the sea. Their storm riders, blue cruisers, and dreadnoughts were marvels of lore. By contrast, the inhabitants of Castlemere and Schalberg sailed the seas in conventional, sturdy ships. They preferred the luster of gold to the glow of runes.

The harbor at Castlemere was wide and deep enough for scores of ships to dock and berth. The wooden planks of the numerous piers rose and fell with the tide, and the ocean breeze blew constantly, with the smell of salt strong in the air.

Miro waited at the docks with Amber, Ella, and Rogan.

They would part ways here. Ella would turn back the way she'd come and travel overland to Mornhaven in order to resume her work with Evrin, and Rogan would take a ship to Seranthia, where he would continue his work holding the fragile Empire together.

Miro's journey would be of an altogether different nature. Equipped with Toro Marossa's directions to the Ochre Isles, he would take a free cities ship to hopefully find strange new lands and, most importantly, to find answers.

After seeing Miro off, Amber would travel back with Ella, as far as Sarostar, before returning home to Tomas.

Amber wanted to be by her son's side in case he woke, although Layla's opinion hadn't supported that outcome. Layla's words had been direct as only she could be: Tomas wouldn't wake without treatment.

Miro's conversation with the Council of Lords had followed the same path as the conversation he'd had with Ella. They wouldn't listen to talk of him staying and were anxious to discover more about this threat from the sea. He knew this plan was desperately dangerous, uncertain at best, but he was resolved to do whatever he could to help his people, and the woman and child he loved.

Amber's eyes were red but Miro recognized the grim tenacity in the set of his wife's mouth. Ella looked at Amber with concern, reaching over to squeeze her friend's hand.

Rogan turned to Miro. "I need to go. Good luck. Come back soon, and come back whole." The two men embraced.

Rogan then took Amber's hand. "Fear not. All will be well."

Amber nodded, and after bidding farewell to Ella, Rogan left.

They were silent for a few moments, the three people staring out to sea, loath to be the first to say good-bye. As the silence stretched,

Miro saw a graceful ship slide slowly past. Seeing the glow of runes on the ship's deck, Miro leapt into motion, running out onto the pier to get as close as he could.

Sailmaster Scherlic's form was unmistakable, standing with legs outstretched, activating the runes that would soon see the *Infinity* speed past the vessels around her.

"Why won't you help me in my time of need?" Miro cried, standing with his arms at his sides and fists clenched.

"I cannot!" Scherlic called, the sound carried on the wind.

"Miro," Amber said, running forward and catching hold of his arm. "Let him be. You don't need him. You have a ship."

"He knows something," Miro said. He called out again: "If you won't take me to these isles, what can you tell us of the people across the sea?"

"There's only one thing I will say," Scherlic cried. "Long ago, we promised never to cross the Great Western Ocean and never to seek them out. It's a promise we will never break. Not for you, Miro Torresante, and not for anyone."

The *Infinity* sped past and soon was lost from sight. Miro stood stone-faced as he watched the Buchalanti vessel disappear. Finally, Miro sighed.

"Which is your ship?" Ella asked.

"Pier thirteen," Miro said. "That big galleon, over there."

His eyes were on a three-masted ship with a raised forecastle at the bow and an even higher poop deck aft. Sailors swarmed over the vessel as they prepared her for the greatest voyage of her life.

"Not the newest ship," Ella said.

Miro spread his hands. "Who would agree to a voyage like this?"

"When do you sail?" Amber asked.

"The broker said with the ship loaded for such a long journey, she'll be heavy in the water, so we have to wait for full tide in order to clear the harbor. You two might as well go now; there's no point in waiting all day."

Ella was the first to open her mouth, and Miro could see she was unsure how to say good-bye. Who could say when they would see each other again?

At that moment a man in the *raj hada* of an Alturan courier came hurrying up, puffing and panting. "Enchantress, I finally found you. An urgent message . . ."

"It's Evrin's seal," Ella said, looking at Miro and breaking the wax.

Miro and Amber exchanged glances.

"What does it say?" Miro asked.

Ella swiftly scanned the note. As she read it her eyes widened, and then she looked at Miro. "Here,"—she held out the note—"you'd better read this."

"Just tell me what it says," Miro said.

"Evrin went to Stonewater to examine the broken machines. While he was in Seranthia, he decided to check on the portal at the Sentinel. Miro, he said the essence is gone, drained away. The seals failed for a short time, and he thinks something crossed over. Something . . . or someone." Her green eyes regarded her brother gravely.

"Killian?" Amber said.

"Evrin doesn't think so," Ella said. "And the crossing happened some time ago. If it was Killian, where is he?"

Miro didn't know what had existed between them, but he was sure Ella didn't want to be reminded of the man who had entered the portal, never to return. "The fact that we were attacked at the wedding and now Evrin tells us someone crossed . . . It can't be coincidence." He paused. "Is this it? Are we facing our ancient enemy?"

Ella looked up at Miro. "If Evrin doesn't know, then neither do we. I'm going to see if I can join Rogan's ship to Seranthia and meet Evrin there."

"What about your things?" Miro said.

Ella hoisted the bag on her shoulder. "An enchantress always has her tools with her."

Amber patted her own satchel. "We've learned the hard way."

"You'd better hurry," Miro said.

"Please take care," Ella said. "You don't know what you'll find out there. Just get the cure, and come back in one piece."

Ella quickly hugged Miro and Amber in turn, and then she left.

Miro and Amber were again silent for a time, both watching the galleon being loaded.

"Miro," Amber said, "you don't need to do this."

Miro turned to Amber in surprise. "What are you talking about?"

"It's dangerous."

"Amber, if there's even the smallest chance of finding a cure, I have to try. Layla's better than any of our healers, and I trust her to look after Tomas while I'm gone, but I also trust her when she says we need a cure. This is more important than anything else. Evrin's message only confirms it."

"He's my son . . ." Amber said.

Miro rounded on her. "He's my son too! Get that straight. I don't want to ever hear you doubt me again. Never, do you hear me?"

"Is this really our only hope?"

"We can't just wait for Tomas's condition to worsen. I can't sit by and do nothing."

"I can't either," Amber said, "but I have to. I have to stay here while you go. I have to stay here in case Tomas needs me. But what if you need me?"

"I always need you," Miro said, attempting a smile. "I'll return. Nothing will stop me. I promise. Now go."

"I don't want to."

"Go, Amber. Please. It's hard enough saying good-bye."

Amber looked down. When she looked up again, her eyes shone with tears. "Good-bye."

"Don't say it like that. I'll be back as soon as I can. Now go."

They kissed, and then Miro squeezed Amber's hand and sent her away with a gentle push.

As he watched her departing back, he took a few deep breaths to calm himself. By the time his wife was gone from sight, Miro was once more in control.

Looking on the busy ship, Miro decided it was time to meet the captain.

As he approached the galleon, feeling the wooden planks of the pier move gently beneath his feet, some of the sailors carrying barrels and sacks looked at him curiously. Many bore the stocky look of the denizens of the free cities, but there were also those with the curly locks of the Halrana and even some with the darker skin of the southern nations. One of the sailors touched a finger to his forehead, but he did it in a way that made Miro unsure whether the man was mocking him.

The galleon soon dominated his vision, with brawny sailors swarming the decks and rigging like birds on a tree. The vessel's name was attached to her side, the big brass letters screwed to the wood tarnished by her many voyages: *Delphin*.

Miro stood at the foot of the gangway, wondering how he would find the captain, when he heard a throat clear behind him.

Two men stood side by side. One was slim and well dressed, if slightly shabbily, in a white shirt, black vest, and tight crimson trousers. He had long graying hair, tied back in a ponytail, and red eyes, as if he hadn't slept well.

"Lord Marshal?" the slim man said in a voice clearly refined. "My apologies if that's not correct; I can never get my head around Alturan titles." He smiled and shook Miro's hand. "I'm Captain Roslen Meredith."

"Thank you for agreeing to the voyage, Captain," Miro said.

"Wait until we get there," Captain Meredith said with a smile and a deprecating shrug. He turned to the man at his side. "And allow me to introduce my first mate, Julian Carver."

The second man held a small chest in his arms, obviously heavy, for he leaned back, the muscles in his arms tensed. First Mate Carver had small eyes and a ratlike face, with scraggly whiskers and a balding pate. Yet his shoulders were broad, and when he spoke, his voice was authoritative. Miro's intuition made him wary about Carver. There was something about the first mate's beady eyes he didn't like.

"A pleasure," Carver grunted. "Cap'n, I'll just go put this in your cabin."

"Yes, of course," Captain Meredith said.

"A man of few words," Miro said as Carver ascended the gangway.

"Don't mind Carver," Captain Meredith said. "He has a fine reputation as a man who does his job well. There will be others for you to meet: our helmsman, quartermaster, and second mate, to name a few. However that can wait until you're aboard ship." He turned serious. "I don't need to tell you this is a major expedition, with only Toro Marossa's notes to tell us our destination is even there. It will take us the better part of the day to load supplies and fit the ship while we await full tide. Please, the Port Royal is one of the finest inns around and has been made available for your use. I'll send one of my men to fetch you when we're ready to go."

Amber had expected to be traveling back to Sarostar with Ella, but she now walked the narrow avenue lining Castlemere's harbor alone. She'd only just left Miro, but now, consumed with worry, she kept tossing her parting words with her husband over in her mind. She hadn't even told him she loved him.

Amber frowned when she saw two swarthy men talking while they smoked pipes. She wasn't far from the docks, and she could see their eyes on Miro's galleon. One pointed the stem of his pipe right at the ship, and Amber moved closer to hear what they were saying, pretending to rummage in her satchel as they spoke.

"The *Delphin* won't return from this journey. I'd be laughin'—if I didn't feel sorry for the lot of 'em," the taller man said.

"I'm no friend of Cap'n Merry. I'm laughin'," said the other, a well-dressed seaman. "Still, look at her. The *Delphin*'s old, but she's sturdy enough."

Even as she covered her eavesdropping by looking through her bag, Amber scowled. Miro was risking his life and so was the ship's crew. Amber felt inclined to scold the men, but something told her to hold her tongue.

"I didn't say it'd be the ship's fault. It's her crew. You know Cap'n Meredith as well as I do. He's not a strong man," the tall man said.

The well-dressed man guffawed. "Well, you never know. He could surprise us yet."

"Ah, but the pair of 'em. That's the problem."

"Eh?"

"Meredith and Carver," said the tall man. "Meredith don't know it, but the arbiters are writin' out a warrant for Carver's arrest. Carver's a good sailor, but he tried to bribe the wrong councilor when he got caught smugglin'."

The well-dressed man laughed again. "You mean the bribe wasn't big enough."

"You got that right." The tall man chuckled. "Still, Carver knows what's comin'. I reckon it's the only reason he took the job with Meredith. I don't reckon he's the type to face justice with a smile. Ten copper cendeens says either Carver or the *Delphin* don't come back."

"I'll take that bet. You're on."

Amber wondered at what she was hearing. Miro's journey would be difficult enough without making it with the wrong crew. These men obviously didn't think much of the captain, and Carver sounded like a man potentially fleeing justice.

Amber needed to discuss what she'd heard with Miro.

She turned back the way she'd come.

Retracing her footsteps, Amber made it back to the pier, relieved to see the galleon still being loaded, though it was late in the day. She encountered a rat-faced man on the gangway.

"Excuse me," Amber said. She tried to keep her face still as she wondered if this was one of the men mentioned. "I'm the lord marshal's wife. Can you direct me to his cabin?"

The rat-faced man grunted a series of directions, and Amber boarded the ship, even as sailors called to one another and forced her to dodge out of their way. It still took Amber several minutes to find Miro's cabin; the vessel was larger from the inside than it appeared.

She mistakenly entered a hatch in the main deck before realizing her error, turning back when open doors revealed scores of hammocks where the sailors obviously slept. Resurfacing to the open, she found a ladder leading upward from the main deck to the aft quarterdeck.

With the crew busy loading the hold under the main deck with supplies, the raised quarterdeck was the only place on the ship devoid of activity. Climbing up the ladder, Amber crossed the quarterdeck and then opened a door to descend another companionway.

Finally, in a corridor of cabins, Amber saw Miro's familiar travel bag propping a door open. Peeking inside, she saw a thick book sitting on a cot: Toro Marossa's *Explorations.*

"Miro?" Amber called, entering the small cabin.

Amber thought she would have seen Miro if he'd been on the deck. Yet now that she was below decks, far from the scurrying sailors in the rigging and the hold, she saw he wasn't in his cabin either.

Amber wondered what to do. She needed to talk to Miro, but he evidently wasn't on the ship.

She looked around the cabin's interior. This was where Miro had planned to sleep, night after night. The narrow cot looked tiny for such a tall man.

Amber's lips thinned as she thought about the bet the two men at the docks had made. She decided she didn't want Miro traveling on this ship at all. They would get the broker to find them another ship—and another crew.

Deciding to pack Toro Marossa's journal inside Miro's travel bag, taking both with her when she left, Amber picked up Miro's bag and placed it on the bed.

With a creak the cabin door closed, shutting with a click.

Turning in surprise, Amber looked at the door. She tried the handle. The door was locked.

Blood drained from Amber's face, and her mouth opened in horror.

The enchanted lock was coded. As a paying passenger, Miro had been given a door that could be locked for privacy. A simple activation sequence opened the door.

Without knowing the words, Amber couldn't open the door. The wood wasn't thick; a strong man could break it. But to Amber it might as well have been steel.

Breaking a coded lock was one of the hardest tasks for an enchantress. It meant reversing and unraveling the flow of the runes, finding the activation rune, which was often intentionally obscured. Ella would be able to open this door, but Amber's chances were slim.

Amber thought about the satchel on her shoulder. She had essence with her, and a scrill. But in the time she had, all she could do was set the door on fire, not a good idea on a wooden ship.

"Help!" Amber cried, pounding at the door. "I'm trapped!"

Amber looked at the tiny pattern of runes around the lock. Miro had said the ship would sail with full tide.

Amber cried and punched the door even as she examined the symbols. She didn't know when the tide would change, but she prayed she would have time enough. If she couldn't break the lock, and if the sailors didn't hear her cries against the chaos of departure and the bulkheads between them, Amber could only hope that Miro would come to his cabin before the ship sailed.

Miro leaned on the wooden rail of the galleon's poop deck, where a multitude of people had leaned before, watching the harbor recede in the vessel's wake.

At sunset Captain Meredith had declared it was full tide, and without further ceremony they were away. As soon as they were into the channel, Captain Meredith ordered full sails set, and the *Delphin's* canvas snapped in the wind as she picked up speed. Miro watched as first the dock became a thin line, and then he could see only the masts of the ships and the tallest buildings behind. Finally, the land became a shapeless blur of brown and green, and then it was gone altogether.

He watched in silence, thinking deep thoughts. As he continued to stare at the same part of the blue horizon where he had last seen land, even though it was much the same as any part, Miro thought about where he was going, and why.

Miro's quest was daunting beyond comprehension, yet all he could wonder was when he would next see his wife, his son, and his homeland.

"We're well underway, Lord Marshal," Miro heard a voice behind him, and turning, he saw Captain Meredith.

"Call me Miro, Captain," Miro said.

"I'll try to remember." Captain Meredith smiled. "If you're ready to head below decks, one of my men can show you to your cabin."

"I think I'll stay up here awhile," Miro said.

"The sea makes you think." Meredith nodded. "I've always found it so."

"How long will the voyage take, I wonder?" Miro asked.

"Who can say? Six weeks? Ten? We've had a fortunate start, however, for the wind is directly behind us." Meredith nodded in the direction of a passing ship, headed back toward Castlemere. "I pity anyone heading back to port. A day's journey for us would take them a week in the other direction as they try to make headway against this wind."

"A good start then," Miro said.

"Indeed. If there's nothing you need?"

"I'm fine here." Miro hoped he wasn't curt, but he wasn't in the mood for conversation.

"Very well, then. You'll have to excuse me, Lord Marshal. There are a few tasks that need seeing to. We'll be serving our evening meal in an hour. I will see you then."

Miro had hardly eaten in days. The thought of eating now sent a wave of gnawing nausea through his stomach. "I'll have to miss this first dinner, I'm afraid. It . . . It's been a difficult few days."

Captain Meredith nodded in sympathy. "I understand completely. The cook will keep a plate for you regardless, and if you change your mind, you can eat later on."

"Thank you, Captain," Miro said.

Miro turned back to the sea as Meredith left. He watched as first one, then another star appeared in the sky, until the dome of night sky overhead became littered with silver lights. Hours later, he watched as a golden moon rose above the horizon. He heard the ship's bell striking the change in watch, and listened to the calls of the officers and curses of the sailors. Miro was exhausted, but sleep remained far off.

Finally, much later, Miro shivered.

Leaving the rail, he found the rat-faced first mate and asked directions to his cabin. Carver wiped at his eyes and gruffly told Miro where he could find it.

Miro found the companionway in the quarterdeck, descending into the corridor where the passengers' cabins lay side by side with the officers'. He thought once more of food but decided against eating. More than anything, he needed sleep.

Miro reached his door, but cursed when he tried the handle and found it locked. Miro muttered the activation sequence he'd been given and felt the lock click open.

He pushed open the door.

"Oh, I'm sorry," Miro said, seeing a woman asleep in the bed. Turning away, he made to depart but frowned. He looked at the woman more closely.

"What in the Skylord's name . . . ?" Miro whispered.

There, asleep in his bed, was Amber.

"I don't understand," Amber said, squinting against the sun. "Why can't we just turn back?"

Captain Meredith sighed. "It's not that easy, I'm afraid. We're provisioned for a very long journey, but even so, supplies are limited.

Every day counts, and our agreement states that the moment we start bringing stores up from the lowest hold we turn back. We have a strong tailwind, which is fortunate if we wish to make good progress westward, but works against us if we try to head back to Castlemere."

Miro and Amber exchanged glances. Amber's face was pale.

Meredith continued, "It would take us a long time to reach port if we have to tack against this wind, and we would need to time our arrival to another full tide. In that time we will be consuming stores, all of which would need to be replaced for us to make a second departure."

"How much time would be lost by turning back?" Miro asked.

"At the end of it all, at least two weeks, perhaps more."

Amber put her hand to her mouth, her eyes wide. She looked at Miro. "What choice do I have?"

Captain Meredith addressed Amber. "I have a possible solution. There's a good chance we'll pass a ship heading the other way, back to port. We can transfer you across, and you'll make it back while we continue our journey."

"Can you guarantee it?" Miro asked.

"No, I'm afraid I cannot. I know these waters, and it's a good bet, but one can never be certain."

"I'll leave you now to make your decision," Captain Meredith said. Bowing, he left Miro and Amber alone on the quarterdeck.

Miro and Amber exchanged glances. Amber had immediately shared with Miro the discussion she'd overheard at the harbor, yet Meredith's words hung in the air.

Miro wondered whether to turn back, but who could say another captain would be prepared to make the journey? Meredith seemed competent enough, and Miro was a bladesinger, so Carver could be handled. If Miro continued with the *Delphin*, at least he would be armed with the knowledge that there could be trouble with the crew.

Miro felt every moment passing with urgency. Even so, he did know one thing—he wanted Amber off the ship.

"I can't decide for you, Amber," Miro said.

"If I can get off the ship, you'll continue on?"

Miro hesitated. "Yes," he finally said. "I have to."

Amber looked at Miro, and then sighed. "Then it's out of our hands. If we can find a ship to take me home to Tomas, I'll get on it. Otherwise . . ." she trailed off. "Otherwise, I'll be with you on this journey, for good or ill."

6

The *Delphin* rose as she climbed a wave and then plunged as she fell into the trough behind. She hit the water with a mighty thud, sending a quiver through the ship and making her timbers creak alarmingly. Spray shot up from the bowsprit in a fountain, the galleon's foremost point plunging under the tops of the bigger waves. Occasionally, a swell hit the ship from the side, and she rolled, dipping and twisting like an overweight dancer.

On the decks, the shade from the sails provided blessed relief from the scorching sun, but in the rigging the bare-chested sailors had little opportunity for respite. They worked continually, given rest only when the striking of the ship's bell indicated a change in watch.

After two weeks, an apologetic Captain Meredith told Amber her chances of finding a ship home were slim. The passage of another week told Miro and Amber they would certainly now be seeing the journey through together. Amber constantly worried she'd made the wrong decision, and nothing Miro said could help.

As they traveled westward the color of the sea deepened until it was the shade of an evening sky when the first stars appear. The waves grew larger, and as they changed course, First Mate Carver called out for a luffing sail to be trimmed. The rat-faced officer appeared to give most of the orders aboard ship while the red-eyed Captain Meredith spent much of his time alone in his cabin.

Toro Marossa's journal gave directions to the islands he called the Ochre Isles, but from overheard sailors' remarks Miro knew most of them thought it a fool's errand. At noon Captain Meredith would take a bearing from the sun to calculate how far north or south they were, while determining their final position using dead reckoning given their speed and direction. He marked their position on a chart, but Miro heard a sailor comment there was little purpose in making a mark on an endless expanse of blue.

Miro and Amber both avoided falling prey to seasickness, earning them the grudging respect of the men they dined with every night in the officers' mess. The meals were basic: boiled beef and potatoes, occasionally varied with pickled cabbage and bacon. Miro reminded himself that the fare of the common sailors would be simpler still. He and Amber would be having the best food the ship's cook served.

At these dinner sessions Miro met and came to know Second Mate Beck, Quartermaster Ulrich, and Helmsman Werner, all from the free cities. Conversation was forced, with little common ground between them. Captain Meredith often arrived late to dinner, smelling of spirits. Miro wasn't going to say anything to the captain on his own ship, but he hoped the man's drinking wouldn't affect his judgment.

The tiny cabins and narrow cots weren't made for two to sleep side by side, and Miro and Amber slept in separate cabins across the passageway, with the other officers' cabins on either side. Miro would have happily slept on the floor, but even Amber wouldn't fit into the space beside the bed. However Miro and his wife often spent time together in his cabin or hers, talking late into the night, making plans for the future, plans that always included their son as if he were well and they were on a simple voyage from which they would return home soon.

Now Miro was alone on the deck, watching the sun sink into the horizon, melting into the blue water like a crucible pouring liquid gold. He paced back and forth, feeling pent, thinking about his quest and about love.

Since Tomas's poisoning, physical love had dried up between the newlywed couple. Miro didn't pressure his wife; he was anxious to be there for Amber in whatever capacity she most needed him.

Miro sighed, concerned for Amber, feeling happy to have her close but worried for the danger of the journey and her fear for Tomas, growing more distant with every moment.

As if thinking about her brought her close, Miro sensed movement beside him.

"You've been here awhile. What are you thinking?" Amber said.

"I was just thinking about the officers," Miro lied.

"Captain Meredith doesn't seem like a bad man," Amber said.

Miro nodded. "A little soft though. These sailors are tough men. I just hope he can keep control of them on such a long voyage."

"They're being paid well," Amber said. "Sailors like to get paid."

"I'm sure you're not wrong there," Miro said, smiling. "Out of interest, though, do you know anything about sailing?" He felt helpless trusting their fates in the hands of these men.

"A little," Amber said, and Miro's eyebrows went up. "My father had a fascination with ships. He had a big book he used to show me, and tell me about what kind of ship it was we were looking at. We sailed little boats on the river once or twice, but it was actually big ships he was interested in. It's funny, we never once went to the free cities to look at the real thing."

Being on a ship reminded Miro of the time he'd sailed aboard the *Infinity* and pitched in just like one of the Buchalanti sailors. That had been a younger Miro, leaving Altura for the first time, on a voyage to Seranthia.

This journey was altogether different. The last time Miro had thought these dark thoughts he'd thought himself alone on this voyage.

Now they were two people who might never see their home again.

———◆———

The following Lordsday, Miro saw Captain Meredith on the forecastle, giving some sailors on the deck below him words of encouragement or perhaps reproach. Miro's eyebrows went up when he saw Meredith turn his back and one of the sailors make a rude gesture to the captain's back.

Descending from the poop deck to the quarterdeck, Miro surprised some junior officers smoking pipes in a sheltered part of the ship. They stopped speaking when Miro approached and gave him dark glares.

Miro hoped Captain Meredith could keep his men together long enough to see the voyage through.

He wondered if there was anything he could do. Miro wasn't sure how he could help, besides wishing the ship would go faster.

Reaching the companionway, Miro decided to head back to his cabin. Fighting the rocking of the ship, he pushed open his door and closed it behind him.

He sat on the foldout bed that doubled as a seat and took a heavy book from out of the wooden trunk.

Miro once again opened Toro Marossa's *Explorations*.

Contrary to what you may believe, I had never set out like this before, pointing myself in a direction and hoping to come across land. I've always traveled where I could see something on the horizon, and if this tacking back and forth across the unbroken ocean unnerved even me, imagine the feelings of the superstitious sailors.

I believe I could easily find the Ochre Isles again. There is a strange haze that hovers over them and is visible from leagues away, and between my extensive experience mapping uncharted lands and the captain's own skill with charting, the directions in these pages can be relied on.

But these long distances bring challenges even I was not prepared for. I can only thank the stars we found freshwater on the island I named Sofia, or we would never have made it back to civilization. I had hoped we would find the homeland of whoever had abandoned the Ochre Isles not far away, but alas, much to my frustration, it was not to be. I convinced the captain to continue onward, but even I could read the mutinous mood of the crew.

We had been out of port for eleven weeks. We were running out of food and water, and in the end the captain would go no farther. Against my arguments, we turned back for Castlemere. I still maintain that the Great Western Ocean is not endless, merely very large. Perhaps the barren islands we discovered could be used as a staging point for another mission. Perhaps the Buchalanti will answer my questions if I ask them in the right way. I would give anything to see what is on the other side of the world.

Miro started when his cabin door opened, and then relaxed when he saw Amber push back her long hair and shut the door behind her.

"Ho," Miro said, smiling. "I wasn't sure if you were taking a nap."

"You're still reading that book?"

"It's fascinating. Toro Marossa found these islands, yet the people who once lived there were all gone. He tried to find land farther on but had to turn back. Who were they?"

"Don't tell me you want to go exploring, Miro."

"If the islands are still abandoned, we have to face the fact we may have to travel further."

"Don't say that! I don't want to spend a moment longer on this ship than I have to."

Miro sighed. "Nor do I. Don't worry; I understand."

"I'm not sure you do," Amber said. "Miro, I need to talk to you. I went into the hold to see if there was any fresh fruit; this diet is making me ill. I overheard some of the sailors. They were expressing . . . misgivings."

"What did they say?"

"They swear a lot," Amber said, "but they aren't happy. One of them said if we don't find the islands soon, he's going to knock some sense into the captain. Another said something worse about us."

Miro's mouth tightened.

It was time to speak with Captain Meredith.

Miro thought about Amber's words as he climbed out to the open quarterdeck. Before looking for Meredith, he paused for a moment to watch the crew as they worked on the decks and in the rigging.

Miro hadn't had an opportunity to spend time with the sailors, but he had commanded soldiers, and he knew how to read the mood of a group of men. More than any factor, morale determined who would win on the battlefield. Some commanders would say training, but Miro knew that training influenced morale, rather than the other way round.

The morale of these men was low.

"A fish stinks from the head," Miro muttered to himself. It was a saying he'd picked up somewhere along the line. It meant that sloppy commanders created careless officers, who led undisciplined soldiers. It meant that if something appears wrong at the bottom, it generally pays to look at the top.

Scanning the galleon, Miro saw two skinny men scowling as they swabbed the decks. Another sailor in the rigging clutched onto the main mast and stared into the distance, looking at nothing, his work forgotten. Near the bow a junior officer struggled to break up a fight between two bigger men.

Miro didn't know how much Meredith paid his men, nor how much food he gave them. But these sailors were thin, and filled with resentment. Miro turned away, shaking his head.

He finally found Meredith on the bridge, conferring with the helmsman, and politely waited a short way away for them to finish.

Helmsman Werner, an unassuming man with sad eyes and drooping moustaches, nodded at something the captain said and then returned to the helm.

"Lord Marshal," Meredith said warmly, coming over, "what can I do for you?"

Miro smelled rum on the captain's breath.

"Can I speak with you alone?" Miro asked.

"Of course. Actually, there's something I want to show you. Please come with me."

Meredith took Miro down to the lowest deck and brought him to the rail on the port side of the ship. "We're now eight weeks out of port," he said. "See?" He indicated the heaving sea. "The water here changes color, becomes darker. The ocean here is deep, as deep as we ever voyage on—perhaps close to a thousand fathoms in depth. The water beyond"—he gestured ahead—"is deeper still. Deeper than we can, or would be willing to, measure. The waves will become much bigger. We are leaving the open zone and entering the deep zone."

"It must be difficult for your men," Miro said.

"My men?" Meredith turned, wobbling slightly, and Miro realized the man was quite drunk. "They're superstitious fools, but their fear is warranted. I know of no ship that has intentionally voyaged into the deep zone."

"Toro Marossa did," Miro said.

"Or so he says," Meredith said wryly. "His stories were always a bit fanciful for my liking. He returned from his first voyage, wrote *Explorations*, and then made a second voyage, from which he never returned. A similar fate may await us. But never fear, Lord Marshal, we're following the course he's described. If these islands are there, we'll find them."

"Your men are what I came to speak with you about, Captain," said Miro. "They seem discontent. What if they were to . . . try something?"

"Carver's a good man, Lord Marshal. He knows how to keep them in line."

"It's Carver I'm worried about," Miro said.

"Now, Lord Marshal," Captain Meredith said, lifting his chin. "I realize you've chartered this vessel, but I am captain on this ship . . ."

Miro held out his hands in placation. "I meant no offense. But, Captain, haven't you looked around you? Can't you sense the mood of your men?"

"It's nothing I haven't seen before," Meredith said. "I have captained hundreds of voyages, Lord Marshal. Tell me, on how many have you traveled as passenger?"

Miro looked about the deck, his soldier's eyes taking note of marlinspikes for grabbing wayward lines and axes for cutting through thick hemp rope in an emergency.

"What about weapons? Are there any real weapons aboard the ship? Cutlasses and the like?"

"We have an arms locker," said Meredith, "but I'm the only one with the key. Please put your fears to rest, Lord Marshal, and have faith in my men. They'll get you to these islands, if they exist, and home again."

"I hope you're right, Captain."

Miro decided it couldn't hurt to be seen in his armorsilk from now on. He knew Amber also had the tools of her trade with her—she and Ella now carried them everywhere—but it would be best if his wife stayed in her cabin as much as possible.

Miro hoped they would find the Ochre Isles soon.

7

Helmsman Werner coughed at the foul smell, tasting rancid air and damp as he waited for his eyes to adjust to the darkness. He took a step forward, and his left foot sank into viscous liquid reaching up nearly to his calf. Another step forward saw his other foot plunge even deeper. The stink was overpowering: urine and rot and the sweet stench of corruption.

Finally Werner's eyes adjusted, and he ignored the wetness on his legs, pushing forward through the liquid, occasionally kicking the ribs of the ship with his bare feet. Below him he could feel the smacks the *Delphin* made as she hit the water again and again. Creaking and sloshing sounds came from all directions.

There was a light ahead; a figure held a shuttered lantern, silhouetting seated men, creating garish shadows.

As Werner grew closer, he saw it was Julian Carver holding the lantern. The *Delphin*'s first mate was sitting on a barrel where some of the supplies had been put into the bilge to provide extra ballast. Also sitting on a barrel was Ulrich, the quartermaster, a fat, balding man who probably dipped his hand too often in his stores.

"Why choose here to meet?" Werner asked, finding himself a seat on a water cask. "I'm a helmsman, not a bilge rat."

"Can you see that Alturan and his fancy wife comin' down here to check on things?" Carver said.

Werner heard a snort from a newcomer and saw Beck, the second mate, a thin, wiry man with an earring and oily hair.

". . . Or old Merry takin' his lips off the bottle to sample some bilge water?" Beck quipped, taking a seat.

Fat Ulrich and Carver both laughed.

"What have you asked us here for, Carver?" Werner said. "You're the senior officer here. You organized this meeting."

"He's here to talk some sense into you," a voice spoke from behind him. Another latecomer sat down, a huge sailor with legs like tree trunks and a broken nose.

"What's he doing here?" Werner asked.

"This is Gus," Carver said. "He represents some of the sailors. Ain't that right, Gus?"

"That's right," Gus said. He looked at Werner. "I don't know 'bout you, helmsman, but we ain't too keen on sailing to the edge of the world and past. They don't call it the endless sea for naught. I'll say it plainly. Meredith's a drunk and we'll follow Carver here instead if he turns us back from this madness. It's been two weeks since we crossed into the deep zone. We want to turn back, 'fore it's too late."

"What about the captain?" Fat Ulrich whined. "The Council back in Castlemere'll have our heads for mutiny."

"Shh," Carver hissed. "I don't want to hear that word uttered here, not once. Look, the ship's surgeon has an expensive mistress back in Schalberg. If we pay him a gold dinar, he'll write up that the captain took sickly, know what I mean?"

"It's a big secret," Beck said, the lean second mate tugging on his earring. "All it takes is one man to break."

"That's why we're the only ones who'll be privy to it. As far as the men will know, the captain actually did take sick, and they'll be so happy to be turnin' back from the deep that they'll think of nothin' but their warm beds back home."

Werner remained silent. Carver seemed to have an answer for everything.

"So we kill the cap'n and give him a funeral service at sea, all right an' proper," Beck said. "That just leaves one other loose end."

"Here's where it gets tricky," Carver said, "but if we work together, stick to our stories, and—most of all—keep the men out of it, we'll be all right."

"Let's hear it," Beck said.

"So here's what we've got so far. The captain's turned sick, and with the surgeon in our pocket he'll back us up on that. The Council back in Castlemere knows Cap'n Merry as well as we do; they know he's not a strong man. You know Meredith, Ulrich. What do you think he'd do if he turned real sick?"

"Order us to turn back," Fat Ulrich said.

"That's exactly right," said Carver. "He'd order us to turn back. Now, the Alturan . . . Tell me, fellows, do you think he's the type to turn back without a fuss?"

"No," Beck said. "Him and his woman, their son's been poisoned. They're lookin' in these islands for a cure or some such."

"Right again." Carver nodded. "And if this Alturan bladesinger, a man consumed with his quest, threatens our captain and tries to force him to keep goin', who do we support? Our sick captain? Or a grief-mad foreigner?"

"The captain," Fat Ulrich and Beck said together.

"And if this Alturan threatens violence, and happens to be killed in a struggle, well, it's unfortunate, but we did the right thing."

"Who does the killin'?" Ulrich said.

"I'll say it was me," said Carver, "provided you all back me up as witnesses."

Beck nodded. "You're cunning, I'll give you that. Remind me not to cross you when you're captain. You're forgettin' someone, though."

"The woman's the easiest of all," Carver said. "You've seen her—she's a mess. Her husband dies, and we're turnin' back from the only hope she's got of saving her son, so what's she goin' to do?"

Gus, the broken-nosed sailor spoke, grinning. "Throw 'erself overboard."

"Three problems solved," said the rat-faced Carver, "with a tragic, but convincing tale to tell, and all of us bearin' witness. Three deaths: one by illness, another by violence, and the last by suicide. No need to involve the crew, except for our friend Gus here and a few of his friends, and even the surgeon only knows a part of it."

Helmsman Werner looked from one face to the other. "It's not as easy as that. You're talking about takin' on a bladesinger. He's taken to wearin' his armor these past two weeks. Even all of us at once wouldn't stand a chance. How do we take care of him?"

"He doesn't sleep in his armor, though." Gus grinned. "And that sword of his is too big to wield below decks."

"How do you know?" Werner challenged.

"'Cause I lowered m'self down the rail and peeked in the window, that's how. Did the same with his wife. Didn't see her sleep in no armor either, heh."

"Bastard," said Beck, rubbing his thin face. "I'll do more than look at her though when she's captured."

"Cut it," Carver said. "Let's just worry about taking the ship first. So, Werner, in answer to your question, we take the ship in the dead of night. But we'll get to the plannin' in a minute. I need to know everyone's in. Second mate?"

"In."

"Quartermaster?"

"In."

"Helmsman?"

Werner hesitated. "In."

"Seaman?"

"In," Gus said.

"Good," Carver said. "Gus, how many sailors can you trust? And I mean trust proper-like. All the other seamen need to think the captain's been taken ill."

"I've picked two," Gus said. "Fischer and Rawl. Both big men. Both trustworthy."

"All right. We move tomorrow night, no point in waitin'. We've already been out here long enough, no point searchin' around to reprovision on islands that don't exist."

"All right," Beck said, "tomorrow night. When?"

"About four hours before dawn, you'll hear the watchman strike the third bell of the middle watch. That's when we strike. With Gus and his seamen, there'll be seven of us. Gus, you and your two mates go straight for the bladesinger. He'll be the most dangerous."

Gus held up a huge fist, the fingers calloused by work. "I'm dangerous too."

"Me and the second mate here, we'll take the woman. The Alturan won't fight long when she's in our hands. Ulrich, you and the helmsman take the cap'n."

Fat Ulrich looked at Werner and nodded.

"Last time Merry drunk himself comatose, I searched his cabin and found the key to the arms locker. Here."

Carver reached behind to a roll of canvas Werner hadn't noticed before. He unrolled the sailcloth, and Werner saw the flash of steel as a bunch of sharp swords jangled.

"Good sharp cutlasses," Carver said. He handed them out, giving three to broken-nosed Gus. "Take them back to your berths, making sure you're not seen. I've cleared the decks until the next change of watch so you should be right. I shouldn't need to tell you. If you're caught with these, you're dead."

There was a noise in the bilge, a splash that sounded like a footstep, and in a flash Carver closed the shutter on his lantern so that Werner's vision went black.

The five conspirators waited in silence, each breathing as quietly as possible, knowing that if caught, the secret of their mutiny would be out.

Then Werner heard a squeal, followed by a screech of triumph and another splash. He heard Carver sigh, and then the first mate slowly opened the shutter a crack.

Cugel, the ship's cat, shone triumphant eyes on them as he held a dead mouse in his maw. He was often left to hunt mice in the hold, and he must have somehow made his way into the bilge.

First Ulrich and then Beck started to chuckle. Werner shook his head side to side, and Carver smiled ruefully before hushing them.

"Here's a thought to keep you warm tonight," Carver finished. "Merry has gold in his cabin. It's the pay from the Alturans. He doesn't trust moneylenders and prefers to keep it in his cabin, the fool. It's enough for us all to have a tidy bonus when this is done. Remember, tomorrow night, at the third bell of the middle watch. You'll do fine."

Helmsman Werner thought about what he'd heard about Carver's run-in with the authorities in Castlemere. With that much gold, Carver could buy his way out of trouble.

He looked at the cutlass he held in his hand.

There was no turning back now.

8

Captain Roslen Meredith added a mark to the chart spread over his desk, before making an entry in the ship's log and signing it with a wavering hand. He absently tilted his heavy-bottomed glass, waiting for the warm rush of alcohol to slide past the back of his throat, but frowned, seeing it was dry.

Tomorrow's course would be much the same as today's, just as yesterday's had been the same as the one the day before. His agreement said that on the day strict rationing commenced, the *Delphin* would head back to Castlemere. In three weeks, perhaps four, low stores would force him to turn back with an unhappy lord marshal and a crew already angry from reduced provisions. He must have been drinking when he negotiated that deal.

Meredith hadn't always been a drinker—not until the trip when he'd returned to find his wife in bed with his cousin, an underwriter whose work allowed him to stay in port while Meredith was gone for weeks or months at a time.

The underwriter was better connected than the ship's captain, and Meredith's wife divorced him, marrying his cousin and taking a large portion of Meredith's wealth. Captain Meredith now had debts he couldn't manage and prematurely gray hair. To keep up with his repayments to the moneylenders, he'd had to take on this foolish quest, a voyage no sane captain would have agreed to. But the interest on his debts was crippling, and here he was. Meredith hated moneylenders nearly as much as he despised underwriters.

Meredith sighed and looked at the chart as he refilled his glass. By the stars, they'd traveled an incredible distance. Once, this journey would have ignited excitement within his breast—an infinite horizon and an epic voyage to uncharted lands. Who knew what lay out there? But now, Meredith just wanted to drink.

Captain Meredith's eyes started to droop, and he heard the watchman strike the first bell of the middle watch.

∗

Alone in her tiny cabin, Amber couldn't sleep, thinking of Tomas. She hadn't told Miro about her difficulties sleeping, not wanting to add to his worries, but it had gone on for too long now, and she wondered if she should speak with the ship's surgeon. She'd stopped by the infirmary once before, which doubled as the surgeon's sleeping quarters, and the surgeon seemed like a man who could keep a confidence.

The ship creaked and groaned, lifted up on one wave before smashing into the next, always with the same up and down, rolling motion. Amber couldn't get the image of a cork being tossed around in a bathtub out of her mind. What made it worse was that she knew her model was all out of proportion. If the cork stayed the same size, the bathtub needed to be scaled up by several orders of magnitude. The thought made Amber giddy.

Amber rolled again and turned onto her side. Would it be better if she tried sleeping on her back? She tried it but wasn't sure whether it was an improvement. Her cabin was stuffy, but the seas were too strong to open the tiny glass porthole.

Her thoughts turned to a time soon after the war, when she and Miro had returned home to Sarostar. Amber hadn't been home since she'd led the Dunfolk to the great battle at the Bridge of Sutanesta. So much had happened since then.

Her long-awaited homecoming could have been tinged with sadness, but Amber had been surprised to find she was so excited about the future that the past held no power over her; it was simply the past.

Miro had taken her straight to the Crystal Palace as if it were the most natural thing in the world. He'd carried Tomas, still a tiny babe, in his arms, and whispered to the child. If Amber hadn't stepped closer, she wouldn't have heard.

"Welcome home," Miro had whispered in the babe's little ear.

He'd then shuffled Tomas to the crook of his arm and taken Amber by the hand, before leading her up the wide marble steps to her incredible new home.

Amber had been speechless, and Miro hadn't even noticed.

She ran the events of her wedding day through her mind. Lord of the Sky, it had been a perfect day to end with such horror. She'd never had a chance to find out what words Ella had written or have her first dance with her new husband. She'd never heard her father make a kind speech, or her mother direct a well-intentioned yet scathing comment to one of the guests. There was going to be music and dancing and incredible food. Tomas would eat too many sweets and then fall asleep. For once, Amber would have all the people she loved in one place, and it wouldn't be because of some great danger.

A tear formed at the corner of Amber's eye, spilling out to run down her cheek. What was she doing here? Shouldn't she be with her son? Had she made the right decision not to force Captain Meredith to turn back?

A vivid image came to her of Rorelan's back, burned red and raw by the explosion. As always, the next image was the mottled pink and purple of Tomas's legs, perfect from the front, yet touched by evil on their backs.

Who would send a device of such malevolence to a wedding? What dark and warped mind would do such a thing?

Amber's heart began to race as her pain turned to rage, and breathing evenly, she tried to calm herself and slow the beating down. She realized her fists were clenched and her legs tensed, and gradually she let herself relax.

But the release of sleep still wouldn't come.

Amber heard the watchman strike the second bell of the middle watch.

Miro woke, startled by a sound as the watchman struck the third bell of the middle watch. What time did that make it? About four hours before dawn.

Surely the bells didn't wake him? They were such a constant presence that they were simply part of the background noise of the ship. He heard a crash, followed by the sound of a man cursing under his breath.

Miro looked to where his armorsilk hung on a peg behind the door. He felt down to where his zenblade lay on the floor, stretched along the length of his narrow cot. Miro gripped the handle and raised himself up, feeling the weight of the sword, comforting in his hands, yet realizing it would be difficult if not impossible to use the long weapon in the cramped confines of the ship.

What was happening outside? Was he overreacting to one of the officers stumbling around after too much drink?

Miro heard a scream from the direction of Amber's cabin.

"Amber!" he shouted, leaping off the bed.

The door to Miro's cabin crashed open, and two strangers rushed into the compartment, cutlasses in their hands.

Miro cursed. The cutlasses were short and perfect for fighting aboard ship, whereas Miro's zenblade was far too long. Both were bare-chested sailors, big, brawny men with deep chests and arms like ropes.

What was happening?

The first man had a pockmarked face and graying hair. He snarled and thrust out with the short cutlass while the second man, a tattooed sailor Miro recognized, came around behind his friend and raised his weapon, poised to strike.

Miro dodged to the side, coming up against the cabin wall, while the cutlass cut the air where his abdomen had been. Cursing the limited space around him, he swore and dropped his zenblade.

What in the Skylord's name was going on? These men weren't trying to subdue him. They were trying to kill him.

The pockmarked sailor attacked again, cutting sideways with his sword. Miro was too tall to duck, and the ceiling was too low for him to jump. As his attacker came in, Miro grabbed the thick copy of Toro Marossa's *Explorations* from the ledge beside his bed. He blocked the sailor's sweeping cut, feeling the blade bite into the book. The sailor came closer, obstructing his tattooed ally, and the next time he attacked, Miro again blocked with the book and then smashed his fist into the man's pockmarked face.

He put everything he could into the blow, and with a wide-eyed expression of surprise, the pockmarked sailor went down.

The tattooed swordsman now came forward, and Miro could see from his stance that he was the more formidable opponent. Grunting, the tattooed sailor feinted and then hacked at Miro's torso. Miro saw the feint, but this time when he blocked, the cutlass cut through the book and opened up the skin below Miro's armpit. Miro felt wetness on his side, and the tattered halves of the book fell out of his hands.

With a look of triumph on his face, Miro's attacker came in for the kill.

The door to the cabin crashed back against the wall as yet another sailor, a huge man with a broken nose, came in, his expression murderous.

The cabin door swung on its hinges, and Miro again saw his armorsilk, hanging on a peg.

The tattooed man raised his cutlass to strike.

Miro shouted a series of activation sequences, turning his head so he wouldn't be blinded.

The armorsilk flared up with stunning brightness. A sudden burst of heat washed from it, and the huge broken-nosed sailor screamed in pain.

Miro's assailant shied at the commotion, and in that instant Miro attacked.

He turned from a side-on position, using the twisting of his body to generate as much force as possible. His fist crashed into the side of the tattooed man's head. Miro followed it with a series of blows to the sailor's chest.

The tattooed sailor attempted to swing his cutlass, but Miro came in close, butting his head against his opponent's nose, feeling the crunch as he crushed it against the man's skull. Miro hit the same spot again, and the tattooed man's eyes rolled back in his head as he crumpled. Miro swiftly squatted and took the cutlass.

He was now armed with a weapon more suited to his environment.

The broken-nosed sailor's hair was singed, but Miro hadn't been able to call forth the full power of the armorsilk; it was too dangerous on a wooden ship. The huge man's face distorted with rage, and his mouth twisted as he growled.

Yet Miro was armed, and his enemy didn't stand a chance.

A woman screamed.

"Amber!" Miro cried in anguish.

"We have your woman, Alturan," a voice called from outside the cabin. "Throw down any weapons and come out with your hands empty."

"I don't believe you," Miro called.

"I have a dagger at her throat."

Miro recognized the voice of the first mate, Julian Carver. Miro cursed and threw the cutlass to the floor. Looking warily at the broken-nosed sailor, he stepped toward the door, moving past the huge man.

As Miro opened the cabin door wide, the broken-nosed sailor punched Miro's kidney.

Miro gasped with pain and staggered to the floor. Stars burst in his vision, and for a moment he didn't know where he was.

When awareness returned, Miro rose slowly back to his feet, still wheezing. There were several men in the passageway, and behind him Miro sensed the huge broken-nosed sailor, eager for any opportunity to avenge his fallen comrades.

Carver stood behind Amber with one arm holding her close and the other holding a shining knife at her neck. Beside him Miro recognized Beck, the wiry second mate, also standing with cutlass bared.

"I'm sorry, Miro," Miro heard, and there was Captain Meredith, just outside the captain's cabin, a dagger also at his throat. The plump quartermaster, Ulrich, held the knife.

"Shut it," Ulrich said, pressing the point hard against Meredith's throat. A thin trickle of red ran down the captain's pasty skin.

Standing beside Ulrich, the helmsman, Werner, also held a cutlass. All the officers were present except the ship's surgeon. Miro wondered if the entire crew was in on the mutiny.

Miro turned back to Carver. "Don't hurt her." His eyes met his wife's. "Don't worry, Amber; we'll get through this."

"Gus, here," Beck said as he tossed the broken-nosed sailor behind Miro some twine, and Miro felt his wrists pulled behind his back. The huge sailor, Gus, expertly tied them together, the cord painfully biting into the skin.

There was nothing Miro could do.

"Stop," Amber said.

All eyes were suddenly on her.

"I'm warning you," she said. "Let us go."

Carver snorted. "You're warning us? How about I give you a warning?"

The rat-faced first mate nodded at Ulrich. Without a word, the fat quartermaster drew his knife along Captain Meredith's throat, slicing it neatly from one ear to the other. Meredith's head lolled back displaying the gaping wound for all to see, and then with a gurgle blood began to gush out.

Miro cried out. He watched as the life left Meredith's eyes.

Ulrich released the captain, and let the man's body slide to the floor.

"Looks like I'm the captain now," Carver said.

"Stop!" Amber screamed again.

Miro tried to smash his head backward, but the big sailor behind him easily avoided the blow. Another blow to Miro's kidney made him cry out, but he fought with all his strength to remain standing.

"Be still, woman," Carver said. He nodded past Miro's shoulder. "Kill him."

Amber raised a hand, and Miro saw a ring on her finger.

"Stop," Amber said, her eyes flicking to the ring. Even standing in her nightdress, with a dagger at her throat, there was strength enough in her voice to make the mutineers pause. "Don't make the slightest move. I have an explosive device in the hold, in one of the store boxes."

Miro's eyes widened. He wondered if she was bluffing, but he remembered how wary she'd been of the sailors. She had her tools with her, and some essence. It was possible.

"If I speak the activation sequence, the device will explode," Amber said, in a voice of steel. "Let us go or I'll do it."

"I don't believe you," Carver said.

"You should," said Miro. "She's an Academy-trained enchantress."

"We need to be quiet," Beck said. "The men might hear."

"Let's get this over with," Carver said.

He nodded again to the huge sailor behind Miro. Miro sensed the cutlass come up at his side. He struggled with desperation as he saw Carver's knife cut into Amber's throat.

Amber gasped an activation sequence. *"Lithia-tassine."*

The ring lit up in a flash of red. A great thudding boom sounded below their feet, and the ship trembled like a wounded animal.

For a long instant no one made a move. Then the shouts and screams of terrified men from outside broke the silence. The other officers looked uncertainly at Carver, who gaped while his mind worked.

The companionway door crashed open, a sailor's head poking in. "Captain! Anyone! We're taking on water!"

The sailor drew back in shock when he took in the situation. His eyes moved, and he gasped when he saw the blood-drenched body of the captain.

Carver swore. He turned to Beck and Ulrich. "The plan's changed. Tie them and gag them while we figure out what to do. We need to save the ship."

"You," he said to the helmsman, "come with me."

Another sailor looked in and saw the captain's body, his face draining of color.

Through the open companionway, Miro heard the cries of panicked men. The remaining mutineers threw Miro and Amber roughly to the floor, shoving gags of cloth into their mouths before binding them hand and foot.

If the ship sank, they couldn't even try to swim.

9

Ella's voyage from Castlemere to Seranthia was long but uneventful. She'd found herself in good company: The captain was a congenial man with a host of stories from his adventures at sea; the officers were simple men, yet took evident pleasure in their work; and the presence of Rogan and his family ensured she felt she was among friends.

As the ship slid into Seranthia's great harbor, Ella couldn't help but stare up at the eerie statue of the Sentinel. Now that she knew the secrets the Sentinel guarded, Ella felt fear where before there had only been awe.

Someone had crossed over. Where was that person now?

The massive statue stood astride a wide pedestal, almost entirely occupying the rocky island barring Seranthia's harbor. There was now a small pier on the island, from which men hurried back and forth, carrying heavy stones from a barge.

They took the stones to where a wall was under construction, a wall around the perimeter of the island. Even from her distance Ella could see runes on several of the stones—the builders of Torakon were constructing this wall. Since his recent discovery, Evrin was taking no chances. He couldn't destroy the portal, but he could wall it up.

Progress was slow and the wall was low. Ella could see it would take a long time to complete, particularly if Evrin intended to enclose the entire statue.

Even then, would it be enough?

Soon the ship was a scene of organized chaos as the crew readied for docking, clearing the decks and reefing the sails. Ella descended to her cabin to get her things, and by the time she'd returned above decks, they were tied up at the quayside.

"Enchantress, we've lowered the gangway. You may now disembark," the captain said, giving Ella a small bow.

"Thank you for getting us here safely, Captain," Ella said.

A sailor helped her descend the gangway, and soon she stood on the firm wooden planks of the dock, feeling them sturdy under her feet. Ella felt a strange sense of rolling motion, even though her head told her there was none: a legacy of the voyage. She hoped it would go away soon.

Ella looked around for Rogan, finally spotting him descending the gangway, Tapel and Amelia in tow. He thanked the captain and the two men shook hands.

With the return to Seranthia, Ella could see the lines of stress return to Rogan's forehead. He waved to the men on the ship and came over to where Ella stood waiting.

"There's one carriage," Ella said. "Why don't you take it?"

"Are you going to be all right?" Rogan said.

"Evrin can't be hard to find," Ella said.

"This city can be a dangerous place." Rogan frowned. "Why don't you come with us to the palace?"

"I'll stay at an inn," Ella said. "I doubt I'll be long in Seranthia in any case."

"Let the girl be," Amelia said. "She's a grown woman."

Ella grinned, wondering if Amelia realized she'd called her a girl and a woman in the same moment. "I'll be fine," Ella said.

"You're needed more than I am. Take the carriage. I'm sure I'll see you soon."

"Just be careful," Rogan grumbled.

Ella bid farewell to Rogan, Amelia, and Tapel, and then looked around the harbor. If there had been any messengers for her, they would have arrived by now.

Evrin had once mentioned to Ella that he usually stayed at the Cedar Palace, one of the finest inns in Seranthia. It was in Fortune, the area closest to the market houses, where the richest merchants had manses.

Ella started to walk.

Fortune was a reasonable distance from the docks, and Ella's journey took her through several unsavory neighborhoods before the scene improved.

Near the harbor, there was at least enough activity to keep the streets busy and taverns maintained. Ships always came to Seranthia, disembarking passengers, fish, cargo, and news.

Farther from the docks the winding lanes grew quiet, and shop fronts had been boarded up. The people who walked the streets were thin and poorly dressed, and they stared at Ella in a way that made her uncomfortable.

Finally, she was able to relax slightly as she reached the first of many markets. Here, she only had to watch out for pickpockets and swindlers.

At the food markets, the wares on display were pitiful, and the merchants and tinkers in the goods markets hawked desperately; it seemed no one was buying. Ella found it strange, walking through market after market. She couldn't see enough goods, or buyers, for so many extensive markets. Once, before the war, this must have been an incredible place, where the citizens would have spent hours at a time, examining one thing after another until something took their fancy. Ella hoped prosperity would return to Seranthia.

The atmosphere drastically changed as Ella climbed a hill and entered the district of Fortune. For all the woes of the common people, Fortune appeared lofty and prosperous. Tall fences barred entrance to the expansive grounds of the manses, but Ella could still see through the bars to the façades of the extraordinary houses. In Seranthia, lords and merchants were often the same thing, with marriage between fading aristocracy and wealthy merchant families common. If these people were having hard times, it wasn't apparent from looking at their grand residences.

Ella felt confident enough here to ask directions.

"Excuse me," Ella asked, stopping a thickset woman with a boy at her side, "could I get some directions?"

The woman looked at Ella askance but noted the cut of Ella's traveling dress and hooded white cloak. "What are you looking for?"

"I'm looking for an inn. Do you know where I can find the Cedar Palace?"

The boy at the woman's side tried to pull on her hand, but she stopped him with a glower. "If you turn left at the next junction, the Purple Star is about ten minutes walk," she said. "The Cedar Palace is further down the street, past the Purple Star. It's directly above Barlow's."

"Barlow's?"

"It's an eating house. One of the best in the area. Good luck," the woman said, before taking the boy and leaving Ella behind.

Ella heard bells in the distance, signaling the middle of the day. Something in her chest told her she was close. Perhaps it was the rumbling of her stomach; she hadn't eaten since leaving the ship.

Resuming her walk, Ella passed a series of boutiques. Fortune's residents didn't shop in markets; they went to specialty stores for hats, shoes, dresses, or cloaks. She passed a dignified row of terraced houses, and then an eating house with black iron bordering the large windows and the name announced in letters of shining brass.

Ella looked into the window as she passed Barlow's, and there was Evrin Evenstar, a napkin tucked into his collar. Today he was dressed in fine garments, yet his piercing blue eyes and white hair spotted with ginger were unmistakable, even through the window.

Breathing a sigh of relief, Ella approached the entrance but drew back when a stiffly dressed man with moustaches opened the door. "Yes, madam?" the doorman said.

"Ella!" Evrin cried, seeing her from his table, drawing the attention of several patrons.

Seeing Ella recognized, the doorman drew back, allowing Ella to enter. She smiled and handed the doorman her satchel. Diners looked at her curiously before returning to their meals. Ignoring the waiter hurrying toward his table, Evrin rose from his seat and held a chair for Ella.

"It's good to see you. How are you? Did you just get here? You're just in time for lunch," Evrin said.

Ella shuffled in her seat and allowed Evrin to push her chair in before he returned to his seat.

"I came as soon as I got your message," Ella said. The tables were spaced far apart, and amid the low murmur of the other patrons there was little chance she could be heard, but Ella still felt uncomfortable in the dignified eating house. "Can we go somewhere to talk?"

"Barlow's is safe," Evrin said. "You should order. I've just asked for the bluefish in orange sauce. Sounds unusual, but the orange and dill work in perfect harmony . . ."

Evrin flagged the waiter, indicating Ella.

"Madam?" the waiter inquired.

Ella realized there was a dining card in front of her, a tall rectangle listing exotic-sounding dishes. "Umm . . ." Ella said. "I'll have the trout."

"Very good," said the waiter.

"Oh," Evrin said, catching the waiter's attention before he departed, "we can't drink too much, so perhaps just one bottle of wine. I'm thinking a light red. Perhaps a Louan gremandy?"

"An excellent choice, sir." The waiter departed with a nod.

"How do you pay for the meals here?" Ella asked. She couldn't help but think of all the skinny people on the streets.

"I don't," Evrin said. "Barlow, the owner also runs the Cedar Palace, the guest house upstairs. Once, I helped him with the streetclans. He's good at what he does, and they wanted a piece of the pie. Barlow supports several charitable ventures—why should he pay the streetclans money that could go to the poor? Let's just say, I helped him, and now, on my visits to Seranthia, Barlow doesn't charge me."

Ella realized the picture was more complicated than she'd initially thought.

"I came as soon as I received your message," Ella said. "I also have some important news."

Ella was suddenly silent as the waiter placed small morsels of savory-smelling pastry in front of them, each a different color and shape. "What's this?" she asked.

"They're to excite your appetite," Evrin said. "You haven't been somewhere like this before? Oh, you're in for a treat."

The waiter came back with a tall glass bottle that he opened with a loud pop. He sniffed the cork, although Ella wasn't sure why, before starting to fill Evrin's glass. Ella was surprised when he suddenly stopped and waited, looking at Evrin expectantly, with just the smallest amount of wine in the round glass.

Evrin picked up the glass and swirled the liquid inside, before tiling his head back and filling his mouth. He looked pensive, his eyes thoughtful, before he swallowed and a broad grin spread across his face.

"Lovely," he said.

The waiter then filled Ella's glass before filling Evrin's glass also to the level of Ella's.

Ella watched, bemused. There was a process being followed here that she didn't understand.

The waiter departed, and Ella saw Evrin pop a savory parcel into his mouth. He closed his eyes and sighed, before taking a sip of wine.

"Go on," he said to Ella, grinning. "Try it."

Ella picked out an orange morsel, wondering what the fluffy white filling was, and put it in her mouth. An explosion of sweet pumpkin and salty fish converged on her senses. She'd never had anything so delicious.

Ella looked at Evrin and smiled.

"Now take a sip of wine," Evrin said.

What Ella had to discuss was important.

But perhaps it could wait, just these few moments.

———

Finally, the bottle was finished. Ella swallowed the last mouthful of sourmelon and cress; she'd already finished the trout, unable to slow herself.

The waiter brought out a dozen chocolates resting in a row on a long tray. Evrin sighed with contentment.

Most of the other patrons had left, and they had their section of the dining room to themselves. The waiter kept an eye on them but maintained a discreet distance.

"Evrin?" Ella asked.

"Yes, my dear?"

"Did you send a gift for my brother's wedding?"

As Ella thought of the wedding and its terrible end, the bitter chocolate suddenly tasted like ash in her mouth.

Evrin was nonplussed. "Well . . . I've . . . I've been busy, you see."

"Don't worry," Ella said, sighing. "I didn't think so, and I have a reason for asking. Someone sent a monstrosity to my brother's wedding, saying it was a gift from you."

"A gift from me?" Evrin asked.

"It had the look," said Ella. "I don't know how to describe it, but it had the look of the chambers inside the Sentinel . . . the same look as the temples dedicated to the Evermen, here in Seranthia. For that reason, we believed."

"Dear stars," Evrin said, "what was it?"

"I didn't think it was from you, though," Ella said. "Your taste is a bit . . . different."

"Ella, what happened?"

Ella didn't want to say the words. The moment came back to her with horrific clarity. The sound of the device as it exploded. Amber's scream. Rorelan and Tomas's nightmare illness.

"It was some kind of explosive device," Ella said, clearing her throat as it caught. "It charred a wide circle of earth and nearly killed most of the Empire's leaders. We were lucky, and the guests were saved, but some weren't so lucky. High Lord Rorelan's health was critical when I left, and little Tomas will not wake."

"Oh, Ella," Evrin said. "I'm sorry, my dear. I truly am."

"Who would do such a thing?" Ella asked. "I doubt it was the Akari. Dain Barden actually went to the wedding."

"Good for him," Evrin said. "Who do they think it could have been?"

"There are those trying to point blame at the Veznans, and others who say it was disgruntled templars from Aynar," Ella said. "There's no basis for their opinions, though. And while I hear this man Bastian is worth worrying about, I can't see him doing such a thing."

"And you believe it's something to do with my message?" Evrin said the words that were in Ella's mind.

"I need to know what you know," Ella said.

"I don't know much," Evrin said. "As I said in my message, someone has crossed."

"Could it have been Killian?" Ella asked.

"No," Evrin said, shattering Ella's hope with the bluntness of his speech. "Killian would have made his presence known, and there are signs that make me believe the one who crossed had power, the kind of power Killian never knew how to use."

Evrin looked at Ella with that disconcerting way he had of shifting from levity to gravity.

"Ella, I believe one of the Evermen is in Merralya, and has been for some time. I think that deep down you know there is a link between the attack on your brother's wedding and this crossing of worlds."

"How could someone cross?" Ella asked.

"I don't understand it, but the essence drained away from the pool. Essence has never been corrosive, yet somehow it ate through the wall bordering the pool . . . even the stairs were melted away. Without power, my seals faded. The portal would have only been open for a moment, yet that moment was enough."

"Why attack the wedding?"

"He would be powerful, Ella, but not all powerful—not yet. After crossing over he would have found one thing very difficult."

"No essence," said Ella.

"Correct. You've always been quick. An Everman has the potential for incredible power, but he needs both essence and the skill to use it. My guess is his first objective would be to seek out essence, but his main quest is to reopen the gateway and help his brothers return. The portal requires a large amount of power to open for long enough to allow all the Evermen to cross in safety, and surrounding the Sentinel is a great empire filled with soldiers. He needs time, and he needs to subdue his enemies. Taking out the Empire's leaders would be a big stroke of luck. All of this is conjecture, but we must fear the worst."

Ella shuddered. "So where is he now?"

"I don't know. He could be anywhere. And by now he will have essence. Even on his own, he will be a force to be reckoned with."

"We need help," Ella said.

Evrin shrugged. "You're right there. Rogan's barely holding the Empire together, but it's imperative that he does. I'm troubled, more than I can admit. Even at the peak of the Empire's strength, with essence plentiful and the houses joining their strongest units, facing one of the Evermen would be a terrifying proposition."

"Before the war, we had over seventy Alturan bladesingers," Ella said. "Now, we have six, including Miro and Bartolo."

Evrin nodded. "Bladesingers, golems, nightshades, avengers . . . We would need them all."

"Can you do anything?"

"My efforts are best spent getting the machines working," said Evrin, scratching at his beard.

Ella held her breath, and then released it with a sigh. "I have an idea," she said. "There is someone who could possibly help us against one of the Evermen."

"I hope you're not thinking of me," Evrin said. "I have the skill, but I no longer have the power. Essence doesn't harm me, but that's all."

"If we could find a way to open the portal, we could bring Killian back and he could help us."

"No, Ella." Evrin's reaction was instant. "It's a bad idea."

"He's your descendant!"

"No," Evrin repeated. "There's too much risk. And I told you, Ella. You can never cross."

Ella decided to leave it. "Then what do we do?"

"All we can do. The builders of Torakon are constructing a wall around the Sentinel at my request. We're also guarding the Sentinel with as many men as will fit on that scratched island. I'm rebuilding the machines as fast as I can. There is something you can do, though."

"What is it?" Ella asked.

"We need to find the one who crossed. Where would you go, if you needed essence? The Empire's as dry as the Hazara Desert."

Ella started. "The Akari."

"They're the only ones with essence. Go to Ku Kara and speak with the Dain. See if they know anything."

"There's no use waiting," Ella said. She stood. "I'll leave tomorrow morning. Thank you for lunch."

"I'm sorry, Ella. About Killian."

Ella squeezed Evrin's shoulder and left him sitting, watching her go.

———◆———

That night, after the meal of thin soup served at her simple lodgings, Ella retired early to her bedchamber.

She sat on her bed and took something square and heavy out of her satchel.

It was a book, but unlike any other book, for its pages were made of a strange metallic material, and the edges were curled and withered as if from intense heat. The book was badly damaged, but some of the words and diagrams were still legible.

Ella had found it in the chamber inside the Sentinel. If Evrin knew she had it, he hadn't asked for it, and she had studied its contents endlessly.

The primate had possessed this book, but Ella was sure he'd understood little of what it described. Even Ella, having worked with Evrin for two years, had difficulty comprehending its contents.

She thought about what she had learned.

Only the Evermen could cross the threshold of the portal and live, or someone with one of the Evermen by their side. Evrin's powers were taken from him long ago; he could not cross.

This explained why Evrin had said Ella could never cross over to find Killian.

In addition, words needed to be spoken on crossing back from the other side, words Killian hadn't known when he'd gone over. It was a safety mechanism the Evermen had built in to prevent danger entering Merralya.

Even if she were able to open the portal, Ella couldn't cross to the other world unless she had one of the Evermen by her side. Yet without crossing over, it was highly unlikely Killian would be standing by, knowing the words, ready to pass through the shimmering curtain back to Merralya.

Additionally, the portal required power to open, even for a short time—a great deal of power.

Ella knew the Empire needed Killian's help. The only one who could challenge one of the Evermen would be someone who also possessed their powers.

It had been over two years since he'd crossed over to wherever that shining doorway led, but Ella knew in her heart he was still alive, trapped and unable to return home.

The thoughts and ideas whirled around in her head.

Ella only had the germ of an idea.

But visiting the Akari fit in with her plans neatly.

10

Rogan Jarvish returned to a city of seething tensions.

The city had changed in his time as lord regent. Seranthia's great wall was no longer used as a quick and easy way to execute dissidents, leaving their corpses for the dogs. The rebuilding of the wealthy districts and squalid slums was well underway, and the market houses of the *raja* were again sacrosanct places where emissaries and trade delegations could engage with each other effectively. Yet there was little trade between the houses, for basic needs such as food and shelter surpassed requirements for Louan-made timepieces and Alturan-made armor. The streetclans still dominated the poorer districts, a problem unfortunately low on the list of issues to address.

The lord regent of the Empire rumbled along the Grand Boulevard in a drudge-pulled carriage, heading directly for the Imperial Palace. With him were his wife, Amelia, and adopted son, Tapel. Lost in thought, Rogan's soldierly instincts suddenly made him look around.

At first he wasn't sure what had alerted him. Then, as the carriage drew in sight of the Imperial Palace, he knew there was going to be trouble.

The Grand Boulevard was a broad avenue as straight as a rule, so wide a stone couldn't be thrown across it, and so long one end could not be seen from the other. Manicured parks with beds of scarlet flowers lined both sides of the street, and the statues of famous figures from the past frowned down on the people below.

These people were now all heading in one direction. They were shouting and waving their arms.

Rogan could see a huge crowd assembling in Imperial Square, where the palace looked down haughtily on the common people below. Nothing in Seranthia was done on a small scale, and the Imperial Palace was no exception. A monumental edifice of crenulated walls and towers, with peaked white roofs poking from behind the battlements, the hundreds of windows only hinted at the size of the interior. Highest of all, rising from the palace above Imperial Square, stood a tower with a railed balcony, from which the emperors of the past had addressed the people of Seranthia.

Before he could open his mouth to alert the driver, the crowd grew thick around the carriage, and Rogan knew it would be impossible to turn around. He leaned out the window, heedless of the people shouting in the street.

"Forward!" he growled at the driver. "Get closer to the palace!"

The drudge picked up speed, and space opened up in front of the carriage so that they were able to properly enter Imperial Square.

"Scratch it!" Rogan cursed. They were so close! He hoped the soldiers would see his carriage and send out some men.

He turned to Amelia and Tapel, both looking frightened. When they'd docked after their long voyage from Castlemere, he'd been so concerned about the state of affairs, he hadn't bothered waiting for an escort to arrive. His poor judgment might now have jeopardized the lives of his family.

"Don't worry," Rogan muttered. "I'll sort this out."

The drudge could go no further, and the carriage drew to a halt. Seeing this display of wealth at a time when farmers had no drudges to plow the soil caused a wave of resentment to surge through the densely packed crowd. Stones bounced off the carriage, and the angry people began to rock it, causing Amelia to shriek.

Someone up ahead cried out to the mob, making speeches from a wagon cart, with the crowd responding to each remark with a roar. Rogan began to get seriously worried for Amelia and Tapel. He didn't have his armorsilk with him; with supplies of essence dwindling, it was expensive to maintain, and the same applied to his zenblade. He wondered if he should have left his family back in Sarostar, but he knew Amelia would never have listened. Or would she have? When it came to her son's safety, Amelia was all ears. He should have at least left Tapel in Altura.

Through a gap in the crowd, Rogan saw the speaker. Of course it was Bastian; he'd never had any doubt. Rogan had tried to open serious talks with the tradesman-turned-troublemaker, but the man always refused.

If Bastian turned the mob against them, they would die.

Bastian was pleased. He'd never managed to gather as many followers in one place before. And now some lord or lady was here, with Bastian holding his or her life in the palm of his hand. It gave him a heady sense of power.

"The Evermen haven't deserted us!" Bastian cried. "It's we who have deserted them!"

The crowd replied with a roar.

"There are those who say the Evermen weren't gods; that they never looked over us. Of course they were! Think about the wonders of Stonewater, the great machines and the golden light of the

Pinnacle, now destroyed by the Alturans. What about the Sentinel, now off-limits and under guard? Who knows what our western occupiers plan to do with the statue that has guarded our harbor for an eternity?"

The crowd surged and ebbed. A hundred paces away, the carriage of whatever fool noble was trying to get into the palace rocked from side to side.

"It's a plot to control the people, yet it's a plot that cannot work, for the evidence is there for all to see. I follow the Evermen, and no one can take that away from me!"

People shouted their approval. Bastian decided it was time to change tone.

"My name is Bastian, and I am a stonemason. My father before me was a stonemason, and back when Xenovere was the emperor, my father led a team of a hundred men in his workshop. Xenovere made sure the Toraks didn't get all the building work. Who needs Torakon's lore when you're building a man's simple house? Yet now they have the Toraks building a wall around the Sentinel and none of the work has gone to a single man from Tingara or Aynar!"

"That's not fair!" a man in the crowd cried.

"What does that mean? The Toraks build with lore, and essence is twenty times the price it was before the war. So for the cost of that wall around the Sentinel, we could rebuild more of the city, and we'd all have jobs!"

"They destroyed our city, so they should fix it!" a woman shrieked.

"Meanwhile, what are all these foreign soldiers doing here? We're plowing the land by hand, and our farms can only feed so many. Why should our farms feed foreign pillagers when the people of Tingara are starving?"

As Bastian's words took effect, the rocking of the carriage increased. The wrought-iron gates of the Imperial Palace opened, and a squad of soldiers came forward, but they were far from the carriage and struggled to push through to come to the occupants' rescue.

The carriage door opened, and a man stepped out. Someone raised an arm to strike him but was thrown back ten paces himself, before falling to the ground, dazed. People surged toward the man but were either tossed back or fell away to let someone else take their place. He was like a rock poking its head above the ocean, but a rock that steadily moved. As he walked through the crowd, none could touch him, and now that the occupant of the carriage had exited, the mob left the vehicle alone.

The tall gray-haired man neither rushed nor faltered as he moved toward Bastian's makeshift podium atop the bed of a wagon. The mob fell back from the man's stare but followed in his wake. As he drew close, Bastian realized with a smile that the approaching man was the head of the beast, the subject of many of his speeches.

Bastian had under his power the Lord Regent Rogan Jarvish.

With a warrior's agility, the Alturan leapt atop the wagon. Disconcerted, Bastian couldn't help but draw back.

"Lord Regent." Bastian smiled, his voice loud so the mob could hear. "So pleased you could come to answer for what you've done."

"I haven't come to answer for anything," the tall man said. He looked out over the crowd and continued. "I've come to explain some hard truths—truths you won't like but must face up to."

Bastian was taken aback. He'd learned to project his voice by helping his father on the masonry floor, shouting commands in an environment where a misinterpreted word could mean instant death from the heavy blocks of stone. The lord regent's parade-ground voice could easily be heard across Imperial Square, and the crowd was stilled.

Rogan continued to address the crowd, ignoring Bastian. "The truth is that things are tough for you here, I know," he said. "But they are little better in Petrya or Halaran, Vezna, or Torakon."

"What about Altura?" a man in the crowd yelled.

Rogan's face was sober. "In Altura the high lord is near death, with the lord marshal's son also poisoned, in an attempt to shatter this fragile new order."

Some in the crowd looked down. Even Bastian was taken aback; this was the first they'd heard of it.

"We've had enough of bloodshed, haven't we? We're working hard to give work to your men and put food on your tables. I choose to bring my wife and son here because I have faith in this city, that it's a safe place where things are getting better day by day. At the moment we're having to make do without essence, which is difficult, but we're making progress. The harvest will come in soon, and it will be the largest harvest yet made without drudges to till the soil. The new aqueduct is bringing water into the city without the use of any lore. I have faith that Seranthia won't just be the city she was before; she will be something even greater. I have faith in all of you. Don't do anything to make me lose that faith."

"When will the essence return?" someone shouted.

Bastian realized he'd lost control of the crowd. They now looked to the lord regent, where before they'd turned to him for answers.

"As we speak, the machines are being rebuilt. Lignite is being stored, ready to process. It will be soon, I can promise you."

"Why is it you use a carriage when we starve?" a woman cried.

"I use a carriage because when I returned only hours ago from Castlemere, I saw this opportunity to address you all and wanted to get here as quickly as possible."

Bastian sneered; he knew it was a lie.

"But," Rogan held up his hand, "this day I will take the drudge to the fields and give it to a farmer who needs it."

Bastian snorted but was forced to admit to himself that, for a soldier, Rogan knew the right things to say.

The lord regent turned to Bastian and gave a small bow in the Tingaran manner. He then turned back to the mob.

"Thank you for the opportunity to address you all. My wife and son have had a long journey by sea, and I have a great deal of work to do. Working together, we can make this city great."

As the lord regent descended, there wasn't exactly a cheer, but people made way for the commanding figure, and one or two even shook his hand.

There would be another opportunity, Bastian knew.

The coming harvest would never feed them all. Parents were less easy to reason with when it came to the fate of their starving children.

Rogan reentered the carriage, his shoulders slumping with weariness. The crowd opened up, and the drudge got underway.

"You did well," Amelia said. "I'm proud of you."

"I had to lie, something I promised myself I'd never do. Bastian wants power. Can't they see it? Scratch that man!"

"Sometimes you need to say whatever it takes. The worst thing that could happen would be for you to let the city fall to mob rule."

"What will I do, though, if the mob gets truly violent? Will I call out the army—my men, many of them Tingarans—to fight their own people? How do you think that will stand, having an Alturan order soldiers with swords to strike down the hungry citizens of Seranthia?"

"We're not at that point yet. You did well today."

"It's not over yet," Rogan growled. "Not by a long shot." He looked out at the common people passing by. "Evrin Evenstar, you had better get those machines working soon."

11

Miro woke to a burst of pain as a boot crashed into his head. He ducked his head into his body as he was kicked again.

He looked up, into the rat-like face of the *Delphin's* new captain. Carver rose when he saw Miro was awake. He stomped over to Amber's comatose form and kicked her savagely in the ribs. Amber moaned, and Miro wanted nothing more than to kill him.

They were in the brig, an iron-barred room half the size of Miro's old cabin. A tiny window let in fresh air and sea spray, and Miro and Amber were both wet and bruised. They'd suffered through more than one beating. Fortunately, the cut on Miro's side wasn't deep.

Carver nodded to some men, who entered the brig and cut the bindings on their ankles, dragging them both to their feet. Carver's men marched Miro and Amber out of their cell and down a series of passageways, finally emerging on the main deck. They continued to drag the captives across the deck, finally halting at a barked command from Carver.

Miro weaved on his feet as he stood near the side of the ship, with the rough water crashing not far below, squinting in the bright sunlight. Carver had evidently ordered the sails reefed, and the ship now bobbed on the water with little power or steerage.

He looked at Amber. She looked both terrified and filled with pain. One of her eyes was half-closed, and she had a blue bruise next to her mouth. Miro seethed with rage as he wondered what would happen next. They were far from home, and apparently Carver now had full control over the galleon and her crew. What story had he given his men?

Still trussed and gagged, Miro and Amber stood with hands tightly bound behind their backs. Sailors knew how to tie knots, and Miro had no chance of breaking his bonds.

The huge sailor with the broken nose hovered near Amber.

"Do it, Gus," Carver said, nodding.

Gus marched Amber to the rail at the side of the ship. Without a word he picked Amber up, his muscles bulging, and tossed her over the side.

Miro roared through his gag: a sound of primal rage. His arms burned as he pulled and twisted at his bonds, to no avail.

Carver waited a moment, and then nodded to a seaman who held a rope in his hands. The seaman dived off the side of the ship, the rope running free behind him. Miro counted the breaths. The blood throbbed in his head, and he twisted and strained, receiving a sharp punch in his gut from one of Carver's men. Two big sailors at the rail held the other end of the rope the diver had left with. After a length had vanished over the side, the rope went taut, and the sailors started to haul.

Miro finally saw Amber being pulled back over the side of the ship, with the end of the rope tied in a loop around her waist. The diver climbed up a ladder as his mates helped him over.

Amber flopped onto the deck like a fish. Carver strode over and with a flick of his wrist yanked her gag away. Tears of frustration poured down Miro's cheeks as she coughed and a large amount of water came out of her mouth. She twitched and spluttered, yet while she was still gasping, Carver stuffed the ball of cloth back in.

The newly made captain came over to Miro. "We can do this as many times as we like. Klaus here is a strong swimmer, but who can say if he'll find her again the next time? Or I can simply tell Klaus not to bother. Do we understand each other? I'm goin' to remove your gag now. I've learned not to let this one speak. She can breathe through her nose. Or not at all, as far as I care."

Miro nodded, and his gag was removed.

"You're no enchanter, but I've heard a bit about what bladesingers can do," Carver said. "Take a look."

Miro's head turned to where Carver gestured. "Stop!" he cried.

A sailor flung his arm, and Miro's armorsilk caught the wind like a kite, flying far into the distance before falling to the sea, finally swallowed by the waves. The sailor then tossed Miro's zenblade over the side. Amber's satchel followed.

"Now you're nothin'," Carver said.

"What do you want?" Miro said. He knew he would do anything to prevent Amber being thrown over the side again.

"Thanks to the lovely lady here . . ." Carver frowned down at Amber's still form. The sheer nightdress she'd worn when they were captured had ridden up to the backs of her thighs, the material now made transparent by the water. It clung to her breasts, and the sailors leered at her nipples. "Cover her up!" Carver roared.

A sailor threw a blanket over her.

"Where was I?" the rat-faced man asked. "Thanks to the lovely lady here, we've lost most of our provisions. Whatever her device was, it destroyed half our food and water and put a hole in the hull. The seawater ruined much of what was left in our stores. We've managed to stabilize the hull and pump out the water, but we're now in a predicament."

Miro looked around, trying to gauge the mood of the sailors. Those close by were definitely Carver's men, but some of the men in the rigging watched stone-faced. Miro guessed that Amber's device had made Carver's plans go awry. He'd probably planned to kill them all quietly and make up some story for the authorities. Now, with the sailors witness to the mutiny, there would be no turning back for Carver and his supporters.

Miro received an enigmatic look from Werner, the helmsman. He remembered that Werner had done little more than wave his cutlass around, and wondered if he had a potential ally in the man.

"So," Carver continued, "we've been left with no choice. We have to find these islands of yours in order to reprovision. That book by Toro Marossa you revere so much was cut to ribbons. Where are the islands? What can you tell us?"

Carver looked significantly at Amber. Miro had read over Toro Marossa's directions enough to commit them to memory.

Miro told him everything he knew.

Amber moaned through her gag.

"What is it?" Miro asked.

She wriggled until her back was to Miro and he could see her hands. Her wrists were tied too tightly, with blood seeping at the edges of the twine, and her hands were white with pink spots.

Looking through the bars of their small cell, Miro couldn't see any of Carver's men. They'd been left to their own devices as Carver fought to keep control of the ship and make as much headway as possible. If Carver couldn't find the Ochre Isles, they would all die of thirst.

Miro threw his body flat onto the ground, feeling the pain of his own bonds cut into his wrists. He kicked with his legs until his mouth was close to Amber's hands.

Miro took some cord into his mouth until his tongue found one of the tough sailor's knots, and he began to chew.

He kept his ears pricked for the sound of anyone coming to the brig; often the barefoot sailors were difficult to hear. If he managed to free Amber's hands they would be punished, but there was no use worrying about the future. Amber must be in excruciating pain, and Miro needed to do something about it now.

Miro managed to loosen one of the knots. He worked at it with his teeth and tongue until he could feel the cord stretch and give. Amber moaned again.

Miro moved to the next knot, learning the knack of it now. His teeth hurt and his jaw ached, but he kept working until he felt the knot go. Amber wriggled her hands, and he felt her sigh with relief. He continued until the cord fell away and Amber's hands were freed.

She rubbed at her wrists, her eyes closed and chest heaving, and then she pulled the gag away from her mouth.

"What about your hands?" she whispered.

At that moment Miro felt the regular pounding of the ship on the waves slow, which could only mean Carver had reefed the sails. The motion of the ship calmed, and for the first time in an eternity, the *Delphin* wasn't rolling on huge waves. Miro scampered over to their tiny window and looked out, then gasped.

"What is it?" Amber said.

"We're here," said Miro.

Miro was surprised at the pleasure he felt in seeing land for the first time in what felt like forever. Outside the window birds wheeled over a nearby rocky outcrop. Miro's view was restricted, but he could see the galleon had just passed through a narrow channel, with a headland on one side and the treacherous darkness of a barrier reef on the other. The water was a vivid light blue, and they'd entered a tranquil lagoon. He wished he could properly see land, but all he could see were the rugged trees that spotted the headland.

He heard the stroke of oars rumbling in their rowlocks, and then a longboat entered his vision, pulling away from the ship with each of the men's strokes. Barrels stood stacked side by side on the vessel, and Miro recognized Beck, the second mate, leading the provisioning party.

There was the grunting of men, and then a mighty splash signaled the throwing of the *Delphin*'s anchor. The anchor sank swiftly, plummeting through the water on a thick hawser of gnarled hemp.

Miro heard a throat clear outside the bars of their cell.

He twisted his body and saw the helmsman, Werner, standing and watching him silently.

"Here to beat us?" Miro asked, kicking with his legs until he was in a sitting position.

"Now that we've found your islands, I'm not needed for some time," the helmsman said. "Carver's going to have you both killed as soon as the ship has water and whatever food we can find. As we speak, the sailors are all fishing, so it's complete chaos out there. Divers are scraping the hull clean, and workmen are patching up the hole your wife here put in our hold."

Werner paused, and Miro wondered what would come.

"So, overall, Carver's keeping the men busy, but what you may not know is he's only just holding onto power. He made up some improbable story for the crew about you attacking the captain after he made a drunken pass at your wife, but no one believes him."

"Can you help us?" Miro said.

"That depends on you," the helmsman said.

"What do you mean?" asked Amber.

"With too many witnesses to the true story, Carver and Beck plan to turn this ship into a raiding vessel and prey on merchant ships," Werner said. "That was never my plan. The crew and I, we just want to go home, so I need Carver and the others out of the way, then we can blame all this on them. We can nominate a new first and second mate, but without me, the men know they'll never make it back. The captain and I were the ones who got us most of the way here, and the crew know they need me." He paused. "Most of the men didn't sign up for a mutiny, yet no one wants to go home to the noose. Even if we can deal with Carver, Beck, Ulrich, and Gus, there'll still be a hell of a story to tell to the Council back in Castlemere. I think it's best if I'm the only officer to tell it. Those with me don't want any loose ends confusing the picture, if you know what I mean."

"I don't understand," Amber said.

"He's saying he'll help us, but he doesn't want us returning with him," said Miro. "He doesn't trust us not to tell our version of events. That's right, isn't it?"

"But then how will we get home?" Amber asked.

Miro looked at the helmsman. "We don't."

Werner nodded. "We'll put you ashore and give you food and water, but you won't be returning with us."

"We'll never make it back!" Amber cried.

The helmsman shrugged. "It's the only option you've got. I suggest you take it."

"We'll take it," Miro said. "What do you want us to do?"

"I want to make a bargain. You take out Carver, Beck, and Ulrich, and I'll make sure you both come out of it alive. When one of the men comes to give you your food tonight, he'll leave your cell door unlocked. He'll also leave a knife inside your gruel. I'm sure you can figure the rest out."

"Not much risk for you, is it?" Amber said. "We risk our lives taking out Carver and his men; meanwhile, your hands aren't bloodied, so if we fail, no one can trace anything back to you."

The helmsman shrugged. "It's life, and I'm a practical man."

"How do I know I can trust you?" Miro asked.

"You'll have to take my word on it," Werner said. "Kill Carver, Beck, and Ulrich, and I'll see you set ashore. It's where you wanted to go, after all." He turned to go, leaving them with his parting words. "You do your part, and I'll do mine."

12

"Here's food," a voice said as two sailors approached the brig. The first man held a lantern in one hand and a hooked marlinspike in the other, and the second held two bowls of steaming gruel.

Miro's heart skipped a beat. Werner had said there would be only one man. Had something gone wrong?

He and Amber both sat on the floor with their hands held behind their backs, although since Werner had left, Miro had freed his hands. Miro had replaced the gag over Amber's mouth. To all outward appearances they were tied and defenseless, with only Miro able to speak.

The first man put down the lantern, keeping his marlinspike raised. "Back against the wall, both of you."

Miro met Amber's eyes as they both shuffled backward until they were leaning against the wall. Her eyes widened slightly, the only way she could communicate.

The man with the marlinspike inserted a key into the lock, and the cell door groaned as he opened it. He then made way for the second man to place the two steaming bowls on the floor, just inside the door, while keeping an eye on the two prisoners the entire time.

The man with the marlinspike leaned forward to yank Amber's gag out of her mouth. "You can eat like dogs," he said. "You won't be no trouble. I know enough to know enchanters need rings and the like." The cell door closed, the key once more jangled in the lock, and he bent to pick up the lantern. The two men left the prisoners in darkness.

Miro waited for the space of ten heartbeats, and when his eyes readjusted to the darkness, he pushed at the cell door. He didn't want to make it swing wide, just to check whether it was open. He held his breath.

The cell door was unlocked. It opened with a creaking moan, both Miro and Amber cringing at the noise. Miro sighed in relief.

He pulled the door tightly closed again, so it would survive a cursory check. He didn't want to strike during the evening meal; they would wait until the middle of the night.

Miro kissed Amber gently on the side of the mouth, avoiding her puffed lips and the big ugly bruise above her jawline, discernible even in the low light.

"Look in the gruel," Amber said.

Miro went over to the two bowls and brought them to where Amber still huddled against the wall. He handed one to Amber and dipped his finger in the other. A feeling of disappointment sank into his stomach when he felt nothing but gruel.

Then Amber held up a sharp knife, little more than a paring knife, but a weapon nonetheless.

"Now we wait," Miro whispered. "We should eat. We'll need our strength."

They ate the gruel, scooping it up with their hands, and then they waited. If Carver or one of his men decided to check on them, or if Carver decided it was time to rid himself of his two burdensome prisoners for good, they were done for.

The waiting was the hardest part. Miro's arms and legs were tensed, yet he still sat in the same position against the wall. He tried making conversation with Amber, but the terrible risk of their plan and the fact they might not survive the night left them mute.

Miro heard the closing bells of the last dogwatch, and then one bell to mark the shift change to the first watch. He closed his eyes but didn't want to sleep. He heard six bells strike, which made it an hour before midnight. Finally, Miro heard one bell strike.

"We'll wait a few more minutes," Miro whispered to Amber. "Then we'll go."

In the now complete darkness, Miro could sense Amber shiver beside him. He squeezed her hand, and she squeezed his in return.

"All right," Miro said. "Now."

He decided to push open the cell door in one motion, rather than drag the sound out. Taking a deep breath, he thrust the metal door open quickly. At the same time, Miro coughed as loudly as he could, hoping to disguise the sound.

He winced at the screeching, howling sound of rusted metal moving against metal. There was no point in waiting to see whether anyone would come to investigate. Miro stepped out of the cell, leading Amber by the hand behind him.

Fortunately, he remembered the way to the main deck; without Carver's demonstration on the deck, it would have taken them an age to find their way to the open. It was dark in the passageways, but behind these doors were scores of sailors, swinging in their hammocks and snoring.

Luck was with them, and they reached the companionway that led to the main deck without encountering anyone on the way. Miro climbed the ladder-like steps and was about to push the hatch open when he felt Amber squeeze his hand sharply.

Miro heard faint footsteps, barely discernible but growing louder, the stump of a barefooted man as he walked on the deck above. The thumps grew in volume until they were directly over-head. Would someone open the hatch and try to descend the steps? But the footsteps continued past them, and over time drew away until they were no longer perceptible.

Without thinking too hard about what he was doing, Miro pushed open the hatch. He peered out, the deck well lit by the stars overhead. The cool sea breeze sent a wave of pleasure through him after the cramped brig, but Miro waited until he could see the deck was clear before he climbed out, pulling Amber up after him.

"Who's that?" a voice challenged. A sailor sleeping under some canvas in a corner sleepily sat up.

"Klaus," Miro said, walking over to the sailor and squatting down.

"You're not Klau . . ."

Miro's knife silenced the man as he stabbed firmly into the sailor's chest, bringing the tip of the knife up to find the heart.

He turned back to Amber. Their next step was to head up to the quarterdeck and find the officers' quarters. Carver would be in the captain's cabin, by far the most comfortable quarters on the ship.

Miro's agreement with Werner said he would kill Carver and the officers supporting him: Ulrich, the quartermaster, and Beck, the second mate. Werner obviously wanted to be the only officer who could bear witness to the mutiny, with no one to challenge his story to the authorities in Castlemere.

Miro saw the longboat, recently used and raised up on the side of the ship, ready to be lowered when next needed.

Rather than risk his and Amber's lives further, Miro decided to change the plan.

He led Amber to the longboat. "Here," Miro said, "help me put some of these barrels into the longboat."

"What are you doing?" she whispered. "Someone will see us."

"Hurry," Miro said, grunting as he lifted a barrel.

"What's in them?"

"Water, probably," Miro said. "Food if we're lucky."

He heaved a second barrel into the longboat, wincing at the sound of wood striking wood. Amber managed to lift a barrel up, and Miro helped with getting it the rest of the way in the boat. They threw two more barrels in before the commotion sparked shouts behind them.

"Get in the longboat while I lower it," Miro said.

Without hesitation Amber clambered over the gunwale. Miro heard more shouts and then turned as he heard a hatch crash open. A sailor ran toward him and Miro smashed a fist into the man's jaw. The sailor fell down.

The ship's bell began to ring, sounding again and again to raise the alarm. Shuttered lanterns opened, and light spilled out onto the deck.

Miro's breath caught. The broken-nosed sailor Gus stood revealed in the light, filled with menace and holding a sharp cutlass in his hand.

Miro charged him, and the cutlass clattered to the deck as they both went down in a pile of limbs. As they rolled over and over, each trying to gain advantage on the other, Miro caught Amber watching from inside the longboat, her eyes wide with fear.

Gus's body twisted, and suddenly he was on top of Miro. The huge sailor wrapped his hands around Miro's neck, pushing two thumbs into his windpipe.

Miro's right hand held his opponent's wrists back, but only enough to prevent his windpipe from being crushed. Miro's vision went dark as his lungs were starved of air. He once more shifted his left arm.

The broken-nosed sailor's eyes went wide as the knife in Miro's left hand found the man's side. Miro stabbed in a second time, the blade finding his enemy's kidney. The pressure on Miro's throat relaxed as Gus gasped, looking for the source of the terrible pain. Miro again thrust the knife in between the sailor's ribs, where the thick muscles of his chest wouldn't stop the small blade from entering.

Gus quivered, and then his eyes closed. He became still.

Miro rolled the body off him, coughing and looking around. Only moments had passed, and for now the deck was clear.

Discarding the knife, Miro picked up Gus's cutlass and ran over to the longboat.

"Hold on tight," he croaked to Amber.

He unwound the line that held the boat up by the back, keeping a grip on it through the cleat. It dropped through four feet suddenly, making Amber shriek. Miro tied the line back up again and then ran to the line hooked to the front of the longboat. As he loosened the line, the longboat's front also lowered, until it was only two feet above the water. Miro held the line in his hands, his muscles bulging with the effort, as he ran again to the line at the back and unwound it completely. Miro let go of everything, and the longboat hit the water with a splash.

"Look out!" Miro called as he tossed the cutlass down into the longboat below. There was a strong current but Amber was already managing the oars; she'd grown up on the banks of the Sarsen, and rowing was part of life in Sarostar.

Miro looked around for one last item. Finally spotting it, he ran over to the mainmast and took a heavy axe from a loop of cord around the mast, placed there for emergencies.

As sailors poured onto the deck, Miro raced over to the ship's rail and leapt over the side, axe in hand, nearly missing the longboat in his haste. He tumbled into the bottom.

"What next?" Amber said.

"Row," panted Miro as he gathered his strength. He gestured to the prow of the ship, where the bowsprit jutted out from her front. "To the front of the ship." Miro pointed. "There."

Amber pulled at the oars as the longboat traveled along the side of the galleon. Up on the decks, confusion reigned.

"Keep going," Miro said. "There, stop." He grabbed hold of the anchor rope, the hawser stretched taut by the strong current.

Miro looked up, and in the light of the clear night sky he saw Carver striding forward, a cutlass in his hand. The rat-faced mutineer snarled when he caught sight of them and came rushing to the front of the ship.

Miro grinned without humor and raised his axe. Carver's mouth dropped open and his face showed real fear.

With all of his strength, Miro swung the axe at the hawser. Threads of hemp popped and snapped. Lifting the axe over his head, he swung again.

After the third blow, the rope holding the ship in place parted with a mighty snap.

The current was strong, and flowing in the direction of the jagged barrier reef that bordered the lagoon. The ship was doomed.

As Carver bellowed and the crew of the *Delphin* realized what was happening, the screams of terrified men pierced the still night air.

Amber began to row away from the ship, and a sailor leapt over the rail, trying to reach them and the safety of the longboat. This sailor could swim, and he grabbed hold of the gunwale, his face showing his desperation.

Miro recognized him. It was Klaus, the diver who had swum after Amber with a rope, when Gus tossed her overboard.

Finally releasing the rage he'd held in check for so long, Miro smashed the axe into Klaus's face. The man screamed with pain and sank into the water.

The galleon picked up pace, and the shouts and cries of her crew became desperate as it became clear the *Delphin* would run straight onto the reef. More sailors jumped off the sides, and Miro saw triangular fins pierce the water. The sharks would feast tonight.

Tearing his eyes from the *Delphin*'s impending doom, Miro also took a pair of oars, aware of the risk of joining the galleon on the reef. With two rowers on the benches, the longboat managed to fight the pull of the current and draw away.

When a safe distance between the longboat and the reef had grown, Miro and Amber waited and watched.

The *Delphin* picked up even more speed, and taken unawares, there was little the crew could do to save themselves.

The once proud galleon hit the reef with a sickening crunch. Her momentum was so great, the *Delphin* immediately began to break up. In the light of a sky full of stars, Miro saw scores of sailors struggling in the water, men who'd jumped at the last instant, and the water frothed as the struggles of the sailors brought more sharks in to feed.

Miro stood up to watch one last man actually make some distance, swimming in their direction. He caught sight of them and waved his arm. The swimmer called out in a voice that carried across the water.

It was Carver.

When he saw the longboat wasn't coming for him, he shouted and bellowed. Carver thrashed in the water and looked desperately at the distant shore.

Carver screamed as something took hold of his legs. The scream became a gurgle as a shark took him, pulling him down under the water.

Miro sat back down.

"What about the plan with the helmsman?" Amber asked.

"He was a mutineer," Miro said, "and you were almost killed. I don't respect people who can't choose sides."

He began to once more pull at the oars. "It's life." He repeated the words of the helmsman. "And I'm a practical man."

13

The summer sun made the trek to the icy north infinitely easier, yet even so, Ella wasn't sure if she would have made it without her traveling companions. The journey through Tingara, Torakon, and Loua Louna took Ella through lands she knew nothing about, and then came the cold.

Initially, the snow was wet and slushy, heated by the warmth of the sun's rays as soon as it fell. The going was tough, and often Ella waded through pools of snowmelt, freezing cold water that soaked her feet. When they reached colder foothills in the north and the snow hardened, Ella was initially thankful; finally, she was dry. But at night, even her thick clothing couldn't keep the cold at bay.

Ella's companions lit blazing fires while it was still light enough to see, allowing the flames to settle down to red coals. She slept huddled next to the heat, and thanked the stars she wasn't traveling alone.

She journeyed with three tall Akari, two men and a woman, who had traveled to Seranthia as emissaries of the Dain and were now returning home. All three used skis, and they had been kind enough to bring an extra pair for Ella when they left Seranthia together. After some practice on Ella's part, the party of four slid across the surface of the snow like ducks on water.

The two men were brothers, and so alike Ella had difficulty telling them apart. Doelan and Straun both had gray eyes and braided blonde hair to their shoulders. They carried short-bladed swords scabbarded at their waists, and the brothers wore the gray clothing and furs that were ubiquitous among the Akari.

Doelan and Straun had seemed brooding and sullen in Seranthia, yet as soon as their journey took them far enough north to see snow, their mood improved immeasurably. The trek from Seranthia to Ku Kara saw them transform from uncomfortable city folk to capable northerners, happy and resilient.

Ella's final travelling companion was Ada, the eldest of Dain Barden's three daughters. Stern as a mountain, she took a long time to warm to Ella, but gradually her attitude changed. Ella asked Ada countless questions about Ada's culture and Ku Kara, the fabled ice city. The Akari were used to foreigners being afraid of them, and people's fear often turned to hostility. When Ada saw Ella's genuine curiosity, she slowly began to answer, and Ella found the woman's answers fascinating, each response opening up further questions. Ella wouldn't say they were friends, but they made good traveling companions. Ada's hair was a shade lighter than even Ella's, so pale it was almost white, and she wore it in a thick braid. She was perhaps five years older than Ella.

The road ahead was now well traveled, the snow packed hard. Markers of gray stone now lined each side of the snowy road, and Ella realized she wasn't aware of where the markers had begun.

"Useful in a white out ," Ada grunted, noticing Ella's attention.

Ella wasn't sure if she wanted to know what a white out was.

"We're here," one of the brothers said.

Ella squinted against the sun shining on the ice, reflecting into her eyes and dazzling her. She tried to look ahead, but tears formed in her eyes.

Still ungainly on her skis, she stumbled and blushed when she heard one of the brothers snort.

"Leave her alone," Ada said.

Ella waited a few more minutes, and then she looked up again, holding her hand in front of her eyes to shield the glare. She gasped.

Two fragile towers of ice stood on either side of the road, beautiful and ethereal in a way no structure of stone could be. Each tower had a ring of points on top and was somehow designed so the weight above tapered to a slender base. On the left was the word "Ku," while the right-hand tower bore the second word, "Kara."

"Well done, Enchantress," Ada said. "You've made it when not many outsiders have."

"With your help," Ella said. She looked at the brothers. "All of you."

One of the brothers—Ella thought it was Doelan—laughed. "I hope you were paying attention."

"Why do you say that?" Ella asked.

"When you leave, it'll be on your own."

Ella wondered if they'd be met once inside the city, but it seemed the Akari weren't overly preoccupied with ceremony, treating one another more like a large family than anything else.

Ahead, Ella saw wide avenues filling the spaces between single-storied houses made of ice. Some were larger, others smaller, and some appeared more functional: storehouses or places where men worked at manual labor.

The brothers, Doelan and Straun, whooped and set off, bidding farewell to Ella with little more than a wave. Ella felt a little let down after their journey together, but she knew the two men were happy to be home.

"Come with me," Ada said. "We don't have inns like your people, but I know where you will be welcome."

Ada led Ella down one straight road and then another. Unlike Seranthia, at least this city was laid to a grid. Ella was confident she'd soon be able to find her way around.

Tall Akari nodded to them as they walked past, some alone, others in groups of three or four. Ella saw men carrying children in their arms—rearing a child here obviously wasn't just a woman's responsibility—and women carrying fish in baskets, fresh from the catch.

Ada stopped them at a house with a door of dark wood, no different from many others they'd passed. She knocked.

"Yes?" An old woman's face poked around the door. "Ah, Ada! You're back, are you?"

"Only just now," Ada said, smiling. "It's good to see you, Oma Jen."

"And you're seeing me before paying respects to your father?" Oma Jen frowned, but Ella could see the woman's eyes sparkle. "Off with you, and not another word."

"Oma Jen, this is Ella. She's a guest of my father's."

Ella opened her mouth to disagree but closed it again. She'd come to Ku Kara uninvited, but Ada probably knew what she was doing.

"A foreigner, are you?" Oma Jen regarded Ella, her wrinkled features peering through thin white hair.

"From Altura," Ella said.

"I have absolutely no idea where that is," Oma Jen said. "Come in, I'll give you a room and you can refresh yourself after your journey. The hearth's warm and you look half frozen. Once you're defrosted, you can tell me where Oltoorah is."

Ada grinned at Ella. "My father will no doubt host a feast tonight at the palace. Rest yourself, Ella. I'll send someone to come and get you."

"Thank you," Ella said.

She watched Ada go with a sense of loss. She was in a strange land far from home, and Ada was the closest thing to a friend she had here.

"Are you coming in?" Oma Jen said. "You're letting the cold air in."

"Of course," Ella said, stepping inside as Oma Jen held the door.

"Call me Oma Jen," the old woman said.

"Thank you for having me, Oma Jen," Ella said.

"Now that's more like it. Are all Oltoorah girls so pretty?"

Ella smiled as Oma Jen fussed over her. Perhaps she would like Ku Kara after all.

———————◆———————

At this time of year and so far north, it stayed light late into the evening, and Ella had difficulty knowing what time it was. She made herself ready early, not wanting someone to show up and be waiting for her, and now she sat in the bedchamber Oma Jen had given her, staring into the mirror.

Ella wore a thick dress of dark silver. Gray was the chosen color of the Akari, and she wanted to make a good impression. Killian's pendant on its chain sparkled on her neck.

She regarded her green eyes seriously.

Ella was nervous.

This was a situation Miro was more experienced with. Ella had only met Dain Barden twice, once inside the chamber in the Sentinel and again at Miro's wedding, which obviously hadn't ended well.

There was a soft knock on the bedchamber door, and Ella stood up. She opened the door, expecting to see Oma Jen standing on the other side, and drew back in shock.

She faced the white-eyed stare of a revenant. He had died an old man, and most likely died recently, for his flesh hadn't yet begun the process of decay. His back was hunched and he had a small white beard. The revenant looked at Ella and spoke.

"Summons," he drawled.

Ella wondered what he would do if she said no. How much of the creature's thought process remained? Could it think independently? It must possess some of its old character. Perhaps he had been a servant in life.

Even as she was repulsed, Ella was fascinated by the lore of the Akari. She was here to ask Dain Barden about his essence; the Akari possessed the only replenishable supply, and if one of the Evermen crossed, he might have come this way. But she was also here on her own, private quest.

Ella's kernel of an idea involved learning the Akari's secrets and discovering how the Akari managed to animate the dead.

It was her only chance of bringing Killian back home.

———◆———

The revenant led Ella to the Dain's palace, a sprawling structure with a grand entrance of wide steps. The entry hall's roof was supported by hundreds of thin pillars of ice, a forest of crystalline trees, each as thick as Ella's arm.

A living steward welcomed Ella, and thankfully the revenant disappeared. The steward was a thin man with a sepulchral voice.

"Welcome, Enchantress Ella," he said. "The Dain is celebrating the return of his daughter and is pleased to invite you to feast, however unexpected."

It was a subtle way of reminding Ella she'd come to Ku Kara uninvited.

"I'm not here in any formal capacity," Ella said. "I'm just an enchantress. My brother is the Alturan lord marshal, but he never gets me to act on his behalf."

The steward smiled. "Please let me lead you into the reception hall."

Revenants played music, served food, and poured drinks, while guests mingled as naturally as at any social gathering.

Ella saw a female revenant offer a tray of small glasses to a man, who took one without a word, his eyes saying enough. The serving women had obviously been chosen for their beauty, and wore diaphanous gowns with nothing underneath. Ella blushed. She knew the women were dead, but the men could see everything.

Ella's heart raced as her nervousness increased. Here she was, uninvited, at someone else's party. She wondered how she would last the night. Who would she talk to? She didn't know a single person here.

"I'll leave you here," the steward said.

Ella nodded and gulped, wondering what to do next. Should she take one of the small glasses? The liquid inside was clear. Was it water?

"Look who it is," a guttural voice said. "On a list of the last people I expected to see here, you're close to the top."

The voice took Ella back to a tent in the Hazara Desert, when she had first met the trader who could often be found with those the houses shunned.

"Hermen Tosch," Ella said, turning and smiling as she greeted the free cities native. "What in the Skylord's name are you doing here?"

"I could ask you the same thing," Hermen said.

Hermen hadn't changed. His hair was still cut short, and he had the same stocky build. Ella remembered him as an unassuming man who rarely smiled, strange qualities for a trader, yet he must possess a strong talent for commerce to even be here.

"I'm sorry, but I can't say," Ella said.

Hermen raised an eyebrow. "Sounds ominous."

Ella shrugged. "Not ominous, just boring," she said in a way she hoped was disarming. "Lore and essence, you know how it is."

"Not particularly, no," Hermen said. "But I'll leave you to your secrets. I generally get to the bottom of these things, at any rate."

"Why are you here, then?" Ella asked.

"The Akari are once again trading with the Empire," Hermen said. He grinned. "I'm here to make sure things go as smoothly as possible."

"And make some gilden along the way, I'm sure," Ella said, grinning along with him.

"That's true," Hermen laughed. He suddenly looked past Ella's shoulder. "I regret I must leave you. I'll see you at dinner," he said, bowing and withdrawing.

Ella wondered what had caused Hermen to leave, when she saw a tall couple regarding her seriously.

"Thank you for inviting me tonight, Dain," Ella said. Not knowing what else to do, she touched her lips and then her forehead in the Alturan manner.

Dain Barden Mensk was tall, even for his race. He towered over Ella and regarded her with brooding eyes somewhere between blue and gray. The Dain's long ice-white hair was braided at the back of his head, and his forked beard was woven with silver chain. His face was unlined and his age indeterminate, but his brow was cruel and his lips turned down in a perpetual scowl. A mantle of silver fox fur lined his broad shoulders, and the muscles in his bare forearms bulged as he looped his fingers in his belt.

"Ella," the Dain said, neglecting any title. "My daughter says you wish to speak with me but that you wouldn't say what you wish to speak about."

"Barden," the woman at the Dain's side said, smiling, "the girl only arrived today. Perhaps it can wait until later?" .

"This is my wife, the Daina," the Dain grumbled. "Mara, this is Ella, an Alturan enchantress."

Ella dipped her head while the statuesque woman smiled and nodded. Daina Mara's eyes sparkled with intelligence. She would have been beautiful as a younger woman.

"How are you enjoying Ku Kara, Ella?" Mara said.

"It's incredible," Ella said. Dain Barden frowned. "Your people make living in the cold look not only easy but enjoyable."

"It's not as simple as it may appear," said the Dain.

"Yet we love our homeland nonetheless," the Dain's wife followed, looking at the Dain fondly.

"I can see why," Ella said. "We're fortunate to have you as part of the new Empire."

"I must check on the dinner preparations," Mara said. "Please excuse me."

"My wife seems to have taken a liking to you," Dain Barden said upon her departure. "Tell me—the attack on your brother's wedding: What progress has been made?"

"Little, I'm afraid," said Ella. "However the attack is part of my reason for being here."

Dain Barden scowled, and Ella realized what she'd said. "Not that there is any suspicion on the Akari. It's not that at all." Ella wished she had Miro by her side.

A bell tinkled, announcing that dinner was being served. Guests began to leave the reception hall, the revenant servers melting to the sides.

"We'll discuss it after dinner," Barden said.

Ella found herself sitting next to Hermen Tosch. She was relieved to have someone she knew to talk to.

"What's the food like?" Ella said.

Hermen paused, gathering his thoughts. "Let me simply say, you may wish to taste a small amount before taking a large mouthful."

"That good?" Ella grinned.

"The Akari diet consists of fish, seal, walrus, whale, and white bear." Hermen sounded as if he were reciting a trader's guide.

"White bear?"

"It's a species of bear that lives up here in the cold. Terrifying creatures, bigger than any other bear."

"Go on."

"Sometimes the Akari cook their food, but much of the time they simply salt it and let it dry. For a change in texture, they keep it warm and let it fester for a time. You might like to use the word 'rot.'"

"Lord of the Sky," Ella muttered. She was in for a treat. "Have you ever been to an eating house called Barlow's, in Seranthia? It's in the Fortune district."

"I should move tables if you keep on like this," Hermen said, raising his hands in mock horror. "How dare you mention Barlow's here? Do you have any idea how long I've been in Ku Kara?"

"How long?"

"Too long!"

"Those little colored pastries are incredible," Ella said.

"And the handmade chocolates," Hermen almost moaned. He obviously had a sweet tooth. "That's enough!"

Ella looked around the long table of bleached wood, curious to get her first good look at the other guests. They were all Akari; she and Hermen appeared to be the only foreigners here, which probably explained why they'd been seated together. There were perhaps eighty or more guests, all invited because Ada had come home from Tingara. The Dain obviously doted on his daughters; Ada had been given a place next to her father, with his wife on his other side. He laughed at something Mara said and clapped his hand on top of hers on the table. The Dain evidently doted on his wife also, Ella noted, when she saw the way he looked at her.

Revenant servers, this time dressed in tailored gray suits, moved down the table. At each place they set a short glass, containing clear liquid, in front of the guest. Ella looked over at the Akari to see what she was supposed to do. She copied the woman across from her, picking her glass up and tilting the contents back into her throat in a single gulp.

Acid burned her mouth, etching its way painfully into her throat and down. Ella gasped and coughed; she could even feel it enter her chest, descending further into her stomach.

"Well done!" Hermen laughed beside her.

Looking across the table, Ella saw Daina Mara nudge her husband and whisper something, chuckling and looking at Ella. The empty glass in front of Ella could only mean one thing.

"What was that?" Ella asked Hermen, placing her hand on her lips and feeling warmth come to her cheeks.

"The Akari call it 'water of life,'" Hermen said. "They ferment rye and distill it before filtering it through charcoal." He rubbed his hands. "What I wouldn't give to sell bottles of it in Seranthia."

Ella wasn't sure if she liked it, but it certainly was strong.

A servant next placed a plate of black strips in front of her.

"Salted seal liver," Hermen whispered. "You won't like it, but you should eat it anyway."

Ella put one of the pieces in her mouth. The texture was firm and rubbery. An oily liquid came out of it as she chewed. Her senses told her she was eating bad meat, and the taste was nothing short of awful. She swallowed and looked around for something to wash it down with.

A revenant placed another small glass in front of her.

After Ella had two more of the strips, fighting the urge to gag, she drank the glass of clear liquid down.

"Just like one of the Akari," Hermen said, grinning.

"Why aren't you eating them?" Ella asked.

"I don't really like them."

"But you said I should eat them!"

"Do you always do what you're told?"

Ella frowned as she realized Hermen was making sport with her, but seeing his grin, she finally laughed and shook her head. At least the Akari across from her nodded approvingly.

The dish was taken away.

"Have you heard the news from the Hazara Desert?" Hermen asked.

"No, what?" Ella asked.

"Ilathor's father is dead. He is now kalif."

Ella remembered Rogan telling her Ilathor's father was ill. "I hope he didn't take it badly," she said. She thought about the proud desert man. Knowing him, he wouldn't have shed any tears, but the way he'd spoken of his father told Ella he would have strongly felt his passing.

"Now that he is kalif, he can no longer help Rogan Jarvish with the regency. His new responsibilities are great. Ilathor is fortunate to have Jehral by his side."

"That's good," Ella said. "Jehral's a good man." Hermen laughed, and Ella frowned again. "Now what?"

"I'm not laughing at what you said," said Hermen. "I'm laughing because I remember saying the same words to your friend, Bladesinger Bartolo, when he was hunting you down after we . . . borrowed you . . . from your brother."

Ella grinned. Now it was her turn to take pleasure from Hermen's discomfort. "I'll bet he didn't take that well."

"No, not well at all. As I recall, in front of Castlemere's city watch, he pinned me up against a wall and put his zenblade to my eye."

Ella laughed heartily. "That sounds like Bartolo."

Hermen's face clouded. Ella wondered if perhaps she shouldn't have laughed so loudly. Then she remembered the taste of the seal livers. She also remembered her captors being less than gentle with her.

Ella laughed some more while Hermen's expression grew more pained.

———————

At the end of the meal, the guests dispersed one by one. A revenant in gray came over to Ella, saying nothing, just staring at her with sightless white eyes.

Ella knew when she was being summoned. She bid good night to Hermen and followed the revenant to a smaller chamber nearby.

Dain Barden crouched in front of a hearth, holding his hands toward the embers.

"I'm a plain-spoken man, Ella, and I will appreciate it if you're direct in return. Why are you here?"

Ella gathered her thoughts, wondering where to begin. "We think the attack may have been directed by an ancient enemy of all of us."

The Dain turned, his eyebrow raised. "You mean one of the Evermen?"

"Yes." Ella met his gaze. Dain Barden had witnessed Evrin's revelation at the Sentinel.

"I didn't see any lore," Barden said. "I saw some kind of chemical explosive, a substance that is also toxic when introduced to the blood."

Ella was surprised at the Dain's insight. He didn't rule his people by might alone.

"There are other reasons," Ella said. She thought about Evrin's words. Someone had crossed. "I need to know. Have any strangers come to these lands, seeking essence?"

"Now I'm getting worried, Enchantress," the Dain said.

"Perhaps it's time to be worried."

"Yes," said Dain Barden, and the one syllable sent chills through Ella's spine. "I can't say for certain that a stranger came here, but Renrik, one of my most senior necromancers, fled, along with a dozen others of his order. I am the only one who can access our essence reserves, but they took several flasks with them. They also took a ship."

Ella was surprised. "You have ships?"

"We don't like those of the houses to know, but yes, we have ships. They took the *Icebreaker*, one of our best open-water vessels."

It had to be, Ella realized. Evrin was right. One of the Evermen was in Merralya, and he had necromancers with him.

"Is it enough?" Ella asked.

"Enough for what?"

"You know what I'm asking! Did they take enough essence to build the vats? Enough to extract essence from the dead?"

"Yes," the Dain said, sighing. "They took enough."

"How long ago did this happen?"

"Some time ago."

"Why didn't you say anything?" Ella cried.

"Who are you, woman, to question me in my own palace?" Dain Barden growled, rising to his full height.

Ella reminded herself she needed the Dain's help, not his ire. She calmed.

"Where could they have gone?"

"Where?" Barden said. "I have no idea. And now that I've answered your questions . . ."

"There's something else," Ella said.

"What is it?"

She took a deep breath. Ella knew Evrin would never teach her the things she needed to know, and this was her only chance.

"I need you to teach me."

"Teach you? Teach you what?"

"I need you to teach me how to bring the dead back to life."

The Dain chuckled. "I learned my lesson with that one. No, never again will we share the knowledge outside my people."

"There must be something I can offer you that will change your mind."

"Ha," Barden snorted. "Nothing. You may stay in Ku Kara one more night after tonight, Enchantress. I know it has been a long journey north for you. But then I'll ask you to leave."

14

The day after the feast, Ella wandered about Ku Kara. It took her hours, but she walked from one end to the other, watching the Akari at work and play, opening her mind to their way of life.

She thought about Killian.

With no idea what strange world lay on the other side of the portal, Ella couldn't even imagine where Killian was, what he was doing, or whether he was even alive. When she tried, she simply saw him as she'd last seen him, bare chested, near naked, looking at her with eyes that spoke volumes as he took a step into the unknown.

Ella held his necklace as she walked, rubbing the worn pendant between her fingers. Lost in thought, she was oblivious to the cold.

Was he cold, also?

His face floated in a void of darkness. Ella again saw his fiery red hair and intense blue eyes, a shade she'd only seen before in Evrin.

Killian had been raised an orphan and had become a street thief in Salvation, under the gaze of Stonewater. He had been offered a chance at a normal life when he'd joined a performing troupe, and with his lean, athletic build, Ella was sure he could have enjoyed a life of success.

But the emperor had destroyed the troupe, murdering the only family Killian had ever known. Lost, Killian had returned to Salvation. The primate had found him and turned the young thief to his own evil ends.

Yet Killian had met Ella, and somehow, she knew she had touched him, and he'd been saved again.

All he had ever wanted was to find his own family and to feel a sense of belonging. Evrin had given Ella part of the story, revealing that Killian was descended from Evrin himself.

Sadly, Killian was already gone. He hadn't been present to hear Evrin's confession. And the mystery of Killian's upbringing remained. Who were his parents? What happened to them?

Ella remembered the promise she'd made at the Sentinel. She had made a promise to bring Killian home.

Her plan was still in its infancy, but it depended wholly on learning the lore of the Akari.

What could she do to make Dain Barden agree to teach her their secrets?

The problem was, Ella could think of plenty of things the Akari might want, but nothing they seemed to need.

Heating stones? Nightlamps? Enchanted weapons?

Ella thought again about the revenants she'd faced in the war. The idea of Akari revenants wielding anything more destructive than steel weapons made her blood run cold.

Even so, Ella knew the promise of enchanted weapons wouldn't be enough. The Dain simply didn't need them.

Just that morning, Ella had asked Dain Barden if someone could show her around Ku Kara. She'd felt that if someone taught her enough about Akari culture, she would find something they needed.

Barden had been pleased, in his way, and asked Ada to show Ella around. Ella knew the Dain felt that if the houses knew more about Akari culture, they would cease to be so filled with fear and revulsion.

Ella had learned a lot but still hadn't found anything the Akari needed.

Alone now, she thought about Dain Barden Mensk and the forces that drove him.

As it grew dark in Ku Kara, Ella finally realized what it was she could offer.

———◆———

"What is it?" Dain Barden asked.

"I wish to speak with you," Ella said.

With a nod, the Dain dismissed the aide he'd been talking to.

"Well? How did you find the tour my daughter gave you? Was it insightful? Are my people degenerate?"

Ella decided honesty was the best approach with the forthright ruler of the Akari. "You know that's not how I feel. And I still need your help. So I looked for something I could offer you—some magic device or tool to make your lives easier. Perhaps some toy or entertainment."

"And what did you find?"

"Your people are content, and there is little I can offer."

"I could have told you that. So you'll be leaving in the morning, then? You can save your farewells for the morrow."

"Whether I leave depends on you, Dain," Ella said. "After learning more about your people, I think I do know what I can offer you, and why you should teach me your lore. I believe I can offer you what no one else can."

The Dain's lips thinned. "And what is that?"

"People fear your lore, Dain. They don't understand it, and what they don't understand frightens them." Barden frowned, and

Ella grew earnest as she saw his interest was piqued. "Dain Barden, I've been shown the secrets of the Hazaran elders and been taught animator's runes. I've been instructed by a Petryan elementalist, and I'm a qualified enchantress from the Academy of Enchanters in Sarostar. People know me as someone who tries to understand the different schools of lore and how they fit together."

"Go on," he said warily.

"I've also known the lord regent, Rogan Jarvish, since I was young, and my brother is the lord marshal of Altura. My friend Shani, an elementalist, is an adviser to the high lord of Petrya and the kalif of the Hazarans is . . . a close friend of mine. You yourself saw who came to my brother's wedding."

"What are you getting at?"

Ella steadily met Dain Barden's steely gaze without flinching. "Teach me your lore, Dain. Let me explain it to them. Let me show the world there's nothing to be afraid of."

Barden turned away, and it was some time before he spoke. "What if we teach you, and what you learn frightens you?"

"Lore is never frightening, Dain. It's what people do with it that keeps me awake at night."

The Dain was silent for so long that Ella wondered if he would ever speak. Finally, the words slowly came. "Go back to your lodgings," he said. Ella felt disappointment sink through her. Barden spoke again, and Ella's eyes lit up with hope. "Someone will fetch you in the morning. We'll see how frightened you get."

Ella woke fresh and excited. She dressed quickly and then paced in the main room of Oma Jen's small house until the old woman made her sit down.

There was a knock on the door, and Ella jumped up, throwing on her cloak and opening the front door before Oma Jen could come close.

A plump Akari in a gray robe bowed when he saw Ella. He wore a circle of bones around his neck, and his robe bore the Akari symbol, the withered tree.

"Enchantress, I am Aldrik. The Dain has spoken to me about you. Please come with me."

Ella felt her excitement rise as she followed the necromancer through the city and down a hidden stairway cut into the ice. Aldrik muttered a word, and a barred door opened. Ella's heart raced as she prepared to set foot in a place she knew few foreigners had seen.

Aldrik started by giving Ella a tour of the vast chambers beneath the city. Deep underground the necromancers did their grisly work, patching up the dead, bringing them back to a semblance of life, and recycling their bodies when their long service to the Dain finally ended.

Slabs of ice stood laid out in neat rows and columns. On each a body stared sightlessly up at the ceiling high above. The necromancer took Ella to one of the closest.

"A new arrival," Aldrik said. "She was killed in a whaling accident."

The woman had been middle-aged, yet was obviously fit and strong. A wide gash bared her ribs to the world. The blood must have been washed away.

"She was caught in the trailing line of a harpoon," the necromancer said matter-of-factly. "There was no way to save her."

Ella fought to maintain her composure. She couldn't show weakness, or the Dain might decide she was too squeamish and that she would portray his lore negatively. "What happens next?"

"Today, before she grows stiff, we will stitch her wounds and wash her skin with an acid solution. The skin must be completely clean before we can begin work on the runes."

"I see," said Ella.

"She will then wait here with the others until we are ready to bring her back. Here, let me show you another."

Aldrik led Ella past the rows of dead bodies to a raised platform. On the platform, four wooden tables stood side by side.

Only one of the tables displayed activity. Half a dozen necromancers in gray robes hovered around a body, their moves smooth and synchronous.

Aldrik took Ella close enough to see something of what they were doing without getting in the way.

"It's a complex process," Aldrik said, "and we never work on more than four at a time. First, the frozen body is thawed in warm water and cleaned a second time. Then it's brought here"—he gestured—"and the work begins."

Ella watched the men at work. They used scrills and protective gloves just like enchanters, dipping them in tiny vials of essence and drawing runes with smooth strokes.

"Will you teach me the runes?" Ella asked.

"Yes, yes," Aldrik said. "Later."

Ella thought about her real reason for learning. "How much of the original personality remains? The woman we saw earlier, you said she was a whaler. What will she become?"

Aldrik hesitated. "It's something we don't speak of much. Her skill memory remains, but she will not remember her loved ones— to them she is dead. If ordered, she will be able to throw a harpoon as well as she could in life, but that does not necessarily mean she would make a good whaler. There is more to being a whaler than possessing a good throwing arm; it's the team working together that brings in the whale."

"So what will she be?"

"A warrior, most likely. She will join the Dain's armies, I should think."

"Will she be able to speak?"

"Ella," Aldrik said, taking her aside, "I am perhaps not explaining myself well. You see, we choose not to bring back much of the draug's personality."

"Why?"

"There can be . . . problems."

"What kind of problems?"

Aldrik sighed. "A draug's eyes are turned white by the process of our lore. This is the sign of a healthy draug. There are some, servants and the like, whom we bring back with a little more of who they were, so they may speak. If you look, you will see their eyes are tinged with pink. We don't do this often because they require more essence to bring back, and they do not last as long. Also, there is a risk."

"A risk of what?"

"It happens only once in a while, and only to the draugar we bring back with more of who they were. Sometimes the eyes turn entirely red, and the life leaves them." The necromancer's voice turned ominous. "But before they go, they become berserk."

Aldrik's words stayed with Ella as he next took her to the vats. The knowledge complicated her plan, a risk she hoped to mitigate by applying herself and learning as much as possible.

Ella suppressed a shudder as she saw the huge vats, as large as trees. She remembered seeing them in Tingara, when the primate's mad plan saw multitudes murdered for the essence in their bodies.

There were six of the great vessels, with steam rising from vents in the sides. Ella wrinkled her nose at a putrid smell in the air. Aldrik said there were more, elsewhere under the ice city.

"When the energy leaves a draug, we bring the body here," the necromancer explained. "The process is simple to perform—a fool could do it—yet the runes on the vats are complex. Only the wisest of my order truly understand how they work."

"Is Renrik one of those?" Ella asked.

"Yes," Aldrik said stiffly.

Ella could see she was discussing a sore point. "What do you do with the bodies?"

"There's a door in the side. First, an activation sequence is spoken to bring the temperature down. Then the door is opened, with the operator careful to avoid the escaping gases. The body, or bodies, are thrown in. We wait."

"How long?"

"Only a few days. Can you see that tube coming out of the side? It leaves this chamber and flows down into the vault, an area only the Dain can access."

"Do you only insert the bodies of draugar?" Ella asked.

Aldrik rounded on her, and his eyes blazed. "Certainly! This idea of murdering people for the energy in their bodies is something only you people of the houses would come up with. It's an abomination. Do you hear me?"

"Yes," Ella said. "I hear you, and I apologize if I've offended you. The Dain has told you, I'm here to learn and to understand, so I can explain to those less tolerant. I haven't seen anything here to warrant the prejudice of those in the south. Thank you, Necromancer Aldrik, for showing me."

Mollified, Aldrik led Ella out of the underground chambers and into his workroom.

There, Ella's instruction began in earnest.

15

Days passed, with Ella learning from dawn to dusk, and the prickly necromancer trying to hide his surprise at the pace of her learning. He hesitated when Ella asked to take some of his books back to her room to study, but Ella again mentioned the Dain, and he grudgingly acquiesced.

Ella's dreams became filled with the whorls and bridges of runes, circling through her consciousness and joining together to become the complex matrices of the Akari's lore.

Aldrik said she would be able to try animating her first draug after a month. Ella was ready after a week.

Aldrik chose the body of the woman killed in the whaling accident.

Deep beneath the city, Ella stood silently over the corpse laid out on the wooden table, recently thawed and ready for the essence. Her eyes ran over the pale skin, no longer seeing it as a woman, but as a canvas for the runes. She put on the protective gloves before taking a scrill and vial of essence from a stand nearby.

Aldrik and three other necromancers looked on as Ella began to draw.

She kept her hand steady, a thin line of vapor rising from the symbols as Ella drew them one by one. She kept her head turned to the side; if the vapor got into her lungs it would make her quite ill.

Ella's heart fluttered. If she made the slightest mistake or drew a line out of place, she would fail. Unlike a work of enchantment, this wasn't a sword or armor; this was a woman's body. If she failed, the woman wouldn't even go into the vats; she would be burned to ash.

In Ella's mind she turned to pages in the books she'd read, adding symbols where they seemed appropriate, inserting a gap between matrices to delineate them. She added activation sequences, scores of them. This wasn't a nightlamp, with a sequence to bring light and another to restore darkness. This was a draug, a revenant; it would be woken once, and once only.

Ella lifted the scrill away from the body. Her arm was tired, and she stretched slowly, careful to avoid making any fateful motions.

Ella looked at the men watching her. Her eyes widened in surprise.

Dain Barden stood with the necromancers, his arms folded across his chest. His expression was inscrutable as he saw Ella dip her scrill in the essence and continue.

Finally, Ella was done.

She put away her tools and the essence, before removing the protective gloves. She leaned backward and heard her back crack painfully. How long had it been? It was hard to tell down here, under the ice city.

"Your work is not complete," Aldrik said.

"I know," Ella said, frowning at him.

Ella looked down at the rune on the revenant's cold chest. She placed her fingers on it, tracing the heart-rune, larger than the rest, as she spoke. *"Mordet-ahl. Sudhet-ahl. Suth-eroth. Soth-eruth. Mordet-suth-ahn."*

Ella continued to chant as the woman's eyes suddenly opened. Ella fought to remain impassive and still the raucous beating of her heart. Her palms sweated, even though the air was frigid. It wasn't over yet.

"*Tsu-tulara-ahn. Morth-thul-ahlara. Sudhet-ahlara-ahn. Shah-lahra-rahn!*"

Blue light traveled from the heart rune to the matrix beside it, a fiery glow moving in a spiral pattern as it lit up the symbols covering the revenant's body. Ella saw the light move down the woman's chest, over her hips, and down to the runes covering her legs. The arcane symbols on her arms began to glow eerily, from her shoulders to her hands. Her face remained clear, but her eyes were solid white, the color of the frozen snow.

The revenant sat up.

"Rise and stand," Ella commanded.

She stood back to make space around the wooden table. The revenant slid off the table and rose to stand tall, looming over Ella, her dead eyes filling Ella with fear, but also accomplishment.

"Well done, Ella," Aldrik said. "Working alone, you brought a draug back in ten hours. Quite an accomplishment, I must say."

Ella looked at the Dain, who nodded at her and then walked away. Was he pleased? The three necromancers also left, leaving Ella standing with Aldrik and the revenant.

"What is your name?" Ella asked the woman.

The revenant stayed silent.

"Ella," Aldrik said, "you know she can't speak."

"Walk to the wall, touch it, and return," Ella directed.

The revenant didn't move.

"Your instructions are too complex, Ella," the plump necromancer said. "She will only understand the simplest commands. For fighting draugar, we actually inscribe a system of battle sequences into the runes. It makes for more coordinated action, although a draug can generally fight on its own when challenged."

Ella was frustrated. "I need to know how to bring back more of who it was. Not much more, but more than this."

"Ella, that's enough for one day. There are more things I can teach you, but they are elements of detail, such as how to give a group of draugar a formation and teach them to fight cohesively. You have learned all I have to teach."

"Can I ask you one last question?" Ella asked.

"What is it?"

"How long can you wait? If a body has been in the ground a long time, how long before it can't be brought back?"

"I don't know what you intend, Enchantress, and I'm not sure that I want to know. But I will tell you one thing."

Aldrik met Ella's gaze.

"I have shown you our process. This is the only way it should be done."

———————

Ella paced around Oma Jen's house, wondering where she would be able to find the knowledge she needed. She'd read Aldrik's books from cover to cover, but there was still something missing.

Oma Jen opened the front door, entering with a basket of groceries in her arms.

"Here, let me get that for you," Ella said. She took the basket from the old woman's arms and followed her into the kitchen.

"You look unhappy," Oma Jen said. "I heard you impressed the Dain today. Why the glum face?"

Ella wondered if she could open up to her host. "It's Aldrik. Or perhaps it's all of them. I need to know more."

"You should visit Barnabas," Oma Jen said.

Ella put down the basket of groceries. "Who?"

"Barnabas. He was Renrik's teacher. They expelled him from the order, but in his day there wasn't anyone better."

"Why did they expel him?"

"He never took much notice of their rules. You might not understand, but morality is a constant source of contention for the order. Barnabas did things they considered . . . questionable."

Ella's eyes lit up. "How can I find him?"

"He has a small house on the far side of the city. You can't miss it; it's the one with the bones scattered out the front. He's an odd one."

Ella remembered the house. "Do you mind if I go there now?"

"You'll do what you need to do," Oma Jen said, smiling. "I'll save your dinner."

"Thank you," Ella said, touching the old woman's shoulder.

Oma Jen turned back to her groceries, smiling and shaking her head.

"What is it?" a voice grumbled when Ella knocked. "Don't you know it's late?"

Ella knocked again, and finally heard the stumping of footsteps. A moment later, the door opened, and a withered face peered at her.

Barnabas might have once been tall, but he was now stooped with age. Ella guessed he was blind in one eye, for it was rheumy and wept fluid.

"Well, hello there," Barnabas said. "Never mind what I said, it's never too late. Pretty young thing, aren't you?"

"I'm Ella. I'd like to speak with you. May I come in?"

"Ella . . . Ella . . . Where have I heard that name? Of course you can come in." Barnabas stepped aside. In the light, Ella could now see he wore a dirty gray robe, stuck to his thin frame like a sheet caught on a tree.

"Now," Barnabas said as Ella entered the house. "How does this work? Kayan sent you for my birthday, did he? Has he paid you?"

"No," Ella said, bemused, "no one sent me."

"Then why are you here?" Barnabas said, gesturing for Ella to take a seat on a padded chair and then seating himself.

Ella looked around the small house. Bones were everywhere. A human skeleton stood erected on a frame in the corner, and a dozen skulls lined the mantel above the hearth. In another corner, a huge white stuffed bear had been manipulated into a snarling pose of attack.

"I'm an enchantress, from Altura. I'm learning . . ."

"Ah, now I remember. I do stay in touch, you know. You've been learning from young Aldrik." His face fell. "Which means you're not here for my birthday."

"No," Ella said, smiling. "I'm afraid I'm not."

"And how are you finding Aldrik?"

"He's been very helpful," Ella said.

Barnabas snorted. "Helpful? He's not even third order. He wouldn't know how to raise a flag."

"Oma Jen said I should talk to you," Ella said. "She said there's no one better."

"She did, did she? Will you do something for me, Ella?"

"Of course."

"Make me a hot mug of spiced wine, will you? Everything you need is over there."

Flustered, Ella went to do the old man's bidding. She filled a copper pot with wine from a bladder and added spices from jars on a rack. She wasn't sure which to add, or how much, so she put in a small amount of each. Taking the copper pot over to the fire, Ella waited until steam rose from the pot. She filled an earthenware mug and took it to Barnabas.

"Ugh," said Barnabas. "This is foul. What did you put in here? Redspice?"

"Will you teach me?" Ella asked.

Barnabas took another sip. "It depends. What do you want to know?"

"I want to know how to bring back someone who has been in the ground a long time. I also need the draug to have some memory, more than what Aldrik showed me."

"Only a master can do that," Barnabas said.

"You were a master, weren't you?"

"Still am!"

"Of course. That's why I came to you."

"Take a look at that bear in the corner, would you?"

Ella walked over to the white bear, looking up at the jagged teeth lining its open mouth.

Barnabas suddenly spoke an activation sequence. Somehow, Ella knew it; she'd heard it before.

The bear's huge paw moved, taking a swipe at Ella's head.

Ella spoke without thinking. *"Taun-tah!"*

The bear was still.

Barnabas chuckled. Ella was perplexed. The bear hadn't been brought back like she'd brought back the woman. It was just a stuffed bear.

She stepped back and examined the bear again. Now that she was looking, she could see symbols on the fur, faint but unmistakable. This wasn't the lore of the Akari.

Ella turned to Barnabas, shocked. "You were using animator's runes."

Barnabas nodded. "All the great masters are those who figure out how to merge runes from the different schools together. I needed to see if you were ready."

The old man put down his empty mug and looked at Ella out of his one good eye. She could see he was treating her differently now.

"The limbs of an old body can't move themselves anymore; they don't have the strength. Animator's runes are required, just like a golem."

"What about the mind?"

"The mind is different. It can never be fully restored. Our lore is not a way to achieve eternal life. If you're looking to bring back a loved one, then I have bad news for you."

"No," Ella said, "that's not it."

"Are you sure?"

"Yes."

"Aldrik told you the problem, about what happens when the mind snaps?"

Ella gulped. "Yes."

"Then perhaps you are ready. But first things first. We need to agree on a price."

"What do you want?"

The old Akari put his feet up on a stool and kicked off his slippers. "It's my birthday," Barnabas said. "I'd like a foot rub."

Killian had better appreciate this, Ella thought.

Sighing, she knelt down next to the old man's feet.

16

Miro and Amber had made it to the Ochre Isles. Weakened, worried, stranded far from home, they had little cause to celebrate.

They slept that first night on the floor of the longboat, a deep sleep of exhaustion, with a piece of canvas used to ward off the night's chill. As it grew light, Miro woke first, leaving Amber to rest while he exited and took stock of their situation.

They'd drawn the longboat up on a short, sandy beach. Small waves knocked against the shore, and in the distance, white breakers outlined the barrier reef. Flotsam lined the shore: planks of wood, barrels, and even clothing. There were no bodies.

Miro stretched his arm, looking at the wound he'd taken on his side. Fortunately, it had crusted over and was already healing. He gazed out at the reef, shielding his eyes from the rising sun, but the *Delphin* was gone: broken up, scattered, and sunk. He felt the sand crunch beneath his bare feet as he walked down to the water and scanned for anything worth salvaging.

Seeing some barrels, Miro decided to carry anything undamaged above the high water mark. Two barrels were filled with seawater, their contents lost, but another three were still sealed tight. He grunted as he lifted each barrel, struggling with it to the longboat before fetching the next.

When he was done, Miro went over to the longboat, reaching in to take the cutlass. They needed to see whether the island was inhabited, and Miro wasn't taking any chances.

His movements woke Amber. "Where are we?" she asked as she sat up.

"The Ochre Isles," Miro said grimly. He watched remembrance dawn in Amber's eyes.

"The ship," she said. "Did anyone survive?"

"No. I've saved some barrels that washed up on the shore, but that's all. We're out of danger for now, but we need to think about supplies. Can you tell me what we managed to bring in the longboat?"

Amber rummaged around. She used the axe to pry open each of the barrels they'd taken with them. "Four barrels, all with freshwater. This axe. Three sets of oars. A square of canvas. Two lengths of rope—one longer, one shorter. That's it."

Miro went to the first of the three barrels he'd picked up from the shore. He used the hilt of his cutlass to open the lid and then, looking in, made a pleased sound. "This one has dried fruit." He opened the next. "Oats." Miro dug his hand into the oats. "They're good." The last barrel's lid was stuck, but he finally levered it open. "More water."

"Plenty of water, plus dried fruit and oats," Amber said. "We were lucky."

"Yes," Miro said, remembering his sense of helplessness when they'd been at the mercy of the mutineers. "We were."

Miro looked around, giving the island a full examination for the first time. Farther up from the shoreline, thick brush came down to the sand, a horde of spiky trees with gnarled trunks. He could see the land rising behind the trees, but it was difficult to tell how big the island was. The beach continued ahead to a rocky promontory, where gulls wheeled above the headland. Behind them, the opposite end of the small bay could be judged by a long stretch of rock.

The channel through which the galleon had entered was marked by water that was a deeper shade of blue. The lagoon was calm, but behind the reef the waves were huge.

Aside from the sound of tumbling waves, the cries of gulls, and the ocean breeze rustling in the trees, there was silence. Their voices jarred against the sound of nature. Miro had the feeling that even if people had once been here, they hadn't been in a very long time.

The rock at both ends of the beach was a strange shade of red, the color of rust. Miro now knew how Toro Marossa had come up with the name, Ochre Isles.

"Here, help me out," Amber said.

"Of course." Miro held out a hand, and Amber stepped out of the longboat.

Amber weaved slightly. "It feels good to have solid ground beneath my feet again. Lord of the Sky, what a journey."

Reflecting on their plight, Miro wondered what he could have done differently.

"How will we get back?" Amber asked. "What about Tomas?"

"I'll find a way," Miro said, "I promise. For now, though, we need to think about survival. Here, help me pull the longboat farther up the beach."

It took a mighty struggle, but finally Miro was satisfied they'd pulled it farther than could be reached by the highest tide. They went back for the barrels, stacking them in a row alongside.

Puffing and panting after their exertions, Miro and Amber both drank some of the water, cupping it in their hands.

They were now closer to the trees. Miro took the oars and the square of canvas out of the longboat. "We need to make a shelter while we have plenty of daylight ahead of us. Help me find a clearing with some thick branches overhead. And, Amber?"

"Yes?"

"Keep an eye out for people."

Miro searched for a suitable clearing while Amber also looked a small way away.

"How's this?" Amber called.

Miro came over to where Amber stood in a patch of sand underneath the spread arms of a huge tree. The lower branches were the height of Miro's head. "Perfect," Miro said.

He went back for the axe and then trimmed the horizontal branches to remove the drooping foliage. Then he used the axe to dig holes and planted the six oars in a row, with Amber assisting.

While Miro draped the canvas over the branches to make an improvised roof, Amber disappeared with the axe, returning with a willowy sapling she'd felled. It was long and thin, with green leaves and an easy springiness. Amber threaded the sapling through the oars and then went back for another. Soon, she'd formed a wall.

Miro finished tying down the canvas and stood back to regard the shelter.

It was basic, with just the one wall and a roof, but it was something.

"Where will we put the kitchen?" Amber asked.

Miro turned to her and barked a laugh. Amber smiled and Miro put an arm around her.

They went back to the beach and searched the washed-up clothing, salvaging a hemp sack and a sailor's woolen vest. Miro returned to the shelter and was hanging the clothing on the branches of a tree to dry in the sun, when he heard a cry.

Sword in hand, he ran back down to the beach.

Amber stood in water to her knees, gingerly trying to take hold of a body that had come in with the tide. The sailor was floating on his stomach. Miro waded into the shallows, and Amber stood back while he rolled the man over. The man's eyes stared wide, but he'd evidently drowned, escaping the sharks. Miro didn't recognize him.

"What should we do?" Amber asked.

"Go back to the shelter," said Miro. "Leave it with me."

Miro dragged the body up onto the beach and then farther, until he was up at the trees, a fair distance from the shelter. He didn't relish the task at hand, but although he wore a shirt and trousers, Amber still wore only a nightdress.

Miro stripped the man's shirt and leggings from him, hanging them on a tree nearby. He began to dig at the sandy ground, and kept digging until sweat dripped down his brow and his arms ached.

When he was done burying the body, Miro washed the dead man's clothes in the sea and took them back to the shelter, hanging them with the vest and sack.

Amber had been busy making a mat of thick fronds. She'd also rolled a log to the shelter and was now sitting on it.

"You look exhausted," Amber said. "Sit down. Have some dried figs."

Miro seated himself and then spoke while he ate. "Our needs are water, food, shelter, warmth, and rescue. We now have clothing, and if we tear that sack open, we can improvise a blanket. Warmth shouldn't be a problem: It doesn't appear to be cold in these parts. Rescue, on the other hand, is out of the question. The only way we'll get off this island is if we do it ourselves. Which brings me to the next imperative—exploration."

"We should split up," Amber said.

Miro opened his mouth to object.

"You know we should. There's a whole island to explore, and we need to cover ground as quickly as possible. I can take the sword, while you take the axe."

"I'll tell you what," Miro said. "There's a tall hill that doesn't look too far away. I saw it from the beach. Let's climb there together. We can take a look around and make a plan about where we'll explore."

The clothing was now dry, and Miro dressed himself in the dead sailor's garments and gave Amber his own trousers and shirt. She made a belt out of a piece of rope, grumbling at the over-sized garments.

Miro handed Amber the cutlass, and he took the axe. He led Amber back to the beach, and they walked along it until they were level with the hill, before heading into the trees. It was tough going, and they were both scratched and panting by the time they ascended to the top of the rocky outcrop.

From their vantage they could now see much more of the island. Looking out at the sea, Miro saw two other islands nearby, one close and one far, both surrounded by rings of reef and still blue lagoons.

He breathed a sigh of relief when he saw they were on the largest of the three islands, the one Toro Marossa had named Sofia. This island was still only a few miles long, but Toro Marossa's journal said he had found settlements on Sofia.

"Let's just pray they're no longer abandoned," Miro muttered. "We need to find these people even more now, not just for a cure but for a way home."

His eyes following the shore as he scanned Sofia's shore, Miro finally saw structures surrounding a cove on the other side of the headland. A second settlement could be seen in the opposite direction, past the stretch of rock.

"Two settlements on this island," Miro said.

"Look, there's a third," said Amber, pointing.

On the closest island, Miro saw another set of buildings. The last island was too far away to tell.

Against the green of the trees and the white of the sand, all of the islands bore strange spreading cascades of reddish rock, stretching down to the water's edge. The island closest to Sofia was dominated by a cratered mountain, with mist surrounding its summit so they couldn't see the peak.

Miro heard a low rumbling.

"What was that?" Amber said.

"I don't know," said Miro. "A storm?"

"The sky is clear."

Miro shrugged. "Ready to split up? I'll head for the buildings past the headland, and you follow the beach to the right until you reach the settlement there."

Amber nodded.

Miro pointed at the mountain. "The sun should set over there, behind the mountain. When the sun hits the mountain, turn back, even if you haven't reached it yet."

"What should we be looking for?"

"We're looking for people, but also keep an eye out for small barrels with a symbol on them. Toro Marossa came here a long time ago, but that's where he found the poisonous powder. If we find the barrels, we might also find an antidote. Be careful, Amber, and if you get into trouble, run."

"I suddenly feel foolish for coming here."

"We had to try. If we hadn't come, we would never have forgiven ourselves."

"Do you really think we can find an antidote?"

"I don't know."

Miro squeezed Amber's hand. "The day's passing fast. We should move on."

17

Miro decided to push through the trees rather than head back to the beach and walk around the headland. It was a decision he regretted almost immediately.

Consumed with worry, yet fighting to be strong for Amber, he stepped over fallen logs and ducked under thick branches as he clambered down from the hill. He realized there was no way to tell whether he was heading in the right direction. All he could see were trees and bushes. If the inhabitants of these islands had once tilled the soil here, the signs of their presence were long gone.

The settlement hadn't looked far away from Miro's vantage on the hill, but the ground was steep and treacherous, the distance deceptive. The trees clawed at Miro's clothing and scratched at his legs. Occasionally, he swung at the branches with his axe, but it was little use.

Suddenly the ground leveled, and Miro burst onto an old trail.

His heart sank when he saw it was weedy and overgrown, but he could see where once the footsteps of many men had trodden a path into the earth. Miro guessed that turning right would take him back to the beach where he and Amber had built their shelter. He turned left.

Eventually, he heard the gurgle of running water, a sound that grew louder as he forged his way ahead. He caught sight of a river and then stopped and stared.

The building on the bank had once been a mill, with an elaborate system of cogs and pulleys designed to harness the river's power for grinding meal. The walls of the structure were made of ingeniously fitted bricks, each overlapping the other in a pattern Miro had never seen before. A tall tree had grown up inside the mill and poked its head through a gaping hole in the roof, but it was a testament to the skill of its builders that the walls were still strong after what must have been many years.

Who were these people? Where had they gone?

Miro crossed the river at a sturdy bridge of stone, overgrown with weeds yet still strong. His path took him around a bend, and as he ducked under some trees, he left the river behind.

There's water here, he reminded himself. *At least we won't die of thirst.*

The path became broader; it must have once been a road. Miro heard the sound of waves splashing against a shore a moment before he caught sight of the sea.

Through the trees Miro saw the remnants of a pier. No matter how sturdy it had once been, the action of the waves had taken its toll, and all that was left were thick timber piles and a few planks of wood. Farther away, Miro saw several more piers, forming what was left of a large dock.

The road took Miro to the shore and then turned to run parallel to the sea. Miro's footsteps took him toward the crumbled buildings of what had once been a proud town.

The silence was ghostly, the sense of abandonment complete.

The structures varied in size and shape, but their walls were all made of perfectly fitted bricks in the same style as the mill. The roofs were peaked and tiled, although most had collapsed as their beams rotted and the weather knocked the tiles loose. On the side facing the street, the bricks had been painted, with each building a different color than the next. Even after so much time, the colors were vibrant and alive: turquoise, yellow, emerald, and pink. The façades reminded Miro of multihued sweets.

The people who had once lived here weren't scratching a living. They'd had time to decorate their homes.

Miro stopped outside the closest building.

The door had rotted away, leaving a gaping hole shadowed by the remnants of the ceiling. He stepped over some rubble and peered into the darkness.

It had once been someone's home. Miro pictured a family here: the husband, perhaps a builder or a fisherman; the wife, hanging pictures on the wall and tending the garden while children ran about.

Miro left the house and continued down the street, past several similar buildings. He saw a lumber mill, now wild as the forest, and a masonry yard, its purpose evident by the worked blocks of stone.

Miro entered three more buildings, all houses, and then he came to a shop.

He guessed it was a place where goods had been bought and sold, judging by the earthenware bottles lined up against the wall. The shelves had decayed and collapsed, but Miro could see the pins that once held them in place. Broken glass covered the ground.

Miro held his breath. Perhaps here he would find some sign of the poisonous powder or its antidote.

The bottles were all empty. Whatever the glass had held, he would never know.

Miro left the building.

He pondered as he explored. These people had obviously left in a planned manner, taking their important belongings with them.

It also seemed obvious that they didn't use lore. All of the houses had hearths, blackened by fire, where in Sarostar only the poorest people burned wood or coal for warmth. He'd seen lanterns in two of the houses, and leather harnesses he could only assume were for animals.

Miro entered yet another building. It looked like it might have been an eating house. There were long tables with bench seats, and Miro guessed the next room had been a kitchen, although that part of the building was now rubble. He spotted some small barrels, but they were rotten, and Miro guessed they'd once held wine.

Miro turned to exit the building, when he heard a sound.

His muscles tensed as the sound sent chills along his back. There was no way it could have been natural. Something or someone had moved, dislodging some stones. Miro heard heavy breathing.

Miro held his axe, ready for whatever came. He walked toward the rubble, his eyes straining to see.

A pair of red eyes regarded him, and he heard a growl. The growl turned to a snarl, and a dog came rushing at him, snarling and snapping its jaws, trying to get at Miro's legs.

Miro leapt back. The dog jumped in fright and scurried back to the rubble, once more hiding from the intruder.

Miro felt sorry for it. It was skinny and wild, probably subsisting on birds or forest creatures. There must be more of them, left here either by the inhabitants or Toro Marossa's exploration party.

Thinking of Toro Marossa made Miro remember what he was here for. Toro had found the poisonous powder in an ancient ship.

Miro left the dog to its growling and headed for the dock.

When he reached it, he felt a surge of disappointment. There weren't any ships, and the dock itself was ruined. He couldn't see any signs that Toro Marossa had come this way, signs that would have told Miro he was at least following in another's footsteps.

From the shore Miro could see the next island and the misty mountain that crowned it. The sun was falling toward the mountain. He didn't have much time.

Miro shaded his eyes. Farther along the beach . . . there was something there. The remains of scaffolding? He decided it would be the last thing he investigated today.

Miro picked up his pace as he approached. The scaffolding rose from a wide hole in the ground, big enough to house ten ships the size of the *Delphin*.

He felt a surge of triumph as he arrived.

It was a dry dock, and the ship being repaired was still in it.

Immediately, Miro saw signs of Toro Marossa having been this way. The ship was decayed, but there was a makeshift ladder someone had built to allow descent into the hole. A second ladder rose from the sunken floor to the side of the ship, obviously constructed by the same group. Whoever once lived in the Ochre Isles built well and built to last, whereas the makers of the ladders had hastily constructed them of tall trees and twine, not even bothering to properly trim the saplings. Miro knew the islands' inhabitants hadn't made them.

As Miro reached the side of the pit, he gazed at the ship in awe.

He'd never seen anything so big. It made the *Delphin* look puny in comparison. Even the *Infinity* was small compared to this ship.

She was held in place by huge ribs of wood and had three great masts, but the foremost had fallen down at some point, crashing through the deck and smashing the ship's front. There was a row of wooden shutters along the sides; they looked like they could open, but Miro had no idea why.

He looked down at the ladder descending into the pit. Miro squatted and shook it; the ladder appeared sturdy.

Miro descended the ladder, praying the rungs wouldn't break. It took an eternity before he was on the ground, and then he had an even longer ascent ahead of him to reach the deck. Finally, Miro stood on the planks of the ancient vessel. For some reason, the ship had survived the ravages of time, whereas many of the buildings hadn't. Perhaps she was built of a harder wood. Miro supposed a ship must be stronger even than a house.

Searching the huge vessel would take time, so Miro decided to search level by level until he reached the hold. Planks creaked beneath his feet as he heaved open a hatch and descended.

Discovering the inner rooms on the upper deck all empty, Miro found steps leading down and searched the next level. Also empty.

The next deck below was cramped. Miro saw strange tubes of bronze, now rusted, each leading to one of the wooden shutters visible from the outside. Once, rollers enabled the bronze tubes to be pointed out the side of the ship. It was yet another mystery.

Avoiding the rotten sections of the planks, Miro finally found the hold. Given the cavernous storage area, Miro wondered how large the ship's crew had once been. Now, it was apparently as empty as the rest of the ship.

Exploring the great hold, Miro walked almost the entire length of the ship before he saw them: a score of small barrels, kegs really, each marked with the symbol of a flame.

Miro's breath caught. Long ago, Toro Marossa had once stood in this very place.

Some of the kegs had a second symbol beside that of the flame. It was a skull, an additional warning to stay clear. Next to an open keg, black powder sat in a small pile.

Miro stayed clear of the barrels, but he knew he'd found the poison. He searched the hold meticulously before he gave up.

Miro's heart sank. It was always a long shot.

Just because he'd found the poison didn't mean there was a cure nearby. It was the people who'd once lived here he wanted to find.

With a sigh, Miro decided to return to the shelter.

It was hours past sundown, and Miro was worried. He didn't have the means to build a fire, but the light cast by a crescent moon outlined the white beach. He watched the beach relentlessly, desperate for a sign of Amber. If she walked on the beach, he would see her.

Should he leave the shelter and head toward the second settlement? What if he missed her?

Miro's fists clenched and unclenched. He should never have let Amber go out on her own. Who knew what she'd found? He'd almost put his foot through the rotten planks of the ship more than once. What if she were stuck somewhere? Perhaps a roof had collapsed on her, or she'd been attacked by a dog. She could have come across some of the island's inhabitants, perhaps someone violent.

As Miro's thoughts turned darker and darker, he finally saw a figure in the distance. Miro leapt up and began to run.

She made slow progress, dragging something behind her, something large and square, obviously heavy.

"Amber!" Miro cried.

"Here, help me with this," she gasped.

"What is it?"

"Tell you later."

The light was low, and Miro only saw it was a piece of wood the size of a large door. She must have labored for hours to bring it back to the camp.

"Here," Miro said, "let me take one end. You take the other."

Between the two of them, they managed to get it off the ground and stumble with it back to the shelter. Finally they dropped it to the ground with a thud, and both sank down beside it, puffing and wheezing.

"What . . . is it?" Miro panted.

"Can't see now." Amber coughed. "Show you in the morning. I'm exhausted."

After drinking greedily from the water barrel and then eating a handful of oats and dried fruit, Amber dropped to the ground and was instantly asleep. Miro burned with curiosity as he lay down beside her, yet he knew he needed to let her rest.

The fronds that made their bed felt like soft linen, and the rough canvas sack made a warm blanket. As Miro thought again about the strange things he'd seen, it started to rain, the heavy drops of water splattering against the canvas roof with a steady patter.

They'd survived their first day on the island. They were warm, and they were dry.

Miro fell asleep.

"Lord of the Sky," Miro breathed, as he looked at what Amber had brought, now revealed by the bright light of morning.

"I thought you'd want to see right away."

"So you brought it with you?"

Amber shrugged. "Time is marching on."

It was a map.

"I thought it was a removable panel," she continued, "but then I found the drawing was part of the wall, engraved into the wood itself. The wood was weak, so I decided to bring the wall—the part with the map, that is."

"That's obviously where we are now." Miro pointed to the three islands. "Wherever Altura is, it's not on here."

"But now we know where these people came from," Amber said, "and, most likely, where they are now."

Near the islands, farther to the west, lines marked out a coast-line, stretching along the height of the wall.

Amber had discovered a landmass on the other side of the Great Western Ocean. It wasn't just big—it was immense.

The map showed them a great continent to rival their own.

18

The next day Miro left Amber to rest while he searched the town and the huge ship again. He finally returned at the end of the day, convinced there was nothing new for them there.

Amber's search had uncovered little besides the map. That night, Miro and Amber compared what they'd seen, deciding that the town he'd found was the larger of the two, while Amber had probably explored a small fishing settlement. Yet the discovery she'd made was incredible.

"This new land is closer by far than Altura. Our best bet is to try to make it there. Amber, we still have a chance of finding these people and finding a way home. Our main problem is we'd never survive the open sea in the longboat," Miro said. "So if there aren't any workable ships on this island, our only option is to try the next island."

"What about the ship you found?"

"Too damaged," Miro said. "The bow was smashed up when the foremast collapsed; also the two of us would never be able to work a ship that big."

"How will we get out of here, then?" Amber asked.

"Well, we know these people knew about this poison, and we have a good idea where they are now. When they departed it was planned and intentional; they left nothing behind. We don't know why they left, but most important of all, stuck on this island we're not doing Tomas any good. We need to find a ship."

"What makes you think a ship will still be in any condition to travel?"

"The dry dock kept that huge ship in pretty good condition. A sailboat that's smaller, but big enough to sail on open water, might be out there." Miro smiled without humor. "Unless you have a better idea?"

"How far do you make the distance to the next island to be?" Amber asked.

"Far enough that I think we should take everything with us," said Miro. "We can always build another shelter, but if something goes wrong and we can't come back, at least we'll have our provisions."

"When do we leave?"

Miro looked out at the lagoon. "We'll get the longboat ready at first light. Tomorrow we can row it around the headland so that we're closer but stay on this island. We can beach it and get another night's rest before trying to make the crossing first thing the following morning."

That night, Miro and Amber slept for the last time in their shelter. They dismantled it at dawn, folding the square of canvas and pulling the six oars out of the ground.

After yet another breakfast of oats and dried fruit, they spent the next hour pushing the unloaded longboat down to the water's edge, turning it around so it faced the water. Then Amber sat in the boat while Miro handed her barrels to stow, followed by the oars and the square of canvas.

Miro had considered making the canvas into a sail, but with no keel they wouldn't be able to sail across the wind. He held the option in reserve, although he hoped that with both of them rowing, they wouldn't need to use it.

Amber jumped out of the boat, and they both pushed it until waves lapped against the wood, finally lifting up the bow as the water came underneath.

"Jump in," Miro called.

Amber climbed over the side and immediately fitted a pair of oars to the rowlocks. With the water nearly at Miro's waist, he gave one last heave and clambered aboard. They were away.

"Remember," Miro said, "today is about getting around the headland. We can worry about making the crossing tomorrow."

Miro took a set of oars, and the sound of splashing and wood grinding against wood broke the morning stillness. The sun shone on their faces, and even though they were rowing against the current, Miro was glad to be moving.

As soon as they began to navigate the channel between the headland and the reef, Miro realized the foolishness of his plan.

He could now see sharp rocks poking their tops through the water on the far side of the promontory, an expanse of hazard Miro knew would be perilous to navigate. He'd intended to travel in that direction, but he now realized it would be impossible. There would be no way to tell where safety lay.

Facing backward to row meant they couldn't see where they were going, and as they exited the channel, Miro stopped rowing momentarily so he could turn around and look ahead. Wavelets formed little crests where two currents collided, and Miro looked up at the misty mountain on the second island as their path took them past the reef and into open water.

The longboat rose and fell on waves that grew larger the farther out they went. The current picked up, and now it was taking them away from both islands, out to sea.

"What is it?" Amber said, stopping when she noticed Miro had ceased rowing. "Shouldn't we be turning?"

"Scratch it," Miro cursed. "The current's too powerful to row against, and it's taking us away from the island we just left."

"What do we do?"

Already the longboat was hundreds of paces from the channel.

"We're going to have to head for the second island. If we row at an angle to the current, we might make it. Row harder on your left than your right. Come on."

Miro pulled at his oars, feeling his back strain and wood rub against his palms. He and Amber both had their backs to their destination, making it hard to check their progress, but he could now see in full the retreating island Toro Marossa had named Sofia.

He quickly turned his head. They were speeding through the water, desperately fighting the current as they tried to head for the island and its tall mountain.

Miro saw a beach and could make out the structures of the second island's abandoned settlement.

"We're going to make it," he grunted. "Keep going!"

Amber groaned and pulled hard at her oars, and Miro's muscles felt as if they were on fire.

Miro turned again. The mountain loomed down; the turquoise lagoon beckoned.

There were some breakers ahead.

"Dear Skylord," Miro whispered. He thrust his oar into the water to turn them, but it was too late.

The longboat ran onto the reef.

Planks splintered at their feet, and immediately water surged through a widening gap in the hull. The collision threw Miro from his bench and nearly tossed Amber out of the boat.

A wave hit the side of the longboat, pouring over the sides in a torrent.

"Amber!"

"What do we do?"

"Ditch everything!" Miro cried. "We're going to have to swim to shore, but we have to be careful of the reef. When the next big wave comes, jump out, and try to ride with it over the coral."

"Here it comes!" Amber yelled.

At the last instant, Miro grabbed the cutlass, wrapping it in the woolen sailor's vest and holding it close.

"Ready. *Go!*"

Miro leapt into the water and felt the swell pick him up. Behind him, he heard a crunch as the longboat broke into pieces. His bare feet touched coral, and he felt pain as something sliced his foot.

Then he was over the reef, with a second wave carrying him into the stillness of the lagoon.

Miro looked frantically for Amber. He saw her clinging to an oar, with her hair over her face. She pushed at the water with her free arm, bringing herself closer to him.

Miro's foot stung where he'd hit the coral, and he struggled with the bundled sword. "Are you hurt?" he asked Amber.

"Not a scratch. What about you?"

"Cut my foot."

Miro tucked the bundled sword under his arm and brought up his foot, trying to look at it through the water. He saw a thin gash where the skin had parted. Blood welled up, instantly diffused in the water.

A dark shape shifted in the depths. A sinuous creature, swimming in lazy circles, a deadly form made for power in the water. Its length was greater than that of the longboat.

Amber saw Miro's expression, and her face turned white. "What is it?"

"Amber," Miro said quietly, as if somehow noise would make it charge. "Let go of that oar, and swim to shore as quickly as you can."

Amber moaned with fear, and letting go of the oar, she began to kick with her legs, swimming with an overarm stroke. Miro's heart sounded loud in his ears, and he was suddenly terribly aware of his legs, the part of him deepest in the water. He looked ahead at the distant shore; it now seemed infinitely far away.

He realized there was no use watching the shark. If it decided to attack, it would attack. Yet he couldn't fight the sensation that even now it was coming for his legs. He could almost feel the jaws closing around his calf.

Miro shifted the bundle to his left hand and began to swim using his right arm and kicking his legs. He was a strong swimmer and had spent his childhood in the water, but the waterlogged vest wrapped around the sword slowed him down.

Amber was ahead, frantically paddling for shore.

A dark triangular fin pierced the water between them. It carved a path through the water before lowering again, disappearing below.

Miro's pulse raced, and a chill ran down his spine. He didn't know if it was the same shark he'd seen below.

There were probably more.

He'd stopped swimming at the sight of the fin, but he now resumed paddling with all his strength. Struggling, he took the hilt of the cutlass in his right hand and let the wrapped vest fall away.

Expecting to feel the lunge of gaping jaws at any instant, Miro saw he'd halved the distance to shore. Amber still splashed ahead of him, and then Miro touched the sandy floor of the lagoon with a foot.

The sword would only be of use if he could take stock of his situation and see. Miro swam farther, and when he could rest both feet on the bottom, he turned.

At that moment the shark struck.

Its pointed nose bumped into his side, but Miro was turning, and the gaping jaws missed his skin by inches. The shark kicked its tail, thrashing in a tight circle, and its tail smacked hard into Miro's chest, taking the wind out of him.

Looking back toward the reef, Miro saw the menacing fin of a second shark pierce the water only a dozen paces away. He gathered the sword in two hands, but the shark that had hit him sped away.

Lapping waves pushed Miro slowly and gently toward shore, and he didn't fight the motion, but walked backward, facing the sea.

A sudden swirl of water and the flash of a dark shape beneath the surface told him where a shark was coming at him for another attack. Miro held the tip of the sword beneath the water, and when he saw the gills and jagged teeth, he thrust out.

The sword was sharp, and the shark's rushing momentum carried it onto the point. Blood instantly filled the water with clouds of red.

The wounded shark thrashed and took itself away.

Miro continued to back away, the water now below his ribs, while the blood sent the sharks into a frenzy. He could no longer count them, there were so many, some larger, some smaller. They chopped the water up as they twisted and turned, seemingly fighting each other, perhaps feeding on the shark Miro had wounded.

Another came at him and he again fought off the attack with the sword, this time opening up the shark's soft belly as it turned. Blood and guts spilled out from the gaping wound, and Miro quickened his pace, backing away as fast as he could, to open up space between himself and the dying creature.

A massive shark, the biggest he'd yet seen, opened its maw wide and took a chunk out of its fellow, kicking with its tail to take a second bite.

The water was now at Miro's waist.

Turning, he left the sharks to their grisly feeding and lunged out of the water, wading forward and finally pulling himself up onto the sand, gasping.

He wasn't happy until there wasn't any part of him in the water.

Amber was suddenly beside him, and while Miro wheezed, she rolled him over, checking him for wounds. She finally pried the cutlass from his grip and crouched beside him, waiting until Miro regained his breath and sat up.

"We made it," she said, "but now we're truly stranded. If we can't find a way off this island, this is where we'll spend our final days."

19

This time, when Miro and Amber searched this new island's settlement, it was with a desperation they hadn't felt before.

Like the towns on the other island, it was built near a river, and they both drank greedily when they reached the cool water. Like the other towns, it had once had a dock, but little was left but timber piles.

This island had much more of the strange red rock than the island Toro called Sofia. There were fields of it, like red mud, but hard to the touch, as if a sticky viscous liquid had spilled down to the shore and been frozen in place.

Most of the island was dominated by the mountain, with the town nestled between the mountain's foot and the shore.

"Miro," Amber called as they searched the buildings, "come here."

Amber stood near the remains of a dozen houses. When Miro arrived, she pointed at them. "Look. These buildings haven't collapsed with time. It happened all at once. See? The roofs are covered with black grime. Some of the timbers are burned, as if they were scorched by fire."

Now that Miro looked, he saw almost all the structures had greater or lesser amounts of the substance on their roofs. Several houses had burned down.

A sudden rumbling came from overhead. It was the same sound they'd heard from Sofia, but this time it was louder. Much louder.

"Lord of the Sky." Amber looked up at the mountain. "It's a volcano!"

"Of course," Miro said. "That explains why they left. The red rock—it's from lava."

Miro followed Amber's gaze. As they watched, red sparks shot into the sky.

"We need to get out of here," Amber said. She started on a direct path through the trees, heading for shore.

"We need to search," Miro said. "I don't think we're in any immediate danger."

"How do you know that? There's lava everywhere!"

"The buildings are still here."

Amber continued to push through the trees, aiming for the beach. She stopped in her tracks, pulling aside some branches and gesturing to Miro.

"Not all of them."

Miro realized they'd only been seeing part of the town. The rest was here, now overgrown by jungle. It was an area twice the size of that still standing, and had been reduced to ash and rubble. Hundreds of people must have been killed.

"Look," Amber said, pointing.

A human skull grinned at them, the rest of the body buried under growth. Now that Miro looked, he saw more bones, some blackened from the volcano's devastating hail of fire.

The mountain rumbled again, and the ground shook.

"We need to search close to the shore," Amber said. "That's where you found the last ship, at the dry dock."

Miro could sense Amber's longing to get away from the town and close to water.

"All right," he said. "You follow the shore right, I'll follow it left. The island isn't big. We'll either meet in the middle, or if we can't continue for some reason, we'll meet back here."

As Amber disappeared in the opposite direction, Miro followed the water, scanning the shore and occasionally checking the tree line to look for ships. He clambered over several fields of hardened lava, wondering at the strange ripples and rounded lumps, feeling fear stab his heart every time the mountain rumbled.

As he walked, he looked at the barrier reef that enclosed this island, much as Sofia's reef had done. He rounded the island, passing a ragged cliff, and then he was on the other side.

The water was rougher on the island's far side, and Miro saw there was a wide channel between two arms of the reef, the channel marked with deep blue to indicate the greater depth. Without the reef to protect the lagoon, waves pounded at the shore.

Miro saw Amber walking toward him.

"Find anything?" he asked, filled with hope.

"Nothing. That volcano scares me."

"Me too," Miro said.

"You looked like you were limping," Amber said. "Let me take a look at your foot."

Amber led Miro down to the hard sand near the water's edge. He washed the sand from his foot and then sat while Amber looked at the cut he'd taken on the reef.

"I think we should put something around it to stop sand and dirt getting into it," Amber said. "The last thing you want is an infection."

"It's not deep," Miro said.

Amber looked up at the tree line. "I'll see if I can find some leaves or fronds we can tie around your foot."

Miro watched Amber walk up to the trees. She vanished into the undergrowth and was gone for a long time. He began to worry. Then she returned, waving her arms.

Miro stood up and ran to where she stood.

"You won't believe this," Amber said excitedly.

Taking Miro by the hand, she led him a short way through the trees, barely a stone's throw away.

There was a shape there, a small hill of dark rock, obscured by the creepers.

Amber reached up and tore at the creepers until Miro saw solid planks of treated wood. He realized what it was.

"It's a ship," he breathed.

"Look," Amber said. She took Miro to the front of the ship and pulled some more vines away, revealing the name on the bow: *Intrepid*. "It's one of ours. It's a type of small ship called a caravel. See, it has a single stern castle, a main mast, and a mizzenmast aft. I remember it from my father's book."

It was perhaps half the size of the *Delphin*.

"I know what it is," Miro said, his voice filled with wonder, "or at least how it came to be here. Toro Marossa always traveled with more than one ship. He preferred the safety of numbers in case disaster struck, and he used caravels. This must be from his second voyage, the one he never returned from. We know he made it this far at least."

Aside from a few vines that had crawled up the sides, the ship was in remarkable condition.

"How did it last this long?" Miro wondered.

"Look," Amber said, pointing overhead.

Miro tilted his head to look up and realized he was seeing a roof, built over the ship to protect it from the elements.

"And it's on huge timber logs—rollers—that hold it up from the ground and also mean it can be easily launched."

Miro walked a short distance and looked out at the sea. He realized the ship's prow pointed at the wide channel he'd seen earlier—the quickest way to the open sea.

"Come on," Miro said. "Let's free it and try to get it down to shore."

"First let me do something about that foot," Amber said.

She made a bandage of fibrous plant matter and tied it in place on Miro's foot with tough reeds. Then they set to work clearing the caravel.

As they worked, the mountain rumbled, and after a time their stomachs began to rumble along with it.

"I saw some shellfish on the way here," Amber said. "I'll get us something to eat. Give me the cutlass."

"Here," Miro handed it to her. "I'll see if I can tie some vines to those iron hoops at the front of the ship. If we can loop the vines around that thick tree, we can get the leverage we need to pull the caravel forward on the rollers."

Sweat poured down Miro's brow as he worked, but in his enthusiasm he forgot everything—the lack of food, the close encounter with the sharks, and his own tired muscles.

Amber returned with her shirt cupped full of shellfish, and using the cutlass to pry them open, they both set to hungrily. Afterward, Miro showed Amber his handiwork. He'd made a rope of tough vines that he'd looped around the thick trunk of a tree situated ahead of the small ship. When they pulled on the vines, the caravel should inch forward on the rollers.

"Are you ready?" Miro asked.

Amber took a loop around her wrist.

"Heave!"

"It moved!" Amber cried.

"Of course it did," Miro said, but he was grinning.

By the middle of the afternoon, they'd hauled the ship to the summit of the gently sloping beach.

"It'll move quickly now," Miro said. "We should wait until morning to take her any farther." He brushed away some leaves clinging to the hull, still amazed at the caravel's condition. "Let's climb aboard."

The sides were low enough that Miro could stand on one of the rollers and hoist himself up. He reached down and helped Amber up behind him. She clambered up the side, and soon they both stood on the deck.

The main mast and mizzenmast had been taken down, but Miro was pleased to see the two stout masts lying side by side on the deck. The ship had a single companionway heading below, and the captain's cabin evidently occupied the space below the raised castle on the stern.

She had a tiller rather than a wheeled helm, a horizontal length of wood on the afterdeck that would directly control the rudder. Miro guessed she'd probably had a crew of about twenty men.

Miro found the sails in a forward stowage area while Amber entered the ship's interior and called out to him.

"There are empty water barrels in here," she said. "Also, there's fishing gear."

"We'll fill the barrels at the river tonight," Miro said. "And we'll bring as many shellfish as we can. Hopefully we can use them as bait to catch something bigger."

Amber vanished into the captain's cabin.

"Come and see this," she called. "You were right."

Miro ducked under the door and entered the cabin. The interior was in excellent condition, given how much time had elapsed.

There were no charts spread out at the navigator's desk, but there was a note, written in a decisive hand.

On this, my second voyage to find what lies across the Great Western Ocean, I have lost too many men to crew the three caravels I brought with me. Bold adventurer, the Intrepid *is now yours to command. If you see me in a tavern, buy me a measure of rum. I drink it neat.*

Toro Marossa

Miro felt a shiver at the age of the message, directed to him, yet written so long ago by the famed explorer.

"He must have left it ready in case he passed this way again," Miro said.

"Do you think we can sail it?" Amber asked.

"We can try," Miro replied.

"How will we know where to go?"

"We have to aim for this new land. The sun rises in the east and sets in the west. East takes us back in the direction of Altura. It's a long, long way, and there's a high probability we'll lose our course, die of thirst, or starve. East takes us home to Tomas."

Amber nodded.

"Then there is west. West takes us toward this new land, the great continent we know nothing about. It's much closer than Altura, and I think we can make it. West takes us to the homeland of those who had the skill to build these settlements and the biggest ships I've seen. There's no guarantee, but these people may have an antidote for their poison."

Amber didn't hesitate. "We're going west. We'll find this new world and seek help from its people."

Miro nodded. "Come on. Let's fill the water barrels and mount the masts. We'll sleep tonight in the captain's cabin. Tomorrow, we set sail."

The next day saw the *Intrepid* carve through the waves, Miro at the tiller and Amber keeping the sails trimmed. The caravel moved gracefully through the water, easily navigating the channel and heading out for open sea.

With the *Intrepid* pointed west, the wind came across their beam. While they became accustomed to the ship, they sailed only by the lateen-rigged main sail, which was now opened up wide to catch the breeze. The caravel rose and fell on the crests and troughs, large enough to handle the seas yet narrow enough to slice through the water like a knife.

The wind was gentle, and the morning sun was at their backs. Miro's strength was needed at the tiller, but with the sail set, Amber was free to cast a line over the side, quickly snaring three silver fish.

There was no way to cook them, so she used the cutlass to slice the fish into fillets that they ate raw.

As the days passed, the wind stayed constant, but someone was needed at the tiller, even at night. Amber struggled with its weight, so Miro never slept more than a short amount at a time. It was wearying, and with the monotonous diet of fish, he felt his strength steadily ebb.

With a great continent to aim for, they had little chance of becoming lost. Miro hoped they would find land soon.

They grew more confident, and after two days they hoisted the mizzen staysail. The caravel picked up speed, leaping through the water, flying like a bird.

Miro and Amber sailed this way for six days. They relied on each other in a way they never had before, their relationship becoming strengthened by shared hardship and cooperation.

On the seventh day, the storm struck.

Conditions changed with terrifying speed. Miro saw dark clouds gather in the west as the sun dipped below the horizon. Even as the light faded, he saw the sky change color and then heard the sound of sudden thunder.

Miro felt a surge of fear. He didn't dare change course, yet the storm lay directly in their path.

As the sun disappeared below the horizon, the light faded to black. Then lightning flashed, sheets of white spreading across the sky, and it started to rain. Water came out of the sky in a torrent, heavy drops that stung the skin.

"Amber!" Miro called.

He saw her exit the companionway, silhouetted by the next flash of lightning. "Amber!" he cried again.

He felt helpless, unable to take his blistered hand from the tiller.

"What should we do?" she came forward to hear him.

"We're in the path of the storm," Miro yelled. "I need you to take the sails down. As soon as possible!"

The lightning was now overhead, jagged forks of white energy striking the sea again and again. The downpour increased until Miro could no longer see, the water hitting his face and eyes with ever greater force.

A mighty wave lifted the caravel up and then crashed down on the deck. The prow went under with the next wave, and the *Intrepid* threatened to tip. Miro thrust hard with the tiller, pointing the caravel into the wave. He realized he couldn't hold his course any longer; he needed to ride the waves and prevent a surge from the side rolling the caravel over.

Miro peered through the torrent and could see Amber still hadn't managed to take down the sails. With the sails still set, a squall would capsize the ship. He wondered if he should leave the tiller and fetch his cutlass from the captain's cabin. Perhaps he could cut the sails down—they would lose them, but it was better than drowning.

Miro's decision was made for him when, with a mighty crack, the main mast snapped at the deck, coming down with a great crash.

The ship turned in the sea, and Miro felt the muscles in his arm screaming as he fought to keep the caravel perpendicular to the huge rolling waves.

"Amber!" Miro cried. Had she been injured when the mast went down?

He shielded his eyes, and then in a flash of lightning he saw her. She had the cutlass in hand as she cleared the fallen sail from the deck. Half of the sail was in the water, making Miro's task at the tiller nearly impossible.

Miro was completely soaked, the rain splattering against his skin, stinging his face and back. The size of the waves increased until they were as tall as mountains, mighty walls of water with curling caps. If a wave broke on top of the *Intrepid*, they were doomed.

Amber managed to free the fallen sail, and Miro turned the caravel against the next monstrous wave. The bucking motion of the ship was so strong he felt his grip on the tiller was the only thing keeping him standing where he was.

Then, with another terrible crash the mizzenmast went down. Amber ran across the swamped deck to free the smaller sail.

Miro concentrated on keeping them alive.

The night grew darker, and the thunder grew louder. Lightning flashes seemed to come with every breath Miro took, as the storm became ever more vicious, the howling wind stronger, the waves taller still.

Miro pushed at the tiller, feeling the caravel come round to meet the next terrifying wave.

The wind whipped against the fallen staysail, and a stout length of wood, still attached to a line, flew up into the air.

It snapped against Miro's head with a crack.

He fell down, and everything went black.

20

Ella had now left the Akari, fortuitously traveling with Hermen Tosch as far south as Mara Maya, the Louan capital. She studied both the damaged book of the Evermen and the new skills she'd learned from the Akari on the journey south. After Mara Maya, Ella bid farewell to the trader. She would make her own way to Stonewater.

Barnabas, the cantankerous old necromancer, had taught Ella the things she needed to know. Her plan had advanced one step further.

Evrin had told Ella someone had crossed through the portal, and Dain Barden had said a dozen necromancers had disappeared with essence. She now knew in her heart that a being of incredible evil was in Merralya. The Empire needed Killian.

Ella finally allowed herself to believe that her plan could work. She thought it through again.

Only one of the Evermen could take Ella through the portal.

Killian, as Evrin's descendant, had their powers.

Logically, one of Killian's parents was also descended from Evrin and also had their powers.

Killian had told Ella that when he was young, at the orphanage in Salvation, he'd been told his parents were dead.

If Ella could find Killian's parents, she now had the power to bring them back from the grave. The portal would recognize one of the Evermen, and Ella would be able to cross.

It sounded mad, even in her own mind. But Ella had made a promise, back at the Sentinel. She had said the words to Evrin.

"I promise," she had said. "I will find a way."

Ella had meant every word.

Ella felt nervous about entering Aynar, the land of the templars, a place she'd never been to before. She passed through the forests of Tingara's south before crossing the border, almost surprised to see little change in the landscape.

Then she saw peaks in the distance, the great mountains that stood higher than any other range. The sight of the mighty Emdas told Ella she was now in Aynar.

The road was heavily traveled, and initially Ella wondered where all the people were going, but her initial trepidation turned to pity as she saw the starved masses. Some were heading in hope for Seranthia in the north, but others journeyed away from Seranthia with eyes downcast.

The Assembly of Templars had been a force for good in the world, Ella reminded herself, before the primate's madness took hold. These poor people had no place to go—no home, no work, and no food to eat—and only the templars took them in.

Ella followed the people heading south, deeper into Aynar. Almost certainly those she saw on the road would be traveling to Salvation.

Ahead Ella saw a strange cloud, low and gray, pointed at the top. The cloud solidified as she walked, becoming firm and brown, and Ella's mouth dropped open as she realized she was seeing the famous mountain. It was solitary and massive, jutting up from the plain, visible from a great distance away. Ella was looking at Stonewater.

Ella knew she would find the large town of Salvation at the foot of the mountain. She'd heard it was filled with temples, but poor. Evidently little of the wealth produced by the houses flowed to those who managed the essence.

Killian had grown up in Salvation, first in an orphanage, and then, after reaching adolescence, on the street.

In Salvation, Killian had learned to hate the self-righteous templars, but then later in Seranthia he'd learned to hate the emperor more.

He'd been taken to see the primate in Stonewater and he'd given his allegiance to the man who promised to end the emperor's reign and redistribute the riches of the houses among the poor.

After meeting Ella, he'd finally realized he had more power to affect the world than he'd thought. Killian didn't have to follow the emperor or the primate. He could be his own man.

After leaving Ella in Petrya, Killian had come back to Stonewater with eyes opened. With Evrin's help, he had destroyed the primate's means of producing essence.

Killian's difficult youth had given him a burning desire to know who he was. How had his parents died? Who had they been?

As the mountain grew to dominate her vision and she began to see buildings ahead, Ella wondered if she would be able to succeed where he had failed.

"Yes? How can I help?" the long-nosed, officious clerk asked.

He wore the white of the Assembly, but it was neither the cassock of a priest nor the uniform of a templar. Ella guessed he was simply an official. Stonewater was huge, and Ella supposed priests and templars had other duties of their own.

"My name is Ella Torresante. My brother is Lord Marshal Miro Torresante. I'm here on an information-gathering mission for Lord Regent Rogan Jarvish," Ella said, which wasn't exactly true. "I'd like access to the archives."

Ella wore her green silk enchantress's dress and had combed her golden hair until it shone. It felt unbelievably strange to be boldly displaying the Alturan *raj hada* in what had not long ago been the heartland of the enemy. Yet Altura had grown in stature after the war, and Ella felt her garments would impress, as would her brother's name.

The Assembly had a reputation for keeping meticulous records, and Ella was sure that, with his unique fiery hair and blue eyes, Killian would have been remembered, even at a young age.

Killian had been desperate to know the things Ella intended to find out, but with the war and his own history with the templars, he'd never have been able to do what she was doing now—simply walk up and ask.

The clerk blanched when he peered down from his desk and saw Ella's dress. "Ella, an Alturan enchantress . . . I've heard of you. Why didn't you send word ahead?"

Ella did her best to look impatient. "Because I *am* the word," she said flatly. "I travel light, particularly when the need is great."

"The lord regent sent you?"

"Yes."

"Hmm . . ." The clerk dithered, and Ella knew what would be coming next. "I need to speak with my superior. Please wait just a moment. I won't be long."

"I'll be here," Ella said.

Ella looked around while she waited. She had been directed here by some priests she'd met on her way to Stonewater, following a path that led for a time outside the mountain before an arched entrance took her inside. She guessed she was somewhere halfway up.

This particular level, carved out of the stone just like she'd always been told, smelled of paper and leather. A sign simply named it "Records."

The clerk returned, looking more nervous than before. Ella resumed her irritated expression.

"I am to let you in and also to assist you," the clerk said.

Ella breathed a sigh of relief.

"I need to ask, do you carry any liquids on you?"

She shook her head. "No."

"Any igniters or flint?"

Ella thought of her dress. With it, she could set the entire floor on fire. The templars weren't known for their experience with lore. "No."

"Good. Please come with me."

———

Whatever the clerk's fussy manner, he knew how the records were cataloged, and Ella made swift progress without giving away too much about what she was looking for.

She felt excitement grow in her breast. She wished Killian were with her, but she promised herself he soon would be.

She was going to discover his past!

Ella quickly found that at the time of Killian's youth there had been four orphanages in Salvation. There was one larger orphanage in Seranthia, also run by the templars, but Ella knew Killian was from Salvation, so she started there.

The records of the four orphanages were each kept in a different location in the archives, and it took Ella most of the day to search the records of each orphanage in turn. She was initially pleased to see that, next to the names of the children, hair and eye color were recorded, but there was no mention of a child matching Killian's description.

"Where are the records of the orphanage in Seranthia?" Ella asked.

The clerk licked his lips. "They're stored in the vault." He gestured to a locked door at the end of the room.

"Why?"

"Those records are private." The clerk gave Ella a significant look.

"I don't understand."

"There are a lot of lords and ladies in Seranthia," the clerk said.

Ella was growing frustrated. "Just tell me what you're trying to say."

"Well, sometimes ladies have children before they're married. Sometimes to men who aren't lords. Those babies sometimes end up in orphanages. The families of the ladies are powerful, and they don't want the records available to just anyone."

"Oh," Ella said. "Please open the vault. I don't care about any of that."

"I can't do that," the clerk said. "I've never been in the vault myself. Not even my superior—"

"I see," said Ella.

She walked over to the heavy door. It was made of stout wood, probably oak, and banded with strips of metal. The lock was made of good steel. The door looked thick, and the lock looked strong.

Ella reached into a pocket inside her dress and took out the wand.

"Evermen protect us," the hovering clerk drew back, his eyes suddenly wide with fear. "Please, Enchantress, no flames! The records—they must be kept for posterity."

Ella looked at the wand, a device she'd constructed herself, as long as her forearm. It was made of dark hazel wood, with three facets rising to the tip, crowned with a prism of gold-flecked quartz. The wand was warm to the touch, and tiny runes covered its length, so small Ella had needed a lens to draw the symbols with the finest of scrills.

Ella spoke the activation sequence, and the symbols lit up, a sparkle of blue traveling up the wand's length until the prism burned with yellow fire. Ignoring the clerk, she turned to the door.

"Please," the clerk said again, and she had to admire his courage. "The records . . ."

Ella had no intention of destroying the records, but she was going to open this door. "Stand back," she told the clerk, before walking up to the door.

"*Tourahn-ash-tassine,*" she said softly, words that would moderate the wand's power.

The prism's radiance dimmed by half. Ella touched the wand to the lock and then called forth a bolt of energy.

She quickly pulled her hand back as the lock liquefied, molten steel bursting out with a spray of sparks.

The door fell open.

Ella deactivated the wand and put it away.

She turned around. The clerk was nowhere to be seen. Ella entered the vault.

Ella had learned the templars' system of filing now, and it took her only a short time to find the records of the orphanage in Seranthia.

She scanned the list of descriptions, ignoring the names; a name could always be changed.

The arrival records were organized by day, and Ella scanned them swiftly, perplexed when she still saw no mention of Killian. Then she scanned the dates again.

There was one day missing.

Ella calculated how long ago it would have been. Killian looked to be a year or two older than she was.

The date was a possible match. With no other records matching Killian's eye and hair color, Ella needed to see the missing record.

"Scratch it," Ella muttered.

Wait—there was another file, hidden behind this one. It was an extract from the arrivals at one of the Salvation orphanages. Someone must have thought it important enough to take it out of the regular archives and put it here, in the vault.

Scanning the list, Ella's heart thudded in her chest.

The date of the Salvation arrival matched the missing card from the Seranthia orphanage.

"Transfer from Seranthia orphanage. Hair: red. Eyes: blue."

There was nothing else. Whoever had hidden these records had done their job well. Most shocking of all, Killian evidently wasn't from Salvation, land of the templars; he was from Seranthia, capital of the Tingaran Empire.

Ella decided it was time to go to Seranthia.

21

After yet another journey, this time north to Seranthia, Ella continued her search. She had little difficulty locating the Assembly-run orphanage. The place was huge, bigger than the Crystal Palace back in Sarostar.

It still existed as an orphanage; if anything, the priests and templars who ran the place had more work than they could handle. The war had torn families apart, and the resulting poverty and disease had led to countless sad stories of children without parents. Even now, two years later, new arrivals flooded in.

Ella tried the same tactic that had worked for her back in Stonewater, introducing herself and then getting to the point of her visit.

"I'd like to see your records," she said to the matronly woman who held a little girl in one arm and a lad's hand in the other.

"Records?" the woman asked, frowning suspiciously. "What for?"

"I'm looking for someone . . ." Ella said.

"Oh, I see," the matronly woman's eyebrows went up, and Ella realized the woman thought she was looking for a child she'd given up. "Hold on, and stay here, I'll be back in a moment."

Ella waited in the reception chamber while the woman disappeared with the children. While she waited, a flaxen-haired boy chased a sweet-faced girl into the room, the girl squealing with mock fear and circling back out.

"Now," Ella heard behind her. The matronly woman, absent her charges, held her hands on her hips. "How long ago was the child brought here?"

"He was transferred from here to the Alma orphanage in Salvation in 522," Ella said.

The woman snorted. "That was years ago. Are you pulling my leg?"

"No."

"Listen, I've got bad news for you. There was a fire here in 530, eight years after that. Nothing survived. No records—nothing."

Ella's heart sank. She'd come so close. Once, when just a babe, Killian had been brought to this orphanage. He'd stayed here a short while before being transferred to Salvation. Now the trail had gone cold.

"Oh," Ella said. "I can see you're busy. Thank you. I won't take more of your time."

Ella left the reception chamber and walked back to the wrought iron gates, the bars reminding her of nothing so much as a prison. The children seemed happy. Still, Ella thought it was a sad place. These children hadn't had a choice; their parents had been taken from them, along with any chance of a normal life.

Something small and wild crashed into Ella from behind.

Ella looked down and saw a small boy, with long, unruly hair and dirt on his cheeks. The boy looked up at her and grinned with mischief.

"Come back, Stefan!" a reedy voice called.

Ella took hold of the boy by his upper arm, holding him gently as he squealed, while an old man approached.

He looked as ancient as the orphanage itself, with scrawny limbs, thin white hair, and dry skin.

"Thank you, young lady," the old man said, taking the squirming boy from Ella.

"Happy to help." Ella looked into the old man's eyes. "Have you worked here long?"

"Thirty-five . . . no, thirty-six years, I've worked here," he said proudly.

"May I ask you something? I'm looking for an orphan who arrived here around 522. He was transferred to the Alma orphanage in Salvation."

The old man barked a laugh. "Do you know how many boys I've seen come through these gates? That's over twenty years ago!"

"He would have only been small, and he had red hair," Ella said. "A strange red, the color of bright fire. And blue eyes. The bluest you've ever seen."

The old man's eyes slowly widened, and Ella knew she'd struck a nerve.

"They told me the records were destroyed in a fire," Ella said.

"Run along, Stefan," he said, giving the boy a gentle shove. He waited a moment before speaking. "The records were destroyed long before the fire," the old man said. "I remember, though, I do. You never forget something like that. You're in the wrong place, though, young lady. Try the courthouse."

"The courthouse?"

"The Imperial Courthouse, near the palace. That's where you need to look."

Without further explanation, the old man turned away.

There were three courthouses in Seranthia, each filling a different purpose.

Three blocks from the palace, still in the Imperial Quarter, arbiters in the Commoners' Courthouse ruled against thieves and swindlers, brawlers and cutthroats. Occasionally neighbors fought over the line of a fence or merchants fought for the right to display their wares at a certain place. It was guarded during the day by heavily armored Tingaran legionnaires, and at night huge dogs patrolled the grounds.

In the nearby Military Courthouse, deserters and men who'd disobeyed the orders of their officers or showed cowardice in battle were tried. In the days of Emperor Xenovere V, there hadn't been a day when fresh bodies weren't swinging from the gallows next to the utilitarian building.

By contrast, the Imperial Courthouse was the closest structure to the palace, and the grandest in design. If a lord had an issue to resolve with another lord—perhaps his virginal daughter was engaged to a recently discovered philanderer—here was where he came. Lords paid their taxes here, and a great deal of gilden was stored in the vaults. The clerks also charted and updated the bloodlines of the great families. Even the emperor's offspring were registered and legitimized by the records stored in the archives.

The Imperial Courthouse wasn't a place where Ella could simply walk up and ask to see records.

During the day it was the scene of constant comings and goings. Any large nation needed bureaucracy, and the Tingaran Empire was the greatest nation the world had known. Rogan Jarvish was trying to have the new Empire seamlessly replace the old, and kept the government machine running much as it always had. Examining the building, Ella saw the new device, the nine-pointed star, high above the massive doors, where it had replaced the Tingaran *raj hada*.

Ella could never enter the Imperial Courthouse by force. She was only blocks from the Imperial Palace, and the last thing Rogan Jarvish needed was another disturbance.

She knew the locks would be magical rather than mechanical. With her knowledge of the runes, Ella could decode complex matrices, even when the activation sequence was deliberately hidden within the pattern.

Ella was confident she could solve the codes on any locks she found. She decided to visit the Imperial Courthouse at night.

———✦———

The next day Ella was brought in front of Rogan Jarvish. He wasn't pleased.

"Why were you trying to break into the Imperial Courthouse, Ella?" Rogan said. "Lord of the Sky, last I knew you were on your way to Ku Kara. I didn't even know you were back in Tingara."

Ella shuffled in her seat, trying to think of the right words to say.

"You know there are wards that can detect shadow," he said. "Templars might not have the best knowledge of lore, but Tingarans certainly do. We can't have people tampering with official documents now, can we?" He glared at her.

Ella wore her green enchantress's dress, having used its power to slip past the guards at the Imperial Courthouse the previous night. She hadn't expected wards.

Ella felt frustrated. She was so close! She wasn't ready to talk to anyone yet.

"I . . . I'm sorry," Ella said.

Rogan shook his head. "That's not good enough," he said. "If there's something you need, you should feel you can ask me."

"I'm digging up a secret, but I can't say anything until I have more information. Not even to you."

"Then I'm also sorry, Ella, because I don't like secrets, and if they're going to be 'dug up,' I'd like to know why they were buried in the first place. Do you want me to put you under house arrest?"

Ella's eyes blazed. "I'd like to see you try."

Rogan Jarvish placed his hands on his desk and slowly stood.

Ella looked up at the tall man and remembered the time, long ago, when Rogan had tracked her down in Sarostar to give her Lady Katherine's legacy. With his scarred face and deadly grace, he'd scared her then.

Suddenly he scared her now.

"I can have my hand around your throat before you can speak a word," Rogan said calmly. "You think they don't teach bladesingers how to defeat your kind?"

Ella's neck felt terribly exposed.

Rogan sat back down. "Relax, Ella. Now, why don't you tell me what you're trying to achieve?"

Ella took a deep breath. "I spoke to Dain Barden of the Akari. Rogan, one of the Evermen is in Merralya."

Rogan drew back. "Evrin said he wasn't sure, but he asked me to build that wall . . ."

"Now we know. The essence drained from the pool, the portal opened, and someone crossed. Seeking essence, he went to the Akari. He took some of their necromancers with him, as well as enough essence to build the vats. Right now, he's out there somewhere, Rogan, and I believe he's building an army of revenants. He will come for Seranthia. He needs to bring the other Evermen home."

"And he'll be coming when we're at our weakest," Rogan said. "Lord of the Sky, the people won't let go of their belief in the Evermen. What will they do when one shows up?"

"We need to rebuild the machines. Evrin's doing everything he can—he barely sleeps. We need to hold the Empire together, and I know you're doing everything you can. But there's something I can do."

"What is it?"

"It's about Killian."

"Your young man, the one who crossed . . . the one you say has their powers. I thought it might be." Rogan paused. "Ella, Evrin Evenstar said you could never bring him back."

"Killian has their power. Trust me in this, Rogan. You won't believe the things he's capable of. When the time comes, we'll need every weapon at our disposal."

"I'm with you so far, but what are you planning?"

"It's a long story, but if I can find Killian's parents, I can find a way to bring him back. The trail leads to the Imperial Courthouse."

"How can you be sure that if you open the portal, more of the Evermen won't cross over?"

"I'll only open it for the shortest time," said Ella. "And I won't be waiting for Killian to simply step through."

"What will you do, then?"

"I'll cross over and get him myself."

Rogan thought for a moment. "All right, Ella. I'll have some of my men take you to the courthouse right now. Just don't go digging up any secrets, not without talking to me first."

Ella nodded. "Of course."

With the custodian's help, Ella quickly located the records for the years she was interested in. She started at what she guessed would be about two years before Killian's birth, methodically searching through birth and marriage certificates, custody battles, divorces, and deaths.

After eight hours of searching, she'd combed through about four years of records, but she hadn't found anything.

She thought back to the old man at the orphanage. The way he'd spoken, something had happened that was more than just a trivial event, something that had involved the destruction of records and the elimination of evidence.

Ella decided to study the criminal trials.

These were the cases that were a matter of death or imprisonment for those convicted—lords and ladies weren't frequently convicted for theft or brawling. These trials were for adultery, murder, and corruption. Surprisingly frequently, nobles were put on trial for treason.

The emperor had been a man jealous of his power, and from the trial notes Ella read, he wasn't above sentencing those closest to him to death.

The cases were fascinating, but Ella forced herself to concentrate on the details, scanning each set of notes swiftly before moving onto the next.

Yet she stopped at one thick file in particular, unable to stop reading. This case was from the time the Rebellion had broken out, a time within the span of years Ella was interested in. Over twenty years ago, the Western Rebellion had been the war that saw Miro and Ella's father, the Alturan High Lord Serosa Torresante, executed by the emperor. It was the war that made them orphans.

The story of the war's inciting event was familiar. The Halrana high lord at the time had married his only daughter to Emperor

214

Xenovere. A man of uncertain temper, Xenovere had beaten his new wife in a sudden rage, killing her.

The emperor had tried to cover up what he'd done, but Lord Aidan Alderon, a man married to Xenovere's sister, secretly passed the true story to the Halrana high lord.

The Halrana called on their steadfast allies, the Alturans. The result was the Western Rebellion.

The case Ella now held in her hands was the set of notes from Lord Aidan's trial.

Inevitably, Lord Aidan was found guilty of treason. Lady Alise, the emperor's sister, had pleaded with her brother to save her husband's life. Her desperate words had been recorded, and reading them, Ella felt her throat catch.

Xenovere had been unrelenting, and Lord Aidan was killed by hanging, the penalty for treason. The emperor intended to hang Lord Aidan's body from the Wall for three days. But after further begging from Lady Alise, Xenovere relented, allowing his sister to intern her husband's body in the nobles' cemetery in Westcliff.

The case summary ended there but directed the reader to another file, the trial of Lady Alise.

Ella hunted through the records until she found it. This case continued the sad story of Lord Aidan's family. Unable to look away, Ella read on.

The Rebellion had become a full-fledged war. Meanwhile, unbeknownst to her brother, the emperor, Lady Alise was pregnant with Lord Aidan's child. During his trial, Lord Aidan must have known his wife carried his child, Ella realized. Poor man!

As the war raged, Lady Alise gave birth to a traitor's child. Fearing for her life and that of her son, Alise tried to flee Tingara and her mad brother. The emperor's men caught her trying to find passage to Altura, and after a summary trial, Xenovere's sister was also convicted of treason.

Whatever feelings the emperor had left caused him to exile his sister to the Isle of Ana, a small rock off Tingara's eastern coast. The child was taken from Lady Alise and never seen again.

Ella put down the papers and looked up, absorbed in the tale. She had a sudden thought and found the custodian as quickly as she could.

"Please," she said, "I need to see a register of nobles."

It was a simple request, and soon Ella was turning the heavy pages. It didn't take her long to find the late emperor's sister.

"Lady Alise," she spoke aloud. "Hair color: brown, eye color: brown." She flipped through the pages some more, finally finding it. "Lord Aidan. Hair color: red, eye color: blue."

Ella felt a thrill course through her, but she needed one final confirmation. She again found the custodian, a hawk-eyed man with patrician features, "I need your help."

"What is it?"

Ella couldn't hide what she was looking for and still seek the custodian's help. She showed him the trial of Lady Alise. "The child that was taken from her. How would I find out his name?"

The custodian looked at Ella with grave eyes. "I don't need to search the records to tell you," he said. "The emperor's sister's trial was no small thing."

Ella held her breath.

"I remember it clearly. The child's name," the custodian said, "was Killian."

Ella's heart pounded in her chest.

She had been looking for Killian's parents, but she'd never expected to find this.

Ella needed to know one last thing.

She scanned the register of nobles until it became clear.

"Lord of the Sky," she breathed.

Killian, orphan from Salvation, as the nephew of the last emperor, was Xenovere's closest living relative.

Killian was the heir to the Empire.

22

Miro woke to a fierce headache as blood throbbed inside his head, pounding into his temples with hammer-like blows.

Groaning, he tried to sit up but felt arms pushing him gently back down.

"Please,"—it was Amber's voice—"don't get up. I'm sorry you're still on deck, but I haven't had a chance to move you to the cabin."

Miro's vision cleared as the pain in his head slowly receded. The sun was bright, and the sea was calm. Amber looked down at him with concern. "What happened?" Miro said.

"The mizzenmast fell and something cracked you on the head. The ship came about and almost capsized. You nearly went over the side."

"How did you . . . ?"

Miro could hear the exhaustion in her voice. "Luck, and a very long night."

"You need to rest." Miro tried to move but winced.

"I do, but you need it more than I do. You've got a lump the size of my fist on your head. There was blood. Lord of the Sky, I can't tell you how scared I was, but you weren't cut deeply."

"How's the ship?"

"We've lost both masts and the two big sails. There was a small headsail in the forward stowage area, which I've rigged using a line and what was left of the mizzenmast. We have some steerage, which is better than nothing. At least the storm has passed. Go to the cabin and get some more rest. I'm going to try to catch some fish, using some of the bloody rag I mopped your head with."

The next time Miro woke, he felt much better, albeit unbelievably thirsty. He exited the cabin and looked around the deck.

Amber had been busy, and rather than the chaos he'd expected to see, he instead noticed the emptiness where the mainmast had been. The smaller mizzenmast—what remained of it—was lashed to the mainmast's stump. At the top of the mizzenmast, a stiff line ran to the bowsprit, and a small triangle of sail unfurled from the line, catching the breeze.

Miro found Amber up on the stern castle. She'd lashed the tiller in place but kept an eye on it while she filleted two small fish.

"What would I do without you?" Miro said.

"Drown," Amber said, looking up and smiling slightly. Miro saw blue circles under her eyes; it must have been days since she'd slept. "Here," she said, handing Miro a chunk of raw fish.

Miro swallowed it down, barely chewing, his stomach gnawing as he did, craving more. Next, he gulped down the water Amber offered him.

He waited until Amber finished with the fish, keeping the head, guts, and tail for bait, and then he spoke. "I'll be all right now. It's time for you to get some rest."

Amber stood, wobbling as she did, before clambering to the stern cabin without another word.

Miro sat down beside the tiller and checked their course. He couldn't believe their luck. The storm had come unexpectedly and faster than he could have imagined, but the *Intrepid* had made it through.

He heard splashing sounds and looked down at the side of the caravel with alarm. He relaxed when he saw playful creatures—porpoises, he knew they were called—frolicking and rolling onto their backs. They paced the ship for a time, grinning toothily at Miro and spraying water out of their blowholes, and then they were gone.

The setting sun told Miro he still headed west. The sky was clear, but he frowned when he saw a low line of dark clouds on the horizon.

"Please," he whispered, "not another storm."

A sudden boom split the air, but this wasn't the crash of thunder. A whining sound filled his ears, and a tall splash of water fountained up in front of the *Intrepid*'s bow. At the same time Miro turned and saw the source of the explosion, he realized he hadn't been looking at clouds.

It was land.

Amber came running out onto the deck. "What was that?"

She turned and gasped when she saw the ship.

It was painted in garish colors, just like the façades of the abandoned buildings on Sofia, and was as big as the great vessel Miro had explored in the dry dock. It was much larger than the doomed galleon, the *Delphin*, and though it had a similar construction, with three masts and raised decks fore and aft, it was different in more than just its coloring.

Shuttered windows lined the ship's side, the lids now pulled open by chains. Bronze tubes, akin to those Miro had seen back on the island, poked out of the openings, their mouths pointing out the ship's port side.

There was a puff of smoke, and Miro again heard the explosive sound. It reminded him painfully of the device from the wedding. Water shot up, close to the caravel's bow this time.

"I think they want us to stop," Miro said. "We don't have a chance against those weapons."

Amber scurried to the bow where she furled in the sail while Miro turned the caravel into the wind. They instantly lost all speed.

Miro looked at the looming ship as it drew steadily closer. He could now see dark-eyed men with swords watching from the huge ship, stocky warriors with bronzed skin and uniforms of blue and brown.

"Amber," Miro said, "you'd better go inside the cabin."

The foreign ship hit the caravel with a crash. Looking for the cutlass, Miro found it looped to the makeshift mast by a length of rope. He retrieved the sword, gripping the hilt with one hand as he prepared to face this new enemy.

Miro wasn't sure if they wanted to fight or parlay, but if they wanted to fight, he would oblige them.

A clipped voice called out. The accent was foreign, but the words were clear. "Take the ship. Check the hold," the voice ordered. "Kill her crew. They're in our waters, and they should know better."

"Stay inside!" Miro called to Amber.

A sailor with a curved sword jumped down to the deck, and another followed. Miro crossed the deck to stand guard over the stern cabin where Amber had retreated. He felt the familiar onset of battle rage. It didn't matter now what strange weapons the ship possessed. The captain wouldn't fire on his own men.

The cutlass wasn't as sharp as it once had been, but the handle was ribbed, providing Miro a firm grip, and the hilt encompassed his hand in a protective guard. The blade was curved and heavy at the front, made for slashing combat in confined quarters. The last time Miro had fought on board a ship, he'd been taken unawares, his sword too long to wield. Adrenaline banished any fatigue. This time he was ready.

Miro's first opponent came forward and hacked down from overhead. Miro went in close and slammed the solid metal of the hilt into the sailor's jaw. He kicked his opponent away as the man went down, keeping the deck clear and the sailor where he could see him.

The next swordsman slashed from left to right, coming in fast. Miro shifted to the side as his attacker came forward, spinning around the sailor's back and thrusting into his chest, withdrawing the cutlass tipped with blood. Like the first man, Miro kicked this one to the side, clearing space for his next attacker and making it difficult for his enemies to surround him.

Miro's training at the Pens under Blademaster Rogan had prepared him for this day. The boys Rogan had taught didn't use enchanted blades; they used normal swords, but the practice swords were sharp, and a mistake could be deadly. Miro thanked Rogan that he wasn't dependent on the power of his zenblade and the protection of his armorsilk. Miro was a bladesinger, but he didn't need Altura's lore to be deadly.

A third swordsman followed a feint with a thrust. Miro blocked the thrust, turning his opponent's sword to the side, before punching the sailor's lantern jaw with his left fist. Miro's opponent dropped his guard, and a slash across the throat finished him.

Miro shoved the dying man into the next attacker, and as the sailor stumbled Miro chopped at his neck. Crying out, the sailor fell over the side, splashing into the water with a scream.

Miro's breath came strong, though sweat poured down his face as he fought in the late afternoon sun. He forgot the lump on his head, and any weakness caused by the travails of his journey was now gone. He took down two more men, yet still more attackers took their places, jumping down to the deck of the caravel and roaring as they attacked.

Miro thrust and slashed, leaping up to the rail and dodging behind the mast. All the while, he guarded the stern cabin. He would never let his enemies past to where Amber waited in terror.

He dispatched a swordsman with a series of slashing blows, and another with a cut across the abdomen. More men kept coming, and Miro kept taking them down.

Suddenly Miro heard a cry from the nearby ship. *"Fire!"*

It was followed by series of cracks, and Miro felt a bite on his arm. The sound caused his opponents to halt. Miro glared at his attackers, who glanced uncertainly back at the ship.

"Stop!" a voice called out. It was the same voice Miro had heard order the attack.

Miro looked up at the rail of the foreign ship. A tall man returned his gaze from where he'd been watching the fight, a cadre of officers around him. The tall man wore a dark blue hat with a feather, and Miro knew this must be the captain.

Beside the captain several men held long sticklike devices pointed in Miro's direction. A trail of smoke rose from the ends of the sticks.

Miro looked at his arm and saw a small line of blood where something had cut through his sleeve, narrowly grazing his arm. He had no idea what manner of weapon the sticks were, but they made him think of a bow.

He thought about the explosion at the wedding. At least he'd made it to the right place.

"Draw back," the captain ordered, and the swordsmen on the caravel fell back, leaving Miro exposed to the marksmen. The captain's eyes met Miro's. "Do you surrender?"

"Do you guarantee my safety and that of my wife?" Miro challenged.

"Your wife," the captain said, an amused expression on his face. "Yes, I guarantee it. While on my ship neither of you will be harmed."

"Amber, come out," Miro said. He threw the cutlass to the deck.

The sailors came forward and seized Miro, gripping his wrists tightly. Amber hesitantly exited the cabin before they took hold of her also. Miro scowled but was surprised to see them treat Amber somewhat gently. The sailors marched Miro and Amber to the side of the strange ship. At sword point, first Miro and then Amber climbed a ladder and were soon both under guard on the huge ship's main deck.

A sailor searched the hold of the *Intrepid*, then climbed up the ladder and reported to the captain. "There's nothing worth taking, Commodore," the sailor said.

"Draw away, then sink their ship," the captain said. "Let's give our gunners some practice."

Sails were set, and Miro and Amber watched stoically as the bronze barrels sent shot after shot at the *Intrepid*.

Soon water rushed into a hole in the side of the caravel. Miro felt sadness as the bold ship that had saved their lives sank.

Miro was suddenly too weary to pay much attention to his surroundings. They were on the main deck of yet another ship, and once again at the mercy of her captain and crew.

He and Amber received looks of disgust from the sailors, and Miro realized how bedraggled they must appear. Amber still wore men's clothing, the trousers several sizes too big for her and held up by a piece of rope. Equally disproportionate, her white shirt hung almost to her knees. Miro wore the clothing he'd found on the dead man washed up on the beach, also not his size. The pain from the lump on his head now returned with intensity, and he felt nauseous. Amber was sunburnt, with cracked lips and chafed hands. Miro turned his own palm up and saw bloody blisters on the skin, below every finger and at the base of his thumb.

In contrast, this was the cleanest, neatest crew Miro had ever seen. They wore tailored clothing of blue with brown trim, the seams finely stitched and the material light and supple. Their tan shoes were of a soft leather, and each man's hair was cut short. They presented a striking contrast to the motley variety of the *Delphin*'s crew.

Miro had killed several of their number, yet where a less disciplined crew would have taken revenge on him for what he'd done, these men kept Miro under close guard, yet waited on the orders of their captain.

The tall man with the feather in his hat called out. The bronze tubes rolled back into the ship's interior, and the wooden shutters closed with a series of slaps. Miro learned the tubes were called cannon.

Once his ship was underway, the captain came over to inspect his new prisoners. Miro examined his captor. Without his blue hat, Miro could now see that the captain's carefully combed dark hair topped a handsome face with penetrating brown eyes and a square jaw. His accent reminded Miro of Hermen Tosch, and his dark clothes were of a fine quality Miro had only seen on the richest nobles and merchants in Seranthia. He looked Miro up and down, and then gave Amber a casual glance.

"Put the woman away somewhere before the rest of the men see her," he ordered.

"Aye aye, Commodore."

"Search the man, see that he has no weapons on him, and then bring him to me. I'll be in my cabin. Actually,"—he paused—"wash his face, hands, and hair. The sea gods only know what vermin he's brought aboard."

Miro exchanged glances with Amber as the crew took her away, but couldn't think of anything to say. The sailors then warily searched Miro before leading him to a bucket and instructing him to wash, using a piece of yellow soap. With his wife in the hands of these people, Miro wasn't going to cause trouble.

He wondered why they hadn't killed him with the projectile weapons. Was there still a chance he could rationalize with the captain and explain his situation?

After Miro washed, two sailors led him to a door in the quarterdeck. They marched him down a corridor to another door, this one ornately paneled. Miro waited while one of the sailors knocked.

"Enter," the captain's voice came from within.

The sailor held the door open while the other led Miro inside. The cabin was the most luxurious Miro had seen on a ship. The shipbuilders had selected different varieties of wood to create a harmony of color and grain, and thick carpets lined the floor. There was a long desk at the far end, with two low recliners next to a squat table at the closer end. Two more doors must lead to the captain's personal privy and sleeping cabin.

"Commodore," one of the men at Miro's side spoke, "we've brought the man we captured."

"Thank you," said the captain, rising from his desk and coming around to stand in front. He again looked Miro up and down. "You are strangely dressed for a barbarian, aren't you?"

"I'm not a barbarian," Miro said.

"Of course you're not," the captain said, smiling. "Now, do I have your word that you won't try to harm anyone on this ship? We have your woman under guard."

"I won't try anything."

The captain nodded to his men. "You can stand at ease. Please leave us."

One of the sailors opened his mouth to say something but shut it with a snap.

The captain looked at the sailor and again smiled. "You have no need to be concerned." He reached down to touch his belt, and Miro saw he wore a beautiful sword, thin and perfectly straight, with a ruby set into the hilt. "The Holdfast champion, three years running. As good as he is, our man here is unarmed, and we have his wife. Besides"—his gaze returned to Miro—"I feel I can trust him."

"Aye aye, Commodore," one of the sailors said. He scowled at Miro. "We'll be just outside."

When they were alone, the captain sat down on one of the recliners, gesturing for Miro to sit on the other. Miro was surprised at the hospitality, but he noticed the captain kept his distance, as if Miro stank. Which, he reflected, he probably did.

"My name is Deniz, and I am captain of the *Seekrieger*, the ship you are aboard right now. You may address me as 'Commodore' or 'Commodore Deniz.'"

"A pleasure, Commodore," Miro said warily.

"You are wondering why I didn't have you killed."

"True."

"There are two reasons why you are still alive. The first is that, frankly, you are one of the finest swordsmen I've ever seen. I'm not without skill myself, and I know it when I see it. I've been to the north and fought your people, and never have I come across a barbarian with such skill as yours."

"I told you, Commodore, I'm not a barbarian."

"There you go again," Deniz said. "Of course you are a barbarian. You certainly aren't Veldrin. However, your words do lead me to the second reason I've let you live. You are something of a curiosity." He counted on his fingers. "You sail in a ship that, while obviously inferior, I have never seen in the northlands.

You and your woman—my apologies, wife—both wear men's garments."

Miro opened his mouth, but the captain continued.

"You speak with a strange accent. You sail in waters where barbarians haven't been seen in generations. You are the first barbarian I've seen without a tangle of facial hair—at last! Finally," Deniz had run out of fingers, "you have the light of intelligence in your eyes."

"Commodore," Miro said, "if you'll let me . . ."

"No," Deniz held up a hand, "this mystery is better unraveled by one wiser than I. Save your words, barbarian. We are not far from home."

Deniz stood, and Miro stood with him.

"I promised you I would not allow harm to come to you or your wife while you were aboard my ship. I cannot offer the same promise when you are out of my hands, but I will commend your skill to the emir. You wouldn't be the first barbarian who has gone on to adopt civilized ways and serve. Do as you are told, barbarian, and you may yet live."

Miro was led to a cabin, and breathed a sigh of relief when Amber turned at the opening door. He was surprised to see she wasn't gagged or tied. The door closed behind him, and Miro heard two of Deniz's men talk in low tones as they took positions outside. Given the earlier battle, it could have been much worse.

Miro embraced Amber, holding her close. "These people are strange," was the first thing he said.

"They must have a peculiar code of honor," Amber said. "They hardly touched me. It was almost comical, watching them try to bring me here without putting their hands on my body."

"We seem to have struck a deal with the captain," Miro said. He told Amber about his encounter with Commodore Deniz. "He has guaranteed our safety until we reach port, and I believe him."

"What will happen then?"

"All he intimated was that we'd be handed over to someone else. He finds us curious, yet every time I tried to explain to him, he wouldn't let me. It must be his way of deferring to his superiors, but I found it odd."

Miro moved over to the cabin window. It was large enough that Amber could look also, and they both cried out in wonder at the same time.

They must have entered a harbor, for the wavelets were small and the sea was calm, yet at this stage, all they could see were ships, most at anchor, but some under sail.

More ships than Miro thought could exist in the entire world.

Miro saw scores of mighty warships like the *Seekrieger* and the vessel Miro had found on the island. He knew they were warships now by the rows of wooden shutters—even the Buchalanti would find them formidable. Hundreds of cruisers were still bigger than any ship Miro had ever seen, while smaller boats abounded: flat-bottomed barges, two-masted caravels, three-masted galleons, speedy galleys, and even pleasure craft. Longboats and jollyboats hopped from one vessel to another, ferrying passengers and carrying stores.

Miro saw a lighthouse at the end of a long wall of rock, and realized something he didn't want to admit.

This harbor dwarfed the great harbor at Seranthia.

"Look," Amber said, "the city!"

The buildings were multihued like those Miro had seen at the Ochre Isles. The city spread arms around the harbor possessively in a way that made Miro think these people prized control of the seas over anything else. It rose in tiers, evidently built against a hillside, continuing higher and higher to a tall summit.

The building at the city's highest point could only be a palace, but with its ivory spires and turquoise domes it was like no palace Miro had encountered in all the lands of the Empire.

The sky grew dark as they approached, and lights appeared at the city's innumerable windows. The lights twinkled in a way that told Miro these people used fire.

"Have you noticed?" Miro asked. "These people use no lore."

"We don't know that for sure," said Amber.

"Commodore Deniz has a beautiful sword, some of the best workmanship I've seen. Not a rune on it. Those lights at the harbor front—you can't tell me they're from nightlamps."

"You may be right," Amber said. "We'll see."

They were soon unable to grasp the size of the city anymore; the ship was now too close to the dock. Deniz carefully piloted the *Seekrieger* past ships large and small, finally finding his place and bumping the wooden pier with the gentlest of nudges.

Miro waited with Amber while the crew tethered the ship, wondering what would happen next. Eventually, Amber gave up watching, resting on the bare wood of a bunk bed while Miro looked out the window. She finally sat up. "What's happening?" she questioned.

"I can see Deniz standing beside the ship and speaking with someone in a uniform," Miro said. "Something tells me he's talking about us. Now the man's gone, and Deniz is heading back to the ship."

Moments later, the door to the cabin opened. Miro and Amber's questions went unanswered as they were bundled off the ship and taken to where a contingent of soldiers with blue and brown uniforms waited.

The soldiers surrounded them, and then Miro heard a voice.

"Barbarian." It was Commodore Deniz, the soldiers parting as he approached. "Welcome to Emirald, capital of Veldria. I wish you luck. If you are allowed to live, and the emir is generous enough to give you your choice of posts, choose the navy."

Deniz touched his feathered hat, and then turned away, while the soldiers reformed around their two prisoners. Without another word, the soldiers marched Miro and Amber away. Miro's suspicions were confirmed when they were taken onto a winding path leading upward.

They were being taken to the palace.

⸻

The soldiers marched in a tight formation, with the prisoners on the inside so it was difficult for them to see through, but on the way to the palace Miro had glimpses of a prosperous city of cobbled streets, well-dressed people, and flickering lanterns at every corner. The windows all had glass, and the vivid colors of the façades were matched by the colorful shades of the people's clothing.

Miro could see they were indeed a seafaring nation, with chandlers, sailmakers, and rope makers in abundance. Sailors strolled on the streets and drank in the taverns, and looking back the way they'd come, Miro saw the massive harbor revealed in all its splendor.

Against the clatter of marching soldiers' boots, he heard the sounds of revelry, voices and warbling music carried on the evening breeze.

"What's going to happen to us, Miro?" Amber said.

"I don't know," Miro said.

"No talking!" a soldier growled.

As they approached the palace, Miro saw it was even bigger than he'd originally thought—a series of buildings rather than a single edifice. He saw little of it, however, besides the heights of the domes and towers.

Entering a courtyard, Miro and Amber were separated, but he was relieved when he saw they were being taken to separate entrances of a bathing hall, with hot and cold pools beckoning seductively and braziers to warm the night air.

A guard told Miro to undress, and his clothing was taken from him—more guards stood close by, looking studiously away. A silent older man led Miro to a pool and handed him soap. The old man refused Miro's efforts at conversation, but wasn't content until Miro had passed through all three of the pools. He then made Miro lie on his stomach while he rubbed fragrant oil into Miro's back.

Even as he worried, Miro felt the cares of the journey melt away under the old man's hands, and sighed in pleasure. Finally, the old man gestured for Miro to don loose white garments—billowing trousers and an open-necked shirt. He was given soft boots to wear, and the old man combed another kind of oil through Miro's long black hair, tying it with a cord at the back of his head.

Miro was then handed back to the guards outside the bathhouse. Amber waited, also under guard. She looked clean and beautiful, clad in a white tunic, but her expression was apprehensive.

"Your woman will be looked after," one of the soldiers said, "but an unmarried woman should be kept apart from the men."

"She's my wife!" Miro said, scowling.

"Where is the stone in her nose to show the status of her husband?"

"We come from another land, and we have a different custom." Miro barked a laugh. "But whatever the highest status is, then that's what she would have."

"I am sorry," the soldier said. He nodded to his fellows, and Amber was led away.

Miro watched as his wife was taken from him.

Not for the first time, he wished Amber wasn't with him on this foolish quest.

23

Miro paced the length of his cell, staring at the windowless walls and thinking dark thoughts. He supposed it wasn't fair to think of his quarters as a cell; they were the size of the small house he'd lived in with Ella and Brandon back in Sarostar, and had a sleeping chamber, a toilet chamber, and a room with a table and chairs where he took his meals. But he was a prisoner, so it was a cell.

The uniformed guards brought him an evening meal of dumplings and broth, and then Miro slept, a long sleep of exhaustion, after which he felt like a new man. In the morning he was given another meal, this time of tart creamy cheese and fruit. His midday meal consisted of dark bread and heavily spiced soup.

Miro hadn't eaten so well since leaving Altura.

With nothing better to do, he now awaited his evening repast. He looked at the paneled wooden door; it was heavy and opened inward. Until he found out what these people intended to do with him, there was no use trying to break free.

Miro heard the jangle of a key, and the door opened on well-oiled hinges. Two guards beckoned to Miro, and he followed them out. They obviously weren't here to give him his dinner.

The guards once more led Miro to the bathing house, where he was again washed and had oil rubbed into his back and combed through his hair. This time the white garments he was given to wear were woven with golden thread, as fine as anything made in the Empire.

"Where is my wife?" Miro asked a guard.

"She is well, barbarian," the soldier said.

"Where am I being taken?"

"You are being taken to the emir."

Miro followed the guards along covered walkways and through tiled halls. He quickly became lost but couldn't help but gape at the splendor of the palace.

Passing a series of marble columns, he felt soft carpet under his feet, shimmering silk material reflecting the light of flickering torches. Every column bore a torch in a sconce, and not a single torch was unlit.

It was perhaps an hour past sundown, and Miro again heard the strange warbling music, though far away this time. He passed a room where a group of women ate seated in a circle, but he returned his attention to the path when one of his guards squeezed his arm and frowned.

Miro finally reached an expansive area where carpets and cushions lay spaced around low tables. Light sparkled from a hanging chandelier, the glow of a hundred candles flickering through crystalline shards. Columns supported the high ceiling, and on all sides the chamber was open to the air, affording an unparalleled view of the city and harbor below.

Miro looked again at his guards, examining them as a group under good light. They had the look of the free cities, with their stocky builds and round faces, but they also had something of the swarthiness of the Hazarans, along with the desert tribes' passion for elaborate custom and opulent surrounds. Who were these people?

Long ago, had there been contact between these people and those in the Empire's west?

Miro scanned the chamber that could easily accommodate several hundred men, only seeing two. The closest was a man who could only be a majordomo, standing still and holding a tall pole topped with gold. In the distance, a second man ignored the newcomers as he gazed out at the harbor.

The majordomo lifted the pole and let it fall to the ground, the thump echoing throughout the chamber.

"Kneel," the majordomo called. "You are in the presence of greatness."

The guards pushed Miro to his knees and then followed suit. The soldiers bowed their heads to the floor before returning to their feet, pulling Miro up with them.

The man in the distance turned and came forward, his steps smooth and graceful. He wore a long flowing robe of crimson silk, held at the waist with a belt of gold. As he came closer, Miro saw he had gray in his trimmed beard and silver in his black hair, with a sharp patrician nose and smoky dark eyes. He had a gold earring in one ear and wore a jeweled dagger at his belt.

"The Ruler of the Seas, the Protector of Veldria and the Bearer of the Seal, Emir Volkan," the majordomo announced, clapping his staff to the floor with a boom.

The soldiers again prostrated themselves, leaving Miro standing. Miro placed his fingers over his heart, and touched his lips and then his forehead in the Alturan manner.

"Ah," the emir said, his eyes lighting up when he saw Miro's movements. "So, barbarian, you are familiar with our customs."

"My customs, not yours," Miro said.

The emir frowned. "You're not from the Crown Islands in the west, I can see that. Nor from Gokan, that much is clear. You're not from Narea, that's certain. Nor are you from Oltara or Muttara."

Miro opened his mouth. "Those places mean nothing—"

The emir held up a hand and was pensive for a moment. He looked at the soldiers. "Leave us," he said.

The guards withdrew.

The emir then turned to the majordomo. "Forgive me, Ruben, but I wish you to leave also."

The majordomo bowed, but Miro could see the man frown, before he turned to Miro. "Do I have your word as a man of honor that you will not harm nor allow harm to come to the Ruler of the Seas, Emil Volkan?"

Miro was again surprised that they would trust his word. "You have my word," he answered.

The majordomo bowed again before departing, leaving Miro alone with the emir.

"You are from the lands in the east, are you not?"

Miro wondered whether to lie, but he couldn't see any reason to, and these people appeared to value honesty. "I am. My name is Miro Torresante. I am the lord marshal of Altura, the land of enchanters."

Emir Volkan's expression grew pained. "Do not speak of lore to me!"

Miro was taken aback. "My apologies—" he began.

"How do you come to be in my lands?" the emir interrupted.

"My ship blew off course—" Miro began.

"That's a lie. Commodore Deniz described your ship to me. You could never have come all the way from the lands in the east in that ship, particularly not with the stores you had aboard. So, tell me again, why are you here? What are a man and his wife doing halfway across the world, far from home? You say you are a leader of some kind. Where are your men?"

"It's a long story," Miro said wryly.

"Save the story. Tell me why you are here."

Miro took a deep breath. "An outside force is causing problems in our realm, and we don't believe the source to be within our lands. We traveled to the three abandoned islands in search of an answer, but our ship ran against a reef, killing everyone except for my wife and me. We found more questions than answers on the islands, and then we found a map that shows this continent. We decided to come here."

Miro thought about the plight of his son. These people must know about the poison, but his intuition told him it wasn't yet the time to bring it up.

The emir stroked his beard. "I sense truth in your words, but I also sense there is much you are hiding from me. We will come back to your journey, and the next time I feel unsatisfied, you will feel my wrath. For now, we are new acquaintances, and the code says we must be civil at all first meetings."

Miro knew he had to speak carefully; this man held their lives in his hands.

"Tell me," the emir said, his hawklike gaze suddenly fierce. "In your lands, are you a master of lore?"

"No, I am not," Miro said.

He decided to reveal nothing about being a bladesinger.

"Good. If you were, I would have you killed."

Miro thought about Amber. Lord of the Sky, he hoped she had said nothing to their captors.

Emir Volkan nodded. "I take it you know nothing of the history of our people and how it relates to your own?"

Miro slowly shook his head, and the emir looked satisfied.

"That is as it should be. Come." He gestured for Miro to follow him.

With stately steps the emir led Miro to the far side of the chamber, where a partition screened a series of benches. Strange sealed tubes and vials of colored powders stood lined up and labeled, though Miro had never come across the words before.

"I am an amateur alchemist, you see," the emir said, "although my skills are as nothing compared to the Guild. Watch."

The stern ruler became animated, and Miro realized he was pleased to have an audience. The emir picked up a bottle containing a large amount of clear liquid.

He held the bottle up. "This is just water."

Volkan poured the bottle into a wide-mouthed glass carafe. He filled it to a depth of six inches and then put the bottle back down on the bench.

The emir then took a second bottle. "Look," he said, swirling the contents.

Miro gaped. The fluid inside shone like steel, yet was obviously a liquid. It slipped and whirled in a mesmerizing way as Volkan tipped the bottle.

"This is an alchemical substance called quicksilver. Have you heard of it?"

"No, I haven't," Miro said.

The emir tipped the silver liquid into a second wide-mouthed carafe to the same depth as the water in the first carafe. "I now have two quantities of liquid. One is water, the other is quicksilver."

Volkan put the bottle away while Miro stared mesmerized at the shining fluid in the carafe.

Volkan then took a small metal sphere and handed it to Miro. "How would you describe this?"

"It's a ball. Heavy," Miro said. "Probably steel."

"It is steel. What will happen when I drop it into the carafe of water?"

"It will sink."

The emir took the ball from Miro and dropped it into the carafe of water. It sank immediately to the bottom, hitting the glass with a clunk.

"Now," Volkan said, "watch."

He took a second steel ball and gave it to Miro to check its weight. He then dropped the ball into the carafe of silver fluid.

Miro watched mesmerized. Even though there was six inches of silver liquid in the carafe, the heavy ball floated on top.

The emir shrugged. "It is a simple experiment."

"How does it work? Did you change the ball?" Miro thought about the runes that made his zenblade feel as light as a feather.

"I did not. The quicksilver has special properties, as do many other substances. Tell me, do the people of your land study such things?"

Miro thought about the Academy of Enchanters. "No, they don't."

The emir reached out for another vial, this one containing a black powder. He removed the stopper and poured a little of the powder into his fingers.

"Come," he said, leading Miro back toward the terrace, where the lights of the city glittered below.

There was a torch near the parapet, ensconced against a supporting column. Without warning, the emir flicked his fingers at the torch.

There was a sudden sparkle in the air and a sizzling sound split the stillness of the night. Miro jumped, and Volkan laughed softly.

"You do not have black powder in your lands, do you?"

Miro smelled the same odor that had hung in the air after the explosion at the wedding.

"No, we do not."

"This is nothing," the emir said dismissively. "The wonders that the Guild is capable of . . . You would be astounded."

"Why are you telling me this?"

"Miro, this is what we are capable of, if we remove the crutch of lore. I mentioned the history of our people. Even many of the councilors don't know this, but I am the emir, my father was emir, and my grandfather was emir before him, so I know."

Miro waited expectantly.

"Long ago, in the lands you call home, there was a great war. This war was fought with the most horrific weapons lore could devise, and the suffering was terrible. Macabre creatures did battle, the forest was brought to life, and golems of wood and iron marched and destroyed all in their path. Fiery swords cut men into pieces, and flying machines rained death on those below."

Miro nodded and thought about Evrin's story and the fight to overthrow the Evermen. This must be the war the emir was referring to. Miro thought about the more recent wars, and Emir Volkan's scathing words struck home.

"We are those who fled. We are those who wanted nothing more to do with lore, with the death and the destruction. Taking pity on us, a group called the Buchalanti helped us make the great voyage across the sea and promised never to reveal our presence to the other houses."

Miro's eyes widened as the pieces of the puzzle finally fit together.

He had a sudden thought. "So your lands are at peace then?"

The emir barked a laugh. "You're a sly one. No, we're not at peace. We have had our own wars, and still do. Technology has come to take the place lore once had, and now inventions like black powder give us a power of destruction almost equal to lore. Note," the emir said, "I said 'almost.'"

Miro looked out from the palace as he listened to Volkan's words.

The emir continued, "Look down at Emirald, our beautiful city. For every advance in war, we have had an advance in peace. We have learned about the way the body is constructed, and we have medicines to cure many ailments. Every year our poor get richer, and our merchants travel Veldria in safety. We Veldrins are safe, not just because we build the best ships and we rule the seas but also because we thirst for knowledge and are the only truly civilized nation in Merralya. To us, all others are uncivilized, and rightly so."

"What of the other nations?" Miro said. From the map he'd seen, he knew this nation's neighbors must all be to the north.

"North of Veldria is Gokan, a small land and the only other that may claim to be civilized. We have fought in the past, but not for a hundred years. Staying strong is not a problem for the Gokani, for the Alchemists' Guild makes its home in their capital, Wengwai."

"And the others?"

"North of Gokan is Narea, a large nation with powerful land-based armies. They are constantly at war with the barbarians. We wish Narea to stay strong, for they protect us from the horde. Where we Veldrins rule the seas, Narea's mighty armies keep our lands safe from the tribes. The far north is where the barbarians call home, a cold land of icy steppes and mountains. They come from Oltara, and they come from Muttara. Sometimes Oltara wars with Muttara, and the people of the south breathe freely. Twice in the past, Oltara and Muttara have joined forces under a single tribal chieftain, and once they sacked Monapea, the capital of Narea."

The names of these nations were strange to Miro, but he gathered that the people of Veldria, Gokan, and Narea lived in constant fear of the barbarians in the north.

He thought about his quest to find the antidote to whatever terrible poison had struck Tomas. It was doubtful that Volkan would have the information he needed.

"You've mentioned a guild. Who are they?"

"The Alchemists' Guild ostensibly makes its home in Gokan, but they rule themselves and keep their secrets close. Their chapter is in Wengwai, and they alone know the secret of the black powder, an invention none can now do without. My two hundred warships are all armed with cannon and need the black powder, as do my five hundred musketeers. Over time, I plan to move all of my swordsmen over to muskets. When you see them in battle, you'll understand why."

Miro wondered if he could look to the Alchemists' Guild in Wengwai for the answers he needed.

"We have a library here," the emir said, and Miro turned his head. "In a week or two, I might give you access. There is much you need to learn."

"Emir, I have one question," Miro said, looking directly into the older man's penetrating eyes.

"What is it?"

"Why are you telling me all this?"

"Why, because you seem a capable man, Miro Torresante, and I am always looking for capable men. You tell me you were a leader among your people, and Deniz praised you to me, telling me you easily defeated a number of his best men. I never turn a good man away, and there may be a place for you here."

"I . . . I'm honored, Emir, but I need to return to my people."

Emir Volkan shook his head sadly. "No, Miro. There is no way I will let you return to your people. By your own admission they do not know our lands exist, and we wish to keep it that way. It is your choice whether you think there is a place for you here."

The emir's last words were final. "But you can never return."

24

The next day, Miro pestered the guards until they gave him a few moments with Amber. They met in a courtyard beside a fountain while the soldiers stood a short distance away, watching them carefully. The sound of the burbling water allowed Miro to speak freely.

He told Amber about his conversation with Emir Volkan, admonishing her not to mention lore to anyone.

"What about Tomas?" Amber said. "Did you ask him about the poison?"

"I can't ask him about it." Miro sighed. "The only thing keeping us alive is the fact he thinks I might enter his service. If Volkan realizes we'll do anything it takes to return, he'll have us killed."

"How do you know that?"

"Amber," Miro said in exasperation, "I know."

"What can we do then?"

"I need to find this library, where there may be mention of the poison. Whether I find the information or not, we need to leave this place. If I'm unsuccessful, these alchemists in the north will know. I'm sure of it. When we have the cure, we can steal a ship and head back home."

Amber started to cry. "I just want to go home."

"I know," Miro said.

"Do you think Tomas is still alive?"

"Yes," said Miro with a certainty he didn't feel, "I'm sure he is."

The soldiers came forward. Their time was up.

———————

That night, when two of the guards brought his evening meal, Miro took action.

He stood behind the paneled door as it opened. He pictured the emir's soldiers scanning the empty room, wondering where he was. He saw a uniformed soldier come forward.

Miro shoved the door with all his strength, bringing it crashing into the two men on the other side. While they were off balance, he came around and pulled first one man, then the other, forward, sending them both stumbling into the room. Miro swiftly closed the door and then squared off to face the angry guards.

Rather than giving them time to draw their swords, Miro cannoned into them, once more sending them sprawling. Miro elbowed a man in the stomach and heard the breath come out of him with a whoosh. He punched the second guard in the face, smashing his nose and sending blood streaming down his chin.

They were all in a tangle on the floor, but Miro was the first to stand. One of his opponents was unconscious, but the other was just angry, wiping the blood from his chin and climbing to his feet.

Miro drew the sword from the prone man's scabbard while the soldier with the bloody nose unsheathed his own blade. They faced each other, each taking the other's measure.

"I don't want to kill you," Miro warned.

"I'd like to see you try," the guard growled.

He thrust at Miro's chest, but Miro moved to the side. Conscious of the sound of clashing steel, Miro chose to duck the next slashing blow. Miro came inside the soldier's guard and rammed the hilt of his sword into the man's bloody chin.

The guard cried out and fell down, dropping his sword. He slumped on the floor, breathing heavily.

Miro kicked the fallen sword out of the way and then squatted next to the guard.

"Where is the library?" Miro asked.

The guard wheezed and coughed. Miro put the point of his sword under the man's chin. The guard's eyes went wide with fear as he struggled to regain his breath.

"I'll ask you again: Where is the library?" Miro repeated.

"Down the path of red stone, past the statue of the sea god," the soldier gasped.

Miro took no pleasure in the guard's pain, but he knew the emir would kill Amber if he discovered she was an enchantress, and Volkan would never allow them to return to Altura.

Miro hit the soldier's temple, and he fell back, unconscious.

Miro examined both men. He knew it would be some time before either woke.

He looked down at himself. He still wore the fine white clothing he'd been wearing when presented to the emir. Fortunately, the clothing was free of blood.

Miro opened the door and walked out, sword in hand.

The palace was a scene of tranquility. Miro saw some soldiers in the distance, but they were walking the other way.

Miro was desperate to free Amber, but he knew he needed to go to the library first. If he were caught, Amber would be innocent and only Miro would be punished. He could have ignored the library, but he knew that if he missed this chance and they made it home, Amber would never forgive him. Nor would Miro forgive himself.

He remembered where he'd seen the statue of the sea god, a tall man of marble holding a trident. Keeping to the shadows, Miro fought to control his labored breathing and weaved from one column to the next. He had to cross a spacious courtyard, but fortunately heard no sound of alarm. Finding the red stone of the path, he began to walk down it, thankful for the silence of his soft boots.

Miro froze as he heard voices ahead. He looked left and right, finally jumping into some shrubbery beside the path. He burrowed into the bushes, cursing his white garments; they would stand out to even the most cursory glance.

Fortunately, the three soldiers who approached were deep in conversation and paying little attention to the path.

"It is dire news—we must tell the emir immediately," a man with golden epaulettes on his shoulders said.

"I still cannot believe it," spoke a second man.

"Our sources are reliable."

"Who will tell him? It should be you, General."

"We will tell him together. No one could have seen this coming."

Their voices softened to a murmur as they departed the area where Miro lay in hiding. He wondered what they were discussing, but he had greater concerns.

Miro emerged from the bushes and continued down the path, finally arriving at a temple-like structure. The grand columns and peaked roof were a brilliant shade of light blue, and at the top of the wide stairs Miro saw a set of double doors.

He crept up the doors and pushed at them, breathing a sigh of relief when they fell open.

Miro entered the library, immediately awed by the tall shelves reaching high to the ceiling and stretching back to the end of the cavernous interior. Where to begin? He walked along the shelves, seeing that the books were categorized alphabetically by subject, and within that, by author. Miro passed along slowly until he came to the letter he was looking for. A moment later, he found his subject.

"Poisons," Miro muttered.

He scanned the books, running his fingers down the bindings until he came to a volume that sounded promising.

"Poisons of the Alchemists' Guild." Miro read the title aloud.

He took down the volume and began to read.

Miro tried to hurry, but there was so much material to go through. Fortunately, the Alchemists' Guild was secretive about its arts, and the author spent more time on historical uses and symptoms than ingredients and formulae. Miro read about toxic liquids and powdered glass, mushrooms that caused visions, and poison used on clothing.

Finally, Miro came to a section describing a poison that could be combined with black powder to devastating effect. The author only knew of the one poison, but it was the one Miro was looking for.

The poison "sleeping death" is the only poison that can be combined with black powder, yet the effect is to make an already deadly substance even more so. Symptoms are spots on the fingernails, vomiting, paralysis, and a lingering coma. The comatose tie up enemy resources and cause panic, a handy outcome. I have heard it said there is a cure, but if there is, only the alchemists know what it is.

Miro put the book down and looked once more at the shelf.

A voice behind him made him rigid with shock.

"Interesting reading?"

Miro turned around. Emir Volkan stood alone, his head tilted as he watched Miro with curiosity.

Miro crouched and his hand went around the hilt of the sword he'd laid on the ground.

"Need I remind you we have your wife in custody?" the emir said, regarding Miro with his piercing gaze. "Ah, but you're thinking that you can kill me and rescue her before the alarm can be raised."

Emir Volkan waved an arm, and soldiers appeared from around the distant shelves, watching Miro warily. "I visit this library often, but I am afforded little privacy. Drop your weapon."

Miro looked around him, counting more guards than he could take on alone. He released the sword and straightened, suddenly realizing he had doomed both himself and Amber. He'd had to try.

"So, Miro Torresante, tell me, what were you looking for?"

The emir held out his hand and Miro gave him the closed book. Volkan glanced at the cover before again looking at Miro. "Now is that time I mentioned, when you will have to tell the truth."

Looking again at the soldiers, Miro thought about Amber. There was no longer any point in dissembling.

Miro glared at the emir. "You might not want my people crossing over to your lands, yet someone from your lands came to mine. They attacked a meeting of our leaders, with an explosive device I now know to be formulated with this black powder. My son was caught in the blast." Miro could hear the emotion in his own voice. "He lived, but the blast also carried a poison."

The emir nodded. "The alchemists can do this."

"My son will never wake without a cure. He needs me, and nothing will stop me from finding an antidote and taking it home."

"I now understand why your wife travels with you," Volkan said. "Tell me, though, Miro, how did you plan to get home? Did you think you could steal a ship from me? Without a crew you wouldn't stand a chance, and the only ship the two of you could crew would be too small to make the crossing."

"I had to try."

The emir was pensive for a moment, and Miro saw his story had touched a nerve. Perhaps the emir had a son also. Perhaps the emir also felt frustration at the whims of the alchemists.

"What will I do with you?" Volkan said. "I cannot have you reporting our presence back to your people."

"Tell me, Emir," said Miro. "Why are you so afraid of lore? Can you not see a future where technology and lore can coexist?"

"Can lore heal? Can it feed? No, lore can only destroy."

"That's not true. We have merchants who use lore to bring goods great distances and build a prosperous economy. We have artificers who use lore to pump pure water up from the ground so that good, clean water is available to all. Our enchanters make heating stones to drive out the fierce cold of winter, and nightlamps to drive out the darkness."

The emir shook his head. "Your idealistic words give you away. If I were to assist you in your quest, no matter how just, I have no doubt men from your land would follow in your wake. You would think contact would benefit us both, and not understand we simply wish to be left alone. We have a prosperous, civilized nation here. You've left me no choice."

Emir Volkan's next words filled Miro with dread.

"I have made my decision. You will spend the remainder of your short life as a slave pulling an oar on one of my galleys. You'll be chained to a bench along with five other men, and the sun will burn your skin while your hands crack and bleed. Your wife . . . I will be generous here, but she also must never leave. I will give her to one of my men. She is young and attractive, and a foreign woman gifted from the emir is a great honor. Her new husband will ensure she stays confined in her new home, as it is a husband's duty to keep his wives out of trouble."

Miro tensed, near to breaking point. He looked at the sword on the ground, and prepared to die. He would never see Amber's face again. He would never again know Tomas's smile.

There was a commotion, and the library's doors burst open. Miro saw the three men he'd overheard on the path, the soldier with the golden epaulettes in the lead.

"Emir, we have urgent news," he said.

Volkan turned. "What is it?"

"There are reports Narea has fallen."

Previously distracted, the emir now gave the soldier his full attention. "That's not possible."

"It is true, Emir Volkan. Our agents in Gokan sent word. Oltara and Muttara have joined forces. and the barbarian horde has moved faster than ever before. They punched through Naiman's Wall in a single day. A week later they were outside the walls of Monapea. Monapea fell three days later."

"How is that possible?" the emir demanded. "What about the Shah's Companions? The Shah's twelve divisions of swordsmen? His two thousand musketmen? His longbowmen?"

"Destroyed in a great battle outside the walls of Monapea."

"I do not believe it," Volkan said, shaking his head decisively. "We would have had reports the barbarians were massing. A month ago Rolan of Oltara and Starin of Muttara were at each other's throats! Where does this news come from?"

"From our people in Wengwai. Refugees fleeing Narea's south have crossed into Gokan, all telling stories of horror. Two of my personal agents in Wengwai have separately corroborated the news. Even so, it is difficult to separate the truth from the fiction.

Apparently neither Rolan of Oltara nor Starin of Muttara leads this army. The rumors say a new leader rose in Muttara and took over from Starin. This leader then conquered Oltara and formed the horde into a single nation."

Another officer entered the library, addressing the man with the golden epaulettes. "Another message, General Hauser. It's from the elector of Gokan. It's dated two days ago. After the fall of Monapea, he fears for Wengwai. Gokan requests our assistance."

General Hauser turned to the emir. "Emir Volkan, if Gokan falls, our ships will have little value when it comes to fighting the horde."

"Gokan won't fall," the emir said. "The barbarians won't be able to handle supply lines stretched so far south. Remember, Monapea is far from here."

"Should we send men to Gokan?"

Emir Volkan was pensive for a moment, before speaking decisively. "For now, send as many men as we can to our border with Gokan. They can easily advance north if need be. Send out messages to the levies and call up the reserves. Recall our ships, and send some warships north to deal with any naval encroachment."

"Emir?" Miro said.

"What?" Volkan said with irritation.

"There may be more going on here than you realize."

Miro saw the thoughts cross the emir's face. He knew Emir Volkan didn't want the lands to the east discussed in front of his men.

"You have your orders; see to it," Volkan commanded, dismissing his men.

The guards remained, keeping a discreet distance, and Miro reminded himself that his and Amber's fates hung on his next words.

"If you're wasting my time . . ." the emir said.

"Emir, there is an ancient enemy we believe may be behind the attacks on my nation. I came here because the signs pointed to these lands, and now a mysterious new leader has risen in your north. Do you really think it a coincidence?"

"What are you suggesting?"

"Let me take my wife and go north, to this land Gokan and its city Wengwai, and farther north if need be. I will learn whether my fears are warranted, and I'll find the truth behind this leader. I give you my word that I'll bring the truth back to you or die trying."

Miro meant every word. He only hoped the emir would believe his sincerity.

"You would give me your word? And what do you want in return?"

"You know what I want. A ship and a crew to take us back home."

Miro held his breath. The emir took a long time replying.

Volkan eventually spoke. "Granted." He called one of the guards forward. "Give him what he needs for his journey. Escort them both out of Emirald."

"At once, Emir."

As he returned the book Miro had been leafing through to the shelf, Emir Volkan was lost in thought.

How could Narea have fallen so quickly? Surely there wasn't any truth to this story of an ancient enemy?

The emir knew how to read men, and he knew Miro truly believed he could find answers in the north. He could also see that the man from across the sea would return to Emirald. Not only had Miro given his word, he needed a ship, something only Volkan could provide.

Yet Emir Volkan did not plan to give Miro the ship he wanted.

Miro Torresante of Altura had foolishly given his word.

But he had never asked Volkan for his.

25

"So Killian is Xenovere's heir," Rogan said, shaking his head. "I can hardly believe it."

"You've seen the proof," Ella said. "There's no doubt."

"How will the people react, I wonder?" There had been another riot, once again incited by Bastian.

"There's something I need you to do," Ella said.

"Another thing, you mean," Rogan said wryly.

Ella looked at Rogan intently. "I need you to send someone to the Isle of Ana. We need to find out what happened to Lady Alise. She may be dead, but Killian's mother could also be alive, perhaps knowing nothing about the changes in the Empire."

"I'll see to it," Rogan said. He looked out his window at Seranthia. "I think this news lends further urgency to what you're doing. It's even more imperative that we bring him back. Ella, you now have my full support. Do you still think you can get Killian back?"

"I can try."

Even if she could enter the portal and cross through to the other side, Ella wondered how Killian would take the news. He was the nephew of a man he despised. He was the heir to a broken empire.

"Rogan . . ."

"I recognize that tone," Rogan said. "What is it?"

"There is one last thing I need your help with . . ."

"Come on," Rogan growled, "out with it."

"You won't like it."

Ella told him.

———◆———

Ella entered the deserted Westcliff cemetery with two of Rogan's men. This late at night there would be no one present to watch a corpse be exhumed—a corpse that had been in the ground for over two decades.

Gnarled trees framed the graveyard, where hundreds of rows of gray headstones stretched from one end to the other. The occasional bunch of flowers leaned against a grave marker, and crypts dotted the landscape. The cemetery was located on a rise, below which Ella could see the twinkling lights of the city, and farther away still, the dark expanse of Seranthia's great harbor.

She wore her green enchantress's dress, the hood pulled over her head. Over her shoulder she carried her satchel containing the tools of her trade. Rogan's two men were strong soldiers, and each carried a spade in addition to the short swords at their waists. Yet as they approached the cemetery, Ella could almost feel the fear washing over them as they gave her sidelong looks.

"What exactly are we looking for, Enchantress?" one of Rogan's men asked Ella.

"We're looking for the grave of Lord Aidan Alderon."

"How will we read the markers?" the other man whispered.

"Here," Ella said, reaching into her satchel and handing two items to the men. "They're pathfinders." She took a third pathfinder out for herself.

"*Tish-shasah*," Ella said, activating her pathfinder. A beam of light shone from the runes, instantly revealing the grave markers at Ella's feet in the glow. Soon all three of them searched the graveyard.

Tingara had seen many lords and ladies pass from life, and it was some time before one of the men called out.

"Enchantress," the soldier whispered as Ella approached, "look."

He shone his pathfinder down at the tombstone. It was simpler than the others, as if whoever had laid this stone had done so out of decorum rather than love. Even the words were cursory.

"Lord Aidan Alderon," Ella read. "Born 484 Y.E. Died 522 Y.E." She looked at the soldier as her second helper approached. "It doesn't say anything more."

Ella felt nothing but sadness. She'd finally found Killian's family, something he'd wanted to do his whole life, yet it was a story of tragedy. The grave was simple and said nothing of the man Lord Aidan was, but he had obviously been a man of principle, who had stood up to an emperor.

Ella wondered again about Lady Alise, Killian's mother, exiled to the Isle of Ana. Had she once looked down at this grave, crying tears of grief? Was she out there somewhere, still alive, wondering what had happened to the red-haired child that was taken from her?

"What do we do now?" the soldier who'd found the marker said.

"I'm sorry," Ella said, "but this must be done. We need to dig up the coffin and put it on the cart we came in."

Exchanging glances, the men set to work.

❖

The coffin was heavy and buried deep. It was hours before it sat on the bed of the drudge-pulled cart they'd arrived in, and by then dirt covered Ella's hands, fatigue setting in after the long sleepless night.

Ella climbed up the cart, glancing back at the stone coffin before sitting in the driver's seat and looking out from her new height. The sky was lightening, and the darkness of night shifted hue through violet and amber. The sun would rise soon, and Ella needed to be on her way.

"Do you need us to open the lid?" one of Ella's helpers said.

"No, thank you," Ella said.

"What are we doing next?"

"Well," said Ella, "it's up to you. I don't require your assistance any more, but if you'd like to hitch a ride for a time . . ."

She tried not to smile when the two soldiers looked at each other and mutely came to an agreement.

"No, that's all right . . ."

"We'll be fine walking."

"Thank you both for your help," Ella said. "I appreciate it, as does the lord regent."

"Good luck with . . . with . . ."

Ella finally allowed herself to smile, and with a few words, she activated the drudge and was on her way.

Ella descended the rise where the cemetery was located, heading down into the city. She'd been given instruction on how to control a drudge by none other than Evrin, long ago when he'd been posing as a Halrana merchant. The words came easily to her, and the rocking motion of the cart on the cobbled stones was soothing as Ella gazed at the waking city around her.

The new essence machines might be being built at Mornhaven, but Seranthia would always be the beating heart of the Empire. The population of Tingara dwarfed that of the other houses; if there were ever a vote on who would be emperor, a Tingaran would certainly be the one named.

Reaching the market district, Ella watched as vendors set up stalls, in a routine they'd probably followed their entire lives. They ignored her lumbering cart and the stone box on its bed, still covered in dirt.

Ella passed an alley where dogs roamed the streets, looking for scraps. She then turned a corner and there was a magnificent temple, devoted to the Evermen. Such contrast in Seranthia, such energy . . . if only it could be channeled in the right direction under a wise leader.

But Tingara's long-held dominance had led to complacency, and then despotism. As the emperors became more and more capricious, so the land fell into darkness. There hadn't always been streetclans in Seranthia, and the poor hadn't always existed in such multitudes. Once, the Empire had been controlled by no single house, but simply had its administration in Tingara. Seranthia had been ruled justly. Laws such as the ridiculous practice of rounding up vagrants and casting them over the walls were a recent invention.

Rogan's prohibition of such laws had led to an outpouring of energy, as those who could never complain before did so with gusto.

The people needed a ruler like Rogan, one who would treat them with decency, but they also needed one of their own— someone who understood how the Assembly of Templars and the Tingaran leadership fit together.

Ella wondered. Could Killian be such a leader?

She turned the drudge again, and in the distance Seranthia's great harbor opened up ahead. Ella could see the Sentinel in the distance, the statue on its island silhouetted by the breaking dawn, its arm raised to the sky imploringly. Fishing boats were returning to the docks, their holds filled with the morning's catch. Imperial warships sailed out on patrol.

Ella guided the drudge down a long street, heading directly for the harbor.

She remembered the first time she'd met Killian. He'd been posing as a merchant's agent, seeking goods in foreign lands. Ella snorted when she thought about how naïve she'd been. Charming and confident, he'd shown Ella what it meant to be carefree, at a time when she'd been forced to grow up ahead of others her age. Brandon, Ella's guardian, had died, and Miro had been consumed with his training. Ella struggled with her studies and the mistakes she'd made. No one had known war was just around the corner.

Ella had fallen in love with Killian, but it was the immature love of a girl. Only later, when she'd seen his true nature, had something deeper sparked within her.

Then came Ilathor, the dark prince of the Hazara Desert, and the conquest of Petrya. She'd seen so much death in those days, and Ella had found herself unable to resist the comfort of Ilathor's arms.

Killian's last words to Ella were to tell her he loved her, before he made a crossing from which he knew he could never return.

If there was one thing Ella had learned, it was that there was always a way.

The Sentinel beckoned. Killian needed her.

Ella was going to get him back.

26

A man in black waited for Ella at the dock, now lit by sunrise, and she breathed a sigh of relief when she saw him.

He walked toward Ella as she called the drudge to a halt close to the water's edge, looking up at her with his dark eyes.

"Jehral," Ella said warmly.

She dismounted from the cart and gave the desert warrior a quick embrace. "Thank you. I was worried you wouldn't come. Did you bring it?"

"Yes, Ella, I brought it." Jehral held up a bundle, wrapped in oilskin.

Two more people came into view, a dark-haired woman in a red robe and a bladesinger with curly locks and a groomed moustache. Both also held bundles.

"You have no idea how difficult this was," Shani said. "If it had been anyone but you . . ."

"I hope you know what you're doing," said Bartolo, running his fingers through his hair.

"Rogan knows," Ella said. "He believes in what I'm doing."

"Does he know about these?" Shani said, holding up her bundle.

"Well . . ."

"Same old Ella." Bartolo grinned.

"What's in the cart?" Shani asked.

"I'll tell you in a moment. Have they been renewed?"

"Yes," said Jehral, "they've all been renewed."

"Can I have them?" Ella stepped forward eagerly.

"Ella . . ." said Shani, holding up a hand, "we've all been given the same instructions. We're not to let them out of our sight. You're going to have to tell us why you need them."

Ella realized these people were her friends; they had a right to know. She wondered where to begin. "One of the Evermen is in Merralya. He has essence, and he's out there somewhere, building an army."

"Are you serious? Lord of the Sky, you are," Bartolo said.

"Do you know this for a fact?" Jehral said. "The kalif must know."

"Challenging one of the Evermen will require the united strength of all the houses," Ella said, "but the Empire's in chaos, with the shortage of essence crushing the economy and fragmenting the new order, just when we need it to be strong. Challenging his army will be difficult. Challenging one of the Evermen may be beyond us. There's only one who could face him."

Jehral looked out from the dock at the Sentinel, now outlined by the glow of dawn.

"Killian," Shani said. She and Bartolo exchanged glances.

"That's right," said Ella. She lifted her chin. "You're going to help me bring him back."

"Ella, how much are your feelings influencing your actions?" Shani said. "Are you sure you're acting rationally?"

"Whatever my feelings are, I know this is right," Ella said. "He crossed over because he was the only one who could . . . because

Evrin told him it was the only way to prevent the return of the Evermen. He's been trapped there for over two years. Worst of all, his sacrifice was for nothing. One of them crossed over. We don't know how, but he did. We need Killian, and I believe I've found a way to bring him back."

"You need to face the fact that he may be dead," Bartolo said.

"He might be. But I have to try."

"And what if entering the portal enables more of them to cross over?"

"It won't. I won't let that happen," Ella said. She looked at her three friends, people with whom she'd shared hardship and the horrors of war. "You'll leave me there, if need be."

Shani, Jehral, and Bartolo looked at each other for a moment.

Finally Shani sighed. "All right. We'll help you. I've learned to trust you, Ella, and I'll trust you now."

Jehral clasped Ella's shoulder.

"I hope you know what you're doing," Bartolo repeated.

"Thank you," Ella said. "I'll feel better, knowing you're on the other side."

She looked at the three bundles held in her friends' hands. Ella had studied the partly destroyed book of the Evermen endlessly. She'd performed the equations, calculated the requirements. The portal's demand for energy was huge, but Ella had found a source of power that would enable her to open the portal, albeit for the briefest moments at a time.

In their hands, her friends held their houses' Lexicons. Bartolo must have fought like a demon to convince High Enchanter Merlon to relinquish the Alturan Lexicon. Jehral would have begged Ilathor, now kalif, to lend Ella the Lore of Illusion. Shani's possessive grip on her bundle said enough.

"Now, what's in the coffin?" Bartolo said.

"The emperor's brother-in-law, Lord Aidan," said Ella. "Killian's father. Here, help me with him."

———◆———

The sun shot above the horizon as the group of four traveled across the harbor on a stout galley; their destination: the Sentinel.

Eight men rowed the galley while another Tingaran piloted the vessel. The stone coffin lay in the center of the boat. The rowers hadn't asked, and the four passengers hadn't been forthcoming with information.

Ella's mind swirled with symbols and properties, activation sequences and lore drain. She'd had little sleep and her eyes were heavy, but excitement and fear coursed through her blood in equal parts.

If she succeeded in opening the portal, she would be crossing over to another world. She had no idea what to expect.

With each stroke of the oars, the looming statue grew bigger until it dominated her vision, massive and unearthly, a relic from another time. He stood tall and bold on the wide pedestal, with one arm raised, pointing up at the sky. A strange headpiece crowned the statue's head, covering the flowing hair, with a rune decorating its front.

As they approached, Ella could now see the low wall being built around the base of the statue. She saw soldiers in Alturan green and Tingaran legionnaires, as well as builders from Torakon in sand-colored robes. Even at this early hour, the island was a hive of activity.

The galley tied up at a small pier where two other boats were docked. Ella wondered if the rowers would help them with the coffin, but they all looked studiously away, and the four friends struggled with the heavy stone until they were on solid land. The galley departed without another word.

"Friendly bunch," said Bartolo.

"Let's see," Shani said. "We've got a coffin, and we're taking it to the one place they're forbidden to set foot, by imperial decree. Oh, and it's the place where rumors say the primate died at the end of the war. Would you be nervous?"

"Well, when you put it that way," Bartolo mused.

An officer came forward, his men behind him, and Ella hoped for someone she knew, but this man wore Tingaran purple, a captain according to his *raj hada*.

"Just what's going on here?" he demanded.

"Captain, we're here on the lord regent's orders."

"I haven't been given any orders."

"Here," Ella said, holding out the pass Rogan had given her.

The captain quickly scrutinized it. "I'll need to have this checked."

Ella knew that with the coffin out of the cold ground, it would warm up. The Lexicons had been renewed, but her three friends had each made a long journey, and with every moment the Lexicons' power would be draining away.

"I'm sorry, Captain," Ella said, "but I'm afraid we don't have time. My name is Ella Torresante. My brother is the lord marshal of Altura. This is Shani, an elementalist and adviser to the Petryan high lord. This is Bartolo, a bladesinger, and this is Jehral, adviser to the Hazaran kalif. You have our pass. We need to enter the statue."

"Two Alturans, a Petryan, and a Hazaran. Need I remind you you're on Tingaran soil?"

Ella was growing frustrated. "Captain, this isn't about house rivalries. This is important."

"What's in those packages?" the captain asked, pointing at the bundles Ella's friends held in their hands. "Give them to me."

"No," Bartolo said. "Ella, I'm not giving this to them. I swore an oath I wouldn't let it out of my control."

"Nor am I," said Shani.

"I will not hand this over," said Jehral.

Ella looked at the captain. He was inexperienced and jittery. Ella guessed this wasn't considered a choice assignment, watching men build a wall. The captain also seemed like the type to take his role seriously, perhaps suffering from an excess of pride. Normally Ella would have applauded the man's duty to his orders, but now she cursed his stubbornness.

The soldiers stood around their commanding officer, and Ella now saw he was trying to save face in front of his men.

"If you allow me to inspect your belongings, you may pass," he said.

"No," Bartolo said. He placed a hand on the hilt of his zenblade.

"Captain," one of the Tingaran soldiers said, "he's a bladesinger."

"Men, at arms!" the captain called.

The soldiers drew their swords. Ella wondered how they'd managed to get into this mess. She didn't want to fight.

"Stop!" Ella cried.

She had their attention, but she knew she had only moments to calm the situation. "Captain, you're doing an excellent job. You're under orders from the lord regent, and you're following them. No one is to go near the statue, is that correct?"

"That's correct." The captain scowled.

"We're here as part of those defenses. I'm an enchantress and I am going inside the statue to add wards to supplement the work you are doing here. That makes sense, doesn't it?"

Ella saw the thoughts crossing the dim-witted captain's face. She'd offered him an opportunity to save face.

"The things we carry with us are dangerous—they must be, to protect this area as effectively as a Torak-built wall and all your men. That's why we can't let you have them."

"I see," said the captain. "Why didn't you say so in the first place?"

Ella smiled. "We weren't sure if you'd understand, but I can now see I was wrong."

"Can I see that pass again?"

"Here."

The captain pretended to inspect the pass once more. "Ah, I see now."

"My apologies for any confusion," Ella said.

"Quite all right. Umm . . . What's in the coffin, then?"

"The emperor's brother-in-law," Shani said.

The Tingaran captain screwed up his face.

Ella frowned at Shani. "It's not a coffin, it's an energy sink."

"An . . . energy sink . . . Of course," the captain said. "Can my men be of assistance?"

"If you could lend us four of your men to help with this, we'd greatly appreciate it," Ella said. "Thank you, Captain."

Ella felt her pulse race as she stood on the pedestal at the base of the statue and saw the circle of runes at her feet.

Shani, Bartolo, and Jehral clustered nervously behind her while four strong soldiers held the coffin between them.

Ella spoke in a loud voice. "*Mulara-latahn. Sunara-latahn. Sumayara-sulamara-latanara.*"

The symbols lit up with a steady green fire, the light traveling from one rune to the next until the circle blazoned with a fierce glow. A grinding sound came from below, and soon the stone disk slid downward, twisting and folding, revealing the stairway underneath.

"I hope you know what you're doing," Bartolo muttered yet again, low enough so only Ella could hear it.

Ella was the first down, remembering the last time she'd come this way. The images came strong and fast, and the pounding of her heart increased to a drumlike tempo.

A soft yellow light with no obvious source lit the passageway below. Descending the steps, Ella reached the floor and continued forward, once again feeling awe at being somewhere she knew she didn't belong. Behind Ella came Shani and then Jehral, with Bartolo close behind. The soldiers struggled with the coffin but managed to tilt it down the stairs until they were all standing in the wide corridor.

"Come on," Ella said.

The straight stone passageway appeared to be all of one piece, with no obvious seams, even at the floor and ceiling. Ella walked forward until she was at the end of the corridor, sensing the others close behind her.

Ella looked up and gasped. Evrin's words came back to her as she looked at the remains of the spiraled stairs leading up. Whatever had happened to the essence in the pool, it had eaten through the stone until the stairway was gone. A ladder leaned against the wall in its stead, evidently placed there by Evrin when he'd last inspected the portal.

Ella turned to the soldiers. "Please, put it down," she said.

With a groan, the soldiers set the coffin on the smooth floor with a clunk.

"Thank you," Ella said. "You may go now."

The four soldiers fled from the corridor, back the way they'd come.

"Ella," Bartolo said, "how do you plan on getting this up the ladder?"

"We can't," said Ella.

"Oh no," said Shani. "You're not seriously suggesting . . ."

"It's the only way. Come on, help me with the lid."

With one of them on each corner of the stone coffin, they removed the lid, coughing at the dust they raised when they removed it, setting it down near the bottom of the ladder.

Ella prepared herself for a grisly sight, but instead saw a second man-sized box inside, this one made of hard wood, unadorned but polished.

"One more lid," Ella said.

They lifted the wooden lid, setting it down on top of the stone.

Taking a deep breath, Ella finally summoned the courage to step forward and look down.

The embalming fluid and sealed container had kept the body of Lord Aidan in surprisingly good condition. He wore faded gray clothing, simple but tailored, with a silver belt buckle and black leather boots.

But the evidence of more than twenty years in the ground was there to see. His skin was dry and white as parchment, the cheeks sunken into his face. Rot had taken hold of the soft skin around his mouth, and half his teeth were exposed, no longer protected by lips. Only the slightest flecks of red indicated the color his hair had once been, the rest was gray and fine, combed against his head in wisps. His eyes were closed and peaceful, but the savage red marks on his neck told the story of his violent death.

Ella felt Shani take her hand as Ella felt tears slide down her cheeks. This was Killian's father. Would he understand what they were doing?

"I'm sorry for this desecration, Lord Aidan," Ella said. "Please understand what we're doing, we're doing to help your son."

"I don't think he can hear you," Bartolo said.

Ella looked up, her eyes burning. "He soon will."

27

Bartolo and Jehral lifted the body carefully from its resting place, grimacing at the weight and the horror of their task.

It took some time to get the body up the ladder, but they made it in the end, and Lord Aidan was once again laid on the ground. The group stood in the strange chamber, staring in silence at the portal.

The essence had eaten away at the wall in what must have started as a trickle and become a flood. The pool was now empty, the stone floor dry.

In the center of the barren pool, a platform of steps rose from the floor. On the summit stood the portal itself, an oval mirror, twice the height of a man and hovering in empty space, held up by some mysterious force.

Where before the mirror had been shimmering gold, shifting to blazing red when the seals were knocked away, it was now dark and still.

Ella felt her heart quiver at the enormity of what she was attempting.

"You can give me the Lexicons now," she said quietly, as if afraid to shatter the silence.

Wordlessly Bartolo handed Ella his bundle. As Ella unwrapped the oilskin and saw the first flash of green, she realized she was trembling. Soon she held the book in her hands, once more seeing the rune on the book's green cover: the number one. The rune glowed softly. If ever that rune faded—if the Lexicon's power were allowed to completely drain—every enchanted item in Merralya would cease to function.

Ella's friends had placed their trust in her. She had to honor that trust.

Ella stepped over the remnants of the pool's boundary wall and placed the book down on the second step, just below the portal.

She turned to Shani. "Could I have the Petryan Lexicon?"

Shani hesitated, but she walked over to Ella and handed her the bundle.

Ella removed the cloth and soon she held a red-covered book in her hands, staring at the glowing rune on the front: the number three. She set it beside the Alturan Lexicon.

Jehral walked to where Ella stood at the portal's base and handed her his bundle. Ella remembered the yellow cover from when she'd helped Ilathor rediscover his people's lore. The glowing symbol on the Hazaran Lexicon bore the number five.

"Three Lexicons, brought into proximity for the first time in eons," Ella said. "How long do you think it has been?"

She looked up at her friends. They were strong warriors, all of them, who'd faced terrifying enemies and held their ground. Now, they looked at Ella with fear in their eyes.

Ella took the device out of her satchel. She'd worked on it ever since she'd had the idea of using the Lexicons to power the portal. She only hoped three Lexicons would be enough.

It was similar to a wand, but it had three legs. At the base of each leg was a clear crystal prism, and where the legs met was another prism, this one a dark red ruby. Ella placed the three Lexicons equidistant from each other and then situated the device so that each leg rested on the books' covers.

She removed the seal from her bag. It was similar to Evrin's draining seals that even now rested on the portal's rim, but Ella's seal was different: larger and more complex. Where Evrin's seals drained the portal's power, Ella's seal would channel energy from the Lexicons to the relic. A ruby on Ella's seal was akin to the ruby on the three-legged device.

Ella stretched tall to place her device on the portal's rim, at the apex of the oval. She hoped this would work.

She left Evrin's three draining seals in place and returned to the other side of the chamber, where Lord Aidan lay on his back, composed as if sleeping.

Ella sat next to Killian's father. She took out her protective gloves and put them on her hands. Finally, she removed a set of scrills and a vial of essence.

Ella again apologized to Lord Aidan for what she was about to do.

The portal would recognize an intruder—only one of the Evermen could cross, or someone in his company.

And only the lore Ella had learned from Barnabas, the old Akari necromancer, would enable her to do what she needed to do. The body was old, and Ella would have to use animator's runes to give it strength.

Finally, against everything she had been taught, in direct conflict with Necromancer Aldrik's warnings, she needed to bring back Lord Aidan's personality, or the portal wouldn't recognize him.

Ella looked at her friends, who watched with dread.

"Get some rest, if you can," Ella said, as she prepared to bring Killian's father back from the dead. "This might take awhile."

None of them took their eyes off Ella for a moment.

She could feel them watching her as she removed Lord Aidan's clothes and cleaned his body, methodically working as she remembered what she'd learned in the icy north. They watched the deft strokes of her scrill while she worked with a constant rhythm, her brow furrowed in concentration as she combined the knowledge she'd received from Barnabas with the lessons of Aldrik.

This was different from working with the Akari woman who'd died in the whaling accident. The flesh was decomposed, mottled with splotches of black and brown. A slight stench came from the body, and the scratches and marks on the skin made it difficult for Ella to draw clean, crisp symbols.

She kept her head tilted to the side as she worked, the hissing sound and chemical sting of the essence coming as a blessing, distracting Ella from the horror of what she was doing.

Ella needed to roll the body over at one point, and found Shani helping her where neither Jehral nor Bartolo would. She covered the corpse in runes, finally stepping back to regard her handiwork.

"Shani, can you help me put his clothes back on? It's safe."

Soon everything was ready.

Ella left Lord Aidan's shirt open, the heart rune exposed.

"What now, Ella?" Jehral asked.

"When I bring him back, we will need to move quickly. What I'm doing is dangerous, and I don't know how long I'll have."

"Can I help?" Bartolo asked.

"When I give the word, remove the three lower seals from the portal, leaving my seal on the top, the one with the ruby."

"I can do that," Bartolo said.

"Anything else?" said Shani.

"Without Evrin's seals, when we give the portal power, it will open, and without power it will close. I've kept the activation sequence for my device simple, and it's important that the portal opens only for the shortest possible amount of time. Listen to me for the activation, Shani. To deactivate my device and close the portal, add *'sula'* to the sequence."

"What are you telling me to do?"

"As soon as I'm through, close the portal. Not a moment after. The Lexicons won't be able to power the portal for long, and I don't know how long it will take me to find Killian, so only open the portal every three days, and then for the briefest instant."

"What's to stop the Lexicons from draining completely?" Bartolo said.

"I've built a safety into the device. It will cut the flow of power before it allows the Lexicons to fade."

"Doesn't that mean you'll be stranded?" asked Bartolo.

"Yes," Ella said simply.

"Ella, it's too dangerous," Shani said.

Ella squeezed Shani's shoulder. "I have to do this. Trust me, everything will be fine."

"What can I do?" asked Jehral.

"All of you must watch the portal. Make sure someone is watching it at all times. If anyone tries to cross who isn't me or Killian . . . kill him."

Jehral nodded.

Ella had never seen Shani look so frightened. "What are you going to find out there?"

"I don't know," Ella said.

"If I only open the portal every three days, how will you tell me if you need it opened sooher?"

"I can't. Just make sure it opens."

Shani nodded. "I will."

"Is everyone ready?"

Shani, Jehral, and Bartolo all nodded.

Ella placed her fingers on the heart rune on Lord Aidan's dead skin. She spoke the words that would give the revenant life, tracing the symbol as her lips moved.

"*Mordet-ahl. Sudhet-ahl. Suth-eroth. Soth-eruth. Mordet-suth-ahn.*"

Lord Aidan's eyes opened. They were completely white, but there were also flecks of red, like blood splattered on snow.

"*Tsu-tulara-ahn. Morth-thul-ahlara. Sudhet-ahlara-ahn. Shah-lahra-rahn!*"

Blue light traveled from the heart rune, spiraling along the runes on the revenant's chest. The light sped from symbol to symbol, and Ella quickly closed the buttons of Lord Aidan's shirt.

He sat up.

Suddenly Lord Aidan put his hands to his throat, moaning and twitching on the ground. Shani jumped back, and Bartolo and Jehral both drew their swords. The revenant slowly calmed, and then his vision must have cleared, for he looked around him, an expression of confusion on his face.

He clambered slowly to his feet.

Ella held her breath. She had never seen this lore performed; these were dark arts, even among the Akari. Even Barnabas had cautioned her about what she was now doing.

"Where . . . where am I?" asked Lord Aidan.

"Lord Aidan . . ." Ella began, and then faltered. She felt tears streak down her cheeks once more. "Lord Aidan, you're dead."

He turned his eerie eyes on her. Red swirled and eddied against the white. Ella felt fear surge through her.

"I remember," he said. "I remember . . . the noose."

"That's right," Ella said, her voice trembling. "I'm sorry, Lord Aidan, but the emperor had you killed."

"Then how am I here?"

"You had a son, Killian." Ella prayed this would work.

"I have a son!" he suddenly screamed, and both Bartolo and Jehral came forward. Ella gestured at the two swordsmen, motioning them back.

"Your son lives," Ella said, "but you've been brought back because he needs your help."

"Where is he? I want to see him."

"Look," Ella pointed, "do you see where I am pointing? It is a portal. Your son is on the other side."

"I . . . I am confused. Where am I?"

Ella blinked the tears away, her heart reaching out to what was left of Killian's father.

"We don't have long," Ella said. "When the portal opens, I need you to cross with me. That's all. Then we can save your son and bring him back from the darkness."

Ella hesitantly took the revenant's hand. Without protest, Lord Aidan allowed her to lead him to the base of the steps to the portal.

"Remove the three lower seals, Bartolo," Ella said.

Bartolo took Evrin's seals from the portal's rim and backed away.

"Listen to the activation sequence, Shani. Do you remember how to add the inflection to deactivate?"

"Yes," Shani's voice quavered.

"Close the portal as soon as I'm across."

"I will."

"*Castrum*," Ella said the single word.

The three Lexicons flared, suddenly too bright to look at. The ruby at the apex of Ella's device began to glow a savage red, and the stone on the seal Ella had placed on the summit of the oval lit up in sympathy.

Ella led Lord Aidan up the steps.

She held her breath, and in front of her the portal began to open.

The dead silver color changed hue, becoming a dirty brown, and then moving to the shade of sand. Suddenly the portal shifted hue to the color of copper, and then it became a sizzling curtain of molten gold.

The beacon called, a terrible sound that rose and fell, bursting inside the head like a thousand exploding stars. It was intended to call the Evermen and could only be stopped from the other side.

Hand in hand, Ella and Killian's father stepped through the molten curtain.

Into the unknown.

28

Ella entered a twilight world. Her first sensation was an intense difference, a factor of the light and the air, the smell and the temperature. She was no longer in Merralya.

She blinked, trying to see what lay in front of her, but all she could see was a dark landscape of rock. Gravel crunched under her boots, and she took a breath to steady her nerves.

The beacon sounded again.

The beacon!

Ella turned back the way she'd come and saw a stone archway, the same height as the oval mirror but different in all other respects. The air under the arch sparked and sizzled while waves of energy shot from one column to the other in bursts.

"Ahh!" The revenant put his hands to his ears and fell to the ground.

Ella looked frantically at the arch, conscious of the time. Killian had stopped the beacon, and she could too.

There! Under the top of the arch was a device. A pendulum swung left and right, timed to the head-splitting cry of the beacon's call.

Ella placed her hand on the pendulum to hold it still.

She screamed. Pain seared her hand; it felt like the device was burning the flesh away from the bones of her fingers. She fought to hold on but it was impossible. Ella had to let go.

The beacon stopped. The pendulum was once again stilled. Ella lifted her hand and stared at her palm in wonder; she was unharmed.

The sudden realization hit her. Her plan had worked. The portal had recognized Lord Aidan as one of the Evermen, and Ella was now in another world.

Wondering at the eerie light, Ella stared up into the sky. She saw a glowing orb but was unsure whether it was the sun or the moon. A thick haze filled the air, so that it seemed neither night nor day, and the orb's light was diffused.

Deciding the orb was this world's sun, Ella turned and examined the landscape. Distances were hard to judge, for the expanse was little more than a rocky field as far as she could see in all directions. A hazy red horizon extended in a blurred line, and the rocks were all shapes and sizes, some small and smooth, others jagged boulders.

The only feature Ella could see was a road.

It started at the stone archway and followed a dead straight line, disappearing into eternity. The path could have been made by the Evermen, or perhaps it had been here before they came. Ella knew one thing, however.

The Evermen had opened a portal into a world of nightmare.

Ella turned back to Lord Aidan. He sat slumped on the earth beside the portal, heedless of the stony ground.

"Come," Ella said.

"No," said the revenant, staring up at Ella with his red-flecked eyes. "I can go no farther."

Ella looked at the faint shimmer of the runes on Lord Aidan's skin. She knew from Barnabas's teachings that a revenant who'd been in the ground as long as Lord Aidan, brought back with so much of who he was, would not last long.

A dark shadow passed overhead, but looking up, Ella couldn't see anything. She shivered. If she couldn't find Killian, Lord Aidan would be her only chance of making it home.

"Lord Aidan, I need to search for your son."

"My son . . ." he moaned.

"Will you stay here? I will be back."

"Stay here."

Ella drew a shaky breath and made herself turn away from the revenant. The portal would only open every three days. She needed to move quickly.

Ella followed the stone path, wondering how long she would need to journey until something would materialize to break the monotonous landscape. She was surprised when, almost immediately, a series of hazy buildings appeared on both sides of the road. The silhouettes appeared decayed and broken, and Ella decided to stay on the path, reminding herself that if it ended at the stone arch, the road must lead somewhere.

Ella thought she saw flickering shadows swirling around the tops of the distant structures. She pulled the hood of her dress over her head, feeling comforted by the extra protection.

Ella continued walking, and after a while the distant clusters of buildings vanished behind her. It was difficult to gain a sense of time in this place. The faded sun hadn't moved, and the strange twilight neither lightened nor darkened. Ella felt neither cold nor warm, yet the bleak sky weighed on her oppressively. She wanted nothing more than to get out of this place and return home.

Ella stopped. There was another cluster of shattered buildings ahead, to the left of the road, but they were much closer this time.

She continued walking, and as she grew closer, she saw piles of rubble, fallen towers, paved squares, and remnants of walls.

Ella decided to investigate.

Leaving the road, she saw that many of the structures were still standing, and the architecture was strange, unlike anything she'd ever seen. The majority of the buildings followed a pyramid-like design, and some were tall, as high as the Imperial Palace in Seranthia.

Ella reached a pyramid and looked up. She could see no means of gaining entry, nor a way of climbing the stepped levels. Whoever had built these structures had possessed some other means of reaching the heights.

The structures were made of a dark stone Ella didn't recognize, and passing a half-toppled wall, Ella stopped and stared.

There was a mosaic on the wall, depicting bizarre creatures flying in the sky and standing in groups on the ground. The bird-like beings had wings and webbed limbs, but Ella could see they were nimble, with clawlike hands. One of the creatures in the picture held a scroll and appeared to be reading to those clustered around him.

Continuing to explore, Ella saw more of the mosaics and came to believe these creatures were the builders of the pyramids and had once occupied this place. Where were they now?

The city was abandoned, and Ella decided to return to the road.

A sudden rumble came from overhead, and Ella saw the sky had developed a pinkish hue. Patches of the haze had formed brown and black clouds, and Ella wondered if she was seeing the beginnings of what this world called a storm. She watched the boiling clouds in fear, but there was no rain, and the rumbling slowly diminished.

The road developed a slope, and Ella felt the muscles in her legs burning as she felt the incline grow steeper. There was something ahead, another pyramid, standing solitary and much larger than the others. It lay directly in front of her.

The object became clearer with every step, and Ella suddenly gasped as she realized what it was.

It wasn't a pyramid—it was a small mountain. The spitting image of . . .

"Stonewater," Ella breathed.

Yet as her footsteps took her closer, Ella saw it was a pale imitation of the great mountain in Aynar, barely a tenth of the size.

The road opened onto steps, and Ella climbed, realizing she was being led up the mountain. There was something too perfect about it. This Stonewater had been constructed, Ella realized. It wasn't a natural mountain at all. Blocks had been placed one on top of the other, in a deliberate mimicry of nature's work, creating uneven slopes and irregularities just like the real Stonewater.

The steps continued, and Ella continued to climb.

There was only one path to follow, and near the summit of the mountain Ella saw an opening. The path leveled, and with trepidation Ella placed one foot in front of the other, with no idea what she would find.

She soon stood outside the dark opening, seeing that it led to a chamber. Ella willed herself to go forward. The interior was as black as pitch.

Ella took her wand out of the pocket of her dress. She rehearsed the words in her mind that would send a bolt of energy flying from the prism on its tip.

Ella stepped into the chamber.

As she did, a soft yellow glow welled up from the floor, the ceiling, and the walls, with no obvious origin. Ella could suddenly see, but what she saw was nothing she could have imagined.

Dozens of clear shells lined the walls of the chamber like upright tombs. Each shell contained the body of a man.

Some of the men were tall, others short, but all had their eyes closed as if sleeping, their hands clasped on their breasts. However long they'd been here, they were unmarked by the ravages of time, but each wore the same cruel lines at the corners of his mouth, the same marks of condescension in the twisting of his brows.

Every one of them had red hair.

In the center of the chamber was a single shell, placed there as if given some special honor. This shell faced the entrance of the chamber, where a direct line of sight would point down the stairs, along the road, and to the stone arch leading back to Merralya.

This shell was empty.

Ella's heart raced in her chest, and her breathing came labored. Filled with fear, she walked along the row of shells. Each had a name above its casing, written with letters of silver.

"Ravathi Roxas," Ella read and then continued to the next living tomb.

"Varian Vitrix." He was a tall man with long hair the color of rust.

"Pyrax Pohlen." This was a striking man with hair of burnished red-gold.

Ella turned and walked to the empty shell facing the chamber's entrance. She looked at the name written above it. "Sentar Scythran."

Ella's mind turned back to the story Evrin had told, when they'd been gathered at the Sentinel after the primate's death.

She looked again at the only tomb without an occupant. "The Lord of the Night," Ella whispered.

Evrin had described him as the darkest of them all. Sentar was the one who first discovered the process of extracting essence from the dead. He was the one who never had any interest in humans, preferring to be served by revenants. It was Sentar who started murdering masses of humans for essence, long ago, without waiting for the people to die first.

Ella felt dread sink into her stomach like a stone.

The Lord of the Night was in Merralya.

She realized her muscles were tense, and she held her wand in a grip of iron. Ella forced herself to relax and then looked at the wand in her hand.

She didn't know how strong the shells were, but there was only one way to find out.

Sentar Scythran may have crossed, but she had a chance, here, to destroy the Evermen forever.

She had to try.

Ella walked to the nearest occupied shell. She looked at Pyrax Pohlen and thought about the great war fought long ago between the humans and their gods. She owed it to those brave people of long ago to do this.

Ella touched her wand to the shell and spoke the activation sequence.

"Tourahn-ash-tassine."

The symbols on the wand lit up as the device came to life. Ella called forth a first-level bolt of energy. *"Asta!"*

Sparks fountained from the clear wall of the shell. The brightness lit up the chamber, sending flickering shadows dancing around the walls and forcing Ella to shield her eyes.

She took her hand away from her brow.

The shell was unharmed.

Taking a deep breath, Ella called up a fourth-level bolt of energy. *"Sahn!"*

The symbols on the wand flickered as the energy left it. Ella felt waves of heat pour from the prism at the wand's tip, and she chanted as she held it to the shell, calling forth the protective capabilities of her dress.

The walls of the chamber lit up white, and when Ella took the wand away from the shell, afterimages danced in her vision.

Still, the shell was unharmed.

Ella sighed.

She sensed sudden movement behind her. Out of the corner of her eye, a black shadow peeled from the wall.

Ella turned to see.

The shadow launched itself at her.

Ella screamed and her hood went over her eyes as she crashed to the ground. She felt wiry muscles and soft clothing, and then her head was knocked back against the stone.

A hand thrust at her face, pushing at her neck and hair, finally finding her mouth and clapping over Ella's lips before she could speak an activation sequence.

Ella fought but her assailant was too strong. She cried against the hand holding her mouth, but nothing came out except a moan.

While she was pinned to the ground, her attacker's other hand pulled the hood back from her head.

Ella looked up into intense blue eyes and hair the color of flame. The hand covered her nostrils as well as her mouth and she couldn't breathe. Looking up at his contorted face, Ella wondered if he was still sane.

"It's not you," Killian muttered.

Ella tried to gasp for breath, her chest heaving and legs kicking at the ground, but her lungs had nothing to draw on. She felt darkness encroaching.

"It's impossible," Killian said. "You feel very real for a vision."

Ella's single free hand smashed into Killian's ear.

He cried out and his hand left Ella's mouth. Killian sat astride her, pinning her down, but Ella gasped as air returned and quickly called on a series of runes, feeling her dress harden to steel. Another activation sequence sent electricity scattering across her form.

Killian screamed as he leapt backward with incredible agility. Coughing and gasping, Ella climbed to her feet. She saw her wand on the floor nearby.

Seeing the direction of her gaze, Killian flicked his wrists in Ella's direction. His hands were empty but Ella saw the silver glow of symbols on his palms.

A ball of fire shot out from his hands.

Ella dived to the side, grabbing the wand as she did, but the flame hit her square on the chest, her dress flaring up as it tried to protect her from the searing heat.

Ella felt her fragile wind knocked out of her as she stumbled to the ground. She sensed her dress failing. Another hit and she'd be dead.

Rolling over, she looked at Killian and saw madness in his eyes. Gasping, Ella pointed her wand at Killian and spoke. *"Sahn!"*

The bolt of yellow light shot out faster than the eye could follow. It hit Killian directly on the chest, but he simply grunted, and Ella's mouth dropped open as the energy haloing his form was somehow diffused. He wore close-fitting black clothing, but Ella now saw more runes on his hands and neck.

Killian pointed his finger, and lightning split the air with a thunderous crash. Ella tried to roll away, but twisting bolts bathed her body in dancing blue sparks. She knew her dress would protect her for moments only.

"Stop!" Ella cried. She dropped the wand and raised her hands imploringly, looking up at him. "It's me!"

Killian ceased his chant, and the lightning vanished. He looked at Ella for a moment, as if thinking, and then he clapped his hands together.

A concussive blast of wind lifted Ella from her feet and she flew through the air, crashing against the empty tomb in the center of the chamber. She lay crumpled and could only look up at him as he loomed over her.

Ella knew her only chance lay in convincing him she was real.

She groaned as Killian looked down at her. "You said you loved me . . . at the portal. I came for you!"

Killian lowered his hands. "Ella?"

Ella coughed. "It's me, you fool!"

"How do I know it's you?"

"Look." Ella held up the pendant on its chain around her neck.

"What?"

"Look! You wore this when we first met."

"I remember," Killian said.

He looked at her quizzically and then started to pace the chamber. Ella kept herself carefully still. In a contest between them, she knew who the victor would be.

Killian stopped pacing, and Ella glanced up.

He was staring at the empty shell. His eyes widened.

"He's gone. Where did he go?"

"I don't know," Ella said.

"He was here before!" Killian screamed.

Killian's sudden rage left him as quickly as it came. He slumped down to the ground until he sat with his arms around his knees.

"Am I going mad?" he whispered, and Ella could only just hear it.

She pulled herself over to him so that she was sitting close.

"It's been over two years. I'm sorry it's taken me so long. Lord of the Sky, I can't tell you how sorry I am. I can't imagine what it's been like for you here."

"It's really you?" Killian looked up.

"Yes." Ella met his eyes. "It's really me."

Killian's eyes were now clear. Seated beside him, Ella wrapped her arms around him and felt a sob shake his body.

"I'm here now," Ella whispered as she held him. "I'm going to take you home."

29

Miro and Amber traveled north, whereas everyone they passed headed in the opposite direction.

They now wore traveling clothes, and both carried satchels filled with food and spare clothing. They had a map and gilden, the coins strange and unfamiliar to Miro's eyes. Miro carried a plain but sharp sword at his belt, and Amber had a stiletto tucked into one of her high boots.

As instructed by the emir, the soldiers gave Miro everything he asked for and even escorted them to the outskirts of Emirald. Miro had told Amber of his bargain with the ruler of the seafaring Veldrin nation, and of his promise to Emir Volkan. Their quest was now twofold: they needed to find the antidote to the alchemical poison, and they must discover the identity of the mysterious leader who commanded the barbarian horde.

They passed through the lands in Veldria's north without mishap. They were obviously foreigners, yet they traveled where everyone not Veldrin was considered uncivilized; there were few chances to make an error of custom.

Miro had expected to stay in simple inns and guesthouses, but everywhere they went, the beds were taken. Merchants and nobles were crossing the border from Gokan in droves, and the roads were congested with those heading to the perceived safety in the south. Only those with urgent business in Gokan went north.

As they approached the border, Miro saw evidence of the emir's soldiers building up their presence. Miro asked a Gokani merchant, traveling with his wife and two sons, about the border crossing.

"It's chaos at Renton, the main border crossing," the merchant said. "They don't care too much about who crosses into Gokan, but the soldiers are checking everyone who comes into Veldria. The emir's not too keen on flooding Veldria with poor refugees."

"We need to go to Wengwai," Miro said. "Would you recommend crossing at Renton?"

The merchant harrumphed. "Recommend? No. It's not that you won't be able to cross, but the crossing is packed with too many people. It'll take you days to make it over the border. Try crossing from Sarina to Maelan. You'll need to take a boat, but you'll save time."

Miro thanked the merchant, watching as he took his family back toward Emirald.

Sarina huddled against the river, a small town earning an income from the trade barges that usually plied the waterways. The typical Veldrin façades colored the buildings in garish hues, and a broad avenue ran down to the water's edge.

Miro and Amber headed directly to the riverside. As they arrived, a barge tied up at the dock, unloading a cargo of Gokani refugees. Veldrin soldiers in brown and blue uniforms shepherded the Gokani to a border station where a team of officials processed them and handed them over to more of the emir's men to be searched.

"Wait here," Miro said.

He found the owner of the barge talking to an official, waving and gesticulating.

"These fees are outrageous!" the bargeman said.

The official shrugged. "How much did you earn from each of your passengers? Tell me, did you charge the normal rate, or did you bump it up? You've given us more work than we can handle, so we need to pay more men to help out. That gilden has to come from somewhere."

Miro waited until the grumbling bargeman handed over several coins.

"Excuse me," Miro said. "Can you take us to Maelan?"

"Aren't you going in the wrong direction?"

"We have urgent business in Wengwai."

The bargeman peered at Miro with calculating eyes. "How urgent?"

"We aren't made of gilden," Miro said, "and I'll warrant you'd be making the journey back empty in any case."

"Two silver crowns."

"One."

"One silver crown and six copper swords."

"One silver crown," Miro said.

Miro saw another barge approaching with a new load of refugees. "Perhaps I should try him?" He gestured toward the barge.

The bargeman turned. "Oh, all right then. Fine. One silver crown. We leave right away, though."

"Perfect," Miro said.

He waved Amber forward.

———

The river was placid and wide, and the empty barge made good time. By early afternoon Miro saw the smoke of chimneys in the distance, and then a cluster of buildings. Gokani architecture was more somber than the vivid style of Veldria, favoring function over form, and the buildings were made of wood and stone rather than brick.

As Miro and Amber waited by the rail, the bargeman stomped over. "Now, where's that silver crown."

Miro handed over the coin.

Looking at the approaching dock, Amber pointed. "Who's that?"

A man of ordinary height stood with the refugees crowding the pier, yet they maintained a careful distance around him. He wore a black robe with a crimson lining. Miro saw an emblem, a triangle bound by a circle, on his breast.

"That's a guildsman," the bargeman said. "Surely you've heard of the Guild?"

"Of course," Miro said smoothly.

The bargeman left them to oversee the docking process.

"What should we do?" Amber asked. "Should we talk to him?"

"I don't know if we can," Miro said. "Look—see that group of soldiers in red uniforms? They're going to talk to us when we disembark. Meanwhile our friend the bargeman is going to load up his vessel. By the time we're finished with the officials, the barge will have left."

"Nothing's ever easy, is it?"

"Don't worry," said Miro. "Something tells me there'll be more of his kind around."

"Disembark!" the bargeman called.

Miro and Amber crossed the gangway and, as the only people crossing into Gokan, were quickly surrounded by soldiers.

The guards herded them to a desk. "What's your business in Gokan?" an official asked.

"I'm bringing gilden for a friend," Miro said.

The official's eyes lit up. "How much gilden?"

Miro hesitated. "A silver crown?"

"That should suffice," said the official. "Here." He handed Miro a small sack. "Place any forbidden items in here, and I'll see they are disposed of. Forbidden items include redberry, heartfire, and black powder."

Miro looked at the surrounding soldiers. He discreetly dropped a coin into the sack and handed it back to the official. "I have no forbidden items."

"Very good," the official said. He gestured to the soldiers. "They can pass."

Miro turned to look back at the barge, but the alchemist had boarded, and the barge was gone.

"Come on," Miro said to Amber. "Let's find lodgings."

They'd made it to Gokan.

Miro pressed his back against the wall and counted for three slow breaths before again looking down the alley.

The alchemist hadn't spotted him.

He'd been following the guildsman for an eternity, looking for an opportunity to question him somewhere quiet. Miro had discerned no obvious pattern to the robed man's wandering. Was he heading home? Perhaps to his place of work? He knew so little about these people.

The black-robed alchemist turned another corner, and Miro crept along the wall, popping his head out before bringing it quickly in again.

This alley was as quiet as he would find in the small town of Maelan. The place was crammed full of refugees, and the alchemist had so far stayed on main streets. This was the time to take him.

Miro ran forward but stopped in his tracks as the alchemist turned to face him. "Why are you following me?" the alchemist questioned, leveling Miro with dark eyes. "Is it gilden you're after?" He shrugged. "Never mind."

Miro sensed motion to his sides. He ducked as a slashing sword cut the air where his head had been, and turned to face his assailants.

There were two swordsmen, both wearing black uniforms with the same emblem on the breast—a triangle bound by a circle. One was stocky, whereas the other was as tall as Miro, with broad shoulders and long arms.

Miro stepped back to give himself space, cursing when he saw the alchemist had left the area.

He watched his opponents' eyes and legs, gauging who would attack first. The stocky swordsman on the left shifted his feet, but Miro didn't accept the feint. The two men watched him warily, circling around him, a mark of experienced fighters.

Then the tall man came forward and thrust twice in quick succession, aiming to pin Miro against the wall. Realizing the trap, Miro dropped to the ground and rolled, coming up between the two men. He faced the stocky man but reversed his thrust behind him, feeling the point of his sword strike home in the tall man's chest. The stocky fighter's sword was extended, but he barged into Miro with his shoulder, knocking him to the ground.

Miro's sword came up to block, and the clash of steel on steel reverberated through the alley. He heard shouts and cries; someone had heard the commotion. More soldiers would be on their way. He had to end it quickly.

Miro swung his sword three times, attempting to wear his opponent down, but the man was strong and held the blows back, his face grim. The stocky fighter raised his sword to strike, and Miro saw his opening. He ducked and thrust, the tip of his sword grazing his opponent's sternum and continuing upward to open his throat.

The two men were dead, and the alchemist was nowhere to be seen.

Miro wiped the blood from his sword on one of the dead men's clothing, quickly sheathing the weapon.

He saw the horrified faces of watching townsfolk. More soldiers would soon be coming.

Miro cursed.

He raced back to the guesthouse where he'd left Amber. Thankfully, it was in Maelan's backstreets rather than near the crowded harbor. As he ran, Miro removed his blood-splattered jerkin and threw it to the side of the street. Finally, he turned a corner and saw the battered front door.

"Amber!" Miro called as he yanked open the door and raced up the stairs. "We need to go!"

Miro was certain the decrepit guesthouse where they'd found lodgings had been a halfway house before the recent flood of refugees gave it a more profitable purpose. Some of the long-term lodgers had a strange look about them, and Miro had felt uneasy leaving Amber on her own.

He came to the thin door to their room and tried the handle. It was locked.

"Amber, it's me," Miro called.

A key rattled in the lock, and Amber pulled the door open, her expression fearful.

"What is it? I heard you calling."

"We need to go. I'll explain later."

"I just handed over two silver crowns!"

"It doesn't matter. Come on!"

It took little time to gather their few possessions, and soon they were running through the streets of Maelan.

Miro swore again when he saw a group of soldiers in the black uniforms of the Alchemists' Guild blocking the street. "Back the other way."

They tried another street, and then slipped between two buildings into an alley. Miro thought if he pointed them away from the river they'd find a road. Behind a farmhouse he saw pasture. "This way!"

It wasn't until they'd crossed the field and come across a narrow path that Miro slowed. As the day passed into darkness, they left Maelan behind.

"What happened?" Amber asked.

"I was asking for directions to Wengwai when I saw another alchemist. I followed him, but—scratch it—he must have realized and led me around by the nose. Two men attacked me in an alley." Miro turned grim. "I was forced to kill them."

"Are you hurt?"

"No, I'm fine. But the alchemist got away, and the struggle raised a cry. They'll be looking for us in Maelan right now."

"Miro, we've just arrived in this country, Gokan, or whatever it's called. I just spent some of our last coins on lodgings. You went to ask for directions, and next thing you know you got yourself into another fight!"

"I was trying to find answers," Miro protested.

"You need to think more," Amber said. "It'll take both of us, working together, to get this cure and return home. We need to use our heads as well as our hearts." Miro heard the fear in her voice. "You'll get yourself killed."

"I understand," Miro said. Looking back, he still didn't know what he could have done differently, but he understood Amber was afraid, not just for herself but for him.

They walked in silence, and soon a crescent moon shone down from the night sky. The narrow trail turned onto a road, and with no better plan they wordlessly followed it away from Maelan.

The road descended into a low valley with copses of thick trees to either side. Amber stopped. "What's that?"

"What?"

"Do you see it?" Amber pointed. "Light—there in the trees."

Miro saw the flicker of firelight. "I'm not sure if we should make our presence known," he said.

Amber rounded on her husband. "It's dark, I'm tired, and we need directions. You seemed happy to use that sword earlier in the day." She set off in the direction of the trees. "Follow my lead."

30

A group of twelve men sat in a circle around the low embers of a cooking fire. A heavy metal pan rested on the coals, and the scent of mushrooms and toasting nuts wafted through the warm night air.

One of the men walked forward and squatted near the fire, stirring the pan with a wooden spoon. The sound of sizzling was accompanied by the melodic notes of a plucked instrument, and Miro saw one of the men held a large gourd between his knees, fitted with dozens of thin strings. He plucked at one string and then another in a haphazard fashion, creating a discordant yet not unpleasant tune, seemingly without structure, but perhaps Miro simply didn't know how to find it.

All the men wore smocks of sky blue and had beards of varying lengths. One older man's beard reached nearly to his waist.

As Miro assessed the men, Amber stepped forward from the trees. "Greetings!"

Miro came forward to stand beside her, keeping his hand on the hilt of his sword.

None of the men jumped or looked at the two newcomers with surprise. Three of the closest turned to regard the couple, while the man stirring the pan brought the spoon to his lips and blew on it, tasting the contents before making a sound of appreciation. The music continued without faltering.

The man with the long beard was one of those closest. "Welcome, strangers," he finally said, as if not used to speaking.

"We're travelers, far from home, and we were hoping to share your fire," Amber said. "We can pay . . ."

"Sit," the long-bearded man interrupted, indicating a space close to both him and the fire. "Make yourselves warm."

Miro met Amber's eyes and she shrugged imperceptibly. They both walked to the place indicated and seated themselves. Miro sighed, pleased to be off his feet.

The twelve men looked at them curiously, but none of them spoke.

"Thank you for letting us join your fire," Miro said.

"Hmm," the long-bearded man said.

The strange melody danced in the air, and the man with the spoon again squatted near the fire and tasted the food, frowning and then sprinkling some seasoning from a pouch into the pan.

The long-bearded man suddenly spoke. "Don't mind my Brothers. They've never spoken and don't know how. I joined the Order late, so I still remember."

"You don't speak?" Amber said.

"Why would we need to?"

Amber appeared at a loss for words herself. "To communicate . . ."

"There are many ways to communicate. Speech is imperfect, and my Brothers and I prefer to speak with our souls. My soul is still impure, I must confess, for I still crave and enjoy speaking with ones such as yourselves."

Miro realized they'd come across members of a priesthood.

"You said you were travelers," the long-bearded man said. "What is your destination?"

Miro opened his mouth, wondering what to say, when Amber spoke for him.

"We're going to Wengwai," she said. "We need to find the Alchemists' Guild. We need to find a cure for a poison."

"Not for someone close to you, I hope?"

Amber's throat caught. "My son."

The long-bearded man turned sorrowful eyes on Amber. "I am sorry. I hope you find what you are looking for."

"Where are you bound?" Miro asked.

"Wengwai, of course," the long-bearded man said, as if it were obvious.

"Why . . . why are you going to Wengwai?" Amber asked.

"You don't know who we are, do you?"

"We come from lands far from here," Miro said hurriedly.

"We are members of the Order of Flowing Water. We are healers, helpers, musicians, and madmen, or so the common people say. We do not take vows of silence, but we prefer not to speak. We do not eat meat, but we are lovers of food. We do not dance, but we are lovers of music. More than anything, we treat wounds and heal sickness. They say a great darkness is on its way to Wengwai, and many will die. We go wherever we are needed, and perhaps we are needed there."

The long-bearded man seemed to run out of breath after his long speech. His Brothers accompanied his words with nods and smiles, but none said a word.

Miro saw the healer with the large spoon filling wooden bowls. Another brother handed out the bowls and gave one to Miro with a smile. The scent, redolent with herbs and onion, mushroom and nuts, made his mouth water. Amber also held a bowl and two carved spoons, and gave a spoon to Miro with a smile.

Miro began to eat, unable to stop himself. He looked up at the healers, hoping he hadn't offended them, but even the man with the gourd had stopped playing his instrument, and all twelve men were eating with gusto.

Amber swallowed and then turned to the long-bearded healer. "May we travel with you to Wengwai?"

"That depends," he said. "Can you cook?"

Miro saw Amber's eyes light up.

———————

It was pleasant to have company, and the journey north was made lighter by the kind-hearted healers' wild food and strange music, their warm fires, and the knowledge that they were headed in the right direction.

The first time Amber cooked, the healers cleaned every plate, and the next night they silently begged her with their eyes. From then on she was the nominated cook for the group, with the bearded Brothers returning from their evening foraging carrying armfuls of wild onions, herbs, berries, and roots.

Miro couldn't believe these gentle men went wherever battles raged, where violent men fought each other with weapons of death. Their courage was of a kind he'd never encountered before, and his respect for them grew.

"Do you ever fight?" Miro asked the long-bearded man one night. He'd asked the man his name but his question had been met with silence.

"No. Never. It is against our nature."

"What do you do if you're attacked?"

"Why would people attack us? We have no wealth, and we exist only to help."

"People aren't always good."

"Even violent people have good in them. They have simply allowed the darkness to dominate, if only for a time. Who are we to judge which side of a man's nature is stronger, whether on the scales of life he will have given the world more violence than love?"

Miro thought about all the men he'd killed. He had difficulty sleeping that night.

———◆———

The first week saw the group of fourteen make their way through a land of rolling hills and green pastures. Villages and hamlets dotted the landscape, and the road was paved with smooth stones. Gokan was evidently a wealthy nation, with a large farming industry and a mill in every village.

The refugees told another story.

Frequently the party moved to the side of the road to let them pass. They fled in groups large and small, with wagons pulled by lumbering beasts loaded to the point of tilting. These refugees weren't just merchants and nobles—those who could take their wealth with them—their numbers now consisted of poor townsfolk and peasant farmers who'd left everything they had by fleeing from their houses, farms, shops, and mills.

On the eighth night, they were attacked.

It was a small group of men, barely Miro's age, who'd come to see whether the camp had anything worth taking. Miro was familiar with war-torn nations; he knew the sense of chaos provoked young men into thinking their deeds could go unpunished.

As the ruffians challenged the group, their voices coming out of the darkness, Miro came forward. He knew their type. If the camp had consisted of rich merchants, they would have been robbed; and if the party had been made up of women, they would have been raped.

He felt his blood rise, but he remembered Amber's admonishments and recalled the words of the long-bearded healer. These were young toughs with a long life ahead of them. Yes, they were here to do harm to the defenseless, but Miro was a capable warrior. He could send them running but allow them to live.

Miro returned to the camp after ten minutes, out of breath, but with a clean sword.

"I'm proud of you," Amber said later as they lay together beside the fire.

"I hope I did the right thing," Miro said. "What if they go on to harm someone else?"

"They won't. You scared the wits out of them."

"I hope you're right."

Amber reached out and squeezed his hand.

"Wengwai lies ahead," said the long-bearded healer.

Miro squinted, but he couldn't see anything.

"When we turn here, we'll be on the main road."

"I thought we were on the main road," Amber said.

"No, this was just the road connecting Maelan and Wengwai," the healer replied. "The main road travels from Wengwai north to Monapea, capital of Narea, and south to Renton, the main border crossing into Veldria."

"How far?" Miro asked.

"To Wengwai? We'll be there tomorrow. Get some good rest tonight; tomorrow will be a difficult day. Have you ever been close to a battle?"

Amber looked at Miro. "Yes," she said. "We have."

Wary of the refugees, they moved deeper into the forest, but there were cliffs barring further ingress, and they were forced to make camp only an hour's walk from the crossroads.

Miro knew it was their last night with the bearded healers in the blue smocks, and silent as they were, he felt he'd come to know them. Each had a face that was as expressive as a child's. They could raise their eyebrows high or curl their faces into fierce scowls. They might not speak, but they laughed, in great big guffaws and girlish giggles.

That night, Amber made a special meal. She had three pans in the fire simultaneously, working and tasting in a finely orchestrated dance, sprinkling spices here, adding herbs there. She caramelized wild onions and sat the mixture on a flat circle of sliced root she'd baked earlier. After serving the savory morsels, she dished out a stew of mushroom and wild rice, seasoned with herbs and spices, rich and fragrant. To conclude the meal, she ground nuts to make a coarse flour and added water, frying circles of the mixture to make pancakes. Amber topped the cakes with berries, handing them out to each of the healers in turn before giving one to Miro with a smile.

"That was the finest meal I've ever had," said the healer with the long beard, leaning back against a fallen log and rubbing his belly with a sigh. "I could die tomorrow and know I'd lived well and eaten the best."

Amber blushed, and Miro grinned. He stood and walked around the circle, taking each man's bowl and walking down to a nearby stream to wash them.

When he returned, the musician with the gourd was plucking at his strings, filling the air with soothing music. The rest of the healers had fallen asleep around the fire.

Miro chuckled and saw Amber smile up at him.

They would part ways the next day. Miro decided that this was how he would always remember them.

Miro jumped awake with a start, suddenly on his feet as he saw people everywhere. So many of them! They weren't looking for the camp—that much was clear; the camp was simply in the way.

He could see even more people over in the direction of the crossroads. They were all running in the same direction: south. What was happening?

Miro sensed Amber beside him. "Draw your knife," he said, as some running men kicked one of the logs that lay over the fire, sending sparks in all directions. "Be prepared."

Miro held Amber close as he led her up a slight rise beside the encampment, near some trees where they would be out of the way of the frantic men and women.

A group of soldiers came out of the trees, running with the others, holding the barest amount of discipline together. There were at least twenty of them.

Miro swore. "Deserters. They'll be dangerous."

"Stop," one of the soldiers ordered his fellows. "We're on the run now—you all know that." He gestured to the camp. "We need food, blankets, gilden—whatever they've got."

Awake now, most of the Brothers were standing, faces showing confusion. They moved closer together while the soldiers searched the camp.

"No food," said one of the soldiers.

"Just a few blankets," said another.

"You," the leader said, pointing at one of the bearded healers. "Where's your food?"

"He's a Brother of the Order," a soldier said. "He won't answer you."

The leader spotted Miro standing with Amber nearby. "These people aren't brothers. Search them."

Miro knew there were too many soldiers for him to take on alone. He wondered whether they would be able to talk their way out of the situation.

The long-bearded healer suddenly walked forward and shoved the leader from behind. "Run!" he cried.

Miro had no choice. He took Amber's hand and ran.

Looking over his shoulder, he saw the leader of the deserters stumble and then spin on his heel, an expression of rage on his face. His sword cut through the healer's chest, sending a spray of blood into the hair of his long beard. Some of the soldiers turned to give chase, but others channeled the fear they all felt into anger. More of the Brothers were cut down by the scared deserters.

Miro held Amber's hand as they ducked and weaved past both trees and running people. He knew if he let go of her hand, Amber would be swept away by the fleeing Gokani. They reached the crossroads, heaving and panting, but there was no one behind them.

"The Brothers!" Amber cried. "Did you see if they escaped?"

Miro thought about the bright splash of red he'd seen as he looked over his shoulder. He knew from experience that when scared men saw blood, their fear would intensify.

"I'm sure they'll be fine," Miro lied.

31

The main road to Wengwai was wide and level, with sloped fields of grass at both edges. This close to the Gokani capital, the smooth stones had been laid in a pattern of alternating colors, pleasing to the eye and easy on the foot.

Today, the stones of the main road could hardly be seen through the river of people, all heading in the same direction: to the border crossing at Renton and the perceived safety of Veldria.

Miro and Amber didn't try to travel on the road, instead keeping to the sloped terrain at the side. It seemed they were the only ones heading to, rather than from, Wengwai.

"How can there be so many of them?" Amber asked.

"I don't think they're all Gokani. See? The Gokani wear fitted clothing, carefully stitched. The women often wear those pointed hats with tassels, like that woman over there. A lot of these other people must be from Narea. They would be the ones with the furs. The emir said Narea was a large nation, with Gokan small in comparison."

"So the people of two nations are heading south."

"It looks that way."

The long-bearded healer had said they would be at Wengwai before nightfall, but Miro hadn't asked how far away that meant they were. Then, around noon, directly ahead he saw a large hill in the middle of a plain, with irrigated farmland on all sides.

As he grew closer, he saw it wasn't a hill; it was a city.

"I think that's it," Amber said. "It must be Wengwai."

Wengwai, capital of Gokan, had obviously been built with defense in mind. A thick wall the height of twenty men encircled the city, and round towers marked regular intervals along the wall's length. The buildings within the walls rose in tiers, an effect achieved by each inner ring of structures being a story higher than its neighboring ring. In the center of the city rose an immense tower. It was the tallest tower Miro had ever seen.

Miro and Amber were forced to walk through farmland while the fleeing people thronged the road. In the distance Miro saw Wengwai's huge gates standing wide open, facing onto the main road. The gates were several feet thick, made of hard wood bound with iron.

"What do we do now?" Amber asked.

"The Alchemists' Guild has its headquarters in there," Miro said. "We go in."

At that moment a horn blasted, the sound reverberating through the distant hills, so low that Miro could feel it in his stomach. The sound came from the city.

"What was that?" Miro asked when the horn blast finally faded away.

"Lord of the Sky," Amber breathed, grabbing hold of Miro's arm. "Look!"

Miro saw a distant dust cloud in the north, unmistakably caused by the steps of a great many feet. The cloud grew larger and closer, and Miro now saw the tops of siege towers poking above it. The billowing dust came from the north, extending from one end of the horizon to the other, moving to encircle the city within its arms.

The barbarian horde was here.

The horn sounded again, the intensity of the blast setting Miro's teeth on edge. The city's massive gates began to close.

Instantly, the people on the road began to scream. They were too late to get away now; anyone heading south on the main road would be caught in the horde's grip.

"Can we make it?" Amber gasped.

"We have to. Run!"

The road was now the scene of chaos as the mob turned around, fighting each other as they tried to reach the city before the swinging gates closed. Miro pushed and weaved, his muscles tensed as he held Amber's hand in a grip of iron.

A little girl fell down in front of them and Miro bent down, encircling her chest with his free arm and picking her up. He looked around for the girl's parents, but all he could see were desperate faces twisted in fear, eyes wide and staring at the closing gates.

Miro held the girl to his chest and ran with the mob, holding on to Amber with all his strength. Through the crowd he saw a man go down, tumbling and screaming as he was trampled by the feet of the throng. There was nothing he could do.

The gates were more than halfway closed, and they had only halved the distance to the city.

"We need to go faster," Miro gasped, turning to Amber. "Get back onto the side of the road."

Still holding the little girl to his chest, he pulled Amber through the crowd until they popped out onto the muddied remnants of farmland. The mud sucked at his feet, but with his long legs and the improved space Miro was able to make faster time. He felt Amber struggling behind him—she didn't have his long stride—and used his strength to pull her through the more difficult parts.

They were now a hundred paces from the huge gates, and then fifty. "Back onto the road!" Miro shouted.

He pushed once more into the crowd and saw there was now only a thin crack between the gates.

If they didn't make it into the city, Miro knew they would never find the Alchemists' Guild.

He lunged and shoved, holding the little girl close and keeping his grip on Amber tight. The distance between the gates was less than two feet.

Miro gave a great push, and turned sideways, sliding through the open gate. Amber! He felt her grip on his hand loosen, but he held firm and pulled, heaving her through the tiny gap, feeling her make it only the barest instant before the gates pushed together.

Miro felt rough hands pull him forward as soldiers cleared him away from the gates.

They'd made it.

"Lora!" he heard a cry, and a thin woman with a tasseled hat came running toward him, her arms outstretched. Miro held the little girl out to the woman, who swept her up as tears ran down her face. "Thank you!" the woman cried.

Miro gave her a shaky smile.

———————

The barbarian horde had moved incredibly fast. Emir Volkan had said they wouldn't make it this far south; their supply lines would be stretched too far.

Yet here they were, and Wengwai was now a city under siege.

The great army drew closer as the day progressed, until they spread toward the city walls like an encroaching tide. Miro climbed up to the walls, ignored by the soldiers as he watched the approach. The tall walls were too high for Miro to see individual soldiers, but he saw siege ladders and siege towers, trebuchets and catapults. The soldiers below marched in close formation, squares of troops in tight files forming larger squares, leaving gaps between them so messengers and supplies could move easily through the army.

"This is no barbarian horde," Miro whispered as he looked on from atop the city wall.

He counted along one of the rows: fifty men. He counted perhaps forty men deep. Miro calculated that one of their smaller squares held two thousand men.

Miro counted ten of the smaller squares forming a larger row. Four of the larger rows, one behind the other, made up the army's front. The depth was impossible to see; there were simply too many of them.

Farther beyond that, a cloud of dust obscured his vision.

Miro marveled as he gave up counting: there had to be well over a hundred thousand fighting men.

How could the enemy commander feed, clothe, and control such a large number of men? The logistics would be a nightmare.

Miro watched until the sun began to set in the west; tomorrow the attack would come. He clambered down from the wall, to find Amber resting against the stone, chatting with a group of other women.

"What did you see?" she asked.

"Come on," Miro said. "Let's walk."

Amber stood and soon they were navigating the orderly chaos of a city under siege. Boys ran with buckets of water to the walls. Fathers carried children through the inner gates to the next ring of buildings. Soldiers pulled carts loaded with swords and barrels of what could only be black powder.

"What did you learn from the women?" Miro asked.

"The elector of Gokan and his councilors administer the city from the tower, which occupies the innermost ring. It's called the Eye. That plume of red smoke rising from the Eye is an attempt to summon aid from Veldria."

Miro thought about the emir's soldiers, back at the border. "They'll never make it in time," he grunted. "This city will be overrun before the emir can give the order."

"You think it'll be that quick?"

"Yes. We're in a doomed city, Amber."

"There are seven rings, their equivalent of districts. The Eye occupies the first, and the Alchemists' Guild is in the second," said Amber.

"Good. We need to get out of here as soon as we can. Once we get what we need from the alchemists, we'll work on a plan of escape."

"What about your promise to the emir?" Amber said. "We owe it to our people to find out what's happening here."

Miro cursed. "I know. I also know that time is against us. As the siege progresses, it'll be more difficult to get out. Amber, we'll have to split up. You find the Alchemists' Guild and get the antidote."

"What will you do?"

"There's one place I can be sure to get a good vantage of events as they occur. I'm going to join the soldiers on the walls."

There were seven concentric tiers to the city, which meant Amber had to pass through five sets of gates to get from the walls to the second ring, the location of the Alchemists' Guild.

The first gate was easily traversed; she simply walked through, just another woman returning after final words to her man on the walls. This was a poor district of storehouses, tanneries, and carpenters, along with rows of single-storied cottages, joined together so that they each shared a wall.

There was a single guard at the second gate, casually checking the people passing through. Amber was dirty, but she was dressed in the quality garments the emir had given them, and the guard let her through without a word.

The city's builders had placed each set of gates at a reasonable distance around the circle from the gate before it, most likely deliberately. It meant Amber had to walk around each ring to reach the next gate, rather than the gates being lined up in a neat row, but she guessed it was a safety feature. In the event that a district was overrun, the enemy would have to pass through a killing ground before reaching the next gate.

Amber was now in the fifth ring from the Eye, with three more gates to enter. This was a district of markets and stalls, but today the stalls weren't placed in neat rows and displaying colorful wares; today they had been pulled over and onto their sides, crammed together to form barricades.

As she walked along the ring in a counterclockwise direction, heading for the next gate, Amber passed six sets of barricades. The rows of two-story terraced houses evidently belonged to the local merchants, who looked down at the barricades from their windows. Amber wondered what was going through their minds.

"Do you live in Fairview?" one of the four soldiers who barred the gate to the fourth ring asked Amber.

"My sister," Amber said, thinking furiously.

"Is she as pretty as you?" another guard quipped.

Amber tried for a coquettish smile.

One of his fellows pulled a face. "Don't mind him. You can pass."

Her heart racing, Amber passed the four guards and entered the next district, evidently called Fairview.

It was a residential area, with well-to-do houses joined together in rows. Each house had three stories, with a small garden on the lowest level, a wide balcony on the first floor, and a tiny balcony under the window on the highest floor. It was a pleasant area, with clean gutters and paved white stones underfoot. Yet, like the others, the inhabitants of Fairview were scared.

A group of well-dressed young men, their jaws set in determination, headed past Amber, in the direction of the walls. Older men also pushed past, some holding swords, others wearing antiquated armor or holding hunting bows.

Amber stopped a red-eyed woman who held a basket of oranges in her hands. "Can you tell me which way it is to the next inner gate?"

"Clockwise," the red-eyed woman said. "Please, will you help me take some oranges to the walls? The men are going to need them. The more we take tonight, the more they'll have when the attack comes tomorrow."

"I'm sorry," Amber said, feeling wretched. "There's something important I need to do."

The red-eyed woman's face twisted. "I'll bet if you had a man on the walls you'd help me."

"I do," Amber said.

Suddenly it came to her, the danger these people were in. The danger Miro was in. She saw the defeat in this woman's reddened eyes; she knew they were doomed. This army had conquered Narea, by all accounts a much more powerful nation. Gokan didn't stand a chance, yet Miro would be on the walls even now, looking down at the horde, perhaps even facing them when morning came.

These weren't Amber's people; this wasn't her and Miro's fight. Amber needed to find the Guild, and Miro needed to find something out about who this leader was. Then they needed to get out of here as quickly as they could.

"I'm sorry," the red-eyed woman said, and Amber realized she'd stopped and put her hand over her mouth. "I really am. I'm so sorry.

My husband is there too. The inner gate is clockwise from here. They won't let you in, though—not unless you're a noble or have a pass from a noble."

"I must get in," Amber said. "I have to!"

"Wait," the woman said. "Put out your hand." She set down her basket and pulled something from her finger, placing it on Amber's outstretched palm. It was a ring, undeniably precious, set with sparkling red and blue stones. "Lord Byron gave me this once. It's a long story, but he said it belonged to his mother. The pattern of stones is the mark of House Byron. If you show it to the guards, they'll let you through."

"How can I thank you?"

The red-eyed woman shrugged. "What use is it now?" She squeezed Amber's shoulder. "Good luck," she said, picking up her basket and heading for the walls.

Following her directions, Amber traveled in a clockwise direction, passing the manicured gardens and glowing windows of the district the guard had called Fairview, walking hurriedly until she saw the gate that led to the third ring. If she made it through this gate, she would be only one gate away from the Guild.

The sun had long gone, and twilight now faded into night, a time when most people would be eating their evening meal. Amber wondered if this would help her or make her task more difficult.

There were eight guards, all well armed and alert. Amber guessed the man with the stripes on his shoulders was the officer, and rather than allowing herself to be challenged, she went directly to him.

"Lord Byron said I was to show you this and you would let me through," Amber said. She held out the ring the woman had given her, holding her breath.

"What's your business in the Parklands?"

Amber paused and looked up, as if remembering words she'd been taught. "I'm to tell Lord Byron his son is well and misses him. The officers are looking after him, and he's settled in for the night."

"Oh," the officer said, making way for Amber to get past, "I see."

He handed Amber back the ring, and she nodded and smiled as she passed the guards and entered between the open arms of the ornate gate.

Then she heard a voice behind her. "Wait a minute, Captain. Lord Byron doesn't have a son."

The officer cursed as Amber burst into a run. "Stop her!"

Amber had spent the day running, but she forced fatigued muscles into action, her desperation spurring her on. Behind her she heard the heavy boots of the soldiers as they chased her, and she looked for somewhere to hide.

Tomas needed her. Miro needed her.

True to its name, the Parklands was a district of sprawling manses and public gardens. Amber ran past a brightly lit park and then two large manors, each at least four stories high. There was another park on her right, this time large and dark enough to hide in.

Amber put on an extra burst of speed as she dug her foot into the ground and made a hard right turn. She ran past large clumps of bushes and groves of trees. When she sensed the trees were between her and the soldiers, she forked to the left, and when she jumped over a small canal, she turned right again.

Finally, she passed a series of flowerbeds and then a long hedge. Amber threw herself into the hedge, heedless of the scratching undergrowth and lay still.

Her breath came in heaves, and she fought to slow the rise and fall of her chest. Sweat dripped down from her brow, and her heart galloped in fits and starts.

Amber listened intently. She heard the voices of men calling out to each other. One of the soldiers came close at one point; she could see his form silhouetted against the light of the distant avenue. He turned and walked away.

She stayed hidden in the bushes until exhaustion overtook her. Sleep overcame her senses, and she didn't stir until dawn.

32

Miro woke with the dawn, hearing groans and moans around him as the male citizens of Wengwai, young and old, also woke and realized this was likely their final morning.

The deep horn blasted in one long note, the deafening sound emanating from the tall tower called the Eye, making Miro's stomach tremble in strange ways. No one would be sleeping now.

Miro looked out from the walls. The dust cloud had settled, and now for the first time he could encompass the incredible multitude below. The enemy commander had brought his siege weapons forward, he saw. Any moment, they would attack.

Miro looked along the line of the wall. The battlements were perhaps twenty paces deep, and the wall was long, encircling the entire city. Miro had experience at holding a long line; he could see that there weren't enough Gokani soldiers to man these walls.

He looked back at the city. The next inner wall was perhaps five paces deep. If the elector of Gokan, or whoever was leading the defenders, were wise, he would pull the men back to the next wall at the first sign of trouble. The attackers would be forced to leave their siege towers outside the main wall, and the line of defenders would be stronger with a smaller area to cover.

Miro snorted. What was the point of tactics, facing so many, so disciplined, and so prepared for a siege? The city would fall.

Miro glanced at the closest of Wengwai's round towers, situated at regular intervals along the walls. He wondered what effect the huge brass cannon placed atop each of the towers would have.

How could he discover who led the horde?

The ground began to tremble, and gazing from the height of the wall, Miro saw the great army, miniscule as ants, start to march.

He looked at the Gokani soldier beside him, a young lad barely more than a boy. He was terrified. Wetness appeared on his trousers, but he didn't seem to have noticed.

Miro allowed his own fear to feed his rage. Why did people wage war? Weeks ago the Gokani had been trading and farming, falling in love and raising families. All of the nations in the north had been destroyed by the horde. Two nations remained: Gokan and Veldria.

This continent was as large as his own, and it was about to be overrun.

The enemy marched forward with strange, jerky movements. As distant as they were, Miro couldn't see their faces, but he could see that some held swords, and others, axes. A few held muskets, the sticklike devices he'd encountered when they'd fallen prey to Commodore Deniz and his men. There were also men with clubs and staves, and strangely, there were women in the ranks.

Many in the horde were dressed in furs and skins, with horned helmets and ragged beards; these must be the barbarians from Oltara and Muttara. Others were clad in fine clothes. It made no sense; the different peoples were mixed up together, where usually people of the same nation would fight together. Few wore armor.

The cannon on the tower near Miro boomed, and a puff of smoke rose into the air. The shot was like the first drop of rain in a storm, and the cannon all around opened fire. The noise was deafening. Miro held his hands clapped to his ears and watched the devastation begin below.

Every strike was a hit; the gunners couldn't miss. With incredible force the huge balls of lead struck the plains below, flurries of dirt and pieces of men flying into the air in their wake. Each ball tore a gouge in the sea of men like a scratch on a painting.

Miro expected some of the enemy to break, but not a man did. They simply closed ranks and continued to move forward in tight formation.

Near the front of the army were eight tall siege towers, their frameworks built from strong logs lashed together. The towers rolled on huge wooden wheels and consisted of wooden boxes placed one on top of another, with the topmost box having a hinged door at the height of the walls. Miro could see each tower filled to bursting with men.

The towers lumbered forward, each about five hundred paces from the next. Behind them Miro could see clusters of trebuchets, scores of them, rolling forward with the soldiers. At this range they would devastate the walls. The attackers carried thousands of ladders, incredibly long, to reach the top of the ramparts. The cannon boomed again and again, but there were too many targets.

"Concentrate on the siege towers!" a voice called, relayed from one guard post to the next. The cannon opened up on the siege towers, one scoring a lucky hit. Then Miro heard a sound that stopped the entire battle.

"*Halt!*" The voice boomed in the air like a thunderclap, impossibly loud.

The marching force below stopped in its tracks, only a few hundred paces from the walls. Cannon rumbled but then petered out. The siege towers stopped rolling. The defenders on the walls held their breath.

Miro saw a single figure walk forward through the horde. Although they were pressed together shoulder to shoulder, a pathway parted for him, and he walked alone. He drew in line with the towers and walked past them, until he was in front of the mass of men.

From his vantage, Miro saw a tall figure in a black shirt and trousers, with hair the color of blood.

Miro watched in awe as the man looked up to the top of the wall. The man spread his arms to his sides and rose into the air.

The defenders gasped, the sound audible to all, as every one of them watched the figure in black rise until he was level with the wall, and then higher, until his body loomed high over the horde below. The defenders' heads tilted back, and he stopped, looking down at them from above and floating easily.

He was clad in soft black material, perhaps velvet, rich and tailored to his slim form. His long sleeves opened at the wrists; silver sparkled at his cuffs and from a stone around his neck. He gazed down at the defenders with an icy stare, a sneer of condescension on his face. The hair was pulled severely back from his brow and bloodred, with strange streaks of black at the temples.

"Lord of the Sky, protect us," Miro breathed.

The man's lips parted, and when he spoke, his voice was somehow amplified so that it carried to every last defender, every last woman and child. His first words sent a chill down Miro's spine.

"My name is Sentar Scythran," he said in a tone as dead as the grave. "I am the Lord of the Night."

Miro closed his eyes. His worst nightmare had come true.

"I am your new ruler, and I will conquer your land, as I have conquered the north. Stronger men have failed to stop me. Braver men have failed. You will fail."

The young recruit near Miro moaned with fear.

"Surrender your city now. You have no chance. Surrender your city, and I will give you your reward."

"We'll never surrender!" a voice cried, and an arrow shot into the air. Perfectly aimed, its razor point flew faster than a bird.

The arrow bounced harmlessly off the Lord of the Night, splintering into fragments as it hit his body.

He carried on without interruption. "Fight, and when I take this city you will all be killed. Every last man, woman, and child will die, as I visit the same fate on you I have visited on realms more powerful than yours. Fight, and I will kill your disgusting babes and your sniveling children, and laugh as I do. Fight, and the last thing you will hear is your mate screaming your name as the blood drips from your veins."

The floating man in black clothing paused, allowing his words to sink in.

"Surrender," Sentar continued, "and I will spare your precious women and children. Your men will die, but you may take comfort knowing that your city will stand, a lingering remnant of your civilization. It is the only comfort I offer, and I suggest you take it."

Even through his horror at the man's words, Miro wondered that for all his power, Sentar was making this offer. Perhaps the one who called himself the Lord of the Night wasn't as confident of victory as Miro expected him to be. Perhaps he was instilling fear in those below. If that were the case, from the expressions Miro saw on the men around him, it was working.

Or perhaps Sentar Scythran was simply in a hurry.

A crack signaled a musket shot, but like the arrow, the ball bounced harmlessly off the floating man in black. A second musket fired, and then a third. A volley of weapons fired simultaneously, the shots bouncing off the Lord of the Night like hail.

These people had no lore. They were facing an army led by one of the Evermen. They didn't have a chance.

Sentar looked over the defenders, his lip curled in a sneer. "I have my answer. Prepare to die."

He floated slowly back to the ground, until he once again stood at the head of his huge army. He raised an arm, and the warriors below cried out in one voice, a sound of rage and triumph. It was eerie, the synchronicity of their cry. Miro had led men into battle on more than one occasion, and he knew how men behaved. Something here was not normal.

"*Cannon!*" Miro heard the order.

Sentar waved his arm forward, and the army surged ahead, covering the final distance in seconds. Ladders rose up to lean against the walls, the defenders waiting until their rungs were filled with climbing men before pushing them away with pole-arms. The siege towers rolled inevitably forward.

Miro gripped his sword as a ladder touched the top of the wall in front of him. A Gokani came rushing forward with a pole-arm and shoved it away, but another ladder took its place, and then another. Soon there were five ladders on the small patch of wall, and the man with the pole-arm couldn't keep up.

Miro longed to help, but he knew that now it was clear who was leading them, he should find Amber and flee, if it was still even possible to do so.

He looked at the sword in his hand, wishing it were a zenblade.

Miro turned to depart the walls.

The young recruit nearby cried out in fear, and Miro suddenly couldn't leave. Every part of his being screamed for him to fight; he couldn't leave this boy to face his enemy alone.

Miro faced the ladders as they trembled under the weight of climbing men. A hand reached the top rung and an enemy warrior came forward, a barbarian by his horned helmet.

He clambered up onto the wall and then stared directly at Miro, the whites of his eyes sending a cold stab into Miro's heart.

Miro realized then what he'd been looking at but had been too blind to see. His gaze swept to the left and the right, where more of the enemy climbed ladders and poured over the walls.

They were all revenants.

The largest army Miro had ever seen was an army of revenants.

Everything clicked into place. Sentar Scythran had somehow built the vats and used some of the dead to create essence. He'd used that essence to create revenants, and with his revenants beside him, he'd killed ever larger groups of people. Some of those people fed the vats, and others became even more revenants.

He'd continued doing this until he'd conquered the barbarian nation of Oltara, and by then he was unstoppable. Muttara fell next, and soon every barbarian was either feeding the vats or in his thrall. The next to fall was Narea, unable to halt the onslaught of a barbarian horde that was already dead.

Miro had seen bladesingers struggle to defeat overwhelming numbers of revenants. With no lore, all of the people of this continent were doomed.

The army of the Lord of the Night was like a plague, feeding on those they killed and growing larger in the process, in a cycle that wouldn't end until Sentar Scythran stood inside the Sentinel and opened the way for his brothers to return. He wouldn't stop until every last human on the face of Merralya was dead or enslaved.

Miro shook himself out of his reverie as the nearby cannon boomed, tearing the revenants below into pieces, but they were inhuman, exhibiting neither fear nor hesitation.

Then the enemy trebuchets let loose, huge stones flying between the approaching siege towers.

A boulder hit the wall in front of Miro's feet.

The five ladders splintered in a heartbeat, tearing to pieces the barbarian warrior in front of Miro.

A piece of the wall hit the young recruit, his chest caving in and blood gushing from his mouth.

Miro was lifted from his feet as the entire section of wall exploded into the air.

33

Hidden somewhere deep in the Parklands, Amber heard the great horn call the men to their stations. She felt the ground tremble as the huge army marched toward the city walls. When the Lord of the Night spoke, she heard his words.

Exiting the hedge where she'd spent the night, Amber scanned the area. Now was the time to enter through the final gate and gain entrance to the second tier, the home of the alchemists. They now knew who led the enemy; Amber had to find the Guild.

She picked a direction and started walking, finding the road and following the district in a counterclockwise route, figuring that the last couple of turns had been clockwise.

She saw it instantly, a ramped pathway that split in the middle, the left-hand side continuing high to the innermost circle, where the great tower called the Eye loomed down on the city below. The right side of the sloping path leveled off, taking the visitor away from the district called the Parklands and to the area the Alchemists' Guild called home.

Even from this distance, Amber heard shouts and screams, and prayed Miro would be safe.

Guards stood at the foot of the sloped path leading to the last two gates, but they ran back up toward the Eye even as Amber approached, ignoring her. She stepped onto the path; like the main road, it displayed a colorful pattern of interlocking stones, and its builders must have possessed a striking ingenuity, for it lifted off the ground seemingly without support.

Amber's determined footsteps took her to the lower path as the other side rose to dizzying heights. Ahead of her, six soldiers in black uniforms watched her approach. Each bore the emblem of the triangle enclosed within a circle on his breast.

"I need to speak with someone from the Guild," Amber said simply.

"Who are you?" one of the soldiers in black said.

Crashes and booms started as the enemy commenced a great bombardment of the walls. Amber closed her eyes. She opened them and looked directly at the soldier who had spoken.

"I'm an enchantress of Altura, from across the sea, far from here. I can tell your masters something of the nature of what we are facing. Your people may understand technology, but I understand lore."

The soldiers exchanged glances. Finally the leader made a decision and assigned two men to take Amber farther along the path.

Amber approached a huge structure of red stone, encircling the Eye like a wheel. Her escorts took her inside an open doorway and into a featureless corridor, slightly curved to follow the building's arc. Stairs led both up and down, and doors were set into the walls on both sides.

The soldiers led Amber to a bare room, with just two seats and a table, and told her to wait. She heard the guards lock the door behind her. A mirror on the wall showed Amber how she looked: haggard, worn, and filled with fear.

As she waited, she tried not to think about Miro. She knew their chances of making it out of Wengwai alive were slim.

The door opened, and a man in a black robe entered. He bore the same symbol of a circle bound by a triangle on his robe, and his hair was gray, his eyes dark. He took a seat without a word and looked down a hooked nose at Amber.

"Who are you?" he inquired.

"My name is Amber."

"Where are you from?"

"I come from Altura."

"And where is Altura?"

"Across the sea, a great distance to the east."

The alchemist snorted. "Pish. There's no such place."

Amber glared at the alchemist. "I thought your Alchemists' Guild was supposed to have all the knowledge. At least I have the pleasure of seeing I was wrong."

"You said you're an enchantress. What, pray tell, is that?"

Amber took a breath, calming herself. She reminded herself she needed this man's help. "An enchantress uses lore to give items special properties. An enchantress might, for example, draw runes on a stone to project light. We call this a nightlamp. This is just one example . . ."

Amber looked at the alchemist's sardonic expression and realized he was making sport with her. "Lord of the Sky," she whispered, "your city is falling down around your ears, and you're holed up in your castle with nothing better to do than make fun of me."

There was a knock on the door, and with an expression of irritation the alchemist stood up and turned the handle. He muttered angrily with someone for a few minutes.

"Wait here," he said before once more leaving Amber alone.

Amber wondered how the soldiers on the walls were faring. The thick stone blocked the sounds of the cannon, but she knew that out there people were dying.

The door opened, and looking up, Amber saw a different alchemist this time. He was older, with shaggy gray eyebrows and kind eyes. The triangle on his robe was bound by a double circle.

"Amber," he said in a quiet, winded voice. "Please come with me."

Amber followed the old alchemist out of the room and down a curling set of stairs.

"Who are you?" Amber asked to break the silence.

"My name is Tungawa. I have to apologize for Mendak. He knows nothing of your people."

"He's rude."

Tungawa chuckled. "Yes, rude he may be." He glanced at Amber. "But he is also brave and has volunteered to stay here in our chapter to the very end. When the enemy comes, which they will, he will ignite a device and ensure our knowledge is kept from the hands of evil."

"What about you? Will you stay to the end?"

"Most of my fellow Guild members have long departed. Some fight on the walls, and others have sworn to make the taking of our chapter a costly venture. A few, such as myself, stay because we need to learn more about those we face. When the time comes, I will offer my services to the enemy, and I will keep my eyes and ears open. Perhaps the opportunity may come to learn this enemy's weakness and bring the knowledge to those who can best put it to advantage."

"Isn't that risky?"

The stairs wound down until Amber thought they must now be below ground level.

"Not as much as you may think. The Guild has knowledge that this Lord of the Night doesn't possess. We did work for him once, before we knew his true nature, much as we've worked for gold for many others. He needed us then. He will have use for us now."

"Do you know what he is?"

Tungawa met Amber's gaze. "He is one of the Evermen, is he not?"

Amber sighed. "I'd been hoping to exchange that knowledge for something I need." She wondered how she would get the alchemist to help her now.

The stairway finally ended, and Tungawa pushed open a door, gesturing for Amber to enter. As her eyes adjusted to the low light ahead of her, she saw she was in a cavernous storeroom rivaling any of the huge storehouses she'd seen in Ralanast.

Shelves filled the interior from one end to the other. From where she stood, Amber saw leather-bound books and brown paper packets, bottles filled with colored liquids and jars containing powders.

"Where are you taking me?"

Tungawa walked ahead of her. "Come," he said, "there is a passage from here that will take you out of the city."

Amber abruptly stopped.

Tungawa turned, surprised. "This is why you came here, is it not? You guessed we would have a way out of the city, and you came here hoping to share your knowledge for this secret."

"No," Amber said. "That's not why I'm here. I'm here because someone from your order built a device for our enemy. This device was not just an explosive; it was built to release a poison as part of the blast. The device looked like a golden shrine, but in actuality was timed to explode at a certain hour of a certain day." Amber felt the anger rise to her cheeks and wetness burn behind her eyes. "That day was my wedding day, and that poison took my son. I'm here to find the antidote, and I won't leave without it."

"Why would he attack your wedding?" Tungawa whispered.

"You know about this?"

"I told you we did work for him once, before we knew his true nature. A man in a gray robe came to us with gold. He gave us his requirements, and we accepted his money. We took the device down to the river, and more men in gray robes loaded it aboard a strange ship with a strange name . . . The *Icebreaker*, I think it was. A man watched and waited nearby, staring at me with eyes that sent a chill through my body. That was the first time I saw Sentar Scythran."

"It was you!" Amber said.

Something inside Amber snapped, and her arm lashed out. She slapped the old alchemist across his face as hard as she could. A tear spilled out of her eye as she moved to hit him again.

Tungawa caught her wrist. "I suppose I deserve that." He sighed, rubbing his face with his other hand. "I know it is no consolation, but we've learnt our mistake. Please follow me," Tungawa said, releasing her hand and turning away.

He led Amber along one of the rows between shelves, and then turned sharply, moving so quickly she had difficulty keeping up. He finally stopped at a shelf no different in appearance from the others. He took a flask from the shelf and handed it to Amber. From the sloshing sound, Amber knew it contained liquid.

"Here," he said. "Remember, everything is a poison, there is poison in everything. Only the dose makes a thing not a poison. Never more than one mouthful each day until his health is improved. When the spots leave his fingernails, cease treatment immediately."

Amber looked at the flask in her hand. She couldn't believe they'd come this far and now she had it. *Please let Tomas be alive to receive his cure!*

"I would thank you," Amber said, "but I'll save that for when my son is well again. Can you show me how to get back to the city? I need to get to the walls."

"Are you sure that's where you want to be? Past this chamber is a way out of the city."

"Yes, I'm sure. I need to find my husband."

The first sensation Miro felt was pain as consciousness slowly returned. He ached from head to toe, but the strongest pain came from his temple and his left arm. His right eye was crusted shut, but he managed to open his left eye enough to see.

He'd awakened in a pile of dead bodies. He didn't know how he'd come to be thrown with the mangled corpses of the fallen defenders. Someone must have thought him dead and thrown him in the heap.

Miro couldn't hear anything, just a constant ringing in his ears. He tasted the metallic flavor of blood in his mouth and ran his tongue across a loose tooth.

An armored soldier lay across his chest, and another Gokani covered his legs. He tried to move but knew it would be some time before he could wriggle out from underneath the bodies.

After a while the ringing in his ears faded, and he heard screams and cries, shouts of rage and moans of agony. Tilting his head back, he could see the clear blue sky, and it wasn't until he turned his face further to the left that he could see part of the battle unfolding.

He saw soldiers fighting revenants, their faces filled with fear as they battled decayed corpses with white eyes, corpses that needed to be hacked into pieces to keep down. Miro heard a great crash, like a wooden door slamming open, and suddenly the wall he watched swarmed with revenants, too many of them to count, easily outnumbering the defenders.

A man in black robes ran forward, an alchemist by the emblem on his breast. He threw a flask into the midst of the revenant warriors, and flame rolled forward in a boiling red cloud. A revenant came from behind the alchemist and a sword suddenly protruded from the black robe, jutting out from the man's chest and then disappearing, releasing a gush of blood.

Miro struggled but still couldn't find the strength in his limbs to get up.

The horn blared, two long blasts sounding from the soaring tower in the middle of the city. "Back to the next wall!" soldiers took up the cry. "Retreat to the next wall!"

The few soldiers Miro could see on this section of wall turned to flee but were cut down from behind. Miro watched the rest of the Gokani falling back. Some brave men at one of the cannon posts stayed to the end, sending shot after shot at a distant target below. When the revenants arrived, a final explosion ensured they destroyed both the cannon and themselves rather than let it fall into their enemy's hands.

The retreat was now nearly complete. The enemy now held the thick outer walls, aiming some of the surviving cannon back toward the city.

Miro froze when a steady stream of white-eyed warriors ran past the pile where he lay. He fought to give his eyes the steady look of death as revenant after revenant passed.

Amber was inside the inner walls while Miro now lay on the outside of the remaining defenses, wondering what to do.

———

The gate posts were unmanned now, and Amber ran through the deserted residential district of Fairview, desperate to find Miro on the walls so they could flee this terrible place.

She passed through the gate leading to the area of merchant stalls, where the barricades formed one of the last defenses against the enemy.

There was already fighting at the barricades.

Amber stopped running and put her hand to her mouth. A handful of Gokani soldiers held back an unstoppable tide of the enemy. At a mutual signal they turned and ran from a barricade to regroup and form a defense at the next. The barbarians cut down the soldiers as they fled, and now there were that many fewer defenders to man the next station.

High on the walls on both sides, archers shot arrow after arrow into the horde. Alchemists in black robes threw explosive flasks into the attackers' midst; these seemed to have a greater effect than the arrows.

As Amber watched transfixed, the defenders fell back to the next set of barricades, directly ahead.

"Miro," Amber whispered.

The tall outer walls had been overrun more quickly than she would have thought possible. Miro was one of the best swordsmen she'd ever seen. Surely he was fine? But swords couldn't stop cannon. Nor could they stop . . .

"Revenants," Amber breathed. "Lord of the Sky, no."

"What are you doing?" a soldier manning the final barricade cried at her. "Run!"

Amber drew the thin blade from her boot. She would have given anything for her green silk dress and an enchanted blade.

The soldier who had told Amber to run was swiftly decapitated by a barbarian warrior, a revenant whose decayed lips gave him a permanent grin.

With a surge the barricade was overrun, and with moans and cries, the revenants swarmed ahead.

Amber turned. The gate she'd just passed through was behind her. She needed to close it and give the defenders whatever chance she could.

She started to run, sensing the rushing attackers behind her, feeling their stench on her neck. The gate was fifty paces more, then forty. Amber turned to look back.

She wasn't going to make it.

A snarling woman was the first of the horde to reach Amber. The woman's throat had been sliced open, probably when she was first killed, for the cut was old and the skin around the wound was crusted and dry.

Amber held her stiletto in front of her, preparing to strike, noting her shaking hand.

She thrust out, piercing the woman's breast, and the force of the revenant's momentum took her further onto the blade.

But the white-eyed woman displayed no reaction. Amber tried to withdraw the blade to strike again, when she felt a club strike the side of her head with a force that belied the woman's thin arms. Stars burst behind Amber's eyes.

Amber went down.

34

By late afternoon the battle was won. Sentar Scythran had conquered the great city of Wengwai in a single day.

The defenders fought bravely from gate to gate, ring to ring, inflicting a heavy toll on the enemy, with each defender fighting to his last breath. But the numbers of the indomitable revenants were too great, they were too hard to destroy, and support from Veldria never came.

With one final gasp of defiance, the innermost circle of red stone where the Alchemists' Guild had their chapter exploded as it was overrun, taking thousands of revenants in the blast. The detonation filled the sky with smoke, and thunder rolled across the plains below the city. The soaring tower called the Eye slowly leaned and ponderously toppled, before crashing down on the city below, crushing still more of the enemy as it fell.

Wengwai, the beating heart of Gokan, was no more.

During the final stages of the battle, Miro managed to free himself from the pile of corpses, finding his sword in the process. Checking himself for injuries, he found his left shoulder was stiff and sore, but he was surprisingly unscathed. Wiping his crusted-over eye, he managed to clear the blood away and could now open both eyes.

With the city overrun, Miro found a place to hide, high on the wall in a mountain of rubble, where he could watch the happenings in the city as well as below on the plain. He saw men in silver robes enter the city, coordinating the revenants as they rounded up the living and the dead alike. He frowned as he saw the symbol of the withered tree on their robes; these were Akari necromancers. Miro now knew how Sentar had built his army so quickly.

The necromancers removed the pile of corpses where Miro had been thrown, and soon every dead body was on its way out of the city.

"Let the living walk," a necromancer called. "It saves us carrying them down to the plain."

Miro watched as the enemy marched a long train of terrified Gokani in single file out the open gates. He felt tears in his eyes, but couldn't tell if they were from rage or frustration. Most of these Gokani had hidden in their homes until the very end: old men and their weeping wives, white-faced young women with babes, and small children carrying toddlers smaller still. Any one of those children in the line could have been Tomas.

Outside the city Miro saw an auburn-haired woman, her face scratched and bleeding, help an elderly man stand back up after a stumble.

Amber!

Miro wanted to scream. His fists clenched and unclenched. He thought about the emir's beliefs, and discussions he'd had with Ella and High Lord Rorelan. He thought about the gentle words of the long-bearded healer.

Miro now knew the value of lore, and he knew the power of violence. He would have given anything for a zenblade and armorsilk, anything in the world, and he would have fought like a demon to free his wife and these people from the terrible fate that awaited them.

As it was, he could only watch and wait.

The prisoners formed an unending line, and Miro turned his gaze to the plains below the city, so he could see Amber's destination.

The sun would set in an hour, and as the clear day ended in a radiant sunset more beautiful than any painting, Miro reflected on the last time he'd seen the sun set, casting its rays on this wall. He couldn't believe so much had happened in such a short space of time.

The army still occupied the area below the city, spotted with siege towers that hadn't even been used, but there was also a new encampment in the hills. A dozen tree-sized cylinders stood beside a series of tents.

"He's taking the vats with him as he goes," Miro muttered as he saw them. "He's going to start the killing tonight."

The long file of prisoners led to the cluster of tents. Miro assumed that even with a dozen vats, it would take time to process so many. They would probably contend with the corpses first, simply because they didn't have to worry about the living rotting.

Miro thought, with a sickening feeling, that it would take Sentar longer to extract the essence he needed and raise more revenants to add to his army, than it had taken to conquer a strong city like Wengwai.

Miro took a bearing on the prisoners' location as the sun went down. Then he went back into the deserted city to find the items he needed.

He would try to free Amber this very night.

———◆———

Miro crept toward the vats. His only blessing was that with so many men at his disposal, Sentar was confident, and his necromancers were more concerned with the grisly tasks he gave them than with placing sentries and devising watch rotations.

It was a gloomy night, and though the moon was up, black clouds passed across it so that the night alternated between darkness and light. Miro was forced to time his movements to the periods when the moon's glowing circle was obscured.

Screams and moans filled the air, covering the sounds he made. Scurrying behind a hill, he saw it on the other side: a tall cylinder, high as a house: a vat.

Miro checked the items he had with him. At his waist he carried the fine but plain sword the emir had given him, and over his shoulder was a small satchel. It had taken time, but he'd eventually found a thin quill, an empty glass jar, and a set of gloves.

Lord of the Sky, he hoped this would work.

Miro popped his head over the hill and quickly ducked back. If he sped over the hill, he would be covered by the vat itself on the downward slope.

His heart hammering, Miro launched himself forward, slipping and sliding on the far side of the hill as it fell away more than he'd expected. He rolled to the earth with a thump, his scabbard hitting the bottle in his satchel and shattering the night air with a loud clunk. Miro held his breath as he used the vat to hide himself, waiting to see if anyone had heard.

He waited several long seconds before he was satisfied no alarm had been raised.

Miro examined the vat. He wasn't interested in the lore that enabled it to extract essence from corpses, nor was he looking for the door in which they were thrown. He finally found what he was after: a thin tube that led to a small steel barrel.

The barrel was the size of a man's head. Miro wondered how many innocent people the self-styled Lord of the Night needed to murder to fill the vessel with essence. It must number in the hundreds.

339

Miro took the gloves out of the satchel and put them on. They were made of cloth, which meant they would only prevent the slightest of spills from reaching Miro's skin, but they were all he'd been able to find.

He unscrewed the cap from the barrel, which allowed him to remove the glass tube.

Miro's hurt left shoulder gave a sudden spasm of pain. A tiny droplet of black liquid fell from the end of the glass tube onto Miro's left hand.

Miro hurriedly pushed the tube away, letting it fall to the ground, before looking at his hand in horror. What should he do? Should he take the glove off? What if he took the glove off and made a second spill? What if he didn't take it off and the essence worked its way through the fabric, worming its way to his skin . . .

Miro hastily tugged the glove off his left hand, throwing it into a clump of grass.

He put his left hand behind his back to remove the temptation to use it. With his shoulder hurt, the risk was too great.

Miro turned to the barrel. He felt its weight. It was heavy, perhaps half full. He took the wide-mouthed jar from his satchel and held it between his knees.

This was another dangerous moment. Miro tilted the barrel until its opening was over the mouthpiece of the jar. He tipped oily black liquid, the deadliest substance in existence, into the vessel he'd brought. He almost tipped too much, and brought the barrel back down with a quick moan of fear.

He'd filled the jar, and he was still alive.

Miro spent the next moments replacing the glass tube in the mouth of the barrel and sealing the cap. No one would know he'd come this way.

Screwing a lid on the jar, now filled with essence, Miro held it carefully as he once again crossed back over the hill, taking his belongings with him.

He continued to run, back bent to hide his form, until he found a quiet place far from the vats. A fallen log made a platform, and Miro drew his sword, placing it horizontally on the log in front of him. He placed the jar beside the sword, where it wouldn't slip, and took out the quill.

Miro waited until the moon came out, and then, taking a deep breath, he unscrewed the lid of the jar. He picked up the quill in his gloved right hand and thought about what he was doing.

Miro had been a bladesinger for years. He'd studied hard and trained endlessly. He had carried his zenblade into countless battles, from one end of the Empire to the other.

His sister was an enchantress. She'd left the temple school at a young age; it was the only way she could save the gilden she needed for the fees at the Academy of Enchanters. But she'd continued learning, bringing home books about topics ranging from mathematics to the study of the weather. Most of all, she'd brought home books about enchantment.

Ella had made Miro his zenblade and armorsilk, both now resting at the bottom of the Great Western Ocean. Miro could never create a zenblade himself, but he knew the activation sequences she'd taught him, and with all his experience he knew some runes for lightness and hardness, heat and light.

Miro's hand trembled as he dipped the quill in the jar. Could he really do this?

He removed the quill from the jar and looked at the bared steel of the sword, glinting in the direct moonlight. He began to draw a rune, fighting the urge to tremble as a hissing sound came from the steel where the essence touched it. Acrid smoke rose into the air, stinging his eyes and throat, forcing him to keep his head tilted to the side. He curled the symbol at the end in the flourish he'd seen so many times. Was it correct? There was no way of knowing; he had only his memory to go on.

He moved on to the second rune: The matrix he was drawing contained six symbols. Somehow Miro was able to recall every one.

The first matrix completed, Miro's hand moved along the blade as he started the second group of symbols. This next matrix bound twelve runes together and was the most complex he would try. Miro wanted to give the sword the power to burn and the power to blind. He would make it stronger and harder, sharper and lighter. He would activate it with a single spoken word.

Compared to a zenblade it would be pitiful, but these people had no lore, and an enchanted sword in the hands of a skilled swordsman would be a deadly weapon indeed. A weapon Miro would need if he planned to face revenants.

The hours passed as Miro worked, and as he drew symbol after symbol, he tried not to think about what might be happening to Amber. The moon went behind a long black cloud, and he cursed, forced to stop until it came back out.

His strategy would be simple; this was no time for subterfuge. He would fight his way into the camp, take Amber, and they would flee.

Miro frowned at the sword as he drew the last rune. What was missing? The activation sequence. Miro drew a final matrix close to the hilt, linking it to the other runes with a bridge. There, it was done.

His hand felt cramped and his arm ached as he put the quill down on the log he was using as a table and removed the glove. He had a thought, and looking into the end of the log, he saw it was hollow. Miro decided to leave the items here. He would need to be unencumbered for fighting, and they might be useful to him again.

Miro screwed the cap back onto the jar and filled the satchel, placing it inside the hollow log.

He picked up the long, straight sword with both hands, looking up and down its length. The steel shone, and even in the moonlight Miro could see the silver symbols etched along its length.

Should he activate it now, to see if it worked?

As far as he was from the enemy encampment, Miro was hesitant to light up the hills around him in the event his enchantment had been a success. He would have to wait to activate the sword until he was ready to use it.

Ella had impressed on Miro the dangers of an incomplete enchantment. When they were learning, students had to have every rune checked before they were allowed to move on to the next. Even accomplished enchanters worked with books and other enchanters.

If he'd made a mistake, the sword could fizzle like a candle burned to a stub.

Or it could explode in his hands.

There was no way to tell.

Miro decided he was as ready as he would ever be.

He took the sword and walked back toward the place marked by the monolithic vats, the place where he'd last seen them take the woman he loved.

35

Finally, Miro allowed his rage to surface. Blood throbbed in his ears, and his breath came from his throat in a hoarse wheeze. He held the hilt of the sword in a grip of iron and no longer tried to hide his presence as he walked toward the encampment with long, bold strides.

He saw the vats to his left, which meant the encampment would be somewhere ahead. There were so many tents, it would be impossible to know which held Amber. Some were large and some small. The necromancers probably slept in rich surrounds. One of the tents more than likely held the Lord of the Night.

Miro passed the first tent. He flicked his wrists and the sword sliced through the canvas wall, tearing a hole. Miro stepped through.

"What . . . ?"

He was obviously a necromancer and had been sleeping. Miro recognized the light hair and gray eyes of one of the Akari. The necromancer blinked at Miro in confusion.

Miro opened the necromancer's throat with a quick thrust of his right arm. Blood fountained from the necromancer's neck, and his eyes went impossibly wide. He clutched at his throat with both hands, gurgling and writhing, and then he was still.

Miro walked back out the way he had come in. He listened, cocking his head. No alarm had been raised.

All of a sudden, it started to rain.

The sky opened and water came down in thick, heavy droplets. The darkness closed in, and the tents became dim shapes, confused and ethereal. Thunder rumbled overhead, and Miro was instantly soaked to the skin.

He peered through the vertical lines of water. For the time being, he kept his sword inactive.

Miro strode forward until he came to another tent, larger this time. He cut through the side with two successive slashes and stepped in.

Torches rested against the supporting poles, lighting the space up and allowing Miro to see the horror within.

Two necromancers in silver robes hovered over a wooden table. A pile of corpses lay in one corner of the room, and two revenant guards stood just inside the door.

On the table was the body of a Gokani soldier. His chest was laid bare, and silver symbols covered one side of his body.

The necromancers turned in surprise.

Miro's arms came up, and holding the sword in both hands, he cut down at the neck of the closest robed figure. Even as the man fell, Miro spun on his heel and thrust into the second necromancer's chest, feeling the sword bite through bone.

Miro withdrew the sword as the revenants came at him.

They were barbarian warriors, huge armored men, taller even than Miro, with broad shoulders and heavy broadswords.

Miro had waited until now to activate his sword, but he could wait no longer. "*Shekular.*" He named the rune.

Light sped from one end of the blade to the other, searing white light that grew brighter as it approached the tip. Miro felt the sword come alive in his hands, growing lighter and throbbing with energy.

He lifted his arms as his enemies came forward, snarling and letting his rage take full hold.

The closest barbarian swung first, but Miro blocked, feeling his arms take the blow and pushing back with all his strength. He saw his opponent's broadsword twist and melt where the enchanted sword clashed against it, and Miro pulled back and swung at the barbarian's face, opening up the skin under his eye to the bone. His opponent made no sound but fell back, and the second revenant came forward. Miro attacked in a flurry of blows, eager to finish the two warriors quickly. His sword sheared through this revenant's broadsword and cut deep into the creature's chest.

Yet both warriors kept going. Miro leapt forward and swung again at the first white-eyed barbarian, once more aiming for the head. The glowing blade bit deep into the revenant's neck and continued, removing his head clean from his shoulders. Miro turned to the last warrior and ducked, slashing through both of his thick legs. The revenant fell to the ground, and Miro hacked downward to take its head off.

Miro looked around the tent. Everyone in it was dead; there was nothing for him here.

He ran back out and peered through the pouring rain. Nothing. He ran forward until he saw the dark shapes of more tents. One was much larger than the rest. Miro's feet dug into the sodden earth as he ran toward it.

His blazing sword would draw the enemy to him, and he knew he had little time. He cut a hole in the wall of the long structure and stepped inside.

Moans and screams greeted his entrance. Several hundred prisoners had been corralled inside a pen fenced with spiked wire on all sides and guarded by revenants. With no time to look for a gate, Miro swung down at the fence with his sword, furiously striking again and again. A revenant came at him and Miro twisted his body, taking the creature's head off with a single blow, before once again returning to the fence.

"Amber!" Miro cried. Where was she?

He finally cut the metal into molten fragments, clearing enough space for the prisoners to exit.

"Get out of here!" he shouted. "All of you, *now!*"

First one shot out, and then they were moving in a flood. Miro searched every face as he admonished them to run as fast and far away as they could. He couldn't see her.

When he'd scanned every face, Miro turned around.

Six revenants charged him. With a roar, Miro came in to meet them.

He dispatched the first with a feint and thrust to the throat, following it with a disemboweling blow to the stomach, tearing the warrior in two. The second exploded as Miro cut into him with three swift blows. Blood flew into the air, covering Miro with red gore. The rain made the sword slippery in his hands, but he held on tightly, aware that without it he was dead.

Dancing between the snarling barbarians, he concentrated on the neck and head, slicing through a man's skull and taking another revenant's head from his shoulders. Miro's training at Rogan's hands, and the experience gained from the war, gave him lightning reflexes, and his rage gave him strength.

There were only two facing him now, and he charged them both, smashing into one with his shoulder and lashing out with his sword at the second. He rolled on the ground and spun on his heel as he stood up, cutting a revenant in two. Another blow saw the final warrior go down.

Breathing heavily, Miro let his arm fall down by his side. He suddenly felt exhausted, but he couldn't stop now, not when he was so close.

"Amber!" Miro cried again, heedless now of the noise he was making.

He exited the tent and dashed through the camp, shielding his eyes from the rain. There, ahead—it was another of the long structures. There would be more prisoners there.

Miro ran, feeling splashes and puddles now beneath his boots. He reached his destination in moments, and this time the entrance was ahead of him, two revenants standing side by side at the door.

He tore through them without thinking, letting his muscles control the sword of their own accord. Panting, he looked down, seeing two headless bodies at his feet.

"Amber!" he cried.

Inside the structure Miro saw another pen filled with wailing prisoners. His arms felt like lead, but he smashed at the fence time and again, the enchanted blade making swift work of the steel. The prisoners ran out, and Miro slumped as weariness took hold of him, his chest heaving as he desperately tried to search the crowd, calling out her name.

He sensed motion behind him and spun, the sword coming forward.

"Miro, it's me!"

Amber looked fragile and weak, but she was alive, and she was unharmed. She held Miro's wrist, and he realized he still had the sword raised. He lowered his arm.

"I'm taking you out of here," he said.

"Look," Amber said. She held up her hand.

Miro stared in confusion at the flask she held out to him.

"It's the cure. I have it. I hid it in my tunic. We can go!"

Miro grabbed Amber's hand in his left, his right hand holding the blazing sword. He took her out into the empty space between the tents, wondering which way to go.

A bright light erupted from above, blinding them.

In an instant Miro could see as clearly as daylight.

A man in black clothing stood before them. He held his hand upturned in front of him, runes glowing on his palm, and high above, an orb of pure light rose higher into the air. When he closed his palm, the ball of light stopped moving and hovered there, now still.

Sentar Scythran regarded Miro with amusement.

He looked at the glowing sword in Miro's hand. "You're not from around here, are you?"

Amber shrank behind Miro as he moved to stand in front of her.

"I'd like to find out what you're doing here, so far from home," Sentar Scythran said.

A necromancer in a silver robe walked up to stand beside his master.

"Renrik," Sentar said. "Instruct our minions to round up those who've fled."

"Yes, Master," said Renrik, bowing and moving away.

"Drop your weapon and come forward," Sentar said to Miro.

"No," said Miro.

Sentar raised an eyebrow. He pointed his finger and words came from his lips.

Miro pushed Amber away, diving to the side as lightning filled the space where they'd stood. He rolled on the ground and a blast hit the earth behind him, tearing a steaming chunk out of the sodden dirt. He twisted and weaved, rolling and ducking, each movement bringing him closer to the Lord of the Night.

Miro screamed as his sword came up and he prepared to lunge, his every being burning with the desire to end this man's life.

Sentar leapt away and pointed again with both hands, this time away from Miro.

Bolts of twisting lightning poured from his fingertips.

Miro's eyes followed the stream of blue energy as it bathed Amber in its destructive power.

She screamed, the most terrible sound Miro had ever heard. Writhing in pain, still on her feet, she twitched and shook, and her clothes began to smoke. As Amber's hair caught fire Miro roared in anguish and held his arms out, lowering his sword.

Sentar dropped his hands. The lightning vanished.

"Enough?" he said, looking at Miro.

Miro watched as Amber crumpled to the ground. Her legs trembled, quivering, the only sign she was still alive, and the blessed rain soon extinguished the flames in her hair.

Miro threw down his sword and fell to his knees. He looked again at Amber. "No more," he said, though his mind was filled with hate. "Don't hurt her."

The Lord of the Night walked toward Miro's kneeling form. Miro looked up into the ice-blue eyes, and then without warning the man's clenched fist came forward, snapping Miro's head back. Indescribable pain rocked him to his core; the blow was inhuman in its strength. Blood poured from Miro's nose and mouth as he spat out a tooth.

"Yes," said Sentar Scythran. "I thought so. You're as weak as all your kind."

Miro fell down to the ground, his face landing in a pool of water and the blood from his face mingling with the mud. Looking up, he saw men in gray robes come forward.

"Take him and bind him. Destroy the sword. And also . . . ensure the woman is the next one raised. Choose one of the more painful ways for her to die, and when she is brought back, send her to me.

I'd like to see the expression on this man's face when his mate is made to kill him."

"Please . . ." Miro gasped.

Sentar bent down until his face was close to Miro's. "What are you doing so far from home, little human? We'll soon find out, won't we?"

36

The Isle of Ana was a long strip of rock in the Tingaran Sea, five days' sailing from the coast. It lacked a deep harbor, and the only means of approach was a tiny cove with a crumbling jetty, providing meager protection from the buffeting waves. The tiny island had little importance. Outsiders visited rarely.

The late Emperor Xenovere had found a purpose for the Isle of Ana, deciding to send convicts from Tingara to live on the island in exile. The men and women taken to the island never saw home again.

A deep chasm divided the Isle of Ana roughly into northern and southern halves. The southern half was the larger section and possessed the pier as well as several clusters of rude huts. The convicts lived here, entirely unsupervised, making the best of their situation. Vegetable gardens scattered the landscape, and a few goats rollicked on the craggy hills, seemingly unaware of the precipitous drop to the ocean below. Most of the convicts were old men, their crimes long forgotten by the society they'd left behind. Escape was impossible.

Once, a bridge had crossed the chasm, connecting the northern and southern halves of the island, but the bridge was long gone. Before the emperor's men had destroyed the only route across the chasm, they'd built a house of wood and stone on the northern tip, resting against the side of a hill on a small plateau with an unparalleled view of the sea. They carried tools, building materials, animals, seeds, and provisions to the newly built house. Their prisoner and those of her retinue who volunteered to join her crossed the bridge to their new home. Only then was the bridge destroyed, leaving the northern section of the Isle of Ana completely isolated.

Lady Alise was now over fifty years old. She'd lived on the northern end of the Isle of Ana for nearly half of her life. Two gravestones marked where her gardener and his wife were buried, and only Marlow, her manservant, and Tara, her maid, remained. There were two other smaller houses a few minutes walk from Alise's own house, but only one was occupied. Tara and Marlow weren't married, but they'd lived together for the last ten years.

Alise stared out to sea, thinking back to the events that had brought her here, as she often did. The wind blew strong in her face, so that her brown dress clung to her slim form, and her long dark hair twisted in the ocean breeze, only occasionally flashing a thread of gray.

She knew she would never have survived without those who had volunteered to join her in exile, but even so she'd begged them not to come. They had pleaded with her, in return, to be allowed to come, and in the end Alise couldn't say no. She'd been convicted of treason. They knew a dark fate might await them at the hands of her brother, back in Seranthia.

More than anything, Alise thought about the son who had been taken from her. He would be a man now, perhaps a farmer or a craftsman—if he'd managed to stay clear of Xenovere's clutches. She didn't expect to ever leave the Isle of Ana, but she would have given anything to know about him. Killian had been just a babe when they'd taken him, and she had no illusions that he would remember his mother. His infant features had been rounded and immature, but

Alise knew he would have his father's red hair and penetrating blue eyes. After the death of her husband, she'd loved the babe more than anything in this life. Now she would never know about the man he'd become.

Alise jumped when she felt a touch at her elbow. Turning, she saw it was Marlow, her manservant. He was old now, and eventually it would be his turn to join the others under the gravestones far from home, but his eyes were still sharp, and he stooped only a little. Alise loved him dearly, and dreaded the day when he would be gone.

"M'lady, my apologies—I didn't mean to startle you."

Alise turned and smiled. "You don't need to apologize. My mind was elsewhere."

"There's a ship."

Alise's eyebrows went up in surprise. "Are you sure?"

"Look." Marlow pointed, and then Alise could see it. It was only a speck on the horizon, but the white triangular shape of a sail was clear, and it grew closer as they watched.

"Four years it's been," Alise said, "with no new convicts. I was beginning to think they'd forgotten about us."

"Who knows what's transpired in the Empire?" Marlow said.

"Not that we'll ever hear anything of it. There's much I would give for some news. Still, it's probably for the best. Better that we forget about them."

Marlow shaded his eyes as he peered at the ship. "I'm not so sure about that, m'lady. Something tells me this isn't another load of prisoners."

———◆———

Marshal Beorn scratched his beard as he saw the craggy Isle of Ana loom larger in his vision. From his approach he could see the chasm that split the island into two halves.

"What a terrible place to live," he muttered.

Beorn sensed movement nearby as a man dressed in Tingaran purple joined him at the rail. "Murderers, thieves, and rapists, all of them, Marshal," said Lieutenant Trask, the man who led Beorn's escort.

"I'll wager there's more than a few political dissidents. Why didn't anyone tell us about this place?" Beorn asked.

"You didn't ask."

Beorn scowled at the Tingaran lieutenant. "That's not good enough."

Trask shrugged. "They're self-sufficient, and they've been put here for life. Better they spend their days here than fill our jails and take up the time of our courts."

"We have a new Empire now, Lieutenant," Beorn said, "and a new way of ensuring fair trials for all. Lord of the Sky, we don't even have any records on these people!"

Lieutenant Trask shrugged again, and Beorn had to fight an urge to strike the man.

Calming himself, Beorn looked up at the island. "Where will we find Lady Alise?"

"If she's still alive, she'll be on the northern end of the island."

"Lieutenant?"

"What?"

"Are you forgetting how to address your commanding officer?"

Trask grimaced. "She'll be on the northern end of the island, Marshal."

"But the pier is on the southern end, is it not, Lieutenant?"

"Yes, Marshal."

Beorn felt a vein begin to throb in his temple. "So how do you plan to cross the chasm? I can't see a bridge."

"There was a bridge, Marshal, but they destroyed it after the emperor's sister was exiled." When Beorn didn't say anything, simply regarding the Tingaran with a glare, Trask continued. "They didn't want the convicts crossing to her side, and they wanted to make it hard for her to escape."

"I understand the reasoning," Beorn growled. "Now I'm waiting . . . first to hear why you didn't say this earlier, and second, to hear that you brought materials to build a new bridge."

Lieutenant Trask began to sweat. "I . . . we . . . no, Marshal. We don't have materials to build a new bridge."

Beorn fought an impulse to draw his sword and run the man through, or at least to demote him. He pushed the urge down with a scowl. The Tingaran officers in the army didn't need any more excuses for enmity with the Alturans.

Beorn closed his eyes and breathed slowly in and then out. Rogan had entrusted him with this task, Beorn reminded himself, and he would see it through.

"I . . . I'm sorry, Marshal," Lieutenant Trask said.

"Don't worry, Lieutenant," Beorn said, opening his eyes. "I'll take care of it. I have an idea."

Their small sailing ship tacked twice more before reefing sails as they approached the rickety pier.

The vessel's captain came over, frowning as he checked on his ship's progress as it slid toward the jetty. "Marshal, please disembark quickly. This pier's no good for tying up longer than a few minutes."

Beorn nodded acquiescence. "We'll get the men off right away."

The ship swiftly unloaded her cargo of Tingaran soldiers and drew away from the island, the captain anxious to maintain a safe distance from the cliffs. Marshal Beorn stood on the rickety pier, looking up at the heights.

"Lead the way, Lieutenant," Beorn instructed Trask. "Take me to the convicts."

Trask led Beorn and his dozen men up a precarious path, with wooden steps wedged into the cliff. Beorn felt every one of his years as he grabbed onto the rocky walls for stability, his calves burning and his breath coming hoarse.

"Are you all right, Marshal?" Lieutenant Trask asked.

"Fine," Beorn muttered. "Just keep going."

Eventually they reached the heights, where a series of tablelands made up the place the convicts called home. Huts clustered here and there, with small vegetable gardens outside most. Goats roamed around, bleating and moaning as they scattered out of the soldiers' way.

The convicts had seen the ship coming from far away and were already lined up, scores of them standing with hands clasped behind their backs. Beorn saw mostly old men, with a few of them middle aged. There wouldn't be any trouble here.

"Ask them to come forward, Lieutenant," Beorn said.

"Come forward!" Trask called. "Marshal Beorn wants to speak with you."

Beorn waited until they had taken three steps forward, before speaking. At least he wouldn't have to shout over the wind.

"Emperor Xenovere, the fifth of that name, is dead," Beorn said. The convicts stirred, exchanging glances. "For those of you who want to, there may be an opportunity to go home. Back in Seranthia your cases will be examined, fairly and impartially, and any of you here for political reasons may find yourselves free men."

"Looks like we're all free then!" a voice called out from the crowd.

Lieutenant Trask put his hand on his sword and stepped forward, but Beorn silenced him with a glare.

"The courts will decide your fate, but I can promise you fair trials, with each of your cases independently judged. However first I need your help with something. I've come for Lady Alise."

"What have you come for?" one of the convicts, a tall man with a square jaw, asked. "She should never have been sent here in the first place."

A chorus of support greeted the square-jawed convict.

"I'm here to take her home," Beorn said. "You're correct. She should never have been sent here. I have orders from Lord Regent Rogan Jarvish to free Lady Alise and restore her lands and titles. I'm to take her to Seranthia."

A ragged cheer met Beorn's words.

"I have to ask you for help, however," Beorn addressed the square-jawed convict. "Can you build a bridge over the chasm?"

"'Course we can," the convict said. "We never did in the past though 'cause there are some here who actually belong in this place. The good lady don't want the likes of them creeping up on her in the middle of the night."

"Thank you," Beorn said, "that's all I needed to know." He raised his voice. "Any man who helps build a bridge across the chasm will have their assistance noted."

"We don't need our assistance noted," said the square-jawed convict. "Come on, fellows. There might not be much left for us back home, but let's give the lady help getting off this rock, shall we?"

"Well?" Beorn said, looking at Lieutenant Trask.

"Well what?"

"We've got twelve strong soldiers here, plus the two of us. We might be here awhile. Let's give these men a hand."

The bridge was a makeshift structure of tree logs and nailed planks of wood. Lieutenant Trask stationed his men at each end while he and Marshal Beorn set off to find Lady Alise.

Beorn still had no evidence she was here. What if she'd escaped, or fallen from a cliff, or taken ill? Trudging along the rocky path with Trask by his side, he wondered what he would say when he saw her.

The trail eventually led them around a hill to a small plateau, placed high and sheltered on one side, with expansive views of the surrounding ocean. Beorn immediately knew who the middle-aged woman flanked by an older couple was.

She was tall and brown haired, with a narrow face and sharp features, and there was something . . . regal about the way she held herself. There was silver in her hair, and her brown eyes were shadowed, as if marked by suffering. The skin of her face was pale and careworn; this was the face of a gentle soul taken on a difficult journey. Her brown dress twisted in the wind, and her expression registered alarm.

"Who in the name of the Evermen are you?" the old man at her side challenged. "What are you doing here? Why have you come to trouble us?"

The three of them stood close together, and the old woman clutched at the one who Beorn reckoned was Lady Alise. Beorn wondered what was terrifying them so much.

Then it came to him.

"Stop." He held out his hand to hold Lieutenant Trask back. "These people haven't seen another soul in who knows how long. We're frightening them."

Beorn and Trask kept a distance several paces from the three trembling people.

"Lady Alise?" said Beorn.

"Y–Yes. That is I," the tall woman said.

"I am Marshal Beorn. I know it has been a long time, and neither Lieutenant Trask here nor I wish to cause you any alarm."

"Why are you here?" Lady Alise asked.

Beorn scratched at his beard. He'd rehearsed this moment, but the words suddenly deserted him. "Well . . . there have been changes in the Empire. Your brother, Xenovere, is dead. I don't know how to say this, but I'm here to take you back to Seranthia. My lady, I'm here to bring you home."

"Home as what?" the old man said, scowling.

"Home with titles fully restored. In fact, the lord regent, a man named Rogan Jarvish, wants me to ask Lady Alise to take a place in the new Empire."

Beorn looked imploringly at Lady Alise. If she didn't want to come with them, he wasn't sure what to do.

"My son, Killian, . . ." Lady Alise finally said. Her voice trembled with emotion. "That is all I care about. What happened to my son? Can you tell me?"

"I'm sorry, my lady," Beorn said. "I don't know. But if anyone can help you, it's the lord regent. He's a good man."

Lady Alise turned to the older couple. "I am going to go with them. Marlow, Tara, will you come?"

The old man looked at the woman, Tara, before turning back to Lady Alise.

"No, m'lady," the old man said gruffly. "Tara and I, we'll stay here. This is our home now. They won't have much use for us in the Empire."

"Are you sure?" Lady Alise asked. She suddenly seemed small, like a little girl. "I might need you."

"You'll do fine," Marlow said. "Be brave. There's nothing they can take from you they haven't already taken. Find your son. Something tells me you will."

Lady Alise turned to Beorn. "May I get some things?"

"Of course," Beorn said. Lord of the Sky, he couldn't imagine how hard this must be for her.

She began to move away but then turned back. "My titles and my lands are returned to me?"

"Yes." Beorn met her gaze, now steadied.

"There's nothing I'll take from here, then," Lady Alise said. "Let's go immediately. My son may need me."

37

"How long did you say it's been?" Killian asked.

"About two and a half years," said Ella, looking at him with concern. "How long has it been for you?"

"No," he shook his head. "I think time flows differently here. It's been a long time, but I don't think it's been that long."

"How long has it been for you?"

"A year? More?" He shrugged and smiled shakily. "I don't know."

"Why did you attack me?"

The madness briefly returned to Killian's eyes. "How could I believe it was you? I . . . I can't explain what it's like. Only living here would tell you, and I wouldn't wish that on anyone. The days are living nightmares, and they're incredibly long. Constant threats . . . hunted by dark creatures . . . The nights are short, but they're worse, much worse. I try to sleep in the daylight hours and stay awake for the nights. When I sleep I have dreams . . . vivid, uncontrollable dreams." He looked at her. "You're in them, as are others. People from my youth and from the dark times in my life."

"I hope you don't associate me with dark times," Ella said, attempting a smile.

"No," said Killian, and Ella was pleased to see him smile, however thinly. "I think I dream of times when I was . . . emotional."

Ella looked around the chamber; the shells with their motionless occupants still gave her chills. "You've mentioned dangers. Are we safe here?"

"This is one of the few places we can be sure of being safe. There's nothing here though, nothing except the Evermen, waiting to return. We can't stay here forever."

"You mentioned dreams."

"It's something about the mood of this world. When I saw you, I couldn't believe you were actually here. I've been forced to fight creatures of death. I couldn't distinguish between my dreams and my waking life." He laughed, but it was forced. "I sound mad, don't I?"

"Don't worry," Ella said. "I'm here to take you home. You'll feel better as soon as you're back."

Killian looked up at the empty shell, where the words "Sentar Scythran" gave the name of the one who once waited in stasis. "What happened to him? He was here when I first found this chamber. I'll never forget that face. Of all of them, his face chilled me the most."

"He must have left some time ago," Ella said. "The essence drained away from the portal, and the gate opened long enough for the beacon to sound and wake him. Sentar must have been chosen by the others to keep guard in case the portal ever opened."

"Then why didn't he wake the others?" Killian asked.

"My guess is he didn't have time."

"So Sentar crossed while he could."

"He crossed, and he went to the Akari. He now has necromancers with him, and essence. He sent an explosive device to my brother's wedding . . ."

Ella told Killian about the strange device and Tomas's poisoning, Miro and Amber's quest, and Evrin's revelations.

How would she explain what she had discovered about Killian himself?

"We need you," Ella said. "Will you come home with me?"

"How did you cross over?" Killian asked. "How is it possible?"

"I can tell you as we journey to the portal. I've asked Shani to open it once every three days, but we have no way of telling when it will open next. We'll have to wait beside the portal. There'll be time to explain everything."

"Wait," Killian said. "Before we go . . . There are dangers out there. You need to know something . . ."

"What is it?"

Killian opened his mouth, trying to speak. "It won't make much sense unless I explain it all," he finally said.

Ella looked out from the mountain chamber's opening at the strange twilight that must be what Killian had called daylight. What would night be like? How much time did they have?

Ella took Killian's hand in hers. He looked up to meet her eyes and then lowered his gaze again.

"Go on," Ella said.

"I crossed over as the beacon was sounding. There was a device like a pendulum on the other side. I stopped it."

Ella nodded. "I saw it."

"I followed the road until I came to this chamber. It was the first place I found. I knew though that I would need food and water, and my hunger drove me to explore this land. There was a problem. The first time I slept in the open, I was attacked."

Killian's expression grew strained.

"It was like a shadow, and with the lack of light I couldn't see its form. I thought I must have been dreaming when my blows didn't touch it, but I was awake, and the gouges it left in my back were real. I wasn't wearing much when I crossed, if you remember."

Ella nodded.

"I only survived that night by running. I found the deepest hole I could and hid. I survived night after night in this way. In my explorations I found peculiar buildings left behind by those who dwelled in the cities, and other structures built by the Evermen, places stranger than this chamber by far."

Killian licked his lips before continuing. "There's plenty of water in the cities, so thirst wasn't a problem, but food is another story. The wrains—that's what the original inhabitants called themselves—ate food quite different from what we're accustomed to. So I concentrated on the places where the Evermen met and slept, ate and studied. I eventually found food they left behind, in a place far from here. I found these clothes."

Killian indicated the fitted garments he wore: black boots, soft black trousers, silver belt, and collared black shirt. Ella stroked the material of his sleeve between her fingertips; it was incredibly soft.

"I found chambers the shadows were unwilling to enter. I wanted to return to the portal and examine it, to continue my explorations, but with the shadows now tuned to my presence and somehow resenting it, I had to stay there. That's when I found the library."

Killian spread his hands. "I had little else to do, and I had to find a way to fight the shadows. I found books the Evermen left behind, and I found essence. I learned to develop my powers."

The last time Ella and Killian had met, he'd said Ella had changed. Now it was Ella who marveled at Killian's new powers.

"The first time I left the library, the shadows came at me again and again. I was filled with fear, but I threw fire at them, and where my physical blows did nothing, the fire made them scream. From then on I learned from the books and tested what I'd learned on the shadows. I've fought them too many times to count, day after day. Having a daily struggle for my life made me strong. In a way, I'm now like one of them."

Ella thought he meant like one of the shadows, and then she realized.

"You're different from the Evermen," Ella whispered.

"I continued to explore, and I examined the portal, but if the Evermen couldn't open it, neither could I. I now know the words I need to speak in order to cross from this side, but the portal stayed closed. In my explorations I did, however, learn what befell the denizens of Shar."

"Is that what they called this world?"

Killian nodded. "At first I couldn't read their writing, so I learned what I could from the records left by the Evermen. Much later, I taught myself to read their pictographic symbols, and then I had both sides of the story.

"The Evermen came here long ago. They knew nothing of the world they'd opened a path to, other than that it was hospitable to life. When the humans exiled them from Merralya, they were pleased to discover this world already occupied. They were pleased because here were more creatures for them to enslave. Here was another species they could murder, converting the life energy of those they killed into essence.

"Those who lived here called themselves wrains, much as we would call ourselves human. They were winged creatures and could fly like birds. The wrains lived in hivelike pyramids, each level of the pyramid indicating a higher social status. They made their homes at the level they had achieved, flying up and down with no need for ladders or stairs."

Ella thought of the structures she'd seen in the ruined city. The bizarre architecture made more sense now. "What happened to them?"

"Their numbers were beyond counting. You probably saw the cities near the road. There are more cities like that, more than you could ever know. All of the cities are in ruins. The wrains are long gone."

Killian looked out at the sky, and Ella saw with a jolt that the twilight had faded to black, the deepest, darkest night imaginable. Remembering Killian's earlier words, Ella realized they would need to wait now. She didn't want to be caught outside with whatever dangers were out there. Ella moved closer to him, until their knees were touching, and felt him squeeze her hand.

"Where did they go?"

"The wrains were peaceful creatures: artists and builders, not fighters. Aggression was unknown to them, and the Evermen easily took control. The Evermen reveled in their power over those they saw as too cowardly to defend themselves, and they killed hundreds, thousands, even tens of thousands of them."

Ella looked at the tomblike shells. The occupants had much to answer for.

"The Evermen enslaved the wrains of Shar. They slaughtered them in great numbers to get essence, which they planned to use to open the way to yet another world. The wrains didn't stand a chance, and their great civilization collapsed. Their cities were beautiful, and their culture thrived. Ella, this is what will happen to Merralya if the Evermen gain power."

"Why are the Evermen here, then? Did they get the essence they needed?"

"As far as I can understand from the histories, both those of the Evermen and those of the wrains, one of the wrains' leaders created a new religion, a kind of magic, in his desperation. He gathered his people, all of them, in a great field, and together they performed some kind of spell or religious rite. Every last one of them was there, Ella. When the spell was finished, the wrains were no longer. The field was littered with dead bodies. They killed themselves rather than give the Evermen the essence they needed, and allow another world to be shattered like Shar."

Ella had a sudden thought. "The shadows . . ."

"The wrains evolved into some new state of being. They left their bodies behind, and now they are no longer wrains. They freed themselves from their nonviolent ways. They are now something else. Something altogether different."

"What are they now?"

"I call them wraiths."

Ella shuddered as she digested the information. "Then the Evermen . . . ?"

"The Evermen were suddenly under attack wherever they went, and had no source of new essence. They uprooted every shrub and tree to extract the essence they needed, but it still wasn't enough. Shar's climate was always strange, and with no vegetation, it grew worse. Much worse. Over time the world became as it is now. With Shar inhospitable, the Evermen were left with no choice but to place themselves in stasis, in hope that one day the portal to Merralya would be reopened."

"They're desperate," Ella said in wonder.

Killian nodded. "This Sentar, he will do whatever it takes to aid their return. There's nothing left in this world for the Evermen. They need to return. And we need to do everything we can to stop them."

Ella was pensive for a moment as she scanned the chamber, looking at the shells and their occupants. "So the wraiths hate the Evermen," she said.

Killian nodded. "I learned why essence doesn't harm me. Somehow I have the same abilities as the Evermen." Ella opened her mouth but closed it, deciding it wasn't the right time. "The wraiths sense me and attack me wherever I go. I searched the cities and found the places where the Evermen extracted their essence. Eventually I found some essence, Ella. Not much, but enough . . . enough to help me survive in this place. Without this power I would long be dead."

Killian opened his palm, looking at the silver symbols, running his eyes over them. He began to softly chant and light welled up in his palm, growing brighter and condensing until he appeared to carry a golden sphere in his hand. Killian's voice fell away, and he closed his hand into a fist as the light faded.

Ella looked on in wonder. "Killian, back in Merralya, Evrin is rebuilding the machines," she finally said. "Soon we'll have essence." She met his gaze. "We need you to help us against Sentar Scythran and those who fight with him."

Killian nodded. "I've seen what happened to the wrains of Shar."

Ella looked out at the darkened mouth of the chamber. It was now so dark outside that nothing could be seen at all. She shivered.

Killian opened his mouth, and Ella wondered if he was going to ask her how she had managed to cross the portal. What would she say about his father, who must now be waiting at the stone archway?

Instead, he said, "You're cold. I don't have any food or blankets with me, but here—come close. We're safe here. Get what sleep you can."

Killian shuffled along the ground and stretched out to lie on his side. Ella moved forward and shifted her body so she was in his arms, her head under his chin.

Her mind whirled with everything he'd told her, but overriding it all, she was conscious of his lean body behind her, the strong muscles of his arms and his warm breath on the back of her neck.

Ella hadn't slept since before she'd gone to the cemetery to find Lord Aidan's grave.

She tried to stay awake, but sleep came instantly.

38

The night was interminably long, but the somber sun came once more to the hazy sky, blurred and dulled into a featureless yellow orb. As Ella woke, she looked once more at the sleeping Evermen in their strange shells and shuddered.

Ella wondered how much time had passed in Merralya. Where was Miro right now? Had he and Amber found the cure for the strange poison that afflicted their son?

"Are you cold?" Killian asked.

He pulled her closer to him, and Ella suddenly wanted him more than she'd ever wanted any other man. But they were in a nightmare world, with the Lexicons' power steadily being drained, and they needed to move on, or they would be stranded.

Ella sat up and looked at Killian.

His face was careworn, but he was still the same Killian she remembered. His time in Shar had changed him. He was no longer a confused youth. He'd grown into his abilities the way Ella had always known he could.

Ella thought with a start that she was looking at Xenovere's heir. She was looking at one of the Evermen.

"We need to go," Ella said.

An expression of disappointment crossed Killian's face as Ella drew away, and on impulse she leaned down and brushed her lips against his. It was a chaste kiss, but he smiled and his arm went around her to pull her closer into his embrace.

"No." Ella smiled. "Come on—we don't want to be stranded here."

He stood first and held out a hand to help her up. Ella rose to her feet and looked around the chamber. She had her satchel, but little else to gather. Killian had nothing with him.

As they exited the chamber at the top of the mountain, Ella again marveled that the Evermen had gone to such lengths to build this place in imitation of Stonewater. For a time they traveled down the steps in silence, and then Killian spoke.

"This is Shar's equivalent of daylight, but that doesn't mean the wraiths won't attack."

When they reached the bottom of the mountain, Ella turned and met Killian's gaze as they walked. "Do you remember when we traveled through Petrya, and that strange creature hunted us?"

"I remember."

"You told me your story: about how you were a thief in Salvation until that man from the traveling troupe caught you stealing from him."

"Marney Beldara," Killian said, smiling as he reflected. "He was a wonderful man. Marney said I had to join his troupe to repay my debts. I realize now that he used the excuse to help an orphan of Salvation."

"Were you happy then?"

"I guess I was."

"Then in Seranthia . . ."

Killian's expression darkened. "In Seranthia, Marney said something to the crowd about helping the street children. Perhaps he said more, but it was nothing seditious. The emperor's men came the next day. I was away with Marney's daughter, Carla. We were lovers . . . It was the only reason we weren't there. The Tingarans burnt the big tents to the ground and killed the animals in their cages. They rounded up the troupe, everyone I thought of as my family. We retrieved their bodies from the bottom of the Wall."

"Xenovere was an evil man," Ella said. "I'm sorry to bring up old wounds." She took a deep breath. "How do you feel about Tingara now?"

Killian was pensive. "It's a confused place. As bad as the emperor was, his peace was better than the war the primate brought to the world. Has much changed in the Tingaran Empire these past years?"

Ella thought about the changes, and her words with Rogan. "They just call it the Empire now. Yet Tingara's the largest nation by far, and Seranthia's still the administrative capital as well as the heart of the economy. Rogan Jarvish is acting as lord regent, but he's having a difficult time. A Tingaran would be best placed to lead the new Empire."

"A Tingaran? I suppose that's true, if you want to have someone the people of Seranthia will follow." Killian paused. "Still, I would have thought Altura and Halaran would never again call a Tingaran emperor. Not when a man with the right connections to be emperor would likely be one of the Black Army commanders who devastated Halaran."

Ella nodded, watching Killian's face as she walked. "The right person would be someone who stood up to the emperor and the primate, yet is Tingaran by birth. Perhaps a relative of Xenovere . . ."

"If such a—Look out!" Killian cried.

A black shape with claws outstretched flew over Ella's head. Ducking, she felt the whistle of its passage a hair's breadth away.

The shadow rose into the air again, with an unearthly shriek, and Ella caught her first look at a wraith.

Where the winged beings in the pictures walked erect and were somehow noble, this was a creature whose very appearance inspired terror. Its back was bent as if broken, and its jagged wings trailed lengths of black hair. It turned to look at them, malevolent black eyes glaring from a triangular head. Claws tipped its bony legs as well as the end of its wings. When it opened its mouth and shrieked again, Ella saw its jaw open impossibly wide, displaying rows of dagger-like back teeth and four huge incisors at the front.

The wraith was all claws and teeth and speed and hate. Its body was twice the size of a man, and its veined, outstretched wings made it larger still.

"Look out! It's coming back!" Killian shouted.

Ella reached for her wand, and then watched in awe as Killian pointed his fingers and muttered some words under his breath.

Twisted bolts of lightning shot from his fingers, cutting through the air as he brought the wild blue energy to where the wraith careened in the sky.

Killian hit the creature with twin blasts, outlining it in a wave of electrical discharge. It screamed with a sound of pure agony, sending chills down Ella's spine. The wraith shot up into the air, higher than Killian's power could follow, and sped away, receding into the distance.

Killian lowered his hands. "It will be back, and it'll bring more of them. Come on."

They both started a wary jog, Ella looking ahead while Killian kept watch behind. Ella finally saw the fallen city she'd explored, close to the path on the right-hand side. "If we have to, can we shelter there?"

Killian smiled without humor. "They may not have sensed you, but they sense me. That's one of the places they'll come from."

With a sinking feeling of dread, Ella saw a cloud of birdlike shapes rise into the air above the cluster of shattered buildings. "Here they come," she breathed.

"There's a second group," Killian said grimly, pointing to a closer cloud, falling down from the sky above.

With several spoken words, Ella activated her wand, feeling the hazel wood warm in her hands and seeing the prism on its tip light up with yellow.

"The larger group's mine," he said.

Killian and Ella stood back to back as each faced a flock of shrieking wraiths. Ella aimed her wand and called forth a bolt of energy, sending it streaking through the air at the clustered creatures. Behind her she heard Killian chanting.

Grouped together as the wraiths were, Ella couldn't miss, and a piercing scream answered the crash of her bolt striking a creature. The wraiths dispersed, and one turned and flew back the way it came. They wouldn't be so easy to strike a second time.

Ella's group was now close enough that she could see the foremost wraith's triangular head, teeth bared as it screamed to attack the intruders who long ago devastated its homeland.

"*Tula!*" Ella pointed the wand, tracking the movement of the wraith.

A yellow beam of light shot from the wand, but the wraith rose higher, and the bolt passed beneath it.

Ella could now count them. There were eight of the wraiths attacking her, and striking them didn't seem to kill them, only to scare them away. She hoped there wouldn't be any more.

Killian grunted behind her, and Ella wondered how many he faced. Ella still didn't know the limit of his powers, but she knew it was Killian the wraiths were after.

Ella sent three bolts from her wand in quick succession, striking two wraiths but missing a third. The twisted black creature she'd missed shrieked as it came down at her, claws outstretched as it swooped.

Ella pulled the hood of her dress over her head and chanted quickly.

The wraith hit the dress as the silk hardened to steel. Killian was standing too close for Ella to activate the lightning effect, and the wraith rose back into the air with a howl of disappointment.

Ella pointed her wand and three more yellow beams launched from the prism. She sent one wraith screaming away, but there were still five remaining.

All five came at Ella together. She took one out with a final shout, but the four winged shadows were aimed to hit her with the full strength of their teeth and claws.

Then Ella felt Killian move behind her. He clapped his hands together, and a wave of concussive air rolled out from his hands in a circle. When the solidified air hit the wraiths, they screamed, suddenly tossed backward. They rolled over and over, before gathering again and flying away, shrieking and wailing in defeat.

"Thank you." Ella panted.

"We need to keep moving," he said.

They continued the ground-eating jog, watching the sky, taking turns looking ahead and behind. Ella saw the first distant structures she'd seen when she arrived, and realized they would soon be at the stone archway.

She still hadn't told Killian who would be waiting when they arrived.

"Killian," Ella said, breathless from her exertions, "there's something you need to know."

"What is it?" he grunted.

"I read the book the primate found at the Pinnacle. The portal destroys anyone who tries to cross. Only one of the Evermen can enter."

"Then how did you cross?"

"I read something in the book that gave me an idea, and I found a way. You have to understand . . . I had to come and get you . . ."

"What are you saying?"

Ella saw the stone archway in the distance. "Stop," she said, dragging Killian to a halt.

"We can't stop here!"

"There—just ahead—it's the portal. The beacon will tell us when it opens. Before we get there, I have to tell you how I crossed."

"Then tell me!" Killian said in exasperation.

"I read in the book that I could step through the portal if I crossed with one of the Evermen by my side. I can cross back to Merralya, for example, with you beside me." Ella looked into Killian's eyes and took his hand.

"So you crossed with one of the Evermen? I don't understand."

"To come here and bring you home, I had to find someone with your powers, someone who shared your blood, and the blood of the Evermen. I had to find . . . your parents."

The blood drained from Killian's face. "You found my parents? They told me my parents were dead."

"Wait," Ella said. "Please, you have to hear the rest. Listen to me. Evrin told us, after you crossed, that you're his descendant. That's why you have the powers he once had."

Killian looked away. "So that's why he was looking for me, back in Salvation, when we destroyed the machines at Stonewater. He wasn't just looking for someone to help him . . ."

"He was looking for you," Ella finished.

"I think I understand now. You're saying that Evrin crossed with you."

"No," Ella said. "The Evermen took his abilities from him long ago, when he helped our people gain freedom. Killian, to bring you back I had to find your parents. I knew that either your mother or your father would share the powers you inherited from Evrin."

"What did you find?" Killian whispered.

"Your father. His name was Lord Aidan. He had red hair and blue eyes, just like you. By crossing with him, I was able to come here to get you."

"He's alive? But you speak about him as if he's dead. Why are you saying it like that?"

"He is dead. I'm sorry Killian. He died more than twenty years ago." Ella held her breath.

"Than how did you . . . ?" Killian suddenly pulled away. "You didn't. Not that."

"I'm sorry. It was the only way."

Killian looked over at the stone archway. He started to stride toward the archway, walking on the paved road with brisk footsteps so that Ella was forced to jog to keep up.

A figure appeared out of the mist, standing next to the archway with his back slightly hunched.

As Ella and Killian approached, the resemblance between Lord Aidan and his son was unmistakable, yet his pallid flesh and white-eyed stare beside Killian's youthful vigor was disturbing.

Killian stopped and stared, and Ella saw raw emotion cross his face.

"Has the portal opened?" Ella asked.

"It has not," said the revenant.

"Then we'll have to wait."

Lord Aidan spoke again, and Ella noticed his speech seemed labored. "I do not have long. It grows difficult to stay in this world. A feeling of rage overcomes me. I do not understand it."

Ella saw how much fainter the runes on the revenant's skin had become. The redness in his eyes was stronger.

"Ella," Killian said, and there were tears streaming down his cheeks. "I need to speak with him."

Ella bowed her head. "Of course. I'll wait over there."

As she turned and left, she heard Killian as he walked toward his father and spoke. "My name is Killian. I . . . I am your son . . ."

39

Renrik had Miro bound hand and foot and then carried to one of the tents where Renrik and his fellow necromancers created warriors for the Lord of the Night.

They laid Miro on an iron table so that he was on his back, staring up at the ceiling. A revenant cut through the bindings on Miro's wrists, but before he could surge forward, two more warriors pinned his arms above his head. They then bound his wrists, one to each corner of the table.

Miro's legs underwent a similar treatment, until he was splayed on the table, his chest heaving and body tensed as he wondered what lay in store.

They left him alone for hours.

Whatever they were going to do to him, no matter how loud they made him scream, the sounds would be lost in the other noises shattering the night.

The rain had stopped, and Miro wished it would come back, for now against the ensuing silence he could hear moans of anguish and cries of terror. A woman called out a man's name, again and again, her torment evident in every shrieking syllable. A wailing man couldn't be understood at all, his pain so great that all he could do was scream. Sobbing children and tortured howls came from all directions, so that Miro despaired at the inhumanity of it all.

The waiting hours filled Miro with suffering enough for a lifetime, for every cry reminded him of Sentar Scythran's promise regarding Amber.

There was a regular rhythm to some of the horrific sounds. A scream would be cut off by a wet crunching sound. A chorus of fear would follow, and the cycle would repeat.

Feeling sickness and fear mingle in equal quantities, Miro realized what it was he was hearing.

They had put the prisoners into a queue. One would be killed, screaming as he or she saw the death blow coming, and the other prisoners' voices would rise in cries of horror as they saw the fate that awaited them and their loved ones. The revenants herded the queue forward, ruthlessly quelling any resistance, and the next man, woman, or child would die.

"Lord of the Sky, help us," Miro whispered.

Sentar had promised to make Amber's death more painful than that of the other prisoners. What would he do to her?

Even imagining her beautiful skin marred to the smallest degree filled Miro with hate and rage. He didn't care that Sentar had said Amber would be the one to kill him, as much as he wanted to spare himself the sight of his wife brought back in revenant form; he cared that when she died, she would be in pain, and her last thoughts would be a desperate longing to go home.

Miro hated himself then. Amber hadn't chosen to join him on this foolish quest. He should have taken her back to Castlemere, regardless of the delay.

Someone entered the tent. The pain would begin now.

Miro felt a presence move slowly toward him, and then a face came down to stare into his eyes. He looked into the remorseless visage of the Lord of the Night.

"Your woman is still alive, for now," were Sentar's first words.

"Don't hurt her," Miro said, swallowing his pride.

"Can you hear the slaughter line?" Sentar asked. "Can you hear the beautiful music of my revenge on the human race? If you answer my questions truthfully, and I consider that you are forthcoming with your responses, your woman may join that line. Trust me. It is better than the other fate I can give her. When humans displease me, I go to . . . extra lengths . . . to ensure their last hours are as pain filled as possible."

"Despot tactics," Miro said. His eyes narrowed. "You're no god."

"Ah, you'll be an interesting one to work with," said Sentar. "I can tell you'll do anything to spare your woman, but there's a stiff backbone in there. Which will it be? Will you choose to divulge, or will you let me go to work on your pain centers, and make you listen as I flay your woman?"

Miro gulped. His breath came in heaves.

"Yes, you heard me. I'm quite an artist. When I flay a human, I do so cleanly, so that I eventually remove the skin in one piece. I can flay your woman just outside these walls, so you will only be able to hear the screams and imagine what I am doing to her. You'll hear her last gasp as she dies, and then do you know what I'll do? I'll bring her back with no skin, and that's when I'll lead her in here and show her to you. She'll be my only skinless revenant."

"What do you want to know?"

Sentar's face drew back, so that Miro could only stare at the ceiling and wonder where his tormenter was. "Where are you from?"

Miro reminded himself that Sentar had seen his hastily crafted enchanted sword.

"Across the sea, in the east," Miro said.

Miro's heightened senses told him there was a sudden swift movement in the area of his chest. He tensed his stomach muscles, but nothing could have prepared him for the blow that struck the area under his ribs.

The breath left him with a whoosh, and for a moment Miro couldn't think, had no comprehension of where he was, could only focus on the pain, his mind begging without hope for it to end.

Some time later awareness returned to him, and he realized he was coughing and wheezing. Sentar's strength wasn't natural, and the sadistic Lord of the Night evidently took pleasure in the pain he dealt out to the race he despised.

"I told you I want you to be forthcoming in your responses. Now, let me try again. Where are you from?"

"I'm from Altura, the land of enchanters."

"These ridiculous tribes you humans have separated your-selves into," Sentar muttered. "I know your land. There is one from Altura, a leader, whom I tried to kill along with some of the other leaders. Dogs without a pack leader are just so many curs, you see. What was his name? Milo? No, that wasn't it. Miro. Yes, Miro. I'm sure you've heard of him."

Miro felt his pulse race. He knew he couldn't hold out for long—not when Sentar had the ability to harm Amber. He thought about the things he knew—about the machines being rebuilt at Mornhaven and the numbers of fighting men each house possessed. He knew Sarostar's weaknesses, and which was the most poorly defended port, Castlemere or Schalberg.

Miro realized Sentar Scythran was going to make him choose between the defense of his homeland and the woman he loved. If he told Sentar the things he knew, he would be placing countless soldiers and civilians in harm's way and dooming the people of the Empire to enslavement and death. If he didn't, he had no doubt this monster would do to Amber every last thing he had said and more.

"Tell me, Alturan. What are you doing here?" Sentar asked.

"There was an explosion at the lord marshal's wedding in Altura's capital, Sarostar," Miro said, treading close to the truth. "I was there as a guest, and a strange poison afflicted my son. Looking

383

for a cure, I tracked the origin of the poison to the Alchemists' Guild in Wengwai."

Sentar's face again appeared in Miro's vision. "Better. Where is your ship?"

"The emir's men captured our ship in the waters near Emirald, the Veldrin capital."

"The Veldrins have many ships, don't they? I plan to take my great army south, where the emir's ships will enable me to take my minions across the ocean—to your land, young Alturan, and beyond. Tell me, where did you come by the enhanced sword?"

"I made it in the hours before I attacked. I stole the essence from one of the vats. My sister is an enchantress."

"Sloppy work. You're fortunate you didn't kill yourself, although in your case perhaps I should say 'unfortunate,' for your current position isn't enviable. I saw the way you moved, however. Are you what they call a bladesinger?"

Miro hesitated. "No."

Miro sensed movement and tensed, his body turning rigid, fear coursing through his blood. Suddenly something burning, like hot coals, pressed against the skin of his chest. Miro screamed and convulsed, smelling his skin scorching as he heard the sickening sound of sizzling. The thing pressed to the bare skin of his abdomen was then removed, but the pain continued, working through his body in waves.

"That was just my hand," Sentar said. "Not much artistry there. It's time to fetch your woman. I'll start by removing the skin of her face. You'll be surprised, but that's not the most painful place. Soon you will be begging me for her death."

"Yes!" Miro cried. "I'm a bladesinger!"

Sentar Scythran laughed, a sound of superiority and triumph. It was all the more chilling against the backdrop of screams and anguished cries.

"You are Miro, aren't you?" He laughed again. "Miro Torresante: one of the few men holding the Empire together. Your name is on every man and woman's lips. If I had killed you with my device, ah, what a triumph! Yet my plan evidently worked, even if it was just to bring you here. Saying the device was a gift from my old adversary, the Lord of the Sky, now that was a stroke of genius." Sentar paused, his voice turning dark. "I dearly look forward to seeing him again." His jubilant tone returned. "And now you've come to me of your own accord, and all for the life of your son. You could have sent another, but you've come yourself, and now you're in my power."

"You'll never win," Miro said. "We're stronger than you, and we always will be."

"Humans? Strong? You're always bickering and warring among yourselves. You need rulers like us to keep you from tearing each other's throats out, to keep you in line. This time, though—this time I don't want to rule you, and neither will my brothers. This time, Lord Marshal Miro, we will scour you from the world until you are not even a memory."

"We're better than you," Miro whispered. "We always will be."

Sentar Scythran moved to depart. "I'm going now, but I will be back shortly. I'm going to get your woman and tie her to a pole outside this tent, just as I promised. I won't even ask you another question before I start, I'll simply set to work. Get some rest, Miro of Altura. Open your ears. Prepare to hear her cries."

"No!" Miro shouted. The muscles in his arms bulged as he strained against his bonds, and his whole body quivered with effort. The ties held strong, and he slumped back with exhaustion.

He tried again as he heard Sentar Scythran leave the tent.

And again.

Sometime later, the Lord of the Night returned.

40

Sentar Scythran stormed into the tent, staring down at Miro with his eyes blazing. Something had happened to shatter his previous composure.

"Start talking," he said. "The people of this continent have no lore, which is why I came here to raise my revenant army. I don't understand your bladesingers and golems, avengers and night-shades. You've seen my army. Do we have anything to fear from the lore of the houses?"

Miro opened his mouth, the words initially coming haltingly, and then faster as he spoke. "Yes. Your army has everything to fear. A bladesinger of Altura is worth a thousand men in combat. A golem of Halaran is more powerful, more indestructible than any revenant. Tingaran avengers fight like demons, and if you think of the strength of trees than you can imagine what it is like to fight a nightshade of Vezna. You have everything to fear, Sentar Scythran." Miro finally allowed himself to grin. "She's not here, is she?"

This time Sentar's rage was unrestrained. With his back against the iron table, there was no space for Miro to duck his head. The iron fist smashed into his cheek, and a second blow under his eye rocked his vision.

Even as Miro wondered how Amber had managed to escape, he felt a sensation of intense pleasure overwhelm the terrible pain he was in. He knew he could hold out now, no matter if Sentar flayed him alive, or burned his eyes with pokers. The secrets of the Empire were safe.

A third blow struck Miro, crushing his nose against his skull. The pain was like nails driven into his head as he heard the bones crunch together.

Sentar struck Miro again and again, but Miro didn't feel a thing as his vision narrowed to a tunnel, and unconsciousness enclosed him in its embrace.

Miro hovered in and out of consciousness for days. Sentar's fit of rage was a mixed blessing, for his wounds saved him from torture for a time, yet his enemy's wild fury took Miro close to death.

At some point he was loaded aboard a cart and traveled with the army as it headed south toward Veldria and the great harbor city of Emirald.

Thinking in one of his conscious moments, Miro now knew the Lord of the Night's plan. Gathering numbers as he went, Sentar Scythran would reach Emirald with an indomitable army. After sacking the emir's beautiful city, he would take possession of the emir's ships. Miro had seen for himself how many ships were in the massive harbor. Revenants didn't need food or water. Sentar would cram them on every vessel and set sail for the Empire. The closest nation was Altura.

Miro moaned whenever he woke, unable to prevent the agony from bringing sound from his throat. He sometimes stayed awake long enough to call out questions, which sometimes were answered, but most times were not.

Someone tended to him on the journey south, although he wasn't sure if the healer did so out of tenderness. More than likely the healer had orders to rebuild Miro's strength to the point where he could be tortured further.

The healer did his work well, and Miro began to feel consciousness return for more than a few moments at a time. Miro wondered how much closer Sentar's army was to Veldria. He tried to fake a comatose state, but with dread he heard someone send word to Sentar Scythran.

Eventually, he felt his body being moved. Another indeterminate amount of time passed, and then Miro opened his eyes.

He realized he was once again splayed on a cold iron table, staring at the ceiling of a tent.

This time Miro was naked.

There was a rustle, and the sound of heavy breathing, as someone entered.

Miro tried to lift his head but still couldn't see who it was. He felt his heart rate increase, and sweat broke out on his brow. The pain in his broken nose throbbed as if in expectation of further pain.

Miro wished he could simply die.

He heard further movement and closed his eyes as he waited for the pain to begin. Would Sentar question him first, or would he simply start to slice and burn?

Miro tensed, unable to prevent the involuntary response of his body. With his eyes closed, his hearing was amplified, and he heard a snicker and a snap. With surprise he felt a loosening of the tension on his right wrist. Another snap a heartbeat later, and Miro's other wrist was freed.

He opened his eyes, flexing each hand as he did. A man in a black robe swiftly cut the bindings around his ankles.

Miro recognized the robe of an alchemist, although this time the triangle was bound by a double circle. When the alchemist turned, Miro saw a pair of shaggy eyebrows and kind eyes.

"Get up." The alchemist's voice was thin but curt. "I know you are weak, but we do not have much time. You need to be strong now."

"Who are you?" Miro whispered.

"My name is Tungawa. I freed your wife, and now I am freeing you."

"Why are you helping us?"

"Those words are better saved for a more appropriate time. Here." Tungawa threw Miro a bundle of black clothing.

Miro slid off the iron table and wobbled as he tried to hold himself on two feet. For a moment he thought he would faint. Pain throbbed in his head, blood rushing to the wounds on his face and sending waves of agony to his battered flesh. With a supreme effort of will, he fought the pain, battling it like an adversary, clenching his jaw and holding himself still.

He realized he held a black alchemist's robe akin to the one Tungawa wore. He pulled the robe on over his head and raised the cowl to cover his face.

"Quickly," Tungawa said. "Come."

Miro followed the alchemist out of the tent. Two revenants lay sprawled on the ground outside the entrance.

"A rare but powerful poison," said Tungawa. "It destroys the nerve centers so the muscles no longer respond. Even revenants are susceptible. Please, we must be fast."

Sentar was evidently busy, but as soon as he finished whatever he was doing and went to interrogate his prisoner, the alarm would be raised. Tungawa was risking a terrible fate by helping Miro escape.

Miro kept his head down as he followed the alchemist, trying to move quickly without appearing to run. With his limited perspective he saw the silver robes of Akari necromancers and tall legs clad in furs: barbarian warriors. Miro passed tent after tent, any moment expecting the alarm to be raised. If they were caught, Miro decided he would force his enemy to kill him rather than suffer interrogation and torture at the Lord of the Night's hands.

He sensed they were leaving the encampment and wondered how Tungawa planned to flee without being questioned. Each footstep was leaden, and Miro fought the pain in his head, just to keep moving. He felt he'd been following the alchemist for hours, but he knew it had only been several minutes. Every time he heard a shout or a cry, he thought his escape had been noticed. Fear made the bile rise up in the back of his throat.

They entered a sea of people.

Realization hit Miro like a punch in the stomach. Rather than heading away from the encampment and raising a cry, Tungawa planned to hide in a place where no sane man would choose to travel, yet where they would disappear instantly.

Tungawa led Miro through the revenant army.

The barbarians of Oltara and Muttara formed eerily still ranks on both sides. Mingled through their numbers were the defenders of Narea and Gokan, now fighting on their enemy's behalf in death as they never would have in life. Miro brushed past a huge northerner, and in his haste to avoid the man's touch, he stumbled, falling into a Gokani woman. Tungawa pulled him back upright as Miro stared into the white eyes of the revenant, seeing the slash across her throat where the necromancers had ended her life.

Without orders, the revenant returned Miro's stare but did nothing, and Miro and the alchemist resumed their journey through rank after rank of the undead.

They were the ultimate warriors: perfectly disciplined, needing no sustenance, feeling no pain, and loyal to the end. There was no use counting them; there were simply too many.

Miro stumbled again as weakness washed over him. This time he fell to one knee and cried out with the pain in his head.

"Get up!" Tungawa hissed. "They are slow to think, but some do."

Miro opened his mouth and retched, as the pain sickened him to the point where nothing else mattered. His stomach was empty, so nothing came out. He felt Tungawa's hand under his arm, pulling him up.

"Fight the pain." Tungawa said. "Do it for Amber."

Summoning strength from some hidden reserve, Miro stood up, battling his body's every desire to let unconsciousness close in and take away the pain. He took three faltering steps forward, sensing the revenants around him stir and seeing more and more of them turn their white-eyed stare on him.

He pushed the pain down, and felt his legs strengthen as his footsteps grew more certain.

"We're almost there," Tungawa said. "Just a little farther."

Miro risked moving his head enough to look up. He saw trees ahead, and the sight gave him strength.

A burst of fresh air washed over him as they cleared the ranks of the revenants and no cries sounded behind them. With Tungawa still holding his arm, Miro followed the alchemist into the trees.

Miro concentrated on placing one foot in front of the other, his entire being consumed with that task. He desperately wanted to rest, but he knew that if he stopped, the relief of unconsciousness would overtake him.

Then he could go no more. Miro fell over a tree root and pushed his head up with his hands, but felt the strength leave his limbs.

There was a new voice beside him. A woman's voice.

"Oh, what have they done to you, my love?" Amber sobbed. "Tungawa, help me get him to the grove."

"He nearly didn't make it," Tungawa said. "You know we can't stay here. We're going to have to put him on the cart. The army occupies this entire region, but if we head for the river, I know where there's a bridge to take us into Veldria. The only problem is, it isn't a shortcut by any means. The army will get ahead of us."

"We need to get him out of here. Oh, Miro! No, don't try to speak."

"Thank you," Miro whispered. "I don't know how you did it, but thank you."

"Shh," Amber hushed. "Rest now. We'll go back to Emirald, and we'll get the ship we've been promised. We'll be on our way home before you know it."

Miro fell into the waiting arms of oblivion.

41

"Soon we'll be at the bridge," Tungawa said. "I have to tell you, by now the army will have crossed the main border at Renton. They'll be in Veldria."

Amber looked down at Miro's sleeping form as the ox-drawn cart rumbled along the road. His chest rose and fell with healthy, normal sleep, and the tension in his body had eased; he was no longer struggling with the pain.

She had cleaned his wounds: his lips, split in three places; his cheeks, scratched and puffed so initially he was almost unrecognizable; and the twin lines of red dripping down from his broken nose.

Tungawa had helped Amber set Miro's nose, telling her it would now heal cleanly. Now, three days later, the black surrounding Miro's eyes had faded to blue, and though he still looked terrible, it was nothing like when Amber had first seen him.

Amber and Miro both wore normal traveling clothes, garments Tungawa had somehow procured. In the time since Miro's failed rescue attempt, the scorched wounds Amber had received at Sentar's hands had mostly healed. She had cut her hair short to remove the singed strands after it caught fire.

Amber had also miraculously managed to hold onto the anti-dote, secreting the small flask inside her tunic before the revenants hauled her away. The slow-witted revenants hadn't been too thorough in their search.

Amber had never traveled on a cart pulled by an animal. It was surprisingly similar to being drawn by drudge, although the two oxen needed feeding and gave off interesting smells. Tungawa knew the area in the south of Gokan well, and took them on trails he was sure the revenant army would avoid, particularly when their path was a less than direct way to get to Veldria.

It was late summer, and under different circumstances Amber would have found the traveling pleasant. The road meandered through forests and plains, over hills and down valleys, with the warm sun of summer shining on the treetops and the scent of flowers in the air.

The road developed an incline, and presently Amber knew they must be approaching the bridge Tungawa had mentioned. She pricked her ears; soon she would hear the sound of rushing water.

"I have to thank you, Tungawa."

"For what?"

"For saving me and then for risking your life again to save my husband."

Tungawa sighed. "It was my Guild that built the device that poisoned your son. I feel now that we were wrong to turn our backs on lore. I have no wish to see the end of the human race. If by helping you, I help the only chance of resistance this world has, then perhaps I am selfish."

"No, Tungawa. You are brave. It took extraordinary courage to do what you did."

Tungawa grimaced. "When those wretched Gokani prisoners saw me offer my services to Sentar Scythran after the fall of

Wengwai . . . I was there to learn what I could, but they didn't know that. Words cannot describe how it made me feel."

"You're no traitor. I promise you, we'll fight Sentar to our last breath."

Tungawa nodded as he met Amber's gaze. "Hearing you say that brings me peace."

"What will you do when we get to Emirald?"

"I would like to help you get a ship and travel with you to your homeland. The Guild has accumulated much knowledge. I would see that the knowledge isn't lost. If"—Tungawa's eyes sparkled—"you'll have me?"

"Of course." Amber smiled but then sobered. "Could you tell me something? Will Miro be all right?"

"He took a great amount of trauma to the head, but he is strong, your man. The worst is behind him."

"Tungawa, I have to ask: You said you were going to look for weaknesses. Did you find any?"

"I am sorry, Amber, but it seems nothing can stop this dark storm sweeping across the world. If I had some time with one of your loremasters, there was something . . ."

Tungawa suddenly cursed, making Amber look up.

Before them stood four men, thin and travel worn, their eyes filled with fear and suspicion. Three had swords, and the fourth held a spiked club. The leader, a bald man with round features, stepped forward. Before Amber and Tungawa could react, he took the halter of one of the oxen in his hand, bringing the cart to a halt.

"We want your oxen and your cart. We'll take any food you have also."

Amber and Tungawa exchanged glances.

Hearing loud voices, Miro stirred. "What's happening?"

"Miro, there's danger," Amber called to him. "You'd better get up."

"Well, did you hear me?" the bald brigand said. "There's four of us, and you're a woman, an old man, and an invalid."

"Our lives are more valuable than this cart," Tungawa said. "We should give it to them."

"Listen to the old man's advice. Quickly now!" the bald brigand brandished his sword.

Amber helped Miro get to his feet. Together they climbed down to stand beside the cart. Miro weaved from side to side as Amber held him upright.

Amber gripped the flask Tungawa had given her tightly in her hand. She tried to hide it with her body; this was the antidote they had come all this way to get.

Both she and Miro were unarmed. Tungawa began to climb down from the cart.

"What's in the flask?" the bald brigand said.

"It's nothing," said Amber.

"Give it here."

Amber handed the bald man the flask while Tungawa finished climbing down. She glanced at Miro, who returned her concerned look.

"Please," Amber said, "be careful. It's medicine for my son."

The brigand flicked the catch and levered the stopper open. He sniffed at the flask suspiciously. "Ugh," he said.

Amber watched in horror as he upended the flask, tipping the contents out onto the ground. *"No!"* she cried.

Miro went into action.

He sprang forward, and his fist clipped the bald brigand under the chin while his other hand grabbed at the flask.

The brigand fell down, clutching his head, and suddenly his sword was in one of Miro's hands, the flask in the other. Two of the bald man's followers charged, but the cart was in the way, preventing the fourth man from coming forward.

Miro ducked a slashing sword and thrust into one brigand's chest. As his opponent fell, Miro turned to the next, the man with the club, attacking furiously until he opened up the third man's throat. The fourth man came around the back of the cart, his sword raised and face twisted with a combination of fear and rage.

Tungawa was in the way. The alchemist raised his hands, but the sword came forward to enter his chest, penetrating through the black robe.

Miro leapt at the last brigand before the man reached Amber. Blocking an overhead blow, Miro slashed his opponent's chest, cutting through the flesh and sending a spray of blood into the air.

Miro's arms lowered and he panted, falling to his knees.

Amber came forward. "Tungawa!" she cried.

Blood soaked the front of the fallen alchemist's robe. Amber heard scurrying behind her and saw the bald brigand rise to his feet. She saw the thoughts cross his face as he realized he was the last of his men standing, and then he turned and ran.

Tungawa rolled to his back and stared at the sky. He coughed, and redness splattered from his mouth onto his lips and chin.

Amber felt Miro beside her.

"My lung has been punctured," Tungawa gasped. "I can feel it filling with blood. I won't last long."

"The cure," Miro said. He shook the flask, but it was empty. "You have to tell us how we can get more."

The old alchemist's lips curled in a smile, and his eyes began to glaze. "Reach into my robe. Look for a book."

Miro felt around inside the blood-soaked robe until he found a leather-bound book, thick, but small enough to fit in a pocket. There was blood on the outside, but the pages were protected.

"The knowledge you need is in there. Find the most gifted of your loremasters and give him this book. Not only does the book detail the cure you need, it contains our greatest secrets. When you give it to the loremaster, tell him this."

Tungawa's voice faded, and both Amber and Miro leaned in close.

Finally he spoke again, little more than a whisper. "Tell him everything is toxic, and small amounts of things considered poisonous can do good, whereas large amounts of substances we think are safe can kill. My Guild has helped as many as we have hurt. I hope someone remembers this."

A gurgling rattle came from Tungawa's chest, and his eyes stared sightlessly. The alchemist was dead.

42

They left the alchemist where he lay, along with the three bodies of the brigands. With no time to lose, they took the cart along the road until they saw the bridge Tungawa had spoken of.

It was a narrow span of stones, and with the wide river surging below, the oxen were reluctant to cross but eventually, with coaxing, the beasts pulled the cart over the bridge. The road ahead was infrequently traveled, the alchemist had said, but if they continued south, passing through the forested hills, they would reach the small town of Rengwin. From then on, they would be in Veldria.

Miro and Amber traveled day and night, one of them always with the reins held firmly in hand. They could see the oxen flagging, and gave them short rests, but always they drove on, pushing south, desperate to outrace the army and reach Emirald before the enemy.

It was impossible to say what Rengwin had once been like. The town was in ruins, buildings burned to the ground and timbers lying across the road. The strewn remnants of houses blocked the streets so that they couldn't take the cart any further. The army was definitely ahead of them.

From here on, they would be walking.

Their footsteps angled slightly toward the setting sun, heading south but with a westward bent, a path that would intersect the road to Emirald. Miro and Amber both kept a keen eye out for it.

Shading his eyes, Miro finally called out as he pointed something out to Amber. "Look!"

Like a river of gray stone, the road pointed directly south. In that direction was Emirald. Miro only hoped the emir would keep his promise.

"I can't see the army on the road," Amber said.

"Neither can I. I don't think we've passed it though, which is worrisome. You saw Rengwin. The enemy must be ahead of us."

"We should shadow the road. If we keep it in sight and travel south, there's less chance of running into trouble."

At mid-morning the next day, they came upon another town. Evidently, it had once been a way-stop for travelers journeying on their way north or south. Like Rengwin, it had been razed.

A terrible force had gone through the town like a storm, shattering the brick dwellings and setting fire to anything that would burn. In some places the garishly colored façades of the Veldrin houses still lined the streets. Bodies had been left to rot in the sun, a sure sign Sentar was in a hurry now that Emirald lay before him.

Miro and Amber left the shattered town behind, and still hugging the road, kept watch for the enemy that marched ahead of them.

"Is this what will happen to Altura?" Amber asked.

She looked at Miro when he didn't immediately respond. The marks on his face were still there, plain to see, but strength had returned to his voice. He now wore an expression of fierce determination Amber had seen before, during the darkest days of the war against the primate.

"No, this won't happen to Altura. Not while we're alive to defend it," Miro vowed.

‒‒‒‒◆‒‒‒‒

Two days later, they came across the enemy encampment. It was early evening, and with the low light Miro and Amber almost stumbled across it. Suddenly, Miro's arm shot out, and he grabbed Amber's shoulder, silencing her with a glare.

They were traveling through the forest and couldn't see far into the distance, but they'd entered a clearing. Lazy trails of smoke rose from behind the trees ahead.

Revenants didn't need to rest or eat. But the necromancers who controlled them did.

"I think it's them," Miro breathed in Amber's ear.

"Should we turn around? How can we be sure?"

Miro wore the sword he'd taken from the brigands. He rested his hand on the hilt while he gazed at the thick trees ahead.

"I'll be back," he muttered, and without another word he moved into the trees, leaving Amber behind.

Miro crept forward, stealing through the undergrowth. He maneuvered from tree to tree, finally seeing lights ahead. He heard cries and moans, the sounds of anguish unmistakable. Again he remembered lying on his back on the iron table and felt the fear he'd felt then send a shiver up his spine. It was all the confirmation he needed.

A moment later Miro emerged from the trees, returning to Amber's side.

"Don't do that again," she said. "Well?"

"It's them. I could hear the screams."

"What should we do?"

"We need to get ahead of them," he said.

"How?"

"The road passes through a valley here, so the army's squeezed between the hills on both sides. Sneaking through will be impossible."

Amber scanned the cliffs on both sides of the valley. "The cliffs. There." She pointed. "I'll bet we can climb up there. If we follow the escarpment, we can get past the army."

Miro looked skeptically at the heights. "We'd be killed."

"Do you have a better idea?"

"Shh . . ." Miro held up his hand. "Do you hear something?"

"I can hear running water."

"Exactly."

Miro led Amber in the direction of the tinkling sound of water. They came to the edge of a gully, where a thin stream at the bottom of an old riverbed sent water in a vaguely southern direction.

"Rather than climb the cliffs, we can follow this as far as it takes us," Miro said. "The gully provides good cover, and it's heading in the right direction. Come on." He turned to descend the steep wall to the riverbed. He suddenly felt Amber pull him back.

She held his arm firmly. "You're not going anywhere. How do you know this isn't going to take you right into the middle of the enemy camp, where you'll find some necromancer washing his robe in the water?"

"It's better than your idea of scaling the cliffs!"

"You're right. But you said yourself the army will be occupying the entire valley. That includes this gully. Your plan needs one small change."

"What's that?"

Amber released Miro's arm and folded her arms across her breasts. "We're going to try this in the middle of the night."

Pale moonlight shone through the trees above as the two figures walked in single file along the narrow ravine. The walls rose on both sides, and if anything they seemed to have grown higher, so that the gully was becoming a small canyon. Miro was thankful as he looked up at the steep sides. Even the moonlight failed to reach these depths.

Something splashed in the water ahead; Miro and Amber both froze. They waited several long breaths before resuming their stealthy walk.

The canyon turned slightly to the left, and Miro prayed they were still heading in the right direction; down here, it was impossible to tell. He prayed the riverbed wouldn't loop back around, leading them back to where they'd started.

They had been walking for at least an hour. Miro judged that by now they should be nearing the enemy. Where were they?

Miro jumped when he felt Amber grab his arm, pinching the skin tightly between her fingers. There was something ahead, a great mound, nearly blocking the ravine. Seeing that it was just a hill, Miro wondered why Amber had grabbed him.

Then he realized what the mound was.

It was a pile of corpses, too many of them to count, with bodies thrown from above, one on top of the other, until they'd formed this huge stack. Miro heard voices, and both he and Amber shrank back against the wall as they crept forward.

"Ready. Heave!"

A body flew through the air to land on top of the mound. Miro saw two robed figures on the edge of the gully, dusting their hands on their garments.

"Come on, let's get the next."

"Why do we have to do this?"

"Renrik's orders. These draugar have decayed too much in this heat. Now that we're moving faster, we're not going to process any more until we reach Emirald. There'll be plenty of fresh bodies after we take the city."

"Yes, but why do we have to throw them in the gully?"

"Where else would you put them?"

"Just leave them where they are."

The other man snorted. "That's disgusting."

"After everything I've seen you do, you're calling me disgusting?"

The voices trailed off.

Seeing his opportunity, Miro quickly took Amber's hand and led her past the mound. He tried not to look at the bodies as they passed, but as they skirted along the side, he couldn't help himself.

These were the revenants too decayed to fight on. In the pile were Gokani and Nareans, barbarians and Veldrins. Miro knew the sight would haunt him to the end of his days.

"Who's that down there?" a voice called from above.

"One of them's still alive!"

"You fool! We checked them all. None of them could still be alive. It must be someone else. Raise the alarm!"

Miro knew the time for caution was gone. He grabbed Amber's hand and started to run.

Behind them, Miro heard a commotion as the chase began. He put on a burst of extra speed and felt Amber stumble behind him.

Miro now had to put his faith in the terrain. The steep drop from above provided protection, but his greatest concern was that the enemy would outpace them. He would soon find out when the ravine ended.

He ran until his legs felt like they were on fire and Amber begged him to stop. Their breathing came labored, and their foreheads dripped with sweat, but still they ran on.

Miro and Amber dashed along the riverbed as the canyon veered right and then back left again. Suddenly, the walls dropped away as the gully became shallower. They were near the end.

Miro pulled up short, his hand on his sword. Panting, he scanned the trees at the gully's end, where the stream continued to wander, with gentle banks sloping downward at both sides. For now, they were alone.

"Look," Amber panted, her chest heaving as she pointed at the horizon.

The sun was rising. The sun rose in the east, which meant they were facing south.

"We made it. We're ahead of the army."

"Now we just need to find the road," Miro said. "Come on. We'll keep our heads down, but we'll find it. It's time for speed above all else now."

By midday they'd joined the road, and by afternoon they could see hills and spires ahead. Miro recognized the rising tiers of Emirald, with the domes and towers of the emir's palace a rose and turquoise crown above it all.

The road was deserted; all of the refugees had long departed this area.

The Lord of the Night's great army was behind them, and Emirald lay ahead.

43

Rogan Jarvish stood high on the balcony, overlooking Imperial Square, and wondered where it had all gone wrong.

Days ago the crowd below had started as a mob, but now it was a seething mass of people, an ocean of figures as far as the eye could see. They pressed up against the gates of the Imperial Palace and filled the Grand Boulevard from one side to the other. Most of all, they thronged Imperial Square, where from this very balcony the emperors of the past had given speeches both grand and sinister.

Now, Rogan could only look on as the packed citizens of Seranthia heaved and cried out, rolling and pushing as they gathered together, united in their frustration.

Rogan still didn't know if he'd done the right thing when he'd told the people the truth about the Evermen. He'd always believed in truth; that open eyes see the clearest, and that once caught in a lie, never again could you earn the people's trust.

But try as he might, Rogan had never managed to earn the people of Seranthia's trust. The Tingaran soldiers followed him, and Rogan knew he had their respect, if not their love, but to the common people he was an Alturan oppressor. His words of honesty and empathy spoke to their minds, but not their hearts. Words couldn't fill stomachs, nor could they restore a great nation's pride.

Down below, Rogan saw the troublemaking stonemason, Bastian, standing on top of a wagon and exhorting the crowd to greater frenzy. His words were lost, but he pointed frequently at the balcony where Rogan stood, and shook his fist as the crowd roared in anger.

"Are you going to speak to them?" Amelia asked behind him.

"What can I say?"

"Take back what you said about the Evermen."

"How can I do that? It would be a lie, and they wouldn't believe anything I said again."

"They don't have anything else," Amelia said. "They need hope."

"And food in their stomachs," Rogan said. "The Empire's coffers are empty, and the harvest came up short. What can I do?"

"Maybe we should just go home."

Rogan turned away from the balcony and moved inside, holding Amelia by the arm and bringing her with him. "Will you go? Please, Amelia. Tapel will be safer, and I'll feel better knowing you're far from here."

"You stubborn man. What good can you do by staying?"

"If I leave now, the Empire is doomed. I can't let that happen. Someone like Bastian will take charge in the void, and Tingara will do what it thinks it needs to do, what Tingara has done in the past when in need of resources."

"And what's that?"

"I've kept the Tingaran army whole. The last thing the city needs is more men without jobs. What would you do, if you had a strong army and little else? They'll go to war, Amelia. With Aynar or Torakon—it doesn't matter whom. When there are too many people competing for too few resources, men fight. The battles whittle down the numbers, and to the victors go the spoils. The rest die."

"Does it matter, if we're safe in Altura?" Amelia asked.

"Yes, it matters! I won't have all that blood on my hands."

"But you said it yourself. There are too many people competing for not enough food, and too little work. How are you going to solve that problem? If you don't know how, then you should at least save yourself."

"Evrin Evenstar—" Rogan began.

"—is working on the machines as we speak. I know that, Rogan. You've said it more times than I can count. In the meantime, the people of Seranthia need something to believe in, and now they don't have the Evermen, they no longer have any hope. The people of Seranthia need a sign. Give them something."

"What do I give them? An enemy to fight? A higher power to pray to? I don't know what to believe myself! How do you fight hunger?"

"Give them hope," Amelia said softly.

Rogan suddenly punched the wall, heedless of the hard stone bruising his knuckles. "I don't know how!" he roared. "I'm a soldier, not even a noble. But no one else is willing to take this from my shoulders. If you have an idea for me, woman, then tell it to me!"

Amelia's eyes filled with sorrow as she reached forward and squeezed Rogan's shoulder. "You'll think of something," she said. "You always do."

She turned and left Rogan alone, knowing his moods. He sat down on a chair and put his head in his hands while the roaring crowd outside drove home his sense of impotence.

He had to think of something.

"Damn you, Miro," Rogan said to himself. "You wanted to tell them, so why aren't you here now?"

The crowd was angry now, but soon it would turn violent.

44

The huge harbor was filled with ships. The emir had recalled his warships, merchantmen, galleons, and caravels, so that vessels crammed the port of Emirald, and a person could walk from one end of the docks to the other by clambering from one deck to the next.

The ships had emptied their crews—the coming battle would be fought on land, not on the sea. Sailors hastily formed into military units, taking many of the mighty cannon from the warships and moving them to the walls facing north.

The enemy would soon be here.

Built on a hillside overlooking the water, the city of Emirald had only two faces: the harbor, where twin arms of wood and stone enclosed the emir's floating pride in their protective embrace; and the walls. The city faced the harbor, the palace faced the harbor, and the houses of the city's residents faced the harbor. Only the poor lived in small houses on the rear of the hillside, where they couldn't see the water.

The walls had been added to the landward side of the city nearly as an afterthought. But they were strong walls, thick rather than tall, and soon they would be the only defense against the horde.

Unlike Wengwai, Emirald wasn't built in concentric circles, with a series of inner walls to fall back to. Crowning the city with ivory towers and glorious domes, the emir's palace had been designed with beauty in mind, rather than defense. The emir's navy had always been all the protection Emirald's citizens needed, and the nations of Gokan and Narea in the north had always been an effective buffer against the barbarian horde. The landward walls had been built because . . . well . . . a city should have walls.

Now soldiers lined these walls, all staring grimly north.

Like swarming ants, the horde could now be seen from the heights of the palace. Those gazing out initially didn't believe their eyes. Surely no army could be this big. Where were the supply trains? How could they feed so many men?

A new order circulated throughout the city. Without exception, every male between the age of fourteen and sixty was commanded to join those at the walls.

Cannon were readied and checked, sighted and prepared. Children took buckets of water to the walls and placed countless huge jugs on coals, the smell of heating pitch filling the air. Soldiers placed pole-arms along the heights, ready to push away the enemy's scaling ladders.

The emir stripped his palace of his elite personal guard and sent them to join the defenders. He now looked at the harbor. It was mid-morning, and the sun climbed the sky over the sea, glistening on the water.

The pride he'd once felt at seeing his two hundred warships now tasted like ashes in his mouth. His naval might was powerless against this foe.

Turning away from the harbor and moving to watch the coming battle on the city's other side, Emir Volkan saw his doom unfold. The horde came ever onward and would now likely be visible to the men on the walls. Volkan knew how his men must be feeling, for he felt it himself. There were simply so many of the enemy. How could they ever hold against them?

He'd sent messengers to talk to whoever commanded this force and discuss terms. None had returned.

The refugees who poured down from the north carried wild stories, none of which made sense. They spoke of barbarian warriors who could not be killed and a leader in black who could rise into the air. Emir Volkan wished he knew what he could believe.

He frowned when he saw two distant figures running toward the walls.

———◆———

With the revenant army close on their heels, Miro and Amber ran for the walls of Emirald in one mad dash. As fast as they'd been moving, the enemy had still moved faster. They hadn't realized the army was gaining ground on them until the thunder of footsteps filled the air.

As the city grew in Miro's vision, he saw that the wide gates were sealed shut. Soldiers stared down at him from the walls, which bristled with spears, muskets, and longbows. Cannon peeked out from behind the battlements, ready to rain destruction on those below. There were more defenders than Miro had seen on the walls at Wengwai, but the walls there had been taller, and the Gokani had possessed many more cannon.

The Lord of the Night's army would have grown since the fall of Wengwai. The Gokani dead had been added to their numbers, and northern Veldria had also been ravaged. Miro saw nothing that would stop Sentar from taking this city.

Miro halted when he saw the gates stay shut, his chest heaving as he looked up at the grim faces of the soldiers. Amber placed her hands on her hips, her breath coming in gasps.

411

"Please!" Miro shouted, cupping his hands to his mouth. "Let us in!"

An officer came to the front, pushing through the men occupying the battlements above the gates. He called down to Miro. "We can't open the gates. They've been sealed, and wooden stocks now hold them from behind. Leave this area!"

"I need to speak with the emir!"

"And why would the emir want to speak to you?"

"He knows me. Send word. Tell him Miro from Altura is here. Tell him I have important information about the enemy."

The officer disappeared, and Miro prayed he wasn't simply being ignored.

The ground trembled behind them. It was mid-morning, and Sentar was in a hurry. Would he pause before attacking and again give a display of his power to the defenders? Or would he simply attack with everything he had?

"Hurry!" Miro called up at the walls.

Miro tried to put himself in the mind of Sentar Scythran. The emir's ships were within his grasp. He had his indomitable army, and across the expanse of the ocean the Empire was weak, barely holding together.

Miro realized how desperately he needed to warn the Empire about what was ahead. The greatest threat the Empire had ever faced would come across the sea, and unless they were prepared, this remorseless foe would gain a foothold in Altura and continue the cycle of death and destruction. Miro's people would be added to the revenant army, and then the people of Halaran, and the process would continue all the way to Tingara itself.

The Evermen would return to a world where the humans were once again enslaved. The Evermen would spread like a disease to other worlds.

They had to be stopped.

45

Ella watched from a distance as Killian spoke quietly with his father, Lord Aidan, the man to whom she'd given a semblance of life after over twenty years in the grave.

She wondered what they were talking about. Aidan had known his wife carried his child, but he had never even met the babe. How much of Killian's father's personality remained?

Unlike the energy in a zenblade or the power of a fireball, the unique lore of the Akari could not be quantified. Ella wasn't sure what she believed about death. All she knew was that Lord Aidan wasn't the man he'd been in life.

While the two men spoke, Ella watched the stone archway. There was no way to tell when the portal would open, but Ella planned to move quickly when it did.

She marveled again at Killian's powers. Ella had helped enhance his body once before, but she had treated him like an item to be enchanted. She'd given his limbs the strength of iron, his skin the toughness of stone. What he was now was something far beyond Ella's wildest imaginings.

Against Sentar Scythran, they now had a chance.

Killian's gestures betrayed his emotion. The revenant, in contrast, was wooden and still. Only the occasional tremble of his arms showed Lord Aidan still possessed an element of life.

Ella wondered about the Evermen. What were they? If they weren't human, where had they come from? Had they long ago opened a portal to Merralya and conquered those they found already there, in the same way they'd conquered Shar?

Somehow it seemed unlikely. The Evermen considered themselves more than human, but to Ella, Killian was human, just like her, albeit a man with extraordinary powers. His features were human, and his mother had been a normal person. The fact that Evrin and a human woman had produced offspring led Ella to believe the Evermen weren't a separate race altogether.

Would Evrin know? In their time together Ella had asked him about his youth. Evrin Evenstar was incredibly old, his lifespan many times that of an ordinary man, but he said his oldest memories were murky, like pages of a picture book faded over the years.

Whatever his youth had been like, Evrin Evenstar had been the Lord of the Sky for eons, ruling over his lands and the humans who lived in them. After the war that saw the humans made free and the Evermen exiled to Shar, he'd traveled the land for eons more, looking for a surviving child from his love with a human woman. His memories were piled one atop another, and asking about his youth was searching too many layers deep.

Finally discovering Killian had spurred Evrin into taking action, whereas before he'd stayed silent and let the people of Merralya fight. Evrin had promised himself he would no longer seek to control the destiny of the people he once ruled. He'd stood by and looked on during more wars than he cared to remember, and always he'd stayed his hand. The primate's evil had finally changed his mind. The ensuing events had culminated with Killian crossing over to Shar.

Soon, Ella would bring Killian back home.

Ella hoped talking to his father might bring Killian some peace. She promised herself that if Lady Alise were still alive, she would try to see Killian reunited with his mother.

Ella saw Lord Aidan slump. His head fell, and his arms dropped to his sides. Ella didn't know what Killian was saying, but she saw him take the revenant's arms and shake him.

Lord Aidan's fists suddenly clenched at his sides, and Ella's eyes went wide as she remembered the warnings of Aldrik and Barnabas.

Aldrik's words came back to her now.

"It happens only once in a while, and only to the draugar we bring back with more of who they were. Sometimes the eyes turn entirely red, and the life leaves them." The necromancer's voice had turned ominous. *"But before they go, they become berserk."*

Ella looked again at the revenant. She'd had to bring back much of the man he had been, using the forbidden lore Barnabas had taught her; otherwise, she wouldn't have been able to cross the portal.

Lord Aidan straightened, and a shudder went through his body. His body tensed, and Killian took two steps back.

Ella opened her mouth to cry out, when she heard a series of shrieks behind her, sending a chill through her body.

Turning, she saw a black cloud fill the twilight sky. Wraiths. Dozens of them.

Killian had turned also, and Ella saw him point at the wraiths.

At that instant, with Killian's attention diverted, Lord Aidan attacked.

46

With the horde thundering toward the walls of Emirald, someone lowered a rope and hoisted first Amber and then Miro up to the walls.

"Quick!" Miro felt a hand shove him. "Get out of here!"

The revenant army crashed into the walls, and beneath him Miro felt the stone tremble. A soldier herded Miro and Amber down from the walls even as ladders slapped up against the battlements. Miro saw defenders carry buckets of boiling pitch up to the walls in the opposite direction.

"Do you know the way to the palace?" the soldier asked when they were down.

Miro nodded. "I can find it."

"Good. You'll have to talk your own way in. I'm needed here."

The soldier turned around and ran back up to the walls, sword in hand. Miro admired the Veldrin's courage.

"Come on," Miro said to Amber, taking her by the hand. "We need to hurry. This city won't last."

The climb up the sloping streets was arduous after the sprint to the city walls. Miro picked a path on the deserted roads, leading them continuously upward and toward the heights.

Miro was surprised to see there weren't any soldiers at the palace. He simply walked in, remembering the last time he'd come here under guard, marveling at the ivory spires and turquoise domes, the tranquil fountains and grassy courtyards.

"I'm going to look over the harbor," Amber said. "There's a good view from up here in the palace, and there must be someone ready to flee the city on a ship."

"Good idea," Miro said. "Don't go too far."

She squeezed his arm. "Good luck."

As he watched Amber head to the seaward side of the palace, Miro wondered where the emir would be. He decided to look for a place that afforded a view of the landward side of the city. He spotted a marble-columned structure, and sure enough, a lone figure stood with his white-knuckled hands on a rail, looking upon the unfolding battle at the walls below.

"Emir Volkan!" Miro called as he approached.

The figure turned.

The emir's flowing robe was deep blue this time, the color of the ocean, and belted with silver. His sharp nose and dark eyes were as penetrating as ever, but Miro could see the lines of care around his eyes. Together with the gray in his beard, his worried eyes made him look old.

Emir Volkan was afraid.

"Ah, look who it is, the man I sent north to gather information on the enemy. Tell me, Miro of Altura, what can you tell me about the enemy's numbers?" the emir asked with heavy irony.

Miro joined the emir at the rail. The Veldrin soldiers below were fighting valiantly, and for now their numbers held back the dark tide.

"We now meet under very different circumstances," Miro said.

"What are those creatures?"

"They're called revenants. The dead are given a semblance of life and made to serve in the army they died fighting against. One of the Evermen leads them. He calls himself the Lord of the Night."

"So," Emir Volkan said, "it seems we were both right. Your ancient enemy is here, and lore has destroyed my land."

"We can fight them," Miro said.

The emir barked a laugh. "How do you fight a multitude of warriors who will not die? They say this ruler is a man no blade or ball can harm. We're doomed."

"There's something I can offer you that may help."

Emir Volkan turned and looked at Miro. "Look at you. You've got nothing. You've been beaten. I see it in your eyes. I don't need to see the bruises on your face to tell me. What can you offer me, Lord Marshal Miro? Can you make this Lord of the Night pass us by?"

"No." Miro shook his head. "I'm afraid not. Veldria was his target all along. Here in Emirald you have the ships he needs to take his army across the ocean. He won't stop until your harbor is in his hands, and your people have been butchered or enslaved just like those in the north."

"My people will never be slaves." The emir bit the words off.

"You won't have a choice. You'll serve in death."

"No," the emir said flatly. "I will destroy my corpse before it serves my enemy. I will destroy my body, my city, and as many of my people as I can before I allow us to become slaves. I will not allow us to serve the army that comes to destroy your homeland, as it has mine. You have my word on that."

"There's another way for your people," Miro said, "some of them at least. I have something I can offer you."

"What can you offer me?"

"Safe haven . . . refuge . . . in my land. For as many of your people as we can get out of here aboard your ships."

The emir turned to Miro, looking deep into his eyes. "You would do that? You would welcome my people, feed them, and shelter them? You have the power to offer me this?"

"We can load your women and children into some of your ships and your sailors can bring them to my land. Once there, I'll ensure they're fed and clothed and given shelter. I am second only to the high lord, and I can speak for him," Miro said. "Later, when we've defeated Sentar Scythran, your people can come back to these lands to rebuild. Veldria can live again. As long as the memory of your civilization exists, it can live again."

"I need your word," Emir Volkan said.

"I give you my word. But there's something I'll need in return."

"What do you want?"

"I want your help, and that of your men. Those of your ships that don't make it out of here, we need to destroy. Destroying your ships, all of them, will give us the time we need to escape and to prepare my homeland's defense."

"And I have your word that you will treat my people well?"

"You do. You can come yourself to make sure of it."

"No." The emir turned his gaze back to the surging battle at the walls. A boy raced a bucket of pitch up to some soldiers, who instantly poured it onto the revenants below, following the oil with a tossed torch. Flames rolled up. The viscous oil was proving to be the main reason the walls hadn't yet been overrun. "Do you see the men with their buckets of pitch?" Emir Volkan suddenly asked.

"Yes." Miro's heart went out to the courageous soldiers. They surely knew to a man that to lose the walls would be to doom everyone and everything they held dear.

"The oil comes from the catacombs that worm through the hillside this city was built on. It seeps up from the lower ground, and we collect it and store it in the higher tunnels. I have had our

419

reserves of black powder also taken to the catacombs, to be stored alongside the oil. Do you understand what I'm saying?"

"I think I do," Miro said, seeing the resolve in the emir's eyes.

"I will stay here, and take as many of the enemy with me as I can. I will watch as my ships leave the harbor, and as you destroy those vessels you don't take with you. Then, when the time comes, I will destroy this city and everyone left in it."

Miro nodded, knowing there was nothing he could say.

"You have my word on that," Emir Volkan said.

47

Shani looked at the oval mirror and then crouched down next to the device Ella had placed over the three Lexicons.

Bartolo and Jehral watched her with concern. The group of three had guarded the portal day and night, with the tension affecting them all. What would they do if someone crossed, and their combined efforts couldn't prevent some evil force gaining entry?

The ancient chamber within the Sentinel wasn't a pleasant place to sleep, eat, and share company. There was something eerie about the light that came from all places and none. The decayed wall was a mystery no one could explain, and made it appear as if a dark tide had permeated the chamber, melting all in its path. Shani and Bartolo bickered, and Jehral retreated into himself, becoming silent and moody. They had all put their faith in Ella, and each of them secretly wondered if they'd done the right thing.

"They're fading," Shani said, looking at the Lexicons.

"Are you sure?" Bartolo asked.

Shani glared at Bartolo. "I'm sure."

"Just asking."

"How long do we have?" Jehral asked.

"Opening the portal the first time must have taken more power from the Lexicons than Ella planned."

"How long?"

"I don't know. I've been monitoring them closely. We can't chance it . . ." Shani made a decision. "I'm going to open the portal."

"Shani," Jehral said, "Ella said to wait exactly three days."

"Do you want to leave her stranded there?"

"What if you open the portal, and she's not there?" Bartolo said. "What if you open it and drain whatever power is left, so you can't open it again?"

"If we wait much longer, I can promise you there won't be enough power to open the portal at all."

Jehral and Bartolo exchanged glances.

"Ella said . . ." Jehral began.

"I know what Ella said! She's my friend too. I'm telling you, we have to open it now, while we still can."

Jehral spoke to Bartolo. "I'm no loremaster."

"Nor am I."

"What if she's right?"

"I'm telling you, I'm right!" Shani said. "Men! Jehral, if Ilathor were here, you'd do as he asked without a second thought. Bartolo, you'd be the same if Rogan gave you an order."

"Are you ordering us now?" Bartolo said, smiling to take the sting out of his words.

"I'm telling you what I believe. We need to open the portal."

"I can't let you do it," Bartolo said, growing serious again.

Shani scowled and straightened, placing her hands on her hips. "Let me? You can't . . . *let* me?"

"Please, both of you," said Jehral, his palms raised in placation. "Calm down. We need to make the right decision here. The wrong decision could leave Ella stranded on the other side."

"Opening the portal now is the right decision," Shani said.

"It's the wrong move," said Bartolo.

Jehral sighed, as the elementalist glared at her husband, and the bladesinger returned her glower.

What was happening on the other side of the portal?

They had no way of knowing.

48

While battle raged on the walls of Emirald, orders arrived to recall the sailors among the defenders, asking them to convene in the harbor.

Commodore Deniz was fighting to close a breach when the order came. A skilled swordsman, the Holdfast champion three years running, he fought like a man possessed.

His blade was perfectly straight and custom made from Narean steel. He'd been a lieutenant for six years and a captain for ten. He'd crushed the pirate fortress of Gaskar and defeated Zafra, the pirate king, in personal combat. The emir had personally promoted him to commodore, a rank he'd held for five more years. Deniz had seen his fair share of combat.

Deniz didn't understand this enemy, but he believed all creatures could be killed. The defenders had quickly learned that flame and heat were the best weapons against these unholy warriors, and pitch came up to the walls in a steady stream. Deniz discovered removing the heads was the most efficient means of dispatching the creatures with a sword and made sure to instruct the men accordingly.

Headless bodies now piled the walls in numbers, so that between the waves of attackers the defenders threw them down from the walls to clear space to fight.

As revenants poured onto the walls, Deniz came forward and took a barbarian's head from his shoulders in a single blow. He ducked a slashing sword and thrust into a throat, amazed again when no blood came out. His opponent's white eyes stared at him, and no cry of fear or pain came from the creature's mouth. Deniz hacked at his enemy's neck, once, twice, before the creature fell down. He narrowly avoided being skewered by a spear and turned to face the new threat. Soldiers dashed forward to join him in closing the breach, pushing the enemy back and knocking away the scaling ladders. Deniz dispatched two more of the creatures, and then the wall was clear.

Deniz lowered his sword and stood panting. The defenders around him cheered, though they knew it was only a matter of time.

"Water!" Deniz cried.

Instead, a soldier came forward and handed the commodore a hastily scrawled note.

The order from the emir came as a mystery. Deniz could only assume they were going to try to assemble a naval force and flee. But where would they go?

Deniz turned to the men around him. "I've been ordered to the harbor. Any sailors on the walls are to join me there. Pass the word around."

"What's happening, Commodore?"

Deniz decided truth was best. "I don't know. But I promise you, I'll send word when I find out."

The message had been short.

All naval personnel to report to the harbor. Follow the instructions of the man who carries my signet ring. His name is Miro. Do as he bids.

By order of the Ruler of the Seas, the Protector of Veldria, and the Bearer of the Seal: Emir Volkan.

Miro. The name was familiar, but Deniz couldn't quite place it.

49

Miro stood with Amber at the harbor, looking for some leaders among the growing numbers of confused Veldrin sailors, when a familiar figure came forward.

"You," Commodore Deniz called out. "What's going on?"

Blood covered the well-dressed captain of the *Seekrieger*, and he still carried his fine sword in one hand. He'd obviously come straight from the walls, and Deniz glowered at Miro, evidently believing he was needed elsewhere.

Miro displayed the emir's signet ring. "I need your help, Commodore."

"Explain quickly."

"You said my origin was a mystery. I'm from a land called Altura, in the east, across the sea. It's a long voyage to Altura, but not an impossible one. I am a leader in my homeland, and I have come to an arrangement with the emir."

"What arrangement?"

"Right now, there are women, children, the old, and the young cowering in their homes. The city is lost, and the walls will fall. There is nothing any of us can do to prevent that. There is, however, something we can do for those people. I have offered refuge in

Altura, my homeland, for every man, woman, and child who can make the voyage across the sea. In return, the emir has promised me your help in destroying those ships we don't take with us."

"You want our help in destroying the fleet?"

"This enemy is led by a man who has come to your city with one objective only. He wants these ships so that he can fill them full of warriors and take them across the sea. He cares nothing for your nation. This objective consumes him. He will come—nothing can prevent that—but if we destroy as many ships as we can, we will delay his arrival and give my people time to prepare."

Miro could see Deniz was uncertain. "Commodore," he said, "your city, Emirald, will fall. Veldria will fall, as the nations in your north have already fallen. But if we can take some of your people away from here, they can return one day to rebuild. Their memories will keep Veldria alive, and the future will be brighter for your people than the death that awaits them at the hands of these monsters."

"I see," Commodore Deniz said. "You gave the emir your word, I presume?"

Miro smiled. "As a man of honor. I'll see that your people are safe."

Commodore Deniz nodded. "I will do as you say."

He suddenly burst into action, and Miro recognized a kindred spirit. This was not a man used to sitting still.

"Lieutenant Mustaf." Deniz addressed a man in the crowd. "Do any of the ships still have powder aboard?"

"The emir's ordered all the powder to the catacombs, Commodore."

Deniz swore. "Lieutenant, take fifty men and keep bringing powder kegs down to this position. Don't stop. Keep them coming."

"Yes, sir!"

Deniz pointed to another man. "Captain Arsan, get fifty men together. Send them throughout the streets. Get everyone out of their homes. Tell everyone you can find that we're taking them to safety. Send them down to the harbor."

"Yes, sir!"

"Captain Drefan, oversee getting the new arrivals into the ships. Load up the warships and cruisers first. Start at the vessels closest to the harbor mouth."

"Aye aye, Commodore!"

Deniz addressed another man. "Lieutenant Oster, send ten men to the walls. Spread the word as quickly as possible. Tell those who fight that we're taking their women and children to safety. By the stars, if they weren't fighting before, they will now."

Deniz turned to Miro. "Do you know how to scuttle a ship?"

"I can start a fire."

"That'll do. Start here, close to the city."

Commodore Deniz raised his voice. "You know what we're doing here. Be prepared to act on your own initiative. We're sending our women and children to a new land, and we'll destroy those ships we aren't taking with us, so our enemy cannot follow. When a ship is full, assemble a crew, and set sail immediately. This is our only chance, men. Don't let me down!"

"Aye aye, Commodore!" the sailors chorused.

They quickly dispersed, and Miro realized he had ten men looking to him for orders.

"Where on the ships will we be guaranteed to find tools to make fire?" Miro asked the closest.

"The captain's cabin, sir. It'll be locked though."

"We can break down the doors," Amber said.

"Right. I'll take five men; you take another five. But, Amber . . ."

"What is it?"

"Be ready to flee. When they storm the city, it'll happen faster than you can imagine."

50

"Lord Regent, we must order the men out to fight the mob," the Tingaran captain said.

"They'll storm the palace," said an Alturan officer.

Rogan Jarvish cursed.

He'd gone out to speak with the crowd, but with nothing to add to his promises that things would be better, his words hadn't had any effect. He could hear the shouts now, rising up from Imperial Square, loud and angry.

"The Evermen will return!" a woman shouted.

"Why should an Alturan rule Tingara?" asked an angry voice indignantly.

"The Assembly of Templars is not evil!" came a third cry.

"When will the essence return?" someone asked plaintively.

Rogan paced back and forth, clenching and unclenching his fists with every stride. "I can't countenance slaughter," he said. "And to what end? If they see blood, they'll tear down the gates."

"They'll tear down the gates anyway," the Alturan officer said bluntly. "This is a mob. They can't be reasoned with."

Rogan looked at Amelia, sitting tensed on a chair, gazing at him with trepidation.

"Send my wife and son to safety," he suddenly said.

"We can't. Until we clear the grounds around the palace, we're stuck here."

Rogan swore again.

He thought back to the past few weeks and wondered what he could have done differently. Since the attack on Miro's wedding, nothing had gone right in Seranthia. Back before the madness of Primate Melovar Aspen, the leader of the Assembly of Templars would have soothed a crowd like this, speaking of virtue and sacrifice. Rogan was no speaker. He thought in terms of supply, strength, logistics, and fortification.

He also couldn't send soldiers to battle against civilians. He knew if he sent his men out to subdue the crowd, stones would fly, swords would be drawn, and bloodshed would follow. It was inevitable.

"Could we send out soldiers without swords?"

"I'm not sending my men out there unarmed," the Tingaran said.

"Nor I," said the Alturan.

"Scratch it!" Rogan cursed. He couldn't argue with them, though. These officers had the safety of their men in mind.

"What's that rattle?" Amelia asked.

"They're shaking the gates," said the Tingaran.

"By the Lord of the Earth's name, Rogan, you have to do something," Amelia said. "You've tried talking to them. Send out your men."

"I can't!" Rogan cried. "I won't have all that blood on my hands."

Amelia stood and walked toward him. "I know," she said softly, putting a hand on his shoulder. "It's why you're the man I love." Rogan clenched his fists. "I will only do it if there's truly no other choice," he growled.

51

Smoke poured from four ships lying docked in Emirald's great harbor. Fire blazed from a fifth, and the ocean breeze fanned the flames so that a sixth vessel caught fire of its own accord.

Yet there were thousands of ships. Miro cursed. They weren't moving quickly enough.

Several great warships loaded with the women and children of Emirald had now left, sails raised hurriedly and massive bulks lumbering along under too little wind.

There was no way to tell how the defenders at the walls fared, but the screams and clashes of weapons could be heard across the harbor. It was now early afternoon. Miro wondered if Emirald could hold longer than a day, when Wengwai had not. Commodore Deniz's words to the defenders must have had their intended effect.

The Veldrin soldiers were no longer fighting a lost cause; they were now fighting to give their loved ones time to escape.

Finally, as the sun began to fall toward the horizon, the powder kegs began to arrive at the harbor.

Miro, Amber, and the sailors helping them destroy the vessels no longer had to work in teams. Now all it took was a barrel of black powder placed at a particular part of the hold. A trail of powder made a clumsy fuse. It was dangerous work, and already they'd lost a man whose keg detonated too early. But the pace picked up, and as the heat of the burning ships intensified, the fire began to do the work on its own. The ships were crowded so closely together that they could ignore those nearest the flames.

Soon, more than a hundred ships were burning.

Miro wiped sweat from his forehead as he scanned the dock to find his next target. His face was black with soot, and a burned patch on his arm was red and raw. In the distance he saw the masts of three more ships moving along as still more women and children made their way to safety.

He could see new arrivals on the dock, crowds of confused people milling around as the sailors tried to get them into order. Some sailors had realized they would need provisions and were bringing barrels of rations, taking valuable men away from helping Miro destroy the vessels. Miro couldn't blame them. It was natural for the sailors to work to save their people and ensure they arrived at their destination safely. Hampering the efforts of those who would follow in their wake was secondary to the men of Veldria.

Miro selected his next target, a large merchantman, dwarfing the two smaller ships on either side. He sprinted along the waterfront and grabbed one of the powder kegs, seeing only three more remaining. He swore; the men who'd been bringing the small barrels down from the catacombs must have decided their efforts were needed elsewhere.

Concussive booms sounded as the sailors destroyed more vessels, the noise mingling with the battle cries drifting from the walls. As he scampered along from ship to ship, finally arriving at the high deck of the merchantman, Miro searched for Amber but couldn't see her; she must be deep in one of the holds.

He was growing adept now at finding the shortest path to the hold, and soon Miro was placing the powder keg near the stern of the ship, deep between the ribs of the vessel, in a place dry and confined. He struck a match—still amazed at the simplicity of the invention—and touched it to the trail of black powder leading to the mouthpiece of the laid-down keg.

The powder sparked and hissed, sending a trail of smoke into the air. Miro carefully walked backward, checking that the fire was traveling down the line, and then turned and ran.

He reached the open deck as the powder keg blew.

The merchantman shuddered like a creature in pain. For good measure Miro took some scraps of wood and paper he'd brought from a pocket and started a small fire on the deck, where the flames would hopefully catch in the sails.

From his vantage, Miro saw Commodore Deniz racing along the waterfront. Deniz caught sight of him and waved an arm. "We need to go. Now!"

Miro ran back along the row of ships until he was back on the dock. He took hold of Deniz's arm. "What's happening?"

"The walls have fallen. We're loading the last ship, and if you're not on it, we'll leave without you."

Miro scanned the rows of ships, searching for Amber. The smoke from the blazing vessels made it hard to see. "I have to find my wife. How will I know the ship?"

"It's my ship, the *Seekrieger*. You've seen it before. It's tied at the northern pier. Hurry!"

As Deniz sped away, Miro ran in the opposite direction, his eyes roving over every vessel, peering through the clouds of smoke, desperately looking for the familiar figure.

There she was!

"Amber!" Miro cried.

Amber was sprinting along the deck of a great warship, tied midway along a row of other vessels. Miro felt a jolt of fear when he saw she wasn't aware of the flames at both ends of the row. She was trapped.

A detonation sounded from deep in the warship as Amber's powder keg blew. Choosing a direction, Amber climbed over to the next ship in the row, not realizing that she was boxing herself in.

"Amber!" Miro called again.

He turned as he heard an eerie roar: a guttural scream of triumph. The enemy would be pouring into the city. Emirald's defenders had died to give them this time.

Miro saw the first revenants rush into the harbor as Amber finally heard his cries.

52

Killian's eyes burned with unshed tears. He saw the man who had been his father slump down, as if ready to rest now that he'd shed a heavy burden.

Lord Aidan had just told Killian that his mother was Emperor Xenovere's sister. He also thought she might still be alive. The revenant didn't know.

Killian stepped forward. Taking the revenant by the shoulders, he shook him. "You must know where she is! Why did she abandon me? Is she dead or isn't she?"

Lord Aidan's fists suddenly clenched at his sides.

He straightened and looked at Killian with eyes shifting from white to pink, and even as Killian looked on, the whites filled with blood, turning entirely red.

A shudder went through the revenant's body. Killian took two steps back.

Then a series of shrieks came from behind. Turning, Killian saw dozens of wraiths descending from the sky, screeching and filled with fury. Claws outstretched, teeth bared, they would strike Ella in moments.

Killian opened his mouth to call to her, pointing at the sky, when he felt hands encircle his neck.

Eyes wide with shock, Killian saw that the revenant's teeth were bared, his face twisted in a snarl. The visible runes on his neck and hands had shifted hue and were now bright red. The strength in the revenant's arms was incredible.

Aidan pushed harder, and a growl came from his throat. Killian gasped and choked.

Killian heard Ella chanting behind him and a whoosh was followed by the screech of a wraith in pain. Even against the agony of the revenant's grip, Killian's mind jumped from thought to thought. Could he destroy his own father? Could Ella survive against so many?

Killian wheeled his arms, smashing them down on the revenant's wrists with the iron strength of his enhanced body behind the blow. The runes on the dead man's wrists and hands flared crimson and purple, but his terrible grip held fast.

Killian panicked. His chest heaved as his body tried to suck air from his closed throat. He'd never encountered strength like this before. Unless he fought back with all his power, the revenant would kill him.

From the corner of his eye, Killian saw Ella retreating in the direction of the stone archway. Wraiths swooped at her head, deflected by the raised hood of her dress, but Killian could see she was struggling. The prism-tipped wand she held in her hand was fainter than Killian remembered. The bolts shooting from it in quick succession were smaller and hurt the wraiths less when they hit.

Ella stopped when her back was at the archway. Dozens of wraiths came at her all at once. Teeth grazed her head, and claws scraped at her back. Lightning scattered across the dress, sending three wraiths cowering in pain. Killian wondered how long she could last.

All the while he smashed his arms down on the revenant's wrists again and again. Was there anything of the man who had been Killian's father left in this creature?

"Please . . ." Killian gasped. "Let . . . go . . ."

Lord Aidan released a hand from Killian's neck, but the other kept up the incessant squeezing. He drew back a fist and slammed it into Killian's chest three times in quick succession.

Killian felt ribs snap, waves of pain spreading across his chest. Nothing should have been able to do that to him, not even the strength of a revenant. What was happening?

Lord Aidan was his father. They'd spent the last hours haltingly talking about the man he had been, at least as much as the revenant could drag forth from his confused memories. Killian couldn't destroy him.

A black wing knocked Ella's arm, and she dropped her wand. As she bent to pick it up, two wraiths clawed her back, fluttering and scratching like carrion birds on a carcass. She tilted her head back and screamed.

Ella needed Killian's help.

Killian closed his eyes, and a tear trickled down his cheek. He had to do this.

He put his palm to Lord Aidan's chest and gasped an activation sequence.

The revenant's grip on Killian's throat released as he flew backward through the air, falling against the ground, his head cracking against the stone path. Growling, the revenant climbed back to his feet and again glared at Killian with bloodred eyes. He came forward slowly, remorselessly, taking jerky strides like a Halrana construct.

A fist came toward Killian's head. Killian blocked the revenant's arm with his left arm, ducking underneath and putting all his strength into his right arm. The blow smashed into the revenant's sternum with the force of a mountain. Again Lord Aidan flew backward, and this time when he stood, his chest was caved in, the ancient ribs broken and splintered, poking from the dead flesh. But still he came on.

Killian glanced quickly at Ella. She was on her feet again, but the wraiths sensed her weakness and now pecked and scratched at her, fighting each other to bite at her head and upper body.

The revenant lashed out with hands curled like claws, aiming for Killian's eyes. Killian used his acrobatic training to duck and roll, returning to his feet a few paces away. The wraiths twisted through the sky, flying over and around the stone archway.

Suddenly, the air under the arch solidified, and a shimmering curtain appeared.

The beacon sounded, filling the air with its wailing call, the pendulum under the arch swinging left and right with every peal.

"Ella," a woman's voice called. "Are you there? Can you hear me? This is the last time we will be able to open the portal. If you're there, you have to come through!"

Ella screamed as a pair of curved teeth bit down into her shoulder. Killian pointed both hands at the revenant and finally accepted what he must do.

He shouted an activation sequence, and twin bolts of lightning shot from his fingers, bathing the revenant in deadly radiance. The creature came on, oblivious to the pain, but Killian retreated, walking backward, continuing the stream of fire.

Smoke rose from Lord Aidan's clothes, and his wispy hair blazed as it caught fire. The flesh on his face and hands blackened, sizzling and smoldering. Killian continued the attack as he walked backward and the revenant came on, face curled with hate, eyes red with blood.

Lord Aidan fell to one knee. He attempted to stand again but fell down on both knees. The skin on his face was now featureless; the only part of him recognizable was the redness of his eyes. His clothes burned away from his body, and smoke poured from him in a steady plume.

Lord Aidan fell down face forward, and then he was still.

"Ella!" the woman's voice called again. "Please hear me! You have to cross now!"

Killian lowered his hands. He'd destroyed the creature that was part monster, part his father.

The curtain of the portal shimmered and flickered as the beacon wailed, even louder than the shrieks of the wraiths.

Ella ducked a swooping shadow, launching a yellow bolt from her wand as it passed. Killian prepared to unleash his power on the wraiths.

A creature flew at the portal and disappeared through the curtain. Whatever the wraiths were, the portal's wards didn't sense the shadow creature.

53

Shani stared at the shimmering curtain of molten gold, willing Ella to come through before it was too late.

Bartolo and Jehral both stood with swords bared, ready to face anything that wasn't Ella or Killian. The beacon pealed, and both men grimaced at the intensity of the sound.

Shani looked at the Lexicons. They were fading visibly. The portal would close automatically rather than drain the Lexicons completely. Ella would be stranded on the other side.

"Ella!" Shani cried. "Please hear me! You have to cross now!"

In a lull between peals, Shani thought she could hear something on the other side. Strange shrieks and cries? What was happening over there?

"I hear it," Jehral said.

"Be ready," said Bartolo.

A black creature of nightmare suddenly shot out of the portal, into the chamber inside the Sentinel, filling the room with shrieks. The winged creature bounced off the walls and scratched at the stone. Spotting the two men, it plummeted down with claws outstretched.

Bartolo was already singing, activating his armorsilk and zenblade, filling the room with his voice. The bladesinger flared up as his silken garments protected his body with a hardness greater than any armor. His zenblade became a hue of fiery blue, a sword that could cut through anything.

The creature shied away from the light and went for the black-clad warrior holding a curved scimitar.

Jehral ducked under the sharp teeth, narrowly missing the following claws. Spinning, he hacked at the winged creature with his sword. The scimitar bounced off the shrieking creature as if striking stone. Bartolo leapt into the air and swung overhead, missing the neck but striking a wing. The zenblade should have passed through the wing like a knife through water. Instead, the glowing blade bit deeply, seeming to anger the creature.

"Close the portal!" Bartolo screamed.

"You have to!" cried Jehral.

Shani looked at the portal, consumed with worry for the friend she would be dooming by closing the gateway. Bartolo was a bladesinger, one of the best, but this creature was something none of them had encountered before. She had no way of knowing how pressed he would be or whether more of the creatures would be on their way.

Jehral struck again at the flying demon, his sword again having no effect other than to enrage the creature. Bartolo tried to strike, but the creature flew out of range, shrieking as it batted around the ceiling of the chamber.

Shani had to keep the portal open for as long as the energy would flow. With no other clear path of action, the elementalist said the words to activate the red cuffs she wore around her wrists.

Taking a deep breath, Shani drew her wrists together and a tiny ball of flame appeared between her palms. The flame grew steadily and Shani drew her wrists apart to give the fire room to breathe. The winged creature tried to swoop down once more, and again Bartolo's fiery sword caused it to rear back, retreating to the heights.

Shani looked up at the creature and took careful aim. The ball of flame twisted and sizzled, quivering with pent-up energy.

With a shout, Shani threw the fireball at the creature.

Incandescence bathed the heights of the chamber, and silhouetted in the center, the black nightmare screamed and writhed in the flame. It held together for a long moment, and then the flame triumphed.

Ash fell down from the ceiling, and the creature was gone.

Shani turned back to the portal, ignoring Bartolo and Jehral's pleas to close it.

"Come on, Ella," she muttered. "Where are you?"

54

Flames traveled from ship to ship along the row, spreading in both directions. Caught between two rapidly advancing lines of fire, Amber's face told Miro she now realized her plight.

Miro knew that any second Commodore Deniz would be giving the order, and the *Seekrieger* would be the last ship to depart. The entire harbor was ablaze, flames raging on the decks of countless vessels while masts went crashing into the water. Deniz would have to leave or face the risk that his own ship would catch fire.

Behind Miro, Sentar's revenant warriors rushed into the harbor. The enemy would be on them in minutes.

"What should I do?" Amber cried.

Miro stood on the dock where between them, right in front of Amber, some smaller boats were also ablaze. He realized the only choice Amber had.

"You have to dive into the water and swim under the flames!" he called, his hands cupped to his mouth.

The fire was now at the vessel next to the warship Amber now stood on. She'd retreated back to the warship she'd holed with a powder keg in the hold, and even as Miro watched, the vessel she stood on was sinking. Sparks flew onto the warship's deck, and it was only a matter of time before the sinking ship caught fire.

"Dive!" Miro cried.

Amber ran at the ship's rail and suddenly stopped, fear crossing her face. The warship was as big as the mighty vessel Miro had come across at the dry dock on the volcanic island. Even with the ship sinking, it was a daunting drop.

"You have to!"

Amber climbed up to the rail, placed her hands above her head, and leapt forward. She was in the air for seconds, finally hitting the water with a mighty slap. With only a small patch of water that wasn't home to a burning piece of wood, Miro breathed a sigh of relief when Amber hit at that exact spot.

Miro prayed she wouldn't come up straight away and would swim under the water for as far as she could; there was fire everywhere.

He prayed she hadn't hit something under the water and that she would come up soon.

Miro turned around and saw blood-splattered warriors waving swords and rushing the docks. Lord of the Sky, there were so many of them!

"Come on," Miro muttered. "Come on!"

He stared down into the water. Amber was a strong swimmer, he reminded himself. Could she really hold her breath for that long?

He released breath he hadn't realized he was holding as her head burst from the water, only fifty paces away.

"Hurry!" Miro shouted. "They're coming!"

Amber pulled her body through the water while the sounds of the revenant horde grew louder. Flaming timbers fell into the harbor, hitting the water with a hiss. Miro couldn't see a ship that wasn't ablaze. Surely Deniz would have left by now?

Amber's outstretched arm hit the dock, and Miro pulled her up and out of the water.

She was gasping and sodden, but he took her hand and pulled her along. "Deniz said he won't wait. We have to hurry!"

Miro followed the northernmost of the two mighty arms that enclosed the harbor. Deniz had said he would be at the end of the long pier, as far as possible from the flames.

Miro looked behind him as he ran, and saw the revenant warriors giving chase. He opened up his stride, hauling Amber along behind him. The revenants were fast and right on their heels.

Two revenants blocked the way ahead, both tall barbarian warriors.

Without letting go of Amber's hand, Miro lowered his shoulder and charged. He knocked them back and kept running, feeling hands clutch at his clothes. The two warriors took up chase, and Miro anxiously searched for the familiar bulk of the *Seekrieger* ahead.

There it was! The mighty warship was drawing away from the dock, and already two paces had grown between them, with the gap steadily widening. Miro heard the cries of the chasing barbarians behind him, felt their hot breath on his neck.

As Miro reached the *Seekrieger*, a man flew over the gap, landing with agility on the dock. Commodore Deniz raised his sword to block a blow that would have ended Miro's life.

Miro launched Amber over the gap and then turned to give aid to his rescuer. Deniz needed little help.

With a thrust the commodore skewered a barbarian's white eye, the creature crumpling as the sword entered the brain. He ducked under the second opponent's slash and took the barbarian's head off with a strong two-handed blow.

The main horde still rushed toward them, and the gap was now too wide to jump across.

Miro and Deniz exchanged glances.

"Commodore!" a sailor called.

He threw a coiled rope across the gap, and with a wry smile Deniz handed the end of the rope to Miro. "You've promised us refuge in your homeland. I'm going to make sure you fulfill that promise."

With a grin, Miro took a firm grip on the rope, and felt himself hauled forward as a sailor tossed a second rope to the commodore. Miro landed in the water with a splash and was quickly pulled up until he was standing, drenched, on the deck.

He held out a hand to help Deniz up.

"Thank you, Commodore," Miro said. "I owe you my life."

Even with his fine clothes sodden through, Deniz stood proud and tall on his ship's deck. "Look," he said, indicating the open sea.

As they exited the harbor Miro saw over a dozen ships like the *Seekrieger*, all heading out together, into the open ocean. Every ship was filled with the women and children of Veldria.

"When we arrive in your homeland, you can consider your debt discharged," Deniz said.

Miro nodded and turned to look back at the city.

The docks burned, smoke rising in a heavy black cloud. High above it all, Emirald rose up into the air, and as the sun set, Miro could see the emir's great palace clearly outlined.

He thought he saw a figure there, a proud silhouette looking out over the harbor watching the mighty ships leave for a faraway land.

They would return one day.

"Commodore," Miro said. "Watch." He gestured toward the city.

The walls had fallen and the men of Veldria were dead. The revenant horde now rushed through the city, searching out any still living and gathering up the dead.

The city would be filled with the enemy. Necromancers would be directing their draugar, and perhaps even Sentar Scythran himself would be standing at the wrong place when it came.

The figure at the palace stood motionless, drinking in the sight of his city's death throes, and the final hope under full sail, leaving these lands behind.

It was impossible, but Miro imagined he could meet the emir's eyes. The people of Emirald would never be slaves.

A rumble came from the city, a huge, all-encompassing sound greater than the eruption of any volcano.

The city lifted off the ground as the hillside underneath it exploded. Kegs of black powder ignited tunnels filled with innumerable barrels of oil. A cloud of dirt, stone, timber, and blood rose into the air in a detonation that grew ever greater.

The noise was deafening. Dust and smoke became so thick that the destruction could no longer be seen. Emirald was gone.

"Stars alive," Commodore Deniz gasped.

Miro breathed slowly in and then out, releasing the air in a steady stream. He sensed Amber beside him.

"Will they still come?" she asked.

"Yes, they'll still come," he said. "Emir Volkan would have destroyed a good portion of the army, but there are many towns on this continent yet to be enslaved. Sentar will build more ships, and he will come."

Miro, Amber, and Commodore Deniz watched Emirald until the smoke of the harbor and dust of the city combined to form a distant haze.

Finally, even the plume of smoke was gone.

55

The wraiths regrouped and once more swooped down to attack. Ella glanced over at the remains of Lord Aidan. Killian's father was now a smoking pile on the ground.

Ella took another step backward, bringing herself closer to the shimmering portal. She couldn't enter the portal without Killian by her side, nor could she turn her back on the creatures; to let them take her from behind would be to die.

Suddenly twisted bolts of lightning arced through the sky, scattering four of the creatures. Killian's voice could be heard above the shrieks of the black shadows, calling forth the powers that only he possessed.

Ella sent a yellow beam from her wand to strike another. She saw Killian then launch a flurry of fireballs from his hands, the wraiths screaming in rage each time they were hit.

Ella sensed Killian by her side, gasping and wheezing. The fight against the berserk revenant had taken its toll.

She chanted continuously, sending yellow bolts shooting through the air, striking wraiths, sending them tumbling and shrieking. As three of the creatures dodged the beams of energy and flew screaming at Killian's head, he sent a concussive blast of air into their midst.

Ella could see the wand's energy was nearly exhausted. She called forth three more bolts, seeing two of them strike home, and then the prism at the wand's tip went dark.

The wraiths rose into the air, some fleeing, but most regrouping.

Killian turned to Ella. "Are you hurt?"

Ella grimaced and put her hand to her shoulder. Her fingers came away dripping red. "One of them got through. I'll be all right."

"This is our chance. Are you ready?"

Ella looked again at the burnt remains of Lord Aidan. "I'm sorry."

Killian nodded, his expression unreadable.

"Ella!" Shani's voice came from the other side. "The portal's closing, and it won't open again. If you can hear me, you need to come through now!"

The reddened gold of the curtain started to fade back to silver. When it turned dark, the way home would be closed.

Killian took Ella's hand, and they turned.

Sensing their prey escaping, the wraiths swooped forward in one last attack.

Killian spoke the words, and together he and Ella took a step through the shimmering portal. Ella once more felt the texture of the air change as she left the nightmare world of Shar behind.

As the portal closed behind them, Ella and Killian crossed the threshold and stepped through to the other side.

The wraiths screamed in frustration as the curtain went dark.

The way through was barred.

56

Across the harbor from the Sentinel, in the city of Seranthia, the mood of the mob turned ugly.

"Lord Regent," the Tingaran captain said. "They're about to tear down the gates."

Rogan wiped a hand over his face. He drew in a deep breath and let it out. As a soldier, Rogan had always taught his recruits it was always better to make a mistake of action than one of inaction.

Finally Rogan spoke, the words labored. "Order the call to arms," he muttered. The captain nodded and left the room.

Stone-faced and silent, Rogan stared down from the palace at the heaving crowd below.

Moments later three great horn blasts sounded, followed by a pause, and then three more. The sound reverberated through the city, and for a moment the crowd stilled before once more surging at the gates to the Imperial Palace.

Soon, Rogan knew, the army would arrive. Men bearing the new insignia of the Empire reborn—the nine-pointed star—would hack and slice at unarmed civilians. Rogan would be known throughout history as a murderer.

What else could he do? Barring some miracle, inaction would lead to the palace being stormed. Rogan and his family would be killed, gruesomely no doubt, and the Empire would be no more. Tingara would go to war against some neighbor, committing theft on the grandest scale, and no matter if the new machines were built, the world would suffer anew.

Looking out over the city Rogan saw smoke rising from several quarters. The call to arms sounded again, loud and strident, and the crowd roared in defiance. Rogan saw Bastian below, exhorting those who attacked the palace. The iron gates shook and trembled. Any minute they would fall.

Which would come first, the slaughter of the mob or the storming of the palace?

Rogan wondered where Amelia was. Surely there was some place where she and Tapel could hide. Perhaps they could disguise themselves as servants. Rogan would stay and try to reason with the mob, even as he knew it was a doomed cause. He owed the Empire that much.

As if on cue, Rogan heard Amelia's voice. She was talking to another person, a woman. They entered the chamber together.

The newcomer was middle-aged and tall, with a slender face and high cheekbones. Her eyes were careworn, with lines of worry on her forehead and at the corners of her mouth. The woman wore her dark hair long and loose, with fine braids woven through, held back by a silver circlet. She was clad in a flowing burgundy dress and a silver necklace. The pendant at her chest bore the symbol of a sun and star.

Rogan immediately recognized the *raj hada* of House Tingara. He closed his eyes and sighed, before reopening them.

Rogan Jarvish, lord regent of the Empire, realized he was looking upon Lady Alise, the sister of the late Emperor Xenovere V.

This was the miracle he had prayed for.

"Lady Alise," Rogan said. He placed three fingers over his heart and then touched his lips and forehead, before bowing from the waist.

"Go easy on her, Rogan," Amelia said softly.

"How . . . ?" Rogan asked.

Rogan saw Marshal Beorn standing behind Amelia and Lady Alise. A Tingaran lieutenant stood with Beorn.

"Lieutenant Trask here found a way into the palace," Beorn said, indicating the Tingaran by his side. "We only just made it in. He did well."

The Tingaran looked abashed.

"Well done, Lieutenant," Rogan said.

Rogan turned to Lady Alise. He tried to smile, but it came out as a grimace. "Your first time home in over twenty years, and this is what you come back to. I'm sorry for everything you've gone through."

"I've been . . . out of touch," Lady Alise said. "They sent me to that island, with no way off, no news, and little company. What have I returned to?"

"Your brother is dead, and there has been a terrible war. The war is over, but the Empire's economy is in ruins. We're rebuilding it one step at a time, but the people are angry. They're angry that a foreigner is lord regent—that would be me—and that recent events brought to light that the Evermen were no gods; they were our masters, and we were their slaves. Lady Alise, the people need someone to lead them, one of their own. Will you speak with them?"

Lady Alise opened her mouth and then closed it. "No," she finally said. "I turned my back on the Tingaran Empire long ago. I came here because they said my son might still be alive. Tell me, Lord Regent Rogan Jarvish. Is my son alive?"

Rogan thought about Killian. Part of him wanted to lie, but he knew he couldn't. He shook his head. "I'm sorry, but it's unlikely."

"Then I will trouble you no more."

Rogan Jarvish bowed his head.

57

Ella and Killian tumbled through the portal to fall onto their knees on the other side. "Don't attack!" Ella gasped.

The beacon ceased its pealing, and the shimmering curtain faded to silver, and then a dull gray.

Ella shook her head to clear it, ignoring the pain in her wounded shoulder. The transition back to Merralya was jarring, the air hot and heavy, the light bright and blinding.

Killian rose to his feet, looking uncertainly at the three people watching him warily.

Ella smiled as she stood. "Shani, Jehral, Bartolo . . . meet Killian."

"Are we safe?" Shani asked. "One of those things came though."

Ella looked again at the portal. "It's closed." She detached her device from the Lexicons and put it back in her satchel. "Don't let me forget to throw this in the sea. You can take the Lexicons now. Thank you, all of you."

Jehral wrapped the yellow-covered Hazaran Lexicon in cloth, and Shani came forward and took the red-covered Petryan Lexicon. Bartolo was the last as he took the Alturan Lexicon, and soon all three held their bundles possessively.

"We did it?" Shani asked, looking askance at Killian.

"We did," Ella said. "Lord of the Sky, I never want to go to that place again."

"I . . . I should thank you," Killian said. "Ella told me about all of you. Without your help I would still be there."

Ella saw Shani give Bartolo a meaningful look, and she wondered how difficult things had been for the three of them.

"You owe Shani your thanks, more than any of us," Jehral said.

"You've got that right, desert man," said Shani.

"Come on," said Ella. "Let's go."

They climbed down the ladder, and soon they stood once more on the pedestal of the Sentinel. Ella remembered the last time she'd stood in this place and promised Evrin she would get Killian back.

Killian knew who his parents were now. The leadership of the Empire was his to claim. Ella looked at him, standing tall in his black garments, and she felt a warm sensation inside.

"We arrived with a coffin, and we leave with one man extra," Shani said. "I'm looking forward to seeing the expression on that captain's face."

"You're wounded," Jehral said, seeing the claw marks on Ella's shoulder. "We need to get you back to Seranthia."

"Wait," Bartolo said, gripping Jehral's arm. "What's that?"

Three horn blasts came from the city, the sound carrying across the water. There was a pause and then three more blasts. Shading her eyes, Ella saw smoke rising from several parts of Seranthia.

"It's the call to arms," Bartolo said. "Something's happening in Seranthia. Something big. We need to cross the harbor. Scratch it, that'll take too much time!"

Ella looked at Killian. He returned her look with a slight smile.

Chanting under his breath, Killian spread his arms out to his sides. As they looked on in awe, he rose into the air.

There was a famous scene from the Evermen Cycles, in which one of the Evermen hovered in the air above a crowd of worshippers below.

Ella now knew they possessed this power.

"Can you make it?" she asked. "It's a long way across the harbor."

"I can try," Killian said. "I'm a Tingaran. These are my people."

He continued to chant, rising farther into the air. His body tilted and he increased speed, and then he was over the water. Looking back at Ella, he waved his hand.

Then he was gone.

58

"Lord Regent," a Tingaran officer called, "the soldiers will soon be at Imperial Square."

After Lady Alise's refusal to help, Rogan decided he would try one last time, though he knew it was hopeless; there was nothing he hadn't already said. He walked back out onto the balcony, feeling the wind crisp in his face, carrying up to him the shouts and cries of the heaving mob below.

The balcony was designed for Tingara's rulers to address those below, and Rogan didn't have to strain to make himself heard.

He looked out over the crowd, seeing craftsmen and farmers, builders and merchants. Rogan felt no anger at these people, only pity.

"People of Seranthia, once more I plead with you to calm yourselves. If you send forth representatives from your numbers, I will hear your requests. If they are within my power to grant, I promise you I will grant them."

Rogan saw Bastian below, bellowing as he called out to the crowd. His words were carried up. "We don't have requests, do we? We have demands!"

"Then let me hear them!" Rogan cried.

"Tell us your words were lies! Take back your denigration of the Evermen!"

"There are those of the Evermen who helped us all," Rogan said, "and still do. But they were no gods. I cannot tell you a lie."

The crowd roared in defiance.

Bastian shouted again. "Relinquish your clinging grip on power. Give us back our nation!"

"There is no wish closer to my heart. I promise you that within a month, a Tingaran will rule in my stead."

"That's not good enough!"

Rogan bowed his head. In conscience, he couldn't give them what they wanted. Better that he be known as a murderer for what happened this day than that the fragile Empire be broken.

Someone joined him on the balcony. Turning, Rogan's eyes widened in surprise as he saw it was Lady Alise.

Rogan took a step back, allowing her to come forward.

"Seranthians, Tingarans, my people," she began. "The younger among you won't know my face, but your fathers and grandfathers will know me. My name is Alise, and Emperor Xenovere, the fifth with that name, was my brother."

Rogan saw the crowd still. Bastian's shouts died on his lips. This was news to them all.

"My brother was a cruel, vindictive man. I don't have to explain myself to you; as Tingarans and residents of Seranthia, you know my words are true."

Lady Alise licked her lips before going on.

"Xenovere hanged my husband, Lord Aidan, for treason, for acting against his tyranny. I watched as my husband writhed and struggled on the rope, as his face turned purple, and the life left his eyes, telling me that my love was dead. I tell you this so you know that I am no tyrant, as he was. The madness that inflicted him is not carried on in my blood."

"Where have you been?" someone screamed up. "When we've been dying, where have you been?"

"When I had my husband's child, I fled my brother's wrath. He sent his men after me, and I was captured. They took my child away, and I was exiled to the Isle of Ana. I haven't set foot off that barren island in more than twenty years. If you have suffered, then let me tell you, so have I."

The crowd stirred uncertainly.

"Please return to your homes before this day becomes a day remembered for darkness. Don't let today be the day your sons and daughters are killed, and the Empire turned to chaos. I understand your anger, but together we will get better, day by day. My son was taken from me. Don't let your children be harmed because rage held sway. My son . . ." Lady Alise trailed off. "His name was Killian, and I don't know if he's alive or dead."

Rogan saw a strange shape, rising above the sea of people. As one, the heads in the crowd turned to follow.

A man in black garments held his arms stretched out at his sides as he rose into the air. He had hair the color of fire.

The man continued to rise, until he was high over the surging mass of people.

The crowd looked on in awe.

Rogan's eyes went wide. He looked at Lady Alise. The blood drained from her face.

Lady Alise turned to Rogan, and he spoke, unable to keep the tremor from his voice.

"Your son has the blood of the ancients in his veins," Rogan said. "He gets it from his father, Lord Aidan, and far back, from the Evermen. Believe me when I tell you. Your son is descended from Evrin Evenstar, the Lord of the Sky."

Lady Alise turned back to the crowd, watching openmouthed as the young man continued to rise, drawing level with the balcony.

Rogan looked at Killian and then at Lady Alise. The resemblance was indisputable. "Lady Alise, this is your son."

"Mother?" Killian spoke, his voice quavering. "Is it really you?"

"People of Tingara!" Lady Alise cried. "I am Alise. The mad Emperor Xenovere was my brother." She held out a trembling hand. "And this is my son, Killian!"

In unison, the people below sank to their knees.

A chant began, welling up from the crowd, starting as a murmur and building volume until it became a roar.

Rogan tried to catch what they were saying. Was it "emperor"? Then the voices built until it was unmistakable, the roar rising from the great city Seranthia until it could be heard from all quarters.

"Everman!" the crowd roared. "Everman!"

"Everman!"

59

A stiff wind blew from the west, driving the flotilla of vessels ever onward. Deep blue ocean stretched out in all directions, an endless expanse of curling waves that made the idea of land seem a dream.

Leading the fleet, the warship *Seekrieger* lumbered over each crest before plunging into the trough behind it. After so many weeks at sea, the men and women aboard were weary. Water and food were both being strictly rationed, and doubts grew among those aboard that their destination even existed.

A man with long black hair tied behind his head stood at the rail with a slim auburn-haired woman. Together they stared into the water, sharing a companionable silence, each thinking their own thoughts.

———

Miro thought about the vibrant new world they'd discovered across the sea, only to see it ravaged beyond belief. He thought about the events that had brought them to that place.

Tomas's poisoning . . . please let him yet survive to be cured!

Ella's discovery in Toro Marossa's journal: She'd found the mention of islands; who could have known there was a continent out there?

The mutiny aboard the *Delphin* . . . Amber's discovery of the caravel, the terrible storm, and their subsequent capture by this very ship.

The dark times: the siege at Wengwai; the horrors perpetuated by Sentar Scythran.

The destruction of Emirald.

Miro had seen a land the size of the Tingaran Empire utterly destroyed within a matter of months. He couldn't let that happen to his homeland.

He thought about his conversations with Emir Volkan. He didn't agree with the way these people had turned their backs on lore, yet some of the discoveries they'd made without it were incredible.

The Veldrins had been able to build bigger, more powerful ships than anyone in the Empire, including the Buchalanti. Their houses, mills, bridges, and walls had been conceived with a skill and ingenuity that required no builders' runes to withstand the mighty forces of volcanoes and cannon. The alchemists had known about chemicals and the workings of the human body. Black powder had given these people projectile weapons more powerful than any bow.

When the revenants came, it would be with the power of black powder at their disposal. They would bring ships, and they would bring cannon.

Seranthia had its massive Wall. The Petryan capital had walls around Tlaxor, the tiered city. Ralanast, the great Halrana city, was encircled by walls.

Sarostar, capital of Altura, the city of the nine bridges, had no walls.

Amber also thought about Tomas. He'd only been burned on the backs of his legs. He could now be recovered on his own; it was possible, wasn't it?

She had the book that the alchemist, Tungawa, had given her, but she still wished she had the cure itself. He had said to give the book to the most gifted loremaster.

Amber knew who she would depend on to decipher the wordy descriptions, strange symbols, and formulae. She only hoped Ella would be in Altura when they arrived home.

She was sad the old alchemist had been killed, and in such a senseless manner: in a struggle over an ox-drawn cart. He'd risked his life to rescue her from torment and death, and then risked it again to save her husband.

Amber thought about the refugees of Veldria they carried on these mighty vessels. First she would see to Tomas, but afterward there would be a great task ahead to find them new homes in Altura. Amber decided she would apply herself to the task. The Veldrins would be afraid, confronted by strange people, confusing customs, and alien items of lore. They would know nothing of nightlamps and heatplates, timepieces and drudges. Things that Amber found commonplace would fill them with trepidation, but hopefully with wonder as well. How would they react to the Crystal Palace cycling through its evening colors? Would they shy away from stepping onto the Runebridge? Amber promised herself she would help them adjust and show them that lore could do more than kill.

"Miro,"—Amber suddenly broke the silence—"did I do the right thing by coming? Do you think I should have gone back to Altura to be by Tomas's side?"

Miro was a long time in responding. "I don't know, Amber. We need to look forward now. There's something I do know, however."

"What?"

"You put the device in the hold of the *Delphin*, saving us from certain death at the hands of Carver's men. You found the map on the volcanic islands that told us there was a great land to the west. You found the caravel Toro Marossa left behind. You saved our lives when our voyage took us into the path of the storm. You found the Alchemists' Guild. You rescued me from Sentar Scythran. If you hadn't come, I wouldn't be here now."

———◆———

A week later, Miro and Amber again stood at the rail when the lookout cried out, "Ship ahoy!"

Sailors and refugees soon joined them at the rail as everyone fought to get a glimpse of the vessel.

"Could it be the enemy?" Amber asked Miro.

"I doubt it. I expect Sentar Scythran is salvaging whatever ships we didn't destroy and building new ones. He'll be searching other towns—I'm sure that wasn't the only harbor on the coast of Veldria. No, I doubt they would have made chase this quickly."

Miro's words were proven true when a streamlined vessel came into view, rakish and built for speed. The sails glowed with a multitude of colors, shimmering as the man who controlled the ship activated and deactivated the runes.

Miro broke out in a broad smile. "It's the *Infinity*! What are they doing out here? We're still in the deep zone!"

The Buchalanti ship sped through the sea, tilting down dangerously close to the water as she tacked across the lumbering warship's beam. The *Seekrieger* dwarfed the *Infinity*, but there was something inordinately beautiful about the magical glowing ship.

Miro turned as a newcomer joined him and Amber at the rail.

"Is this ship commanded by the Buchalanti?" Commodore Deniz asked.

"You know who they are?" Amber queried.

"Legend says the Buchalanti saved us in the past, taking us on a great voyage away from a terrible war. Without our saviors, we would never have settled Veldria, nor any of the lands in the north."

"This is your people's first experience of lore, Commodore," Miro said. "I'm glad this is how you're seeing it."

Runes covered the ship, matrices of arcane symbols lit up with vivid colors flickering from hue to hue. Miro saw a broad-shouldered figure standing astride on the deck, his mouth opened wide as he chanted. The sonorous voice of Sailmaster Scherlic carried over to them on the cool sea breeze.

"Reef sails!" Commodore Deniz called out, turning and striding onto the deck to take command of his vessel. "They're going to come alongside us!"

It took some time for the warship to slow. The *Infinity* tacked back and forth, each movement bringing her closer to the *Seekrieger*.

The sailors of House Buchalantas swarmed on the rigging, and Miro could now make out their individual faces. Then Amber grabbed Miro's arm so hard, he jumped. "Look," she pointed. *"Look!"*

A woman stood near Sailmaster Scherlic on the bridge, one hand holding the mast, the other waving to catch their attention. She wore a green dress, and her pale golden hair blew in the wind.

Ella smiled broadly, releasing the mast and waving with both arms. Miro and Amber exchanged glances, both grinning and waving in return.

Both vessels gradually slowed until they drew alongside each other, with twenty paces between them, decks rising and falling as they were tossed in the waves.

"We've been looking for you for a long time!" Ella called.

Miro felt Amber's hand slip inside his, and he squeezed it tightly. They were all smiling.

"We had some trouble along the way!" Miro called.

"I'll bet that's an understatement!"

"Friends of yours?" Commodore Deniz's voice came from behind Miro.

"My sister," Miro said, still grinning.

"Miro, that ship is the fastest thing I've seen on the water. You'll need to prepare the way for my people. We know the way, and I'll make sure we get there. We'll put down a boat to take you across. Go."

"We're coming aboard your ship!" Amber cried.

"I'll see if we have room!" Ella called, grinning. "You can have the sailmaster's cabin!"

Miro shook Commodore Deniz's hand. "You have my word we'll be ready for your arrival, Commodore."

"Thank you, Miro."

Miro took Amber's hand, and together they quickly gathered their few possessions. They followed one of Deniz's men to the side of the ship, where a ladder led down to the waiting longboat.

The sea was as calm as it ever was out in open water, and although boarding the boat was difficult, with a push against the side of the *Seekrieger*, they were away.

Miro and Amber reached the *Infinity*, with Scherlic gazing down at them from above and Ella looking on and grinning.

"Permission to come aboard?" Miro called up to Scherlic.

"Permission granted," the sailmaster said, as sober-faced as ever.

"You first," Miro said to Amber.

He held the longboat fast to the ladder as Amber began to climb.

Miro looked over at the *Seekrieger* and in the distance saw the other Veldrin vessels drawing near.

Boarding the *Infinity* gave Miro a greater sense of pleasure than he could have imagined, but still the greatest pleasure came from seeing Ella again after so long, safe and well.

Soon they would be home.

60

The *Infinity* turned and headed swiftly east, as fast as she could travel, swiftly leaving the Veldrin fleet behind. In under a week she would be docking at the port of Castlemere.

Ella, Miro, and Amber spent their time standing at the ship's rail, feeling the wind of her passage strong in their faces, and talking.

"I have so much news, I don't know where to start," Ella said.

"Ella," Amber interrupted, "have you been through Sarostar? Please, is Tomas still alive?"

"I'm sorry," Ella said. "I took a ship from Seranthia to Castlemere, and then I found Sailmaster Scherlic and made him help me look for you. The last time I was in Altura I was with you."

"Oh," Amber said. She bowed her head.

"I did discover one thing, though. Miro, they need you back in Altura. They're all desperate for you to return. I have some bad news."

"Tell me," Miro said.

"I am sorry, but Rorelan is dead. The decision was unanimous—the Council of Lords barely discussed it: You're now high lord of Altura."

Amber lifted her head to look at her husband. "High lord?"

"Poor man," said Miro. "He was brave, Rorelan, in his own way. I don't know if we could have won the war without him."

Ella turned to Amber. "It'll sink in," she said, tilting her head in Miro's direction.

"They didn't mention Tomas?"

"I'm sorry, Amber. We'll only know when we get back to Altura. There's more news."

"What else?" Miro asked.

"There's a new emperor."

"What?" Miro exclaimed, shock crossing his face. He suddenly scowled. "Surely not one of the Tingaran commanders who . . ."

"It's Killian, although I'm not sure how happy he is about it."

Ella told them the story of Killian's ancestry. "Lord Aidan's revelation of how Xenovere had killed the Halrana high lord's daughter led to the Western Rebellion. He and his wife were both convicted of treason. Lord Aidan was hanged, and Lady Alise, Killian's mother, was exiled. Killian grew up in Salvation, with no idea of who his parents were."

"You brought him back through the portal? How?"

"I found a way to cross to Shar, the world where Killian was trapped. While he was there, he learned to use his powers. You wouldn't believe it, the things he can do . . ."

"I can believe it," said Miro grimly.

Between Miro and Amber, with halting words and haunted eyes, they told Ella about their quest and the terrible things they'd seen.

Ella felt dread well up within her as she listened.

"How long do we have?" she finally asked.

"Several months? A year? There's no way of knowing," her brother said.

"How did you leave things with Killian?" Amber asked, evidently leaving the question open for Ella to answer as she wanted.

"I only saw him briefly before I came to find you. The common people worship him, and he doesn't know how to take it. Even Bastian, a troublemaker, is behind him. They've sent the proclamation to all corners of the Empire. There's a new emperor, and the nine-pointed star now flies from every building in Tingara and beyond. Killian's asked that the name be changed to the Empire of Merralya. I think Rogan approves. Between Rogan and Lady Alise, they'll help him become accustomed to rule. He still can't believe he has a mother, and a home and a people."

"The Empire will need strong leadership," Miro said, "if we're to survive the coming storm. Altura stands directly in the enemy's path, but we can't stand alone. We'll need bladesingers and enchanters, but we'll also need the strength of all the houses combined. We'll need Veznan nightshades, Petryan elementalists, Tingaran avengers, and Halrana constructs. We can't let what happened to the land across the sea happen to our homeland."

"I saw what they did to Shar," Ella said. "The Evermen destroyed that world, and it's now a broken land. The Lord of the Night will do anything to aid his brothers' return. He'll stop at nothing."

"And we have to do everything we can to prevent him," said Miro.

"Ella," Amber said, "I want to give you this."

She held out a leather-bound volume. Splatters of blood spotted the spine and the cover.

"The man who gave it to me was high in the Alchemist's Guild. He knew all their secrets. He said in this book's pages is the cure for my son's poisoning. The poison is something called sleeping death. Do you think you can search this book and find the cure?"

"I'll do everything in my power to help you," Ella promised, taking the book. "I'll study it on the way back to Sarostar, every moment I get."

"Has Evrin Evenstar finished building the machines?" Miro asked.

James Maxwell

"No, he hasn't. When I depart Altura, I'll head to Mornhaven to see if I can help."

"I don't understand. Without a huge amount of essence, how did you open the portal?"

"I used the power of three Lexicons."

"But how did you get them to the chamber inside the Sentinel?"

"Well . . ." Ella smiled. "I asked Bartolo, Jehral, and Shani to request them from their respective loremasters. They met me with the Lexicons, and we were able to open the portal. Only later did I discover . . ."

"What?" Amber asked.

"They didn't request the Lexicons. They knew they would never get permission. All three of them stole them."

61

Chiming music tinkled in the air, carried across from district to district upon the tumbling waters of the Sarsen. The nine bridges of Sarostar thronged with people, all dressed in their finery. Men and women held hands while children skipped and played on the streets. There was a mood of celebration in the air.

This time they weren't gathered for a wedding; it was a coronation. This time nothing would go wrong.

The fountains outside the Crystal Palace shot up into the sky, splashing back to the stone before rising up again. Lords and dignitaries crowded the riverbank close to the palace, all holding glasses and smiling as they chatted quietly. The musicians ended a tune, to be met with applause, before moving onto the next uplifting score.

The rulers of all the nine houses—even Vezna—had journeyed to Sarostar from across the Empire. None would miss being present to see Miro Torresante become high lord of Altura, as his father Serosa had been long ago.

This was a time of coronations, and with the new leaders came new hope. After Miro's inauguration the high lords would travel together to Seranthia to witness the crowning of a new emperor.

The journey would give them an opportunity to talk and to prepare. The Empire was whole, and they had much to discuss.

From the heights of the Crystal Palace two great banners fluttered in the late summer breeze. The first was green and bore a sword and flower, the emblem of Altura. Above it, in pride of place, a second banner of black silk overlooked the people below. In the center of the black banner was a nine-pointed star, with each point colored a different shade:

Red for House Petrya: the color of rust-colored earth and fire
Blue for House Loua Louna: the shade of the artificers
Purple for House Tingara: always the emperor's color
Yellow for House Hazara: the color of the desert
Brown for House Halaran: the hue of the tilled earth
Pink for House Buchalantas: the people of the sunlit sea
Tan for House Torakon: the color of sand and stone
Orange for House Vezna: the shapers of nature
Green for House Altura: the emerald shade of the enchanters

Many were those who looked up at the black banner and felt the hope of a new day stir in their hearts. They waited expectantly for the man they had come here to see, Miro Torresante. Where was he? The multitudes looked around, but neither his wife nor his sister could be seen either.

Everything was ready. Miro would emerge from the Crystal Palace in the high-collared robe of his new office, and his retinue of Alturan lords would fall into procession behind him. He would lead them through the streets of Sarostar, giving the people of Altura a chance to see their new ruler up close, before returning to the Crystal Palace to be acknowledged by the visiting dignitaries.

The Alturan lords shifted and stirred as they hovered to either side of the wide marble steps outside the palace. The great timepiece on the face of the Green Tower began to peal, far off at the Academy of Enchanters. The moment was upon them.

Where was he?

⬤

Everything about the room was white, from the gentle glow emanating from the crystal walls to the linen on the bed.

Amber knelt beside her son's unconscious form, her head bowed as if in supplication. She finally looked up. "Should we give him another spoonful? Where's the bottle?"

Ella came over to stand beside her friend. "No. I know it has been a week, but give him time. The counteragent needs to bind to the poison so that it can be expelled with his bodily wastes."

"How can you be sure?"

"Please, Amber. I know it's hard, but trust me."

Amber leaned forward to stroke Tomas's cheek. "Please come back to me," she said softly.

Sensing movement behind her, Ella turned.

Miro stood by the door in a long robe of green silk, the fabric woven with protective runes. An incredibly high collar framed his head, stiff and striking. With his sharp features, dark hair, and the scar that ran from under his eye to his jawline, he looked imposing and intimidating—regal and commanding all at the same time.

A bell began to peal. Knowing Miro should now be exiting the palace, Ella said nothing.

The burn marks on the child's legs had healed. The poison was another matter.

"Anything?" Miro said. "Scratch it, we tried so hard!"

"Shh," Ella hushed. "We still don't know anything. Be patient. Layla said he's been rebuilding his strength since we gave him the counteragent."

"Why won't he wake up?"

Amber continued to stroke her son's skin, pulling the hair back from his forehead. "He looks so still."

Miro came over to stand behind his wife, resting his hands on her shoulders.

Ella thought about everything that had happened to her brother and her childhood friend. They'd finally had the wedding they had always wanted, and it had ended in disaster. They'd traveled halfway across the world to find the cure their son needed, and it displayed no apparent effect.

Ella blinked and felt a tear roll down her cheek. She wanted nothing more than for Miro and Amber to be happy. Why did they have to endure such pain?

She thought about the alchemist's dying words. He'd spoken those words to Amber and Miro, asking them to pass them on. What had he meant exactly?

"Everything is toxic, and small amounts of things considered poisonous can do good, whereas large amounts of substances we think are safe can kill."

Whatever he had meant, he had considered it important enough to say those words with his last breath.

Ella knew she had made the counteragent properly. Was Tomas too far gone to recover? Only time would tell.

She looked at Miro's face. He seemed unaware that outside the palace they were all waiting for him. Every high lord had traveled incredible distances to be here, and Alturans had traveled far and wide to be present to welcome their new ruler. Yet Miro's concern was for Amber and for the son that wasn't his by blood, but would always be his in every other way.

An eyelid fluttered, but Ella swiftly crushed the hope that began to swell in her breast, unwilling to face the disappointment that would follow. Then the other eyelid moved.

474 ·

Miro knelt until he was beside Amber. He took the child's hand in his.

Amber looked at Miro, and there were tears streaming down her face. Miro put his arm around her, and Ella saw his eyes were reddened also. Ella sniffed and wiped at her own eyes.

The face that had until now been so calm, so serene, began to twitch. "He squeezed my hand," Miro whispered. "He squeezed my hand!"

Tomas opened his eyes.

"Mama?" the child said. He licked his lips. "What's happening?"

"I'm here, Tomas," Amber sobbed. "I'm here."

"Why are you crying?"

"I'm crying because I'm happy."

Ella squeezed Amber's shoulder. Deciding it was time to leave them alone, she exited the room without a word, her own sense of relief and joy overpowering.

She walked through the softly lit chambers of the Crystal Palace, finally reaching the open doors to the main entrance. Ella could see them all waiting, the lords of Altura dressed in their finery and hovering around the steps, waiting for her brother.

Ella descended the steps as the distant bell pealed. A man in an elegant maroon doublet tugged on her sleeve, leaning forward. "Your brother," the lord whispered. "Where is he?"

Ella whispered in the lord's ear, watching the expression on the man's face shift from concern to elation.

She smiled as the lord turned to address the people around him, raising his voice. "Ladies and gentlemen, I have wonderful news. The high lord's son has recovered."

A cheer greeted his words, and suddenly the tension in the lords' bodies left, and they were grinning and passing the news. It traveled through to the guests who stood by the river and a second shout of approval came from the river. From the riverbank the news traveled to the Alturans who crowded the streets and bridges.

Miro exited the Crystal Palace to a mighty roar.

Ella grinned when she saw that he couldn't stop smiling, and she only realized now the tension he'd been under when she saw how much its absence softened his face.

She decided to leave him to his moment. This was his time, and she had important work to do in Mornhaven, where the future of the Empire depended on the new machines.

Perhaps, sometime soon, she would also go to Seranthia.

Later, much later, Miro and Amber strolled along the riverbank, watching the ferryboats crossing the Sarsen and the students in their green woolen gowns crossing Victory Bridge on their way to the Academy of Enchanters.

"Miro," Amber said. "I think you can give me a better honeymoon than that. The beach was very nice, but I'm not sure if the journey was enjoyable."

Miro laughed, the sound filling the air as he roared. Finally, he was able to speak. "Would having a second honeymoon make you feel guilty?"

"Sometimes guilty pleasures are the best. We need to go to Seranthia for Killian's coronation anyway, what if we left a little early? Ella told me there's an incredible eating house I'd really like to try. It's called Barlow's. Apparently they give you these little pastries before the meal, and at the end they give you handmade chocolates."

"Sounds wonderful," Miro grinned. "Do they serve children?"

"Apparently fish dishes are their specialty," Amber said, "although I'm sure you could ask for a meal of children if you really wanted it."

Miro laughed again. His wife was back.

Amber grew serious. "I need to ask you something."

"Anything."

"It's about Ella. She's always alone. Do you think she'll find someone?"

"I sensed something between her and that man from the desert, Ilathor."

"No." Amber shook her head. "She loves Killian."

"I said something about love to her on the *Infinity*." Miro stopped walking and took Amber's hand. "I told her how happy I am now that I've found you."

Amber smiled and leaned forward, brushing Miro's lips with her own. "What did she say?"

"She changed the subject and spoke to me about essence and lore. She asked me about the Alchemists' Guild and the technology of the Veldrins."

"That sounds like her," Amber said. "I said something to her too, you know."

"What response did you get?"

"She said she doesn't have time for love."

EPILOGUE

Ella again traveled alone, back the way she'd come long ago when she'd left Evrin on a journey that started with her brother's wedding and took her to Seranthia, Ku Kara, Stonewater, and the ravaged world of Shar.

Summer was moving into autumn, and the road from Sarostar to Mornhaven was crowded with men and women hauling carts bearing the fruits of the harvest. At Carnathion, Ella again passed the inscription bearing her brother's name, running her hand over it and smiling. More than once she overheard locals discussing the new emperor, the nephew of the old one, a man reputed to possess incredible powers.

This time Ella saw the nine-pointed star flown from buildings in both Altura and Halaran. There was hope in people's eyes and food in their bellies. The rulers of the nine houses were working together for the first time in what seemed like an eternity. Each voice was equal, and all would be heard.

Ella saw the peaks of the Ring Forts long before she saw Mornhaven. She was glad now they'd chosen this place. When the essence flowed, it would flow from here, the midpoint of the Empire, bringing it quickly to those who needed it. The Ring Forts would provide the best possible protection, and the machines' location in the catacombs deep beneath afforded a second level of defense.

Ella arrived at Mornhaven, passing several checkpoints and immediately heading to the tunnel. She found Evrin Evenstar scratching his head and looking at the gaping mouth of the harvesting plant.

Nearby was a wheeled handcart filled to the brim with black lignite. The rare ore was dug up all over the Empire. Now it was being sent to this place.

"Ah, my dear," Evrin said without turning around, "I've been waiting for you. I expected you tomorrow."

"How did you know I was coming?" Ella said.

"News travels fast. I'm pleased to hear your brother's son is well. You were at his inauguration. I knew you would come here next."

"Why were you waiting for me?"

Ignoring her, Evrin called out to half a dozen men entering the massive chamber. "Quickly now. Don't dawdle. Come on—you know what to do."

Ella's eyes widened when she recognized the white robes and the symbol of a black sun on the breast. "Templars?"

"They know how to do this best," Evrin said. "They're good men. The first is Felyan, and the second is Maurix. I've forgotten the names of the others."

"Enchantress," one of the templars said, bowing, and the others following suit.

"Come on," Evrin said. "Hurry up. We don't have all day."

"Yes, Skylord."

"And don't call me that! My name is Evrin. Come on—load it up."

The six templars rolled the handcart toward the massive entry port of the harvesting plant, finally disappearing inside. When they came out, their hands were black from handling the lignite.

The energy of a million blades of grass was pent in each lump of black ore, waiting for the magical machines to unlock its potential.

"Now go and stand over there." Evrin said to the templars, pointing. "Farther! If it explodes, you'll be better off against the wall."

Ella looked at Evrin in alarm, but his twinkling eyes told her he was jesting.

"Why have you been waiting for me?" Ella repeated.

"Why, because I thought you might like to do this. You deserve it, Ella. Without your help we would still be a year away from completion. Now, tell me something: Do you know that rune over there? The one with the triple whorl and the inverted bridge . . ."

Ella walked over to the harvesting plant. "I know it."

"What does it mean?"

"Loosely translated, it means 'awaken.'"

"Fitting, don't you think? Say the rune, Ella. Speak it aloud."

"Alitas," Ella said softly.

"No, loudly! Say it so the world can hear. When you speak, all of the machines will become alive. Let the world know!"

"ALITAS!" Ella shouted.

The symbol Evrin had pointed to flared up with emerald light. The color traveled from rune to rune, sending prismatic colors scattering across the walls of the huge cave. A rumbling noise came from the harvesting plant, and the ground began to shake. Ella could hear nearby hisses and hoots from the extraction system, and a sizzling sound like lightning from the distant refinery.

"Thank you, Skylord," one of the templars said, "for allowing us to be present at this historic moment."

All of the templars bowed in Evrin's direction.

"I told you not to call me that!" Evrin said.

Ella watched, filled with awe, as the work of over three years bore fruition, and she barely noticed as the templars brought another cart of lignite into the chamber.

The lignite would enter at the harvesting plant. It wouldn't become a liquid until the substance was taken through the extraction system, and only at the refinery would essence come into being.

Essence would allow drudges to till the earth and haul goods from one land to another. Pathfinders would shine, heating stones would warm, and timepieces would count the seconds.

But there was more.

Nightshades would come from the forest, the tree warriors bearing the power of nature itself in their gnarled limbs.

Avengers would twist and slash, scattering their enemies with a flail in one arm and a black sword grafted to the other.

Colossi would make the earth tremble beneath their massive forms.

Elementalists would call forth walls of fire.

Bladesingers would fight to their very last breath.

The enemy was coming.

But essence had returned to the Empire.

ACKNOWLEDGMENTS

As I have progressed through the writing of each book in this series, the list of people to thank has grown ever longer. I think that's a wonderful thought.

Huge thanks go to my editor, Emilie, and the team at 47North, for excellent guidance, support, and assistance with every aspect of development and publication.

Thanks go to Mike for (still more) tireless efforts with the editorial development of the manuscript, and for endless dedication and patience. I came very close to inserting an exclamation mark at the end of the last sentence.

I'd also like to thank all of the family, friends, and colleagues who over the years have provided me with constant support. In particular, I'd like to thank Marc M, Sam P, and Jeremy L, who gave me a great deal of help on this novel, and Marc F, for valuable input with too many things to mention.

Thanks to all of you who've reached out to me and taken the time to post reviews of my books.

In pride of place, thanks go to my wife, Alicia.

I will be ever grateful for your constant support.

ABOUT THE AUTHOR

 James Maxwell found inspiration growing up in the lush forests of New Zealand, and later in rugged Australia where he was educated. Devouring fantasy and science fiction classics at an early age, his love for books translated to a passion for writing, which he began at age 11.

He relocated to London at age 25, but continued to seek inspiration wherever he could find it, in the grand cities of the old world and the monuments of fallen empires. His travels influenced his writing as he spent varying amounts of time in forty countries on six continents.

He wrote his first full-length novel, *Enchantress*, while living on an isle in Thailand and its sequel, *The Hidden Relic*, from a coastal town on the Yucatan peninsula in Mexico.

The third book in the Evermen Saga, *The Path of the Storm*, was written in the Austrian Alps, and he completed the fourth, *The Lore of the Evermen*, in Malta.

When he isn't writing or traveling, James enjoys sailing, snowboarding, classical guitar, and French cooking.